Disney

WINGS OF STARLIGHT

ALSO IN THIS SERIES:

Wings of Reverie by Anna Bright

Disney

Wings of Starlight

Allison Saft

RANDOM HOUSE NEW YORK

Random House Books for Young Readers
An imprint of Random House Children's Books
A division of Penguin Random House LLC
1745 Broadway, New York, NY 10019
penguinrandomhouse.com
rhcbooks.com/disney

Cover art by Charlie Bowater
Cover design by Gegham Vardanyan

Library of Congress Cataloging-in-Publication Data is available upon request.
ISBN 978-1-368-09845-8 (trade) — ISBN 978-1-368-11413-4 (ebook) —
ISBN 978-1-368-10110-3 (paperback)

Originally published in hardcover by Disney Press, Glendale, in 2025.

The text of this book is set in 11.25-point Levato Pro.

Manufactured in the United States of America
1st Printing

The authorized representative in the EU for product safety and compliance is
Penguin Random House Ireland, Morrison Chambers, 32 Nassau Street, Dublin D02 YH68,
Ireland, https://eu-contact.penguin.ie.

Random House Children's Books supports the First Amendment and celebrates the right to read.

For those who see the world as it could be:
brighter and full of magic

PROLOGUE

There are things hidden from all except those who know exactly where to look. If you gaze out your window in the early twilight hours, when all the world is still asleep, you might notice an orb of light flitting through the late-summer leaves, each one blushing red in its wake. You might see faint ribbons of gold in the air, shimmering just above the hyacinths pushing through the newly thawed earth. Perhaps, if you are truly observant, you might appreciate the chisel marks scoring the crystal lacework of each snowflake. Alas, few are. And so, few will ever experience true wonder. Few will ever know that even the most mundane thing—the waning of the moon, the flow of the tide, the serendipitous reappearance of a lost trinket beneath your kitchen table—is magical.

All of it, of course, is the work of Never Fairies.

They orchestrate the turn of the season in a single night, then return home. It is said that if you soar past the second star on the right and go straight on till morning, you will reach it, too: the Queendom of Pixie Hollow. Considered from above, Pixie Hollow is like a cake sliced into four generous pieces. At its heart is the Pixie Dust Tree, luminous and golden as a candle in the darkness. To the east is Spring Valley, where the flowers remain forever in bloom. To the south: the Summer Glade, where the days stretch long and languid as a drowsing cat. To the west: the Autumn Forest, cool and crisp and ablaze with color.

Then, to the north, there are the Winter Woods.

The denizens of the warm seasons do their best to keep the Winter Woods far out of their minds. But when they catch a glimpse of it beneath the vast shadow of the mountain, they cannot help thinking of its skeletal trees, or the icicles glittering like bared fangs in the moonlight, or those who dwell in such a gray and lifeless place. The winter fairies—so the warm fairies reason—are best left to their snowy solitude. They have managed their own affairs for centuries. Besides, the cold there is so bitter and cruel it will shatter a warm fairy's wings in an instant. No good would ever come of crossing its border.

Now, most of their fears are baseless superstition. But unbeknownst to the warm seasons, dark forces do dwell within the

Winter Woods. There is a place where all the trees bend backward, flinching away from the frozen lake sprawled beneath them. There, the very air sits as heavy and wrong as a feverish sweat. No one visits this place. No one sensible, anyway, save the young Warden of the Winter Woods.

But if you were brave enough or foolish enough, you could step out onto the ice. Beneath it, you would find not water but a deep, writhing darkness. Even if you could stomach the dread it inspires for more than a moment, you would not be able to make sense of it. The shadows only occasionally arrange themselves into a recognizable shape. Here, a tooth. There, an eye, a claw.

No, few would ever experience such terror. But if you *had* somehow wandered down to the lake on this cold, moonless night—as the Warden of the Winter Woods did—you might have seen what he did: the moment a single crack fissured the surface of the ice. You might have heard the splintering that shook the snowfall loose from the branches. You might have felt the very woods tremble with anticipation.

Then: something—barely a wisp of shadow—rose like smoke from the broken ice. It seethed, then coalesced into a form it remembered from the nightmare that birthed it. In the darkness, it was nearly impossible to see, but its footprints fell heavy against the earth. Then, compelled by some horrible, ancient instinct, it lumbered toward the warm seasons.

1

It was the kind of afternoon made for daydreams: the air golden with sunlight and pixie dust, the meadow humming with the low drone of bees. Clarion perched on the branch of an oak tree, surrounded by the sigh and rustle of leaves. How sweet to find herself alone and—at least, for fifteen glorious minutes—with nothing at all to do.

She almost regretted the thought, as lovely as it was. It was all too easy to imagine Queen Elvina's response, delivered like a royal decree: *The Queen of Pixie Hollow does not sit idle while there is work still to be done.*

But Clarion was not the Queen of Pixie Hollow—not yet,

anyway—and her weekly appointment with the Minister of Summer had ended unexpectedly early. She did not intend to let this rare glimmer of freedom go to waste.

With her coronation looming, her every waking moment was regimented with lessons, rehearsals, fittings, and more meetings than she'd ever thought possible. All essential, she supposed, when she had only one month left to absorb Elvina's hundreds of years of wisdom. And yet, Pixie Hollow was vast and wondrous, and Clarion sometimes suspected she knew nothing about it at all. How could she, when she'd spent almost all her life observing it from afar?

Clarion gazed out at Sunflower Meadow with something dangerously close to yearning. As the golden hour drew nearer, the light-talent fairies emerged, aglow with excitement and eager to face the controlled chaos of their busiest time of day. Through the canopy, she watched them weave through the pollen-thick air, leaving trails of pixie dust in their wake. Some worked in teams to angle the sun's rays ever closer to the horizon line, shouting things like "A little to the left!" and "No, your other left!" Others dipped their hands into beams of sunlight and scooped them into their baskets, as easy as collecting water from a well. It never failed to astound Clarion how many tiny details went into the everyday magic of a sunset. It seemed impossible that soon, on the night of the summer solstice, she would be responsible for all of them.

The prospect terrified her more than she cared to admit.

A high-pitched buzz sliced through her thoughts. Then, something hurtled past her: a streak of black against the brightening sky. Clarion stumbled backward, nearly losing her balance before steadying herself on a branch.

What in the stars was *that*?

With a hand resting against her pounding heart, she peered down through the curtain of leaves. A bee, faltering in her flight, landed heavily on the ground and went terribly still. After a moment, her wings fluttered, and Clarion let out a sigh of relief. *Not injured, then,* she thought. The poor thing must have exhausted herself. Bees were an industrious bunch and tended to overestimate their limits, especially here in the perpetual heat of midsummer. Luckily, it was nothing a spoonful of sugar wouldn't fix—and there was sugar aplenty in Pixie Hollow. The kitchens, no doubt bursting with all manner of sweets at this hour, were back at the palace. Better yet, the hive—and all its honey—was just across the meadow.

A simple problem with a simple solution.

And yet, Clarion hesitated.

Any trouble in the queendom made her itch with the desire to fix it. Once, she'd believed that tendency was a spark of her latent governing-talent magic—one small piece of the whole that finally made sense to her. But now, she understood that her instincts—her compassion—could not be trusted.

The Queen of Pixie Hollow does not belong among her subjects.

Ever since her Arrival—the night she emerged from a fallen star, as all the Queens of Pixie Hollow before her had—Elvina had impressed upon her that she was different. That *they* were different, marked indelibly with stardust. Besides Elvina, Clarion was the only governing-talent in all of Pixie Hollow.

Clarion glanced at the meadow, where teams of animal-talents and garden-talents shepherded their flock of bees. Would they notice one missing? Even if they did, a search would take them all night. Perhaps something as menial as saving a bee was beneath her notice, but she could not stomach the thought of leaving now. What kind of queen would she be if she turned away from the suffering of even the smallest of her subjects?

Now, there was just the matter of getting down from this tree.

A heavy cloak hung around her shoulders, trapping her wings beneath its weight. All fairies emitted a faint aura—one that flared and dimmed with their moods—but thanks to her wings, her glow had always verged on irrepressible. Although the light-talent fairies here in Summer shared her penchant for gold, the resemblance wasn't striking enough to allow hiding in plain sight. Letting anyone see her wings was as good as shouting *Here comes the future Queen of Pixie Hollow.*

If anyone told Elvina she had been here, unattended . . . No, it did not bear thinking about. She would have to climb down. Inconvenient, yes. Dangerous, almost certainly. But she preferred by far the risk of falling to enduring another of Elvina's lectures.

Steeling herself, Clarion lowered herself branch by branch. Her muscles burned and the bark scraped her hands raw, but by some miracle, she managed not to roll her ankle as she landed in the sea of sunflowers. They towered above her, swaying gently in the breeze and casting dappled shadows across the grass. And there, just a few yards ahead of her, the bee lay in a pool of yellow sunlight.

Warily, she approached the bee and knelt beside her. "Are you all right?"

The bee's antennae swiveled lethargically toward her, which Clarion chose to interpret as a yes.

It occurred to her that she had never interacted with a bee before. Many fairies kept them as pets—as much as one *could* keep them, considering they came and went as they pleased. The fairies befriended them with dishes of nectar left on windowsills and home gardens full of their favorite flowers: catmint and lavender and black-eyed Susans. Elvina had never *forbidden* such things, of course, but she had not encouraged them, either. The ease others had with the animals of Pixie Hollow was yet another thing Clarion had never learned.

"Let's get you back in the air," she said. She felt only a little foolish, speaking to a bee as if she could understand. Only animal-talents could truly communicate with their charges. Still, for good measure, she added: "Please don't sting me."

Carefully, she scooped the creature into her arms. The bee offered no resistance, and Clarion would have sworn she saw gratitude in her weary eyes. Her fur was surprisingly soft—and gave off the faintest scent: the brightness of lemon and the earthiness of pollen. This close, it struck Clarion for the first time just how similar a bee's wings were to the rest of her subjects'. They were as fragile and precious as glass and marked with an intricate pattern of veins. It made that protective instinct kindle brighter within her.

Cradling the bee to her chest, she made her way through the field of sunflowers. Through the canopy overhead, she caught glimpses of fairies flitting by. Motes of pixie dust drifted lazily through the air, along with the sparkling sound of their laughter. It filled her with happiness and longing—and also a terrible loneliness. All fairies who shared a talent lived together, worked together, played together. They mingled with others, of course, but there was an innate understanding among those who were made for the same purpose. Sometimes, Clarion wondered what it must be like to feel as though you belonged somewhere—to have so many others to turn to, who all understood you so completely.

They arrived at the edge of the field, where a lofty maple cast its long shadow over them. But it was the hollow in its trunk—a knothole a few feet off the ground, filled with precise rows of golden honeycomb—that caught Clarion's eye: the hive.

Gently, Clarion set the bee down in the grass. "I'll be right back."

She gave an answering flutter of her wings. On some level, perhaps the bee did understand her.

Clarion turned to the tree and drew in a steadying breath. She'd already climbed one tree today. What was another? She hoisted herself up, finding footholds in the grooves of the bark and the caps of honey mushrooms blooming from the trunk. At last, she climbed onto the lip of the knothole. The soothing drone of the bees reverberated within her chest, and the comforting, floral smells of wax and nectar washed over her. Clarion carefully pried loose a cap of wax that sealed the honeycomb. Immediately, honey welled to the surface. In the late-afternoon sunlight, it almost seemed to glow. Clarion plucked a leaf from a branch, then used it to gather honey dripping languidly from the comb.

The journey back down was perilous with one hand, but she managed not to fall. She hurried back to her bee and placed the leaf beside her. "Here you are."

Clarion watched anxiously as she drank. Slowly, the bee began to stir. First, she stood—cautiously, as though testing whether her delicate legs would hold her. Then, clearly emboldened, she took flight. She pirouetted and capered, twirling in circles around Clarion as if to say, *Join me.*

"I wish I could."

Clarion couldn't help grinning. Even if her talent eluded her, perhaps she could do some good.

"Mel?" someone called, her voice frayed with panic. "Mel?"

The bee perked up at the sound of her name.

Clarion looked up to see an animal-talent frantically combing through the sunflowers. "Looking for this one?"

The fairy's tawny face appeared between the petals, confusion writ plain on her features. She blinked hard at the empty space in front of her. "Is someone there?"

"Down here."

She startled, nearly plummeting from her perch. Clarion winced. It was admittedly rare to see a fairy on her feet. Self-consciously, she adjusted the fall of her cloak. Fortunately, the brilliance of the summer sun muted the light her wings shed. What little escaped from the collar only faintly stained her skin, no more obvious than the reflection of a buttercup held beneath her chin. Sweat trickled down her back, sliding between her cramped wings. She really could not wait to be free of this cloak—and the heat, for that matter.

When the animal-talent recovered her senses, her gaze landed on the bee. "Mel!"

Mel careened toward the fairy at full speed, veering away at the very last moment. The animal-talent did not flinch, as though she was accustomed to such displays. She seemed to be fighting back a smile as Mel dove into a sunflower.

"You were supposed to pollinate marigolds today," the fairy groused, but Clarion could tell from the look on her face that she was relieved to have found her.

Mel resurfaced covered in pollen. She shook off the excess like a wet dog, then flew off to join the rest of her hive. Even Clarion could tell she was preening.

"She seems like a handful," Clarion observed.

"Oh, you don't know the half of it." The animal-talent shook her head with fond exasperation, then turned to Clarion. "That was a kind thing you did."

Clarion found herself caught off guard—and somewhat flustered by the praise. Few fairies ever spoke to her without being addressed first. Elvina exuded a commanding aura that enshrouded Clarion in its protection. It kept her in, yes—but everyone else out. She was woefully out of practice with any sort of small talk.

Fighting to keep the formality out of her voice, she said, "It was no trouble at all."

"Even so, thank you." The animal-talent's smile was as warm as summer itself. "I'm sure you're plenty busy without chasing down wayward bees."

Clarion tentatively smiled back. "You're welcome."

"Have I seen you around before?" The fairy frowned, searching her face as if trying to place her features. "You look almost like—"

"Clarion?"

Clarion flinched at the sound of her name—and at the familiar voice of the Minister of Summer. *Exposed.* Dread seized hold of Clarion as she turned to face the minister. Aurelia hovered just behind her with a look of mild surprise. She had deep black skin and eyes as golden as pixie dust. Her hair fell in twists down to her shoulders. Today, she dressed in a gown of yarrow; the tiered skirt frothed with blossoms, arranged in clusters of pink, orange, and white.

"What are you still doing here?" she asked. "I thought you'd have returned to the palace by now."

"I took a brief detour," she replied wanly. "To rest?"

Aurelia brightened at that. She'd been shaped by an eternity of languid summer afternoons and valued peace and quiet above all else. Here in the Summer Glade, there was always time for a nap or a glass of lemonade. But while they dozed during the brunt of the midday heat, they truly came alive at night. Summer was the only season that never truly slept. If Clarion lingered here long enough, those who lived beneath the light of the moon—firefly-talents and star-counting-talents—would emerge from their slumber.

"My brilliant protégé," Aurelia cooed. "See? You *are* learning about Summer."

The praise rang hollow, but Clarion forced cheer into her voice. "Thank you, Minister."

She smiled indulgently. "Now, if you'll excuse me. I have to check in on my light-talents."

With that, she left. Reluctantly, Clarion glanced over at the animal-talent, who had gone quite pale. She opened her mouth to say something, *anything*, to put her at ease. But it was too late. She saw the exact moment it dawned on the other fairy. The exact moment her shock slackened into mortification—and something like awe. Clarion could hardly bear it.

"Princess Clarion," she choked out. "I am *so* sorry."

Clarion held up her hands placatingly. "There's no need to apologize."

"But there is." The animal-talent bowed her head deeply. "Your Highness, please forgive me for my impertinence. If I had known . . ."

Then she never would have spoken to Clarion at all.

What else was there to say? Quietly, she said, "You're forgiven."

The animal-talent bowed her head again. Murmuring a breathless thank-you, she rushed off. Back to her work, no doubt—and back to her friends.

That familiar ache of loneliness unfurled through her like a collapsing star. For a few precious minutes, Clarion had almost been able to forget who she was. Here, there were no guards following her at a distance. No one snapping to attention as she passed. No conversations dying as she approached. No whispers rippling in her wake. But none of it mattered in the end. Even here, she could not escape what she was.

She should have wanted this: respect, deference, impartial distance. But she didn't. More than anything, she wanted the only thing that felt truly impossible: to be *known*. Elvina would never . . .

Elvina.

Oh, stars. If she didn't leave now, she was going to be late.

She unclasped the brooch at her throat and dropped the traveling cloak from her shoulders. She gathered it up hastily in her arms and took flight, bursting from the sunflowers in a flurry of golden light and golden petals. A few bees lazily trundling by swerved off course to avoid her.

As she rose higher into the sky, she dragged a wake of pollen behind her. She allowed herself a single moment to glance back—and regretted it immediately. The light-talents had apparently finished their work for the afternoon. They'd separated themselves into teams and were volleying a ball of light back and forth over a net. Even from this distance, Clarion could hear their shrieks of laughter—and the mingled shouts of triumph and frustration when one team scored a point.

The sight of her subjects, so completely and uncomplicatedly happy, should have delighted her. But right now, it was only a painful reminder of her own queenly solitude. As much as she wanted to, she would never truly belong among them.

2

The Pixie Dust Tree loomed in the distance, stately and lush with its cloudlike canopy. Tiered cascades of pixie dust—as golden and bright as starlight—poured from the heart of its highest branches and pooled in the apex of its trunk. Its limbs curled protectively around the Pixie Dust Well before veering off in elegant arches and whimsical curlicues. Clarion had always thought one looked like an upside-down heart, another like the tail of a curious cat. And just below the well, housed in a hollow of the tree's ancient trunk, was the palace. Windows dotted the bark, each one lit from within.

Even from here, Clarion could make out the glow of the light she'd left on in her bedroom, softly emanating from the glass doors of her balcony. She'd counted on sneaking back in being the hardest part of this little venture, but she had not anticipated the added challenge of her own lateness. Really, she had been on such a good streak of punctuality. Elvina would be so disappointed to see it broken.

If only Clarion had managed to master teleportation, one of the most useful governing-talent abilities. Elvina always made it look so easy: dissolving into a swirl of glittering gold dust, then reappearing across the room. Clarion had once managed to make her left hand disappear before it snapped back into existence with a vengeance. Given her track record with magic, she'd been half convinced that it would vanish forever, or that it would wind up halfway across the room without the rest of her attached.

She landed in the tangle of branches just outside her balcony and dampened her glow. With any luck, no one would be searching for a flash of gold among the foliage . . . although she secretly delighted in imagining how her subjects would react to the ever-dignified Princess of Pixie Hollow breaking into her own quarters. Imagining Elvina's reaction, however, was decidedly less amusing. Mercifully, she'd had the foresight to leave the balcony doors unlocked. She carefully eased them open, then slipped back into her room. As soon as she latched the doors behind her, muffled voices filtered in from the hallway. Clarion instantly recognized both Petra and Artemis.

". . . feeling a little under the weather . . ." *Petra's voice,* Clarion noted with pleasant surprise. It was practically fraying beneath the strain of lying.

Her oldest—well, her *only*—friend had always been terrible at this sort of thing. It didn't help that even after all these years, Artemis—Clarion's guard—always managed to fluster her. Clarion supposed she appreciated the effort, considering she hadn't asked Petra to cover for her. She hadn't even known to expect her today.

What fortunate timing.

Clarion crossed the room and paused in front of her vanity, which was cluttered with bottles of fragrances and cosmetics. A quick glance in the mirror confirmed that she had no pollen streaked across her nose or any stray petals tangled in her hair. She looked a little flushed from her flight, but that was nothing that couldn't be explained away. Petra *had* said she felt ill, after all. Clarion was tempted to use the excuse to beg off her lesson, but there was no sense delaying the inevitable. She'd made little progress in her magic since Elvina began training her, and she did not anticipate a breakthrough before the next one.

A flicker in the corner of her eye caught her attention. The clouds had shifted, letting a wash of sunlight spill into the room. Beyond the glass of her balcony doors, she was greeted with the familiar sight of the mountains keeping their grim vigil over the Winter Woods. In the warmth of the golden hour, the snow cloaking them gleamed a brilliant white. No matter how many times she laid eyes on it, that cold, austere beauty never failed to stun her. As foolish as it was, Clarion yearned to see the mountains up close.

She could almost picture standing atop their summit: the wind in her hair, the snow dancing around her, the beauty of Pixie Hollow seen from that great height. How wondrous it would be.

Elvina had discouraged any line of questioning about the Winter Woods, of course. Even so, Winter did not frighten her as much as she knew it should. From the warm, secluded safety of her bedroom, there was something so peaceful about it—and so terribly lonely.

Just like her.

No one from the warm seasons had visited the Winter Woods in hundreds of years—not since before Elvina was born, and who knew exactly how long *that* was? Governing-talent fairies lived long lives. Clarion had never understood Elvina's lack of curiosity. There was a whole other realm they knew nothing about, filled with fairies no one had ever spoken to. Only the spring and autumn fairies had even *seen* winter fairies—and only at a distance as they crossed the Never Sea each turn of the season.

They're as cold as their season, their reports had said, *and hardly even look our way.*

Clarion tried to envision them, bleak and monochrome against a slate-colored sky, but those spare details had never satisfied her. She burned with questions she might never have the answers to. What must it be like to live in such a harsh place? What kinds of problems did they have? And what was the Warden of the Winter Woods like?

Artemis's voice sounded from the hall: "Out of the way, tinker."

A strangled noise of protest—then, the doorknob jiggled menacingly against the lock.

"Princess Clarion," Artemis called, "I've come to escort you to Her Majesty's chambers."

No avoiding it any longer, then. If she really set her mind to it—or believed Clarion was in genuine danger—Artemis was more than capable of removing her door from its hinges.

Clarion flung open the door, coming face to face with Artemis's fist raised to knock. Petra, clearly in the middle of a valiant effort to thwart her, was scrabbling for a grip on her forearm. Artemis snapped to attention immediately. Petra smothered a yelp of surprise. A flush dusted the bridge of her pale, freckled nose.

Artemis and Petra never failed to strike her in contrast: Artemis, tall with broad shoulders; Petra, with bones as delicate as a hummingbird's. Neither, however, had ever bothered to learn what to do with her hair. Artemis had shorn hers to her chin, and it framed her olive-complexioned face in jagged black strands, as though she'd taken a dull knife to it out of boredom or necessity. Petra boasted a shock of brilliant red curls. Most of the time, it was piled atop her head and pinned in place with whatever she had lying around her workshop. Today, she'd chosen a nail; the metal glinted softly in the light. A safety hazard, as far as Clarion was concerned.

"Your Highness," Artemis said when she had recovered, "are you feeling well?"

Your Highness. As many times as Clarion had asked, Artemis never dropped her formality. The scout-talent had been Clarion's shadow for as long as she could remember: trailing behind her or standing dutifully at her side on the occasions Clarion made public appearances. But in truth, Clarion knew shockingly little about her, other than her frightening competence and her insistence on punctuality. Neither of them was exactly in the habit of sharing her feelings with the other.

"Much better now, thank you." Clarion caught a glimpse of Petra's panicked expression over Artemis's shoulder. She would almost certainly be late to her lesson now, but she could not just leave Petra to stew in whatever worst-case scenario she'd envisioned. Summoning her most queenly voice, she added, "Will you give me just a moment? I need to speak with Petra. Alone."

Artemis—obviously thinking of the unspeakable horror of arriving even one minute late to an appointment—looked agonized. Nevertheless, she said, "Of course, Your Highness."

She retreated down the hallway and folded her arms behind her back in parade rest. No doubt she'd be listening in, despite her studiously indifferent expression. All scout-talents were incorrigibly nosy, but Clarion supposed that was what made them good at their jobs.

Clarion ushered Petra into her bedroom and shut the door behind them. Immediately, Petra latched onto Clarion's arm. In a shrill whisper, she demanded, "Where have you been? I stopped by to say hello, but you didn't answer the door. Then, Artemis cornered me out there to ask if I'd seen you, and I had to make something up!"

"I'm sorry. And thank you. I got—"

Before she could get another word out, Petra slumped to the floor. Her gown, stitched together from green maple leaves, puddled around her. She let out a long groan and cradled her head in her hands. Clarion almost reminded her about the sharp object skewering her chignon but thought better of it. Clearly, she had bigger concerns at the moment.

"I don't know how you can be alone with her every day," said Petra. "She is so *intense.* Have you ever tried to get in her way when she's set her mind on something?"

"As a matter of fact—"

"I covered for you as long as I possibly could," Petra continued, "but once she reports what I've done to Elvina, my days here are numbered."

"Thank you for covering for me," Clarion managed to interject. "But I'm sure that's not—"

"Maybe it's not too late to escape." Once Petra got going, there was not much that could stop her. Every word barreled out of her with increasing urgency. "I've heard some fairies make their living elsewhere, stowing away on pirate ships or—"

Clarion did not know where to begin disentangling that. Instead, she pretended to consider it. "Now, that's an idea. I imagine they'd have a lot of work for a tinker on a ship."

Petra gawped at her. "You're trying to get rid of me!"

Clarion couldn't keep herself from smiling. "Mending nets, repairing the hull, fixing the pots and pans . . ."

"All right," Petra groused, but there was no venom to it. "I get it."

Clarion laughed softly—but quickly sobered at the strangely bittersweet look on Petra's face. Clarion understood perfectly. It had been a few weeks since they'd seen each other, and yet, it felt like no time had passed at all. Although they hadn't been born of the same laugh, sometimes Clarion felt as though they were sisters. They'd always shared some innate understanding: neither of them was exactly what she seemed at first glance.

Few fairies took Petra seriously when all they bothered to notice were the fretful things she said. But Clarion had always loved to watch her mind whir like a fantastical machine. In fact, she considered catastrophizing one of Petra's many charms, now that she knew how to snap her out of it. Beneath it all, she was brilliant and funny and loyal—the kind of fairy who never truly let her fears hold her back, no matter how powerful they were.

Oh, how she missed her, even when she was right here.

Years ago—before Elvina had barred Clarion from roaming freely, before their duties commandeered all their free time—the two of them had been inseparable. They'd sneak out—or perhaps more accurately, Clarion would drag Petra kicking and screaming from her workshop—to explore, with Artemis's long-suffering presence just behind them. Now, Clarion had her training, and Petra had her work.

She specialized in intricate metalwork, but there was little she could not fix or make. Over the years, she'd fashioned everything from jewelry to utensils to sculptures—and dreamed bigger still. She had once spent an entire evening explaining her schematics for a prosthetic limb. Naturally, Elvina had taken a shine to both her art and her ingenuity and appointed her as the Crown's personal tinker. Clarion still remembered how proud Petra had been—how her excitement had made her positively luminous. It filled Clarion up with the purest sort of joy she'd ever known. As much as Clarion longed for those carefree days they used to share, Petra deserved her success.

She deserved happiness.

Clarion offered Petra her hands. When she took them, Clarion pulled her off the floor and guided her back into the air. "I'll see you as soon as I can." After a moment, she added, "I'll let you know if you need to flee for a life at sea."

Petra moaned piteously. "Fine."

Clarion opened her bedroom door. With one last beleaguered sigh, Petra flitted down the hallway. She paused for only a moment to shoot Artemis a lingering look. Artemis, for her part, remained perfectly impassive, but Clarion did not mistake the tension in her shoulders.

Honestly. One of these days, Clarion would orchestrate some sort of intervention. Ten years of pining was long enough.

"I'm ready," she said.

Her bedroom doors opened into a vast chamber: a hollow that had formed in the trunk. Wooden walkways and staircases traced the perimeter, spiraling down to a level of solid heartwood. Beneath that was the living heart of the tree, where magic flowed through it like sap, up to the narrowest veins of its leaves and out to its farthest-flung roots.

Together, they made their way up the winding stairs toward Elvina's quarters. The walls had been worn smooth with time and carved by countless carpentering-talents' hands. Clarion always found something new to admire when she passed. Here and there, an image struck her: an ornate iris, the round eyes of an owl, the bend of the river that cut through Pixie Hollow. In places, the artwork was concealed by swatches of moss and flowering vines, but Clarion could still see pixie-dust-infused paint glittering underneath. No one ever scraped the foliage away; the Pixie Dust Tree, of course, should have a hand in its own styling.

They stopped in front of the massive set of doors that stood before Elvina's chambers, each one engraved in breathtaking detail with a mirrored half of the Pixie Dust Tree. Artemis pushed them open for her, letting a blade of late-afternoon sunlight cut into the walkway. Drawing in a steadying breath, Clarion entered—and was met by the wall of portraits.

Paintings of all the queens that came before her stared back at her, all of them poised and powerful. With centuries between them, each one was done in a radically different style—but all of them had been wrought by a reverent hand. They filled her with a quiet awe. It seemed impossible that her portrait would ever hang beside theirs. When she was younger, she had searched them for any resemblance to her. Some shared her fair skin or hooded blue eyes, others her honey-brown hair. But all of them had the same wings: luminous and golden and shaped like a monarch butterfly's. Now, she only worried that if she looked too closely, she would find disappointment in their faces.

Clarion tore her gaze away from the portraits. At the end of the row was Elvina, her silhouette slashed into the sunlit window. She wore a golden gown with wide, ruffled skirts; the fabric shimmered with the pixie dust woven into it. Golden motes trailed from the train of her gown and sparkled on the floor, swirling listlessly through the air. A crown—the one fashioned by Petra, Clarion noted—sat atop her head; it towered high above her, curling back in the shape of a goat's horns. In it, she looked imposing, exactly as a governing-talent fairy should be.

"You're late," she said wearily. It was not an accusation as much as it was a statement. It had happened before. Both of them knew it would happen again.

Clarion did her best not to wilt at her dissatisfaction. "I'm sorry."

Elvina turned to face her. Clarion couldn't help noticing how tired the queen looked today. Streaks of gray threaded through her brown hair, and the brightness of her gown washed out the cool undertones of her white skin. Even so, her expression brooked no arguments or groveling. There was something unknowable in her green eyes, the remote and uncompromising look of a fairy who had lived a hundred lifetimes. Sometimes, it daunted Clarion, this glimpse of her future.

"For a good reason, I trust," said Elvina.

"Oh, yes. A very good reason." What that reason *was*, she did not know yet. But surely she could come up with some reasonable explanation if prompted.

Elvina made a dismissive sound, as though the particulars did not concern her. Clarion could hardly believe her luck. "Have you been practicing the techniques we discussed?"

Clarion nodded. She had been. Of course she had been. She could not say, however, that she'd made much progress in the last few months—a fact that endlessly dismayed her. From the moment a fairy first opened their eyes, they knew exactly what their talent was: their magical affinity, their calling in life, the thing that came to them as easily as breath. Talents, by most fairies' accounts, gave everyone in Pixie Hollow purpose and joy. Clarion very much doubted her own would ever feel so effortless.

Elvina had told her that governing-talent magic was rooted in emotion—or rather, the absence of it. Only with perfect clarity of mind and complete focus could she find the freedom to manipulate the starlight burning bright within her. But as much as Clarion tried—whether through breathwork or exercise or sheer force of will—she could not empty herself of feeling. She could not shake that desperate hunger for connection.

"Good," said Elvina. "Let me see."

In an instant, Clarion's hands went cold with nerves. No, she could not despair just yet. Perhaps this time, it would be different. She extended her hand. Deep within her chest, she felt that infinite wellspring of magic. If she applied enough pressure to it, if she held on with all her strength, she could bend it to her will.

Focus, she thought. *Control it.*

For a moment, a golden light bloomed in the center of her palm. It guttered like a candle in the breeze, but tentative hope kindled within her. She felt lightheaded from the effort, but with just a little more . . .

The light spluttered, then died. Clarion huffed out a breath, closing her fingers around the dying ember as if she could keep it. She tried not to let her disappointment show on her face.

Across the room, a bright light flared. When Clarion glanced up, Elvina was illuminated by her power. It balanced in her palm like a star in miniature, casting the planes of her face and all the room in stark relief. It gave off such brilliance and heat, Clarion had to resist the urge to raise her arm to shield herself.

Unlike light-talent fairies, governing-talent fairies did not need to manipulate a source of light. Born from fallen stars, they carried wells of starlight within themselves. Their magic could cut through absolute darkness—and most anything else in its path. It could be shaped into a shield to protect the queendom. More than anything, it was a symbol: something the citizens of Pixie Hollow could believe in.

Elvina clenched her fist, and the light extinguished. "Clarion."

Here it comes. Clarion schooled her face into neutrality as she braced for her lecture.

"Your coronation is one month away."

Clarion bowed her head. "It is."

"You still have not mastered the most fundamental skill of our magic."

"I haven't," she said, with the barest hitch in her voice.

The Queen of Pixie Hollow required a mastery of politics, organization, and leadership—but also the magic unique to governing-talent fairies. A magic that Clarion had been struggling to perfect since her training officially began. She could not teleport. She could not produce more than a flicker of light. Evidently, she could not even help a single *bee* without horrifying her subjects.

After a brittle moment, Elvina asked, "Where were you?"

What sense was there in hiding it? She sighed in defeat. "The Summer Glade."

Elvina's lips thinned. She did not need to speak for Clarion to feel the full weight of her disapproval. The look in her eyes said, *It is long past time to set aside childish things.* "Why did you not return here after your meeting?"

"I'd meant to come back on time, truly. But just as I was leaving, there was—" She cut herself off before she could get lost in details Elvina did not want or need. "I thought I would offer my assistance to an animal-talent."

Elvina's surprise was palpable. "That is not your business. I am certain that fairy had their affairs very well in hand."

"But she thanked me," Clarion protested. "Perhaps she needed—"

"I understand you feel constrained by our role. But you cannot help every fairy in need, and you certainly cannot befriend them all. A good queen must focus on the task at hand—and help at *scale*. This is a vast queendom." Elvina floated to the window. Here in the highest branches of the Pixie Dust Tree, they could see half of Pixie Hollow stretched before them. "All of it is your responsibility. You understand what this means?"

"Of course I do."

"You are young." Elvina frowned. "You have not known conflict—not *real* conflict, one that threatens all of the people under your protection. You must be prepared. Until you have mastered the basics, you cannot attempt to solve problems that are far more complicated than they seem at first glance. I am entrusting all that I have to you."

Her tone left room for something unspoken. There were so many things she could fill in. *I will not see you squander it. I do not feel you can handle it.*

"To be a good queen—"

"Is to be as cold and remote as the star from which you were born," Clarion finished for her. It was the tenet that grounded Elvina's philosophy of governance, one that had been impressed upon Clarion since the day she arrived.

Elvina leveled her with a flat stare. "I know it does not come easy to you. But that is the only way you can maintain impartiality—the only way you can make the calculations you need to rule fairly."

But if that was truly the only way, why had she arrived like *this*? When she first emerged from her star, a sense of purpose had smoldered within her. That certainty felt so far away now. Sometimes, she suspected she'd gotten worse at magic the closer her coronation loomed. Sometimes, deeper down, she worried that maybe any day, a new star would crash to the earth and a new heir would emerge, as perfect as Elvina herself. As perfect as Clarion failed to be.

"I understand," she murmured.

Elvina's stern countenance softened. "You are under a great deal of pressure. But it will come to you, Clarion."

But when? The thought stung more sharply than she expected. "Thank you."

"Go and get some rest," said Elvina. "You're set to run the council meeting tomorrow."

She'd nearly forgotten. Weekly, the Seasonal Ministers met to discuss the state of affairs within each of their realms. Anything, from disputes to requests for resources, was brought before Elvina.

And starting tomorrow, Clarion supposed, before *her*.

Tomorrow, then. Starting tomorrow, she would *try* to act like the queen Pixie Hollow needed.

3

The next morning, with Elvina's admonition still ringing in her ears, Clarion prepared for the council meeting: the first she would ever run alone. For good measure, she shuffled one last time through the papers on her writing desk, a collection of briefs from her ministers. Today's agenda was mercifully—and surprisingly—light. Pixie Hollow was at its most bustling in the weeks leading up to each seasonal turn. With the solstice a month away, late spring hardly constituted a lull.

Not to mention, there was the matter of her coronation.

Her coronation. The very thought of it made her nerves flare with renewed intensity. Soon, Clarion would make the decisions that ensured the queendom functioned as it should and that the seasons changed without a hitch. Not only Pixie Hollow depended on her—but also the Mainland and all the humans within it.

The pressure would crack her if she dwelled on it too much. Instead, she would put Elvina's advice to work and focus on the task at hand. If she could not manifest a burst of magic, then she would at least run a meeting with unequivocal poise. Today, Elvina would find no fault in her.

She stood, and immediately, a shudder passed through her. Clarion turned, half-expecting to find someone—or some*thing*—watching her through the glass doors of her balcony. But it was only her own weary reflection staring back at her, framed like a portrait by interlocking branches—and beyond it, the mountains of the Winter Woods. The tallest of them rose into curved peaks, reaching toward each other in the shape of a crescent moon. In the early-morning light, all the snow was washed pink as a shell. Sometimes, she could almost imagine the mountains were staring back at her.

All her life, she'd been told that winter fairies were not to be trusted. Few stories remained that explained the source of their conflict, but Clarion had seen one or two theatrical performances that touched on the conflict that had driven their worlds apart. She still remembered sitting beside Elvina—breathless, with her hands white-knuckled around the railing of their opera box—as Saga, the most gifted of Pixie Hollow's storytellers, wove the tale of Titania, the first Queen of Pixie Hollow.

As she spoke, images shimmered in a cloud of golden dust behind her. Flashes of icicle spears and quill arrows. The Pixie Dust Tree, no more than a sapling bending to the wind. The Warden of the Winter Woods and his cruel, serrated crown, wreathed by a towering darkness.

Privately, Clarion had thought the drama of it terribly romantic. Elvina, meanwhile, had scoffed when one of Titania's trusted advisors died his tragic death. But for all its theatrics, the legend never expounded on the details Clarion craved. It told of only some vague disagreement between the two rulers—and a dark force that had consumed the Warden of the Winter Woods. That, for most citizens of the warm seasons, was enough to discourage any curiosity about their neighbors.

Clarion gathered up her notes and unlatched her balcony doors. Cool air washed over her, and the sounds of Pixie Hollow stirring awake filtered down from above. With a flutter of her wings, she leapt onto the balustrades of her balcony, then into the air.

She ascended, pushing aside leaves and twigs, until she could see the source of the Pixie Dust Well. A cascade of golden dust spilled from a knothole and onto the pink petals of a lily. The overflow dripped onto tiers of pearl oyster mushrooms until at last it emptied into the well, cradled in the spiraled nexus of the tree's limbs.

Pixie dust—the lifeblood of their society—was produced deep within the heart of the tree. No one knew exactly how or why, although dustologists had penned dense academic tomes and quibbled over theories for centuries. All Clarion knew for certain was that magic flowed through it, suffusing all of Pixie Hollow with its vast network of roots. If she let herself pause, she could feel it all around her, warm and comforting. It made the very air smell sweet, like honeyed tea and cinnamon rolls rising in an oven. Its subtle presence never failed to fill her with wonder.

This early, everyone had begun lining up for their daily ration of dust: a teacupful and no more. Dust-keeper fairies stood ankle-deep in the shallows of the Pixie Dust Well, dipping their cups into the pool. With efficiency Clarion admired, they poured it over each fairy. Without it, flight would be impossible; a fairy's wings couldn't support their weight unassisted. All the way down the queue, fairies gossiped and laughed. Some carried cups full of dandelion tea, eager for a kick of energy; others still buzzed with energy from their night shifts. One of the sparrow men below noticed her half-hidden behind a curtain of leaves. She lifted a hand in a sheepish wave. He paled, then looked away, attempting to do something complicated and industrious-looking with the blade of grass in his hands.

Clarion tried not to wilt with disappointment. Petra had always said her expression conveyed a certain *queenliness*, as did her voice. It wasn't as if there were anything she could do about either of those things.

"Your Highness."

Clarion let out a gasp of surprise. She craned her neck to find

Artemis seated on one of the branches just above her. She always managed to hide herself in plain sight—an impressive, if not occasionally terrifying, talent.

"Good morning," Clarion said, a little breathlessly.

Her guard wore an expression verging on sympathetic. It was always difficult to tell with Artemis, who had mastered the subtle art of stoicism. But sometimes, Clarion caught Artemis watching the other scout-talents when they went out on patrol with something like yearning in her eyes. On the one occasion Clarion had asked her about it, Artemis had shuttered completely. Some wounds, Clarion supposed, should not be picked at.

"They're unaccustomed to a queen who welcomes familiarity," Artemis said gruffly. "It's only respect they're offering you."

Respect, was it? Even if she wanted it, she hardly felt worthy of it. Still, Artemis's halting attempts to comfort her never failed to bring *some* cheer. Artemis would never admit it, of course, but Clarion suspected there was a sensitive soul buried somewhere beneath that cool, professional exterior. One of these days, she just might reveal it.

"Of course." With forced brightness, Clarion asked, "Shall we go?"

Artemis nodded.

Doing her best to stay out of sight, Clarion led them to the council chambers, located just below the Pixie Dust Well. There was no door to speak of; rather, the sides of the domed ceiling had been carved so that it seemed to be paned with swatches of open sky. Intricately scrolled designs, rendered in glittering pixie-dust paint, filled the thin strips of bark left between each pane. Hidden within the patterns were the symbols of each season: the Evergreen flower for Spring; the full moon for Autumn; a rainbow for Summer; and a snowflake for Winter. It had always intrigued Clarion. If their realms had always been separate from one another, why had the art-talents included Winter in their designs?

As they drew nearer, the muffled sound of the ministers bickering among themselves reached Clarion through the open ceiling. What there was to argue about this early in the morning was beyond her. She supposed it came with such infinitely long working relationships. There was an endless number of petty squabbles and political slights to dredge up and litigate, the origins of which Clarion had only vaguely pieced together since her Arrival. At any rate, they never tired of debating which of the seasons mattered most. She steeled herself as she entered the chamber.

Inside, the three Seasonal Ministers gathered around a long table that took up almost the entirety of the room. The Minister of Spring seemed to be delivering some sort of impassioned speech, which the Minister of Autumn vacantly nodded along to. The Minister of Summer, meanwhile, looked on the verge of falling asleep where she stood. But as soon as they noticed her, a hush fell over them. It was part of governing-talent magic, she'd learned: an ability to command a crowd's attention. Artemis folded herself into the shadows, falling into a perfect parade rest. Clarion kept her chin high as she made her way to the head of the table, where Elvina usually stood. Somehow, the room looked entirely different from this vantage point.

Closest to her was the Minister of Autumn—Rowan—who flashed her an easy smile. As always, he looked as though he'd just stepped out of the cold; his pale cheeks were stung red. His brown eyes twinkled at her, and auburn hair curled around his ears. He wore a patchwork cloak of autumn leaves fastened with a polished chestnut brooch. Clarion liked him best, if only because he dared to speak out of turn in her presence. He was keen, agreeable, and only *occasionally* prone to bouts of melancholy.

Beside him was the Minister of Summer, Aurelia, who lifted her chin in acknowledgment. Today, she had dressed in the full bloom of her season: a gown of hydrangeas, a necklace of zinnias, and bracelets of roses. She'd arranged her hair in an elaborate bun atop her head.

And then, there was the Minister of Spring—Iris—who offered Clarion a small wave of her fingers. She'd chosen a wide-skirted snowdrop gown, and delicate new growth was woven into a crown around her temples, framing her face in long tendrils. She had a warm, sandy complexion and eyes almost as black as her hair, which fell long and loose down to her mid-back. Like her season, she was light and airy, flighty and eager: a personality bright enough to rouse nature from its slumber.

This had been Elvina's retinue for as long as Clarion had been alive. Still, she couldn't help feeling that they were incomplete with no Minister of Winter. Somewhere across the border, the Warden of the Winter Woods ruled in solitude over their frozen realm. But even if the warm seasons and Winter had been on good terms, it wasn't as if the Warden of the Winter Woods could join their meetings. Warm fairies could not withstand the cold of Winter; after only a few minutes, their wings would turn brittle and shatter. Winter fairies' wings, meanwhile, would melt like frost beneath the springtime sun.

Iris smiled radiantly at her. "Good morning, Your Highness!"

Clarion startled. The cheer she could muster, even at the earliest hour, never failed to strike her. "Good morning."

"I hear you're leading us today," said Rowan, dropping his voice conspiratorially low. "Finally convinced Her Majesty to slow down for a change, hmm?"

Clarion spread her notes out on the table in front of her. "It's nothing like—"

Before she could finish her sentence, the doors opened to admit Elvina. She whisked into the room in a whirl of pixie dust and diaphanous skirts. The ministers immediately snapped to attention, all of them murmuring "Your Majesty" in unison. Elvina, however, did not pause for pleasantries. She said nothing as she took her place at the opposite end of the table. Then, she pinned Clarion with an expectant look. Straight to business, then.

"I hereby call this meeting to order." Clarion cleared her throat when her voice wavered, just barely. "We'll begin with reports from the ministers. Minister of Summer, will you please share any new business?"

"We are nearly ready for the seasonal turn," Aurelia said languidly. "I have little to report on, apart from your coronation."

Elvina said nothing, but she looked visibly discomfited. Clarion did her best to put it far out of mind. The alternative was giving weight to that quiet fear within her: that Elvina did not trust her to assume her role.

"Preparations are proceeding on schedule," Aurelia continued. "We have gathered nearly all the sunlight we'll need, and we've identified the perfect location. When you have a free moment, Your Highness, I'll ask that you come by to approve it."

In her warm, drawling cadence, Aurelia outlined the other projects her fairies had been working on over the past week. By the time she finished, Iris was practically vibrating with barely restrained excitement.

"We'll continue with the Minister of Spring's—"

"I am *so* glad you asked, Your Highness. My garden-talents are hard at work on the floral arrangements. But there are just a few tiny things I want to nail down. . . ." Iris procured no fewer than five bouquets from beneath the table. Rowan looked on in silent wonderment as she placed them in a neat row. "Talk to me about colors. What do you think of these? We could also go in a completely different direction and—"

Clarion felt only a little overwhelmed. “I trust you, Minister. I’m sure it’s going to be beautiful.”

“It certainly will be.” Iris preened. “Ooh! But that still leaves the matter of the dewdrop mosaics. . . . The water-talents have been experimenting with designs. Of course, I can’t bring them here, but perhaps soon, you could come by Springtime Square, and we can go over *all* the details.”

“I look forward to it,” Clarion said, and she found she meant it. Even if she did not have the eye for design that Iris did, her enthusiasm was admittedly infectious. “Minister of Autumn . . . ?”

“I,” Rowan said, ruefully, “have nothing to contribute at the moment—at least not to your coronation.”

It was understandable. Although autumn wouldn’t arrive on the Mainland for months, preparing for the seasonal change took a great deal of coordination and effort. Before she could say so, Iris huffed out a sigh.

“Oh, but you *do*,” said Iris. “I need to borrow some of your fast-flyers.”

“Ah, right.” Rowan tapped his chin. A teasing edge crept into his tone. “Now, why was that again?”

“To carry the petals for— Ugh!” Iris threw up her hands “Listen. If you can’t appreciate my artistic vision—”

“While we’re on the subject,” Aurelia interjected, “I could use some tinkers, if you haven’t put them all to work yet.”

“A more practical concern,” Rowan mused. “But I’m not convinced I can spare them.”

As the three of them wandered down the back roads of their tangent, Elvina fixed Clarion with another speaking look from across the table. This one said, *Well?*

Right. It was up to her to bring the meeting to order.

"If I may," Clarion cut in, softer than she intended. Even so, they fell quiet. Every gaze in the room landed on her again. Determined not to lose her nerve, she continued, "Surely we can arrange a schedule that works for everyone. Perhaps the Minister of Autumn can spare some fairies for one day a week . . . ?"

Rowan glanced at Elvina, as if seeking her approval. Elvina only gave a vague wave of her hand, as if to say, *As she wishes.*

Satisfied, Rowan nodded.

Clarion couldn't bite back a smile. Perhaps she had managed one small victory: a resolution for a problem that had been brought before her. Before she could continue the meeting, however, a scout-talent all but tumbled into the room from above.

All five of them jumped with surprise.

The scout only narrowly avoided crashing into the table. Nevertheless, she saluted Elvina, even as she struggled to even out her breathing. It was as if something had chased her all the way here. Clarion chanced a look back at Artemis. Curiosity and concern warred in her expression, but she did not break from her station.

Elvina stood, once again assuming her role as queen. "What is it?"

"Apologies for the interruption, Your Majesty," the scout-talent wheezed, "but just before dawn, a monster was sighted in Pixie Hollow."

A chilly silence descended over them.

Iris spoke first, her confusion evident in her voice. "A monster? Like a hawk, or—"

"No, Minister," the scout replied gravely. "A monster. I don't know what else to call it. It crossed into Spring from Winter."

A monster? From Winter? Clarion hadn't known anything besides winter fairies and a few animals thrived there, much less *monsters.* But when she glanced at Elvina, the queen did not look rattled at all. Then again, she kept her composure in every situation, no matter how dangerous. As much as it baffled Clarion, she had always admired and envied that about Elvina. A true Queen of Pixie Hollow could show no cracks.

"And what," Rowan asked warily, "did this monster look like?"

"It's hard to place, sir. Something like a fox, but not like any fox I've ever seen. It had something like a glow, or a shadow. . . ." The scout trailed off, growing paler. "We followed it as long as we could, but we lost sight of it when the sun rose."

"Send for the commander at once," Elvina said. "I will see her here."

With the grounding comfort of following an order, the scout regained some of her composure. She snapped back to attention. "Yes, Your Majesty."

"Once you've done that, take your unit and ensure every citizen gets inside," Elvina continued. A troubled frown creased her brow. "Until we can identify the threat, no one goes out."

"Yes, Your Majesty."

Artemis perked up, her fingers twitching toward the sword strapped to her hip. "Your Majesty, if there's anything I can—"

"You will not desert your post at the princess's side," Elvina replied icily.

Clarion felt a pang of sympathy at how Artemis wilted. Bowing her head, she said, "Of course not."

Elvina flicked her wrist at the other scout. "You are dismissed. As for the rest of you, this meeting is adjourned. As a matter of safety, do not leave the palace until you hear otherwise."

"But, Your Majesty, I can't stay here," Iris protested. "If it came in through Spring—"

The look on Elvina's face brooked no argument. "The scouts will handle this."

"Yes. Of course," Iris replied, but Clarion did not mistake the worry in her tone. Aurelia rested a steadying hand on her shoulder and squeezed.

The rustling of paper and low murmurs filled the room. Clarion watched the ministers filter out, with cold dread lodged deep in her chest. *A monster.* How could such a thing be possible?

"You, too, Clarion," said Elvina wearily. "Go to your room."

Indignation flared within her. Was that it, then? Dismissed, just like the others, as though she were nothing more than a child? This meeting—an opportunity to demonstrate her capability—had gone awry. And now, Elvina would shut her out of something so important? "I can help."

"You cannot. This isn't a matter that concerns you."

It should have gutted her to have confirmation of all her worst fears: Elvina did not need her. Instead, that seed of anger flared into full bloom within her. She flitted across the room in a rush, her glow intensifying and casting an amber light on the walls around them. "How can it not concern me? I am expected to govern all of Pixie Hollow within a month's time."

At last, Elvina looked at her—*truly* looked at her. Clearly, Clarion had shocked her, because she did not reply for a long few moments. "I only mean to say that you shouldn't worry yourself with this."

Clarion could not accept that. "But shouldn't I learn how to handle a crisis?"

"There's still time to teach you. That time is not *during* a crisis. Trust me. I have this in hand." Elvina rested her hands on Clarion's shoulders. They weighed heavily on her, and Clarion found her resistance momentarily smothered beneath her shock.

Elvina so rarely touched her, so rarely displayed any sort of tenderness toward her. And yet, Clarion could not forget the way Elvina had looked at her when she first arose from the star on her Arrival Day. She'd helped Clarion out of the crater, then cradled her face with something like wonder and terrible recognition shining in her eyes. It had filled Clarion with such a sadness—one she did not and could not understand.

Before she could reply, in flew the Captain of the Scouts, Nightshade. She was dressed in full regalia—a breastplate, and plates of bark armor strapped to her forearms and shins, all of it gleaming menacingly—and carried a spear in her hand and a quiver of saw-grass arrows across her back. Her blond hair was pulled back into a severe bun at the nape of her neck, which was bronzed from sun exposure.

"Your Majesty. Your Highness." She clasped a fist over her heart in salute. "We should discuss logistics."

"We should," Elvina agreed. "Clarion—"

"Please let me stay," Clarion pressed. "I won't interrupt."

"It is out of the question," Elvina snapped. "Go."

Clarion could only stare at her, stunned. Elvina had been impatient or disappointed in her before, yes—but never had she been so curt. Without another word, she turned toward Nightshade and began to speak with her in low tones. Clarion, bristling all over with affronted humiliation, understood that was indeed the end of the discussion. Elvina had promised to teach her everything she needed to know—and what better way to learn than by observing? Clearly, her insight was not valuable or welcome.

She had half a mind to listen in at the door like a child sent off to bed. She had sworn to do better—to comport herself with the dignity befitting her role. And yet . . .

"Come on, Your Highness," Artemis said quietly. Now, there was no mistaking the pity in her voice. She all but steered Clarion out of the council chamber and back to her room. This time, Clarion felt too raw to protest.

Outside her bedroom window, controlled chaos had erupted in Pixie Hollow. Distantly, she could hear the sound of the horns echoing from the watchtowers high in the pines. Pixie dust streaked the sky as fairies flitted home and scouts soared above the canopy with their bows drawn and their eyes trained on the shadows. Clarion's heart ached with worry. Her people were suffering. Petra was likely terrified out of her mind, and that pained her most of all.

You have to help at scale, Elvina had told her. But she couldn't. Not while she was locked away in her bedroom—and certainly not while Elvina was barring her from duty.

The Queen of Pixie Hollow does not sit idle while there is still work to be done.

Clarion had never been perfect, she knew. But how could she ever be when Elvina's mandates contradicted each other? She would have to choose one. And right now, with her coronation looming so close, she could not content herself with doing nothing at all.

It couldn't hurt to look for the monster herself, could it?

If she came back with something useful, she would never be shut out again. And maybe—just maybe—she could convince *herself* that the stars hadn't made a horrible mistake. Surely, with all the scouts and Elvina occupied, no one would notice her missing. She'd just have to wait until nighttime, when Artemis was finally off duty, to make her escape.

As the hours wore on, the sun sank lower, staining the sky a wildfire red. Just before twilight descended, Clarion eased open her balcony doors. When she stepped outside, shadows settled heavily over her and prickled her skin with unease. A gust of wind set all the branches clattering, and buried somewhere beneath the sound, she would have sworn she heard the distant scream of a fox.

Somewhere out there, a monster lurked.

The thought had no sooner slithered through her mind than her gaze fell on the mountains. The near dark of dusk had transformed them into something stark and shadowed. For the first time, they leered back at her almost expectantly. Clarion could not tell if it thrilled or unsettled her more. Gathering her nerve, she took flight toward Spring Valley—to the border where Spring met Winter.

An eerie quiet had settled over Spring. No birdsong, no breeze shivering through the tall grass, no sound of laughter echoing through the trees. Never had Clarion seen Pixie Hollow quite like this. It felt almost desolate.

Darkness descended slowly, trickling down through the cherry blossom trees and onto the meadows. Far below her, she caught a glimpse of her glow reflected on a pond. Fading sunlight glittered on the water, but with no water-talents to carve ripples into it, the surface was disconcertingly glass-like in its stillness. One of the dewdrop mosaics Iris had mentioned lay unfinished on the shore, clearly abandoned once the scouts had sounded the alarms.

As she neared the border, the sound of rushing water reached Clarion. Gradually, the trees thinned as they shied away from a river's muddy banks. With a flutter of her wings, Clarion descended and landed with a soft thud of her slippers in the grass. Blackberries and sweetbriar grew wild in the underbrush, and the delicate smell of evening primrose perfumed the air. As she approached the river dividing Spring from Winter, she felt oddly exposed, with no woods enfolding her and the glow of her wings undampened by a traveling cloak. She'd never been this close to the border before.

She'd never been this *alone.*

A root of the Pixie Dust Tree twisted out of the earth and spanned the river's breadth. Bridges like this one existed between each season in an unbroken ring: from Winter to Spring, Spring to Summer, Summer to Autumn, and Autumn to Winter. When Clarion first arrived, their existence had puzzled her. What use did fairies have for them, when so few of them walked anywhere at all? Now, she marveled at the powerful magic flowing through them.

The four seasons existed simultaneously in Pixie Hollow, thanks to the roots of the Pixie Dust Tree binding them together in one place. A thought—one she knew very well she should not entertain—bubbled up in her mind: If Winter and the warm seasons were truly meant to be apart, then why did this bridge exist at all?

A distant rustle of the trees snapped her from her thoughts. Unease worked its way down her spine in a shiver. The sound had come from the Winter Woods. When she turned her attention to it, she would have sworn she saw a flash of light disappear behind a row of stark white trees. The dark knotholes on their trunks stared back at her like unblinking eyes.

Perhaps she'd found what she'd come for, after all.

Steeling herself, Clarion stepped onto the bridge. Halfway across, the lush moss carpeting the bark gave way to a thick layer of snow. Icicles dripped off its sides, glinting wickedly in the glare of sunset. Clarion stopped just short of the frost lacing the very edge of Spring.

In the gloaming, everything across the river was painted in silver and charcoal. Flurries drifted lazily through the air, a cold mirror to the cherry blossoms floating down from Spring's canopy. The snowfall seemed to her a veil separating their worlds. It felt more *magical* than she'd anticipated, but she could not let down her guard—or forget why she had come here in the first place.

The shadows seemed darker in Winter, but her wings gave off enough light to see by. Pixie dust shed from them as she moved, the motes glowing like embers in the darkness. The snow blanketing the earth was undisturbed: no paw prints, no divots, nothing. The scout had said this monster resembled a fox. If it was large enough to be seen at a great distance, radiating some sinister aura, where could it have gone?

Suddenly, she felt very foolish indeed. She must have imagined that sound entirely. What had she been thinking, wandering off in search of a monster? At the time, the plan had seemed so obvious—so *sensible*. Now, she saw it for how ridiculous it was. The stress and the doubt of her impending coronation had muddled everything. The truly sensible thing to do would be to turn back now.

But then, where did that leave her? She could not bear the thought of returning to her empty bedroom, or worse, to a council chamber she'd been shut out of.

Besides, she was *here*, so near to a place that had called to her for years. It was so strangely tempting to reach out and catch a snowflake. Even this close to the border, the spring air still held its pleasant evening chill. How close would she have to get to feel the bite of true cold? Very tentatively, she brought her hand to the very edge of the border, letting it hover a bare inch away from the flurries. Finally, she felt the slightest sigh of winter against her skin. Steeling herself, she let her fingers slip through to the other side.

Bone-deep cold seized hold of her, sharp and sudden enough to make her gasp. It raised all the hairs on the backs of her arms. Clarion snatched her hand back and puffed warm breath into her cupped palms. Well, she certainly had no doubts now about her inability to cross. Even so, the sting left her somewhat exhilarated. She'd never felt anything quite like it.

Another flicker of movement caught her attention. This time, she could see it clearly: a faint silver glow glaring out of the darkness. *No,* she thought, *an aura.* The spectral light wreathed a shadow peeling off from the night itself. Clarion fluttered backward a few feet. This was it: the monster.

"Stay back!"

But as soon as the words left her mouth, the shadow came into focus. Clarion tried and failed to swallow her growing mortification. This was no monster.

It was a sparrow man.

He looked to be delicately shaped from snow, with his fair skin and bone-white hair. It fell to his shoulders, with half of it pulled back from his face to reveal the pointed tips of his ears. His wings shimmered like ice beneath the light of the fading sun. Against the stark backdrop of Winter, he was almost . . . ethereal.

A winter fairy.

She had not imagined a winter fairy would be so unassuming. He was just a *boy*, no older than her. And yet, looks could be deceiving. She could not underestimate him.

She arranged her face into some semblance of composure. Too late, evidently, for he lifted his hands placatingly and said, "My apologies. I didn't mean to frighten you."

His politeness surprised her even more than his sudden appearance had.

"You didn't," she said guardedly.

"Well," he replied, visibly taken aback, "that's a relief."

The winter fairy slowly drew closer to the border, his every stride measured, as though giving her the opportunity to retreat. She forced herself to remain rooted where she stood. With each step he took, the snow crunched beneath his boots and her anticipation mounted. He stopped just at the edge of the border.

This close, she could see every plane of his face, from his broad cheekbones to his square jaw. There was no warmth in the young sparrow man's eyes. His gaze was wary and trained on her, as though she were a wounded animal poised to strike. Whatever mistrust Clarion harbored, it seemed it was entirely mutual.

"Who are you?" Clarion demanded. Her voice came out exactly as she'd practiced: authoritative, cool, dispassionate. The voice of a queen, even if it wasn't exactly *her* voice.

"I don't mean any harm," he said. Clarion resisted the urge to laugh. As if simply saying that could put her at ease. "My name is Milori."

"And what business do you have here"—she paused, giving him another once-over—"Milori?"

If he was at all bothered by her skeptical tone, he did not show it. From his neutral expression to his drawn-back shoulders, he was the very picture of confidence. "I've come to request an audience with the Queen of Pixie Hollow." After a pause, he added, "And it seems I've gotten one."

"You know who I am?" In her shock, Clarion abandoned her queenly hauteur. The question sounded far more hopeful than she intended.

"Of course I do." He sounded almost puzzled. A strange glint entered his eye—one not entirely unpleasant but one that she couldn't exactly read.

It hardly mattered to her, because *he knew who she was.*

He knew who she was, and he hadn't flinched away from her or demurred or panicked. She could count on one hand the number of fairies who dared look her in the eye—who dared speak to her unbidden at all. Perhaps they had no respect or love for warm-season royalty in the Winter Woods, but she would gladly take impertinence over reverence.

"May I ask what gave it away?" she asked, trying not to sound *too* eager.

That glint in his eyes intensified. If she didn't know any better, she'd say he looked *amused.* "Your regal bearing."

Clarion glared at him. "I beg your pardon?"

His smirk indicated she had rather proven his point. "And your wings," he added, more soberly. "They're very distinctive—and bright. I saw you coming at quite a distance away."

Self-consciously, Clarion folded them against her back. She suddenly wished she had brought her traveling cloak after all. "I'm terribly sorry to disappoint you, but I'm not actually the Queen of Pixie Hollow. You're looking for Queen Elvina. I'm only the queen-in-training."

And not a very good one, at that, she almost added.

"I see," he replied. All of the mirth drained from his expression. Clarion found she missed it when it was gone; such somberness did not belong on a face like his. "And what do I call you?"

A small part of her knew that she should insist on decorum. No one called her by her name but Elvina and Petra. *Your Highness,* she almost said. But what came out of her mouth was "Clarion."

"Clarion," he repeated. How strange it was to hear her name

in his lilting accent—in that voice as cool and smooth as a pane of glass. It made a shiver pass through her, one that had nothing to do with the cold.

Clarion smoothed her hands over her skirts, doing her best to appear disinterested. "Shall I pass on your message to Queen Elvina?"

"If you would. Tell her that the Warden of the Winter Woods wishes to speak with her. It's an urgent matter—one that concerns both our realms."

Could he be talking about the monster? Her mind whirred with the possibilities. She had hoped to bring information back to Elvina—and what information could be more valuable than something that came from the Warden of the Winter Woods himself?

"She'll never agree to it." It wasn't a lie; Elvina had never exactly encouraged her interest in the Winter Woods. "But perhaps I can meet with the warden."

A rather peculiar expression crossed his features, there and gone in an instant. "That can be arranged, if you wish."

Clarion fought to keep the excitement from pouring out of her. She'd have to orchestrate another escape, which might prove difficult once the situation had stabilized. But for the safety of Pixie Hollow—for the chance to prove herself—she could manage it. "I do. Just tell me when—and where."

"Would here and now work?"

"Here and . . . ?" Clarion nearly toppled into the river as the realization struck her. *Milori* was the Warden of the Winter Woods. The Warden of the Winter Woods was *here*, speaking to her as though it were the most natural thing in the world. She could not keep the accusation out of her voice when she said, "You might have begun with that! Do they not teach propriety in Winter? And what is the Warden of the Winter Woods doing on the border?"

"I suppose the same thing the Queen of Pixie Hollow is." He paused to consider it. "Or the queen-in-training, as it were. You're looking for something."

She could not argue with that. She crossed her arms over her chest and pinned him with a challenging stare. "I suppose I am."

The silence pulled taut between them.

"I'm happy to conduct our meeting from this distance," he said, tilting his head at her. Wryness played over his features as he surveyed the space she'd created when he first emerged from the woods. "But it might be easier if you came closer."

The snowfall thickened, and when a wind gusted by, it swirled around him, partially obscuring him from view. The border was as good as a barrier between them. Besides, if he'd meant her any harm, beyond the blow he'd already dealt to her dignity, he surely would have done *something* by now. Tentatively, Clarion crossed the distance between them again and came to stand just on the edge of Spring. Frost crunched beneath her feet when she landed.

Clarion resented the fact she had to tip her head back just slightly to meet his gaze. His eyes were as gray as the winter sky and steady on hers, and there was such terrible weariness behind them. The realization made her feel oddly off-kilter. What could trouble him enough to wear it so plainly?

Up close, she drank him in anew. A few stray wisps of hair curled around his pointed ears. But what struck her the most were his arms, wiry with muscle and completely bare beneath his lamb's-ear tunic. She couldn't fathom how he wasn't chilled. Passing her hand through the border for one moment had been enough to pierce her to the bone. Would he feel similarly, if he reached toward her? Would *she* be hot to the touch, like holding his hand to a flame? Clarion cleared her throat, determined to end that line of thought.

"What is it, then?" she asked.

The angle of the fading sunlight cast half his face in shadow. "I believe a monster will soon cross into your realm."

It was a grim proclamation, but it had come too late. Still, if he had any information about this monster, this excursion had been worth it. She wouldn't return to the palace entirely empty-handed. "I'm afraid it already has. Our scouts saw it just before dawn this morning."

"I'm sorry," he replied quietly. Something like guilt wrote itself across his expression. "I'd hoped I would have time to warn you before it reached Spring."

To warn *me*? Clarion frowned. "You saw it?"

"And I regret that I could not stop it," he said, as though he could not speak quickly enough. She did not think she mistook the strangled emotion in those words. "But that's why I've come to ask for your help."

"My help?" She couldn't keep the incredulity out of her voice. "Tell me what this monster is first."

Surprise flickered across his face. For a moment, he said nothing, as if he had not heard her correctly. "You don't know."

Clarion was certain she looked just as baffled as he did now. "How would I?"

"Your predecessor has not been forthcoming with you," he said, with a touch of bitterness.

"Excuse me?" She reeled back. How *dare* he fling such accusations? And if he knew what this monster was—if it had come from his realm—then he had no high ground to stand on. "Perhaps you should leash your beasts before letting them tear through the warm seasons!"

Milori looked stung, but he did not try to defend himself. It made some of her anger fizzle out. He extended a hand, as if he meant to reach through the border and still her before she fled. In the end, he must have thought better of it. He curled his fingers into a fist at his side. "Listen to me, Clarion. I can explain, but—"

"I *am* listening."

"—but it's too dangerous to stay here much longer. The monster is only active in darkness."

Clarion was growing sick of being denied information she wanted. "Oh, how very convenient."

He had the grace, at least, to look chastened. "I can be here first thing in the morning, if you'd like."

"I . . ." She *would* like that, if only to satisfy her curiosity. "I can't."

Some of the gravity bled out of him, replaced instead with befuddlement. "Why not?"

"I do not know what duties *you* have, Warden of the Winter Woods," she said, feeling oddly flustered, "but I have obligations. I can't abandon them to go wherever I please—especially not to the border of Winter."

"I see." He raked a hand through his hair, looking somewhat overwhelmed. "The queen does not know you're here, does she?"

"No. I snuck out." Clarion deflated. It embarrassed her only a little to admit it. Perhaps he would think less of her, now that he knew how stymied she was in her role. "Dangerous or not, evenings are the only time that's truly mine."

"Very well," he said, clearly undeterred. "I will see you at sunset tomorrow."

With that, he turned on his heel.

"Wait!" Indignation—and panic—flared bright within her. What if she could not make it tomorrow? What if she needed time to think about what she was committing to? "I . . . I did not agree to that!"

Milori paused, as if considering. "If you are interested in solving this problem rather than avoiding it, you know where to find me. I will be waiting here, at sunset, every night for a week." He studied her face, and the searching intensity of his stare made heat crawl up her neck. Whatever he found made a faint smile curl on his lips. That, she thought weakly, suited him far more than gravity. "Good night, Clarion."

He took wing. Clarion could only stare up at him as he soared deeper into the Winter Woods—and she caught the exact moment moonlight gilded his wings and cast their delicate shadow across the snow.

She threw up her hands, then dragged them down her face in frustration. She had come here for answers, but she would leave with far more questions than she'd had before.

5

Your predecessor has not been forthcoming. Milori's words haunted her as she made her way back toward the palace. What, exactly, did he think she was supposed to know? More concerningly, what did he think Elvina had withheld from her?

It was surely treasonous to even entertain a thought like that. But then, Elvina had been preternaturally calm when that scout crashed into the council meeting, donning her role as easily as sliding on a new gown. If she'd already known about the monster, then . . .

No, *no.* Clarion could not allow herself to go down this road.

Taking information back to Elvina was tempting, yes, but

to involve herself in some sort of—what, conspiracy? That was beyond her, and with her coronation looming, she could not afford to be distracted by the Warden of the Winter Woods and his cryptic words. For all she knew, he was lying to her. And yet, Clarion found it difficult to doubt the genuine concern—and guilt—she'd seen on his face.

She shoved the memory of his haunted expression aside. Sincere or not, she could not meet with him again.

In the distance, the Pixie Dust Tree shone out of the night like the glow of a lantern. But Clarion couldn't bring herself to return home just yet. Milori had warned her that this creature, whatever it was, hunted in the darkness, but below her, Spring Valley slumbered peacefully: no chaos, no terror, and certainly no monsters. Surely it couldn't hurt to check on Petra; it was on the way home, after all. She banked left, the wind guiding her along its steady course.

Tinker's Nook lay nestled at the base of a massive sycamore, surrounded on all sides by sloping earth grown wild with tall grass and drowsing bluebells. Most tinkers built their houses atop the tree's roots, each home crowned with a roof of maple leaves. Delicate stairways of northern tooth mushrooms sprouted from the bark and paved the way to their front doors. Tinkers' creativity always amazed Clarion. Without them, little would get done in Pixie Hollow. Apart from repairing and building infrastructure, they invented all manner of things to make daily life easier.

Their handiwork—and the beginnings of autumn preparations—lay scattered in the center of the clearing: acorn cups filled with the leaf-talents' dye, carefully arranged in a gradient from scarlet to gold; mushroom-cap workbenches scattered with tools; half-assembled carts made of hollowed avocado skins. A short distance away, Clarion spied their chestnut-shell wheels, waiting to be installed. The disarray gave the impression of a place abandoned in a great hurry. But candles and sunlight-powered lamps burned softly on the windowsills, and she could see the vague shapes of silhouettes moving within.

Clarion made her way toward Petra's home, tucked away in a far-flung corner of the village. Unlike most of the other homes, hers was an intricate work of stacked river stones, mortared with mud and pixie dust and thatched with a thick layer of moss. By her own admission, Petra preferred a less "organic" look, but a single mushroom sprouted from the roof as if to spite her.

Clarion alighted on her porch. The door loomed above her, a delicate sliver of a felled tree that Petra had sanded and polished to a shine. She knocked. Immediately, a shriek came from within.

Clarion sighed. "It's me."

"Clarion?" The curtains parted, and Petra's pale face appeared in the window. The door cracked open slowly to reveal her there, clutching a hammer in one hand and the cap of an acorn—a makeshift shield, Clarion presumed—in the other. "You scared me!"

Clarion couldn't help smiling. "Are you so unused to visitors, or did you think a monster would knock so politely?"

As soon as the word *monster* passed her lips, Petra gasped. "What are you doing out there? It's too dangerous to be outside."

Before Clarion could reply, Petra seized her by the arm and all but dragged her inside in a flurry of wild red hair and scattered pixie dust. The house was completely, disconcertingly dark. She blinked hard, willing her eyes to adjust. "Perhaps some light would . . . ?"

"Absolutely not. Your wings are so bright as it is," Petra groused. "You're going to lure it here if you haven't already."

Clarion scoffed. "That's ridiculous."

Petra gave her a meaningful look. "Have you forgotten the Bat Incident? I haven't."

Now, that was low. Once, many years ago, the two of them had snuck off to Autumn under the cover of nightfall, to sit beneath the stars with mugs of hot apple cider. It had taken her days to convince Petra it would be worth her while. What she had not accounted for was her glow disrupting the bats' flight patterns on the way there. Even now, she could see the flash of dark wings—and hear her own laughter over Petra's horrified scream.

"The scout said it looked like a fox," Clarion said. "This time, you're safe."

Petra did not dignify that with a response. Instead, she pointedly drew the curtains. Clarion's wings did indeed brighten the blackness of the room. Their glow traced the outline of all Petra's things, and the pixie dust that drifted off them scattered across the floor, glittering like pieces of starlight. From what little she could make out in the gloom, it looked like Petra's workbench had upended itself on the floor. Clearly, she was in the middle of a project. All other aspects of her life—from socializing to tidying—fell away when she fully immersed herself. It both surprised and disappointed Clarion to realize that she didn't know what it was that had captured Petra's attention this time.

Both of them really *had* been busy lately.

Apparently satisfied with her security measures, Petra slid down onto the floor and fixed Clarion with a bleary-eyed stare. "What are you doing here so late?"

"I wanted to check on you."

Petra sighed fretfully as she began gathering up her hair into a messy knot atop her head. "Oh, well. It's more of the same. Work has been—"

"To see if you're safe," Clarion cut in. "I was worried about you, holed up in here all alone."

"Oh! Yes, as safe as I can be. I don't mind an excuse to stay in here." She studied Clarion almost suspiciously. "Is that really why you came? You look like you have a secret."

"A secret?" Clarion laughed nervously. *Did* she? Going to the border wasn't forbidden, exactly, but if anyone found out she'd met with the Warden of the Winter Woods . . . Well, in truth, she did not know what would happen. It was best not to mention it, partly because she would never be meeting with him again, and mostly because the very mention of a winter fairy anywhere near the warm seasons would shatter Petra's fragile constitution. She already looked one scrap of bad news away from a nervous breakdown.

Besides, Petra was *terrible* at keeping secrets. "No, of course not. What gave you that idea?"

"Oh, no." Petra rested her forehead on her knees. When she spoke again, her voice was muffled. "It's really bad, then, isn't it?"

Clarion's stomach dropped. Was she really *so* obvious that Petra had already figured her out?

Somehow, Petra slumped even further into the floor. She lifted her chin and gazed at Clarion with a look of pure despair. "Elvina really *is* going to banish me."

Clarion blinked hard at her, caught somewhere between relief and confusion. "Um . . . no?"

"Worse? You've come to break the news that we're not going to make it through the night? No, it's—"

"Petra," Clarion cut in, grabbing her shoulders. "You're catastrophizing again."

"Right. You're right." Petra deflated, then forced herself back upright. "So, what is it? The Queen of Pixie Hollow shows up at my door—"

"Queen-in-training," Clarion interjected.

"—unannounced and with no business?"

How sweet it would be to talk through what had happened with her. Clarion sighed and perched on the edge of Petra's table—in what little space there was left for her, anyway. Something jangled behind her, which she slid out of the way. Petra did not shout at her to be careful, so she supposed it was nothing important.

As Clarion studied her friend's drawn, soot-streaked face, an ache bloomed deep in her chest. In moments like this, she could appreciate the true wisdom of Elvina's philosophy. A queen had to carry the weight of her decisions alone. Keeping everyone at a distance made it far easier to resist the temptation to burden others. And so, she said, "I promise I have no ulterior motives, secrets, or terrible news."

Petra did not look convinced. Absentmindedly, she picked up one of her tools and turned it in her fingers, staring intently down at it. "You don't have to be mysterious, Clarion. Not with me."

Don't I? She gestured at the wreckage of Petra's cottage and forced herself to smile. "I know. I've just missed you. Why don't you tell me what all this is?"

"I haven't told you yet?" Petra's eyes lit up, and all the anxiety, all the uncertainty, melted off her. She rummaged through her things until she retrieved two flat sheets of metal. "This could be groundbreaking. I've been developing a new welding technique using sand and . . ."

Clarion let the rush of Petra's enthusiasm wash over her. Even though she hardly understood a word of her speech, the sight of her in her element warmed Clarion like sunlight. And somewhere, deeper down, it stirred a spark of sadness.

What must it be like, she wondered, *to be so certain of your path? What must it be like to share it?*

When she returned to the palace, the balcony doors latched too loudly behind her. Clarion held her breath, bracing herself, but after a few moments, nothing had happened. No alarms blared. No scouts kicked in her door.

A small relief, she thought. Somehow, she'd gotten away with her reconnaissance mission. She felt almost giddy with the rush of it.

She changed into a nightgown, then settled at her vanity to undo her braid. As she worked, freeing the flower petals and pins from her hair, some fanciful part of her believed she could still smell snow and pine resin. Winter, in some way, had followed her even here. She had just picked up her comb when three sharp knocks sounded on the door. Clarion winced. There was no mistaking that authoritative announcement, wordless as it was.

Elvina.

As composedly as she could, Clarion said, "Enter."

When she turned, she saw Elvina framed by the doorway. Despite the late hour, she had not changed out of her regalia. Her expression was unreadable at first glance, but Clarion thought she detected a flash of relief in her eyes. "You're here."

"Where else would I be?" Clarion smiled radiantly at her, hoping it would distract from the hitch in her voice, and swiveled back toward the mirror. She retrieved her comb and set about smoothing out the waves in her hair.

In the reflection, Clarion watched Elvina's expression darken. "You were unaccounted for when I checked on your earlier."

Clarion had no answer for that. If only she'd devised some

clever lie, some excuse . . . But it seemed unwise to contrive something now. "I'm sorry."

Her voice sounded terribly small and pathetic, even to her own ears. Elvina heaved a long sigh. "I thought you had grown out of this impulse of yours. At the very least, I thought you had the good sense to stay out of such obvious danger. I ought to reassign your guard for the oversight."

"It wasn't her fault," Clarion protested. Panic knifed through her. How could she have been so careless? She hadn't considered how it might impact Artemis, whose entire job was ensuring that Clarion stayed out of harm's way. "It was mine."

Any warmth in Elvina's expression vanished. "You disobeyed my direct orders."

"And I apologize for that." Clarion rose to her feet. In her unbound hair and loose nightgown, she felt entirely unequal to the task of challenging Elvina. But perhaps, now that she had her full attention, she could get through to her. "However, I cannot sit idle while our subjects put themselves at risk. The Queen of Pixie Hollow must—"

"I feared the worst!"

The rawness of Elvina's voice silenced Clarion's every coherent thought. It rang in the silence. Elvina's breathing came unevenly, and it was only then that Clarion understood. Elvina was not just furious with her.

She was afraid.

"The scouts weren't able to track the creature," Elvina continued. "It left no trace, as if it just vanished. When I returned to the palace to find Artemis in a panic and you missing, what was I supposed to believe? If it had taken you . . ."

Then there would be no coronation, and Elvina would be free to rule for another thousand years—or until another star fell, one carrying a far more suitable heir. Clarion did not know what was worse: her self-pity or how wretched Elvina looked with her trembling hands.

"Where were you?" Elvina asked, voice low.

Your predecessor has not been forthcoming. Clarion shoved the memory of Milori's words down as quickly as it arose. "I went to check on Petra. You know how she gets."

It wasn't a lie—not entirely.

"I do." Elvina relented. The answer seemed to appease her, and moment by moment, she collected herself. "You are kind to that tinker. But do not disobey me again. Pixie Hollow cannot afford to have its heir going wherever she pleases and putting herself in needless danger. You are too valuable."

Of course. Orders were not for her to question, nor for her to understand. Clarion wrapped her arms around herself. "Elvina?"

Elvina inclined her chin in acknowledgment.

If she wanted the answer to her question, she had to tread carefully. "That scout said the monster came from the Winter Woods. Will the winter fairies be all right?"

Elvina frowned, clearly surprised by this new line of questioning. "The Winter Woods is a dangerous, barren place crawling with monsters. They are used to it by now."

Crawling with monsters. Clarion could not scrub from her mind Milori's look of befuddlement when he'd said, *You don't know.* Struggling to keep her tone neutral, she asked, "Did you know that before today?"

"Only vaguely," Elvina replied guardedly. "There is a reason we haven't attempted to make contact with Winter."

"But it's the Queen of Pixie Hollow's job to keep her subjects safe." Clarion dared to meet her mentor's eyes. She found herself jittery and cold with the thrill of talking back. She did not think she liked it. "Isn't it?"

"Her *subjects*, yes," Elvina said, leveling a flat stare at her. "The winter fairies have managed themselves for centuries and have coexisted alongside those creatures for as long as I have been alive—and much, much longer, I'm certain. Besides, they answer to the Warden of the Winter Woods. The Warden has their own way of doing things, and I assure you that they would not appreciate our interference."

Clarion wasn't satisfied with that answer. How could she be, when the Warden of the Winter Woods himself had *asked* for her help? Elvina demanded she accept her decisions and explanations without question. Yesterday, she might have. But now, Clarion could not deny that maybe Milori was right.

Elvina was withholding something from her.

When Clarion made no reply, Elvina seemed relieved. Her rigid posture relaxed, and her tone softened. "Let us put this behind us. We will remain vigilant, but for now, it seems the danger has passed. Tomorrow, business will continue as usual, and you will be shadowing the Minister of Autumn. It will be good for you to see how he manages preparations for a seasonal turn."

"Yes, Your Majesty."

With a stiff nod, Elvina left the room.

As soon as the door latched behind her, Clarion collapsed into bed. In the dark, the ceiling swam with the golden light emanating from her wings. From her vantage point, she could see the vastness of the night sky through her window. And there, reaching toward the scattering of stars, was the frost-backed peak of the mountain, frozen and forlorn. This time, it felt less like the mountains watching her—and more like a winter fairy. If she closed her eyes, she could practically see it: Milori, his hair like a white flame in the wind, his eyes fixed on the Pixie Dust Tree.

I will be waiting here, at sunset, every night for a week.

6

The next day, Clarion regretted staying up so late. By the time evening settled over the Autumn Forest, she was exhausted from a full day's work alongside the Minister of Autumn—and shivering even in her cobweb shawl.

Rowan, who had excused himself a few minutes ago, returned now with a mug of dandelion-root tea. He handed it to her with a knowing sort of look. "You'll get used to the long days eventually."

"I hope I haven't been dragging too much," she said, equal parts embarrassed and grateful that he'd noticed. "Thank you."

He beamed at her. "Not at all."

Clarion took a sip of her tea. Although she never much cared for the dandelion's bitterness, it made her feel that she somewhat belonged among the living. At the very least, it warmed her hands. The temperature here always landed perfectly on *crisp*, and the foliage blazed eternal in its red and orange glory. It made her long for things she had not enjoyed for quite some time: long evenings by a fire, or diving into an ocean of fallen leaves.

Rowan had recently begun preparations for the arrival of autumn, and despite her distraction, Clarion was determined to commit every detail to memory. This would be the first seasonal transition she oversaw as queen, and after how bitterly she'd disappointed Elvina last night, nothing could go awry. This would be her one opportunity to prove her mettle now that she had dissuaded herself from any further engagement with the Warden of the Winter Woods. Never mind that she had lain awake for far longer than she cared to admit, turning over his every word to her.

Now, Clarion directed all her formidable willpower to putting him far, *far* out of mind. It was admittedly difficult when Artemis lurked a few yards away, staring at Clarion as though she might vanish if Artemis looked away for even a moment. Clarion supposed she deserved her renewed attention—and the guilt that accompanied it. She had landed Artemis in trouble with her little disappearing act.

She hadn't been to Autumn since the Revelry last year, where all the world glowed beneath the light of the full harvest moon. She still remembered the gleam of the autumn scepter refracting moonlight into blue pixie dust—how it had rained down on them, gathering in the trees and catching on her eyelashes like snowfall. She'd rarely seen Pixie Hollow so joyous. Most of all, she remembered standing beside Elvina, placid-faced and aching, as she watched everyone dancing and glittering far below them.

She'd hovered, as she did now, forever out of reach.

Clarion watched the autumn fairies work in the glade below. With Elvina's decree to return to business as usual, it seemed impossible for Clarion to imagine there had been any danger at all. And yet, as the shadows beneath the trees deepened, she could not shake her misgivings.

Waning sunlight dripped through the canopy, patterning the earth in soft rose gold. A few fairies gathered around a leaf-talent dabbing pigment onto an oak leaf carted in from summer, nodding and murmuring approvingly at his technique. A fast-flying fairy whizzed past Clarion. She dragged a great gust of wind in her wake, sending Clarion's hair fluttering—and a flock of monarch butterflies whirling off their course. The animal-talent shepherding them wailed in protest.

"Sorry!" the fast-flyer called without stopping.

"Three thousand miles!" the animal-talent shouted after her, shaking her crook. "They have to go three thousand miles!"

Clarion couldn't help smiling. How wondrous to see her subjects, bickering and laughing and demonstrating their talents. Rowan, meanwhile, seemed entirely unfazed, as if this sort of ruckus was so commonplace as to be unremarkable. He stood with one hand tucked into the pocket of his cloak. In the other, he held a notebook, filled to bursting with his haphazard scrawl. He'd told her it was a checklist, but Clarion could not in good conscience call such disorder a checklist. Items had been scribbled out and tacked on with reckless abandon. His mind worked in leaps she could not follow.

"At this point in the cycle," he said, as if he had been speaking for quite some time already, "we're mainly testing new ideas and ensuring we have all the supplies we'll need. Elvina typically trusts me to handle all the small details. But a few days before we leave for the Mainland, she pays us a visit to give our preparations a final review."

"And how does she know what you've done is acceptable?"

His eyes twinkled at her. "Intuition."

That was exactly the sort of unquantifiable answer that tormented her. No, she could not depend on something as untrustworthy and inconstant as her own intuition. These past few days, it had done nothing but cause her trouble. Surely he was teasing her. Elvina almost certainly had an elaborate system of criteria she'd devised to assess his work. Clarion made a mental note to trouble her for it when she returned to the palace.

Clearly sensing her distress, Rowan laughed. "And a little faith in her minister, of course. I've done this hundreds of times before, Clarion. You're in good hands—or at least experienced ones."

The reminder of his age did little to assuage her. It was only a bitter reminder of how far she had to go—and how she did not have the luxury of centuries to become competent. "Did it ever worry you?"

Surprise softened his face. "What?"

"I don't know," she said quietly. She found she could not say what she really meant. *Did you ever doubt yourself?* Instead, she swept a hand down at the glade below them, where a group of leaf-talents were folding and refolding dried leaves into complicated patterns—an effort to achieve the optimal crunch-when-stepped-upon texture. *A very complicated process,* Rowan had once assured her. "All of this. Everything depending on you. Everyone looking to you."

His loose curls fluttered in the wind, and the shadows of his long eyelashes slanted across his cheekbones. As he considered her, frowning, Clarion could not unsee the stillness of an ancient forest that lived behind his eyes. "I'm sure it did, once upon a time. But it's not in my nature. Autumn is all about reflection and slowing down. As I've gotten older, I've learned not to worry about things before they happen."

"I see." Was that the trick, then? Simply choosing not to worry? It was a truly foreign concept to her, considering her closest friend was Petra, who chose to worry about every possibility.

"You're a governing-talent," Rowan said. "I know it seems overwhelming in the abstract, but once you get into it, you'll know what to do."

Clarion drew her shawl tighter around herself. "Of course."

His smile faded as he drank in her expression. "What brought all this on? Is Her Majesty giving you trouble?"

"We have had our disagreements lately," she said as diplomatically as she could.

"Is that so?" He rested his chin appraisingly in the crook of his forefinger and thumb. "Ever since you were a brand-new arrival, you've tried to make yourself into the very image of her. The same posture. The same voice—you know the one. I can't imagine she's discouraged that."

Clarion wanted to take it as a compliment, but something about his tone suggested he did not mean it as one. Less like a human mother and child, whom she'd heard tended to bear resemblance to one another, and more like a child and her doll. At the plain sympathy on his face—*no,* she thought, *pity*—she bristled. "She only wants to prepare me for the role."

"Of course she does." Rowan quickly backtracked. "And I only mean to say you are a credit to her. You have always been . . . shall we say, rebellious? Still, what disagreements could you possibly have?"

"She says I've gotten my priorities confused. It's more natural to me to address what I see in front of me. An argument. Someone's feelings." *An opportunity to investigate,* she thought. She picked at an invisible loose thread on her shawl. "It distracts me from the bigger picture."

"Ah." There was something unreadable in his expression, as though he was trying to hold himself back from saying what was truly on his mind. "Perhaps what she meant to say is that you can't blame yourself every time things go wrong. Try as you may, you can't solve every issue in Pixie Hollow on your own."

"I suppose not."

He clapped her on the shoulder, an affectionate gesture that nearly knocked her off balance. "You have better instincts than you give yourself credit for."

But I don't. If only he knew. If only he knew just how inadequate she was beneath the façade. When it came down to the things that mattered—the decision-making, the composure, the raw *power*—she would never be Elvina's equal. She offered him a wobbly smile. "I appreciate that. Truly."

His expression grew serious. "Clarion. You know you don't need to—"

The very air shivered, and all the world went deathly, unnaturally silent. Gooseflesh rippled down her arms. Dread gripped her spine in a vise. It felt like the skin-crawling moment before lightning struck, but the sky—dark as it was with encroaching night—was cloudless.

Rowan frowned. "Did you feel that?"

"I did," she said, a little breathlessly.

Artemis appeared at her side in an instant, her fingers hovering above the quiver of arrows strapped to her hip. Rowan tucked his notebook into his pocket. The hem of his cloak snapped in the wind. In the glade below, everyone had frozen. No shadow of a hawk darkened the earth. No scream of a fox rent the silence. But there, at the tree line . . .

Something caught Clarion's attention. Black fog—had fog ever been so thick?—spilled into the clearing, and shadows pooled on the earth. They began to seethe and thrash, as if struggling to take shape. Murmurs of alarm broke out from the glade below.

"What *is* that?" Clarion asked.

"I don't know," Artemis said apprehensively. She withdrew an arrow and nocked it in her bow. A formidable weapon against their natural enemies, certainly, but something told Clarion it'd be useless against whatever *that* was.

Threads of darkness swirled upward, weaving together as they rose. Clarion caught the glimmer of black scales, the flash of venom-bright eyes. *A serpent,* she realized after a moment—although not like any serpent she'd ever seen. It was solid, *real*, and yet its body seemed to be composed entirely of smoke, held together by what looked to be stitches of violet light. Its body looped around itself in coils, dripping and oozing from its seams; the exact shape of it changed from blink to blink, as though it could hardly remember what exactly it was meant to be. It sprouted a limb, then a wing, before reabsorbing them. She could scarcely hold it in her mind. Its long shadow fell like a blade over the autumn fairies.

Monster.

It hissed. That was all it took for Artemis to spring into action. She loosed her arrow. It soared through the air and into the beast's open mouth. Although it skewered the back of its head, the serpent did not even flinch. All the color drained from Artemis's face.

"Everyone, flee!" Rowan shouted.

That was when the screaming began.

As the fairies took flight, the serpent spat its venom. It was pitch black—and glinting with an oily, iridescent sheen. Every fairy it struck dropped from the sky and hit the earth with a sickening sound. They did not cry out; they only lay there, limp, as though they'd fallen asleep mid-flight. Rowan looked on in horror.

Clarion seized his elbow. "We have to do something."

That, evidently, was enough to snap him out of his stupor. He rounded on her, his jaw set and his mouth pressed into a thin line. "Oh, no. *I* have to do something. *You* will return to the palace at once. It's far too dangerous for you to be here."

How many times would she be forced to stay back? Excluded from aiding in the protection of her people? "What good is a queen if she's forbidden to do a single thing?"

"Better than a dead one," Artemis snarled.

Clarion wavered. Considering only one governing-talent arrived every few hundred years, they were a precious commodity. No one knew what would happen if a queen died before her time. Would another be sent, or would Pixie Hollow be left to the wisdom of its ministers?

Artemis fumbled to withdraw a blade of bluegrass from her pocket. She brought it to her lips and blew. The shrill sound cut through the forest. The scouts' alarm. After a few moments, Clarion heard the alarm picked up by another scout in the distance.

"Scouts will be here any minute," said Artemis. "Come with me. It's not worth your life."

"You know she's right," Rowan said, more gently this time. "Go."

"Fine," Clarion choked out. "Just help them."

"I'll keep her safe, sir." Artemis sounded as duty bound as ever, but Clarion did not miss the emotion shining in her eyes.

Regret, she thought. *And longing.*

He nodded, then turned his attention to the glade below. A few brave fast-flyers had stayed, trying to corral the beast away from their friends. They dodged and wove through its shadowy coils, pelting it with whatever they could get their hands on. This time, Rowan did not hesitate. He dove from the knoll, his wings snapping wide.

"Distract it," he shouted. "I'll move the wounded to safety."

Clarion could not tear her eyes away from the handful of fast-flyers. They sliced through the air in wild streaks and flurries of pixie dust. With the beast distracted, Rowan landed and lifted one of the downed fairies into his arms. Just as he began carrying her toward the tree line, the monster rounded on him. Venom dripped from its bared fangs.

No. Clarion saw the moment he turned—and realized what was about to happen. Every second stretched into an eternity. On instinct, her hand shot out. As if she could reach him from this distance. As if she could do a thing. But fear had kindled a spark within her that tore through her like wildfire. She knew that feeling.

Magic.

She gasped as the golden light of her power flared at the center of her palm and launched itself at the beast. Her surprise had made her aim terrible, but the serpent reared back as if burned.

For a moment, Clarion could only stare down at her own hand in dumbstruck wonder. Magic still glimmered like stardust in her palm. It bathed her in its golden light and set Artemis's wide-open eyes aglow. How had she . . . ? No. Right now, it didn't matter how she had done it—only that she could do it again. Scouts were on the way, but they wouldn't be here in time. Besides, arrows had not done a thing against that monster.

But maybe magic would.

She had promised to be good. She had promised to be safe. But if it meant saving lives . . . "Please forgive me, Artemis."

When Clarion took flight, she heard only the faint cry of "Your Highness! Wait!"

By the time she glided down, planting herself between the serpent and Rowan, it had reoriented itself. Where her magic had singed it, its flesh—if it could be called flesh at all—had begun sloughing off in gouts of black liquid.

Up close, it was even more horrifying than it had been at a distance. The nearness of it filled her skull with a droning buzz of fear. And then, it turned the full brunt of its gaze on her. Her mind went entirely blank. Her every muscle seized with some instinctual fear.

She forced herself to lift her hands, but they were trembling. Her magic had never felt so far away. But now, of all times, she had to be perfect.

Control, she thought, through the rabbit scream of terror her thoughts had become. *Focus.*

Her magic sputtered weakly in her palm. The serpent poised itself to strike, its jaw hinging wide. In that moment, the stranglehold she'd exerted on her magic loosened. Two thoughts occurred to her at once. *I am going to die.* And, stronger yet: *If you want to hurt them, you will have to go through me.*

It was the second one that filled her, strangely, with serenity. Golden light poured from her. It flared brighter than the sun, cutting through the low-hanging mist in the clearing.

Then, something knocked Clarion to the ground.

She went sprawling, kicking up a cloud of dust in her wake. A heavy weight settled over her. When the spots cleared from her vision, Clarion was staring up at Artemis, her face streaked with dirt and wild with panic. She could hear nothing over the ringing in her ears and the sound of their ragged breathing. Motes of starlight still glimmered in the air when her vision cleared, drifting like snowflakes on the other side of the border.

But when she dared to lift herself onto one elbow, she saw nothing left of the serpent but a wisp of darkness, slithering frantically back into the shadow of the woods. Venom spattered the earth where Clarion had been standing just a moment before.

Artemis had saved her.

Her relief did not last long, however. Her gaze snagged on Rowan, lying very still amidst the scattered autumn leaves. They reminded her too much of blood.

"Minister!"

She scrabbled to her feet and flew to him. He did not stir at her approach, but his chest rose and fell. *Alive.* Clarion nearly wept with relief. She knelt at his side and shook him. His expression contorted—not with pain, exactly, but . . . fear? His eyes flickered behind their closed lids. It almost looked as though he was having a nightmare.

She shook him again, more frantically. "Wake up."

He made no reply.

Clarion's breaths came heavier. What was happening? Slowly, she stood and surveyed the wreckage around her. All of the fairies' careful preparations were upended. Unconscious fairies lay in the clearing, a few letting out choked sobs as they slept. Panic rose within her. She fluttered to the next fairy beside Rowan and shook her. "Wake up."

Nothing.

She fluttered to the next and the next and the next. None of them stirred.

Nothing, nothing, nothing.

"Wake up," she whispered to herself. "Please, please. Wake up."

By the time she attempted to rouse a sixth from her slumber, a hand landed heavily on her shoulder.

"Your Highness," Artemis said softly. "Stop."

At last, Clarion sank to her knees and buried her face in her hands. She breathed until she no longer felt close to tears. Never in her life had she felt so pathetic, so *unqueenly*. Never had she felt so disgusted with herself.

For the first time, Clarion fully understood why Elvina did not trust her. She understood the true depth of her failures. If she did not master her abilities before her coronation, one day, Pixie Hollow would fall to ruin.

And it would be entirely her fault.

7

Clarion hardly recalled being brought back to the palace.

The scouts had arrived only minutes after the serpent escaped, alighting around her in formation on quiet feet. None of them said a word to her; at least, if they did, she did not hear it. Her grief had pulled a gauze over the world; behind it, nothing felt entirely real. Behind it, nothing could truly touch her. She vaguely remembered the scouts surveying the scene in silent horror. She remembered the dull sensation of pain when she noticed the scrapes on her arm. Then: Artemis steering her away from the Autumn Forest.

Now, she sat numbly in Elvina's quarters, perched on a chaise longue. At some point, Artemis had removed her cloak and wrapped it around Clarion's shoulders. It was warm with body heat, but Clarion still shivered. Someone had also pressed a cup of tea into her hands, but it had gone cold. The room was cozily dark, with the heavy curtains drawn over the windows and candlelight gilding every surface. Shadows flickered across Elvina's face.

"Clarion." Elvina's voice—gentler than she'd heard it in quite some time—jolted her back into her body. "What happened?"

Clarion took a sip of her tea, if only to save herself from answering immediately. She pulled air into her lungs until the haze over her thoughts cleared. "I'm not sure I can describe it properly. It all happened very quickly."

"I understand. But please try."

And so, Clarion did. How one moment, everything had been normal—and how the next, the air had gone cold and heavy. How a shadow had come to life before her very eyes, only half-formed. How fairies dropped like stones from the sky and did not rouse themselves. How dread had felt like a living weight on her when she came face to face with the beast, rooting her in place. The very thought of it made her shudder.

As Clarion spoke, Elvina's expression did not change. No surprise—no horror—registered. She only looked grimly resigned. By the time Clarion finished recounting the evening, a sick sense of certainty washed over her. The doubt Milori had introduced no longer felt so ridiculous.

"You know what they are," she said.

The firelight glimmered in Elvina's eyes. The shadows it threw carved stark lines into her face. For a moment, her expression was unreadable. Would she deny it, even now? Then, with a displeased twist of her mouth, she said, "They're called Nightmares."

"Nightmares?" Even saying it aloud chilled her.

"As you've now seen, they have a terrible power," Elvina continued. "They plunge their victims into a terror-filled slumber. The moment we received the first alarm, I had our healers begin work on an antidote. So far, none of their efforts have worked. The Minister of Autumn and ten other citizens of Pixie Hollow have yet to be roused."

Clarion could hardly process it. Until they developed an antidote, eleven fairies would suffer for as long as they lived. Guilt bubbled up within her, but stronger still was her frustration. Right now, all Clarion could think of was how Elvina had kept this from her. If she had known what she was up against—if she could have prepared herself . . .

"You knew what they were capable of?"

"And I have made plans to deal with it," Elvina replied. Clarion detected the defensive edge to her voice. "The healing-talents will continue to work around the clock until they find the cure. They will keep everyone as comfortable as possible until their task is complete."

No, she would not allow Elvina to keep her in the dark any longer. "What *are* they?"

"No one knows exactly." Elvina settled on the chaise longue

beside her and folded her hands in her lap. She stared straight ahead, her expression oddly vacant. "Once, a very long time ago, queens remembered the origin of Nightmares. But knowledge of them has faded with time. All we have are fragments.

"Titania, the first Queen of Pixie Hollow, entrusted the story to her apprentice—and so on down the line, until now. By the time it reached me, it had grown distorted and vague. It was more like a fairy tale, one worn smooth with repetition until it hardly seemed real at all. All I can tell you is that Nightmares dwell in the Winter Woods, where the nights are long and the cold feels like a familiar embrace. No one had seen them in an eternity, but my mentor imparted this to me: if they ever reemerged, we must act swiftly."

Her words sank in slowly. Over the years, Elvina had given Clarion morsels of Pixie Hollow's history. But no mention had ever been made of *Nightmares*. Clearly, it was a deliberate omission. Before she could stop herself, before she could swallow yet another flash of hurt, she said, "Why didn't you tell me sooner?"

"It didn't seem important."

"It seems important now."

"What would you have me do?" Elvina said through her teeth. "You cannot yet access the full range of your abilities. Legends about things that might very well have never come to pass—that might never have even existed—would only have distracted you."

"You cannot decide what I should and should not know." Clarion's voice trembled with the force of her anger. The attack had shaken her far too much for her to maintain her usual composure. Eleven people wounded because of *her* failures—and because of Elvina's lack of caution. "What else have you not told me?"

Elvina sighed as though the conversation had thoroughly exhausted her. "Clarion. Contain yourself."

Control. Focus. If she could not present herself as a proper queen, Elvina would not treat her as one. Clarion drew in a deep breath, doing her utmost to smooth her features into passivity. This was how Elvina liked her best. This was how she could convince her that she was capable.

"I have to be prepared for all eventualities," said Clarion. "How can I be prepared if I don't know what I'm up against?"

With her composure restored, Elvina regarded her less like a Sprinting Thistle about to tear through Springtime Square. Back into familiar territory, at last. With equal measure, the queen said, "It will be handled."

Clarion set her teacup down on its saucer with a clink as brittle as her nerves. "How?"

Silence descended over them. For a moment, Clarion thought that would be the end of the discussion. But Elvina shocked her by responding.

"We must minimize the risk of repeating another tragedy. I will convene a meeting tomorrow to discuss the safety plan for Pixie Hollow. In the meantime, the scouts will handle flushing out the Nightmares—and disposing of them."

Clarion could only think of how quickly the Nightmare had

struck; of fairies falling from the sky, silhouetted by the bloodred sunlight, pixie dust streaming from their limp wings. There was no way to dispose of a beast like that so neatly. But then she remembered how it had fled when she'd unleashed her magic, like a roach skittering away from a sudden flood of light. Clarion still did not know how she'd done it, or if she could do it again.

But Elvina could.

"They're frightened of our magic."

Surprise passed over Elvina's face. "Oh?"

"I was able to summon my magic—just briefly. If only you could have seen it." Clarion tamped down her enthusiasm as much as she could. She reminded herself that composure, not conviction, would win her mentor over. "None of Artemis's weapons did a thing to it. But if you or I accompanied the scouts—"

"No. It is out of the question, Clarion." Elvina rose from her seat abruptly, her tone turning frigid. "Pixie Hollow is only as strong as its queen."

What good is a queen if she's forbidden to do a single thing?

Better than a dead one.

Her heart twisted. If that were true, then Pixie Hollow should have been unbreakable. Elvina, after all, was the perfect queen. Though now, Clarion was not so certain. Elvina would not hear counsel. She would not share valuable information, which could have prevented all of this from unfolding as catastrophically as it did.

If you are interested in solving this problem rather than avoiding it, you know where to find me. In that moment, she could think only of Milori and his sad gray eyes: someone with a plan to act.

Elvina was not lying to her, surely, but she clearly was not telling her the entire truth, either. Unless Clarion wanted to sit quietly—unless she wanted to completely smother her own intuition forever—she had no options left. For the good of Pixie Hollow, she would swallow her reservations. The moment she could, she would find Milori where Spring bled into Winter.

The next morning, Elvina convened an assembly.

On her orders, everyone set aside their work for the day and poured into the palace's throne room. Ivy and flowering vines hung from the ceiling like royal banners, and sunlight filtered in from delicate fissures in the wood, washing the space in gold.

The throne itself sprouted from the earth: a sapling's trunk, carved into a seat. Twisting branches, lush with summer leaves, formed the armrests and back. It was beautiful, but Clarion had always suspected it to be terribly uncomfortable. Here on the moss-carpeted dais, she towered above the fairies gathered below. It astounded her, just how many lives she would one day hold in her hands. She hadn't seen all her subjects in one place since the day she arrived.

Elvina stood at the very edge of the dais, regal and utterly resplendent. She wore her full regalia today: her horned crown, woven with wildflowers, and her wide-skirted gown, glistering and golden with pixie dust. Clarion stood a short distance behind her, flanked on either side by the Ministers of Spring and Summer. Neither of them had said a word all morning. Without Rowan—without the lively discussion and laughter he sparked—they seemed almost lost. Their silence had suited her fine. Clarion startled at every rattle of leaves in the breeze, at every lengthening shadow.

Murmurs rippled through the gathered masses. In their upturned faces, Clarion saw all her worry reflected back at her a thousandfold. Absently, she reached for that spark of power within her and found nothing. Why had it abandoned her again, when it had come to her so easily yesterday? In that moment of danger, faced with that beast, something within her had given way.

But *what*?

For the life of her, she could not remember what technique she had employed. At the time, her mind had been consumed with a sort of blankness, somewhere between desperation and resignation. It was entirely impossible to replicate here of all places, and she did not know how she could re-create those conditions unless she decided to make a habit of throwing herself headlong into life-threatening situations. Besides, she did not know whether she wanted to find out if—when it truly mattered—she could summon the power she needed to save someone.

Elvina lifted a hand, and a hush fell instantly over the crowd. There was that governing-talent magnetism at work. It never failed to impress Clarion.

"Thank you all for gathering here today," said Elvina. "I

understand this is unusual and that you all have work to finish, so I will endeavor to keep this brief. However, there is a dire situation in Pixie Hollow—one that I am sure many of you have heard of through rumors and speculation. Yesterday, a group of fairies was attacked in the Autumn Forest by a creature that crossed from the Winter Woods."

Gasps and shouts of alarm met Elvina's words.

"I know many of you have questions." Elvina's voice carried above the crowds, echoing off the high ceilings. "I know many of you are concerned. I want to put those worries to rest and assure you that we are doing everything in our power to keep all residents of Pixie Hollow safe. All the victims are alive and in stable condition. While we do not have much information to share, it seems these monsters can ensnare their prey in a slumber they cannot wake from. While we have not been able to rouse the victims, our healers are hard at work to restore them. Now—"

A storm-talent dressed in a gown of rain lilies shot up in the crowd. "With all due respect, Your Majesty, how did this happen? Just the other day, all of us were placed under a curfew—then assured the threat had been handled."

Clarion tried not to let her surprise show on her face. In all her seventeen years, she had never heard someone question Elvina so openly. But many in the crowd nodded their agreement.

"Our scouts did not find any evidence of a continued threat at the time," Elvina replied, with some ice in her tone. "With the information we had—and given Princess Clarion's imminent coronation—it seemed the best course of action to resume normal activity. I very much regret the lack of caution, and I assure you such an oversight will not happen again. What happened was a tragedy, and I accept responsibility. Now, if I may?"

When no one else chimed in, she clasped her hands and resumed. "Eleven of your fellows are currently under our healers' care. One of them, as many of you know by now, is the Minister of Autumn."

Another fairy—a dyeing-talent spattered with pigments—spoke from the back of the crowd. "How will the preparations for autumn be handled?"

Murmurs erupted from the crowd again, their voices low with fear. Clarion hadn't truly considered the impact of it until now. If a season did not arrive on the Mainland in time, the effects could be disastrous. A long summer meant drought. It meant deadly heat waves and wildfires. Crops withering in the soil and waters choked with algal blooms. Nature was a vast network, like a spider's delicate web. If one thread was touched, it reverberated through the whole. There were things not even pixie dust and the work ethic of fairies could help.

That vicious voice in her head whispered, *And it would be all your fault.*

If she were a more competent governing-talent, then . . .

"There are still several months before autumn is due to arrive on the Mainland," Elvina replied, with far more confidence than Clarion could muster. "We will do everything in our power to ensure preparations continue without a hitch. The autumn fairies are knowledgeable, and Princess Clarion and I will manage in the minister's stead. However, I anticipate he will be back on his feet well before we feel his absence."

Some of the crowd's restlessness seemed to dissipate. Clarion thought she saw some of the tension bleed from Elvina's shoulders when their subjects once again fell quiet. The idea that she had been rattled, even for a second, seemed preposterous to Clarion. Elvina had never once shown anything but unflagging conviction in her own plans. She had refused to hear anything different last night.

"Before I dismiss you," Elvina said, "I would like to share the names of those who are recovering from the attack."

Her cupped hands filled with the light of her magic. With each name she recited, she let an orb of light rise to the ceiling. Pixie dust rained softly down on them. From here, Clarion could see fairies holding each other close or joining hands to comfort one another.

"We will deal with the creatures that did this," said Elvina, when all eleven lights burned brightly above them. "But we must not be reckless. Beginning today, I am instituting a curfew again. Now that we have learned these creatures are active in the darkness, no one will go out after the sun has set. There will be no exceptions. Anyone who breaks this rule will answer to me. Are we understood?"

The silence was complete.

Then, a weather-talent, his hair wild from tracking the wind patterns, asked, "And what of Winter?"

There was the faintest note of accusation in it. All at once,

Clarion became acutely aware of the mountain looming to the north—all the windswept, glaring white of it.

Several fairies spoke at once, clamoring to be heard:

"You said those beasts came from Winter."

"Have they set them loose?"

"Have they lost control of them?"

"Have they fallen victim to them as well?"

Elvina held up her hand, demanding silence once more. When the commotion died down, she replied, "The Warden of the Winter Woods has not made contact with the warm seasons in quite some time. However, I do not believe this is their doing. I can only imagine that they must be suffering, too. My thoughts are with them."

Did Elvina believe that, or did she *know*? Clarion flinched at the turn of her own thoughts. She hated this newfound paranoia—this mistrust of the woman who had all but raised her.

"That said, I share your trepidation. We must take measures to protect ourselves in the long term." Elvina canted her chin, and the hooked shadow of her crown stretched across the floor. "I intend to tear down the bridges between Winter and the warm seasons."

If the crowd reacted, Clarion could not hear it over the ringing in her own ears. Horror felt like claws raking down her back.

"It will take time," Elvina continued. "The magic flowing within them is powerful and cannot be destroyed by ordinary means. But rest assured, the plan is already in motion."

This was Elvina's plan? To abandon Winter to the Nightmares—worse, to set them adrift from the rest of Pixie Hollow entirely?

Perhaps Clarion had little experience ruling. Perhaps she did not understand exactly what they were dealing with. But she knew, down to the very heart of her, that this was *wrong.*

When Elvina dismissed the assembly, fairies began filtering out. A familiar voice cut through the gloom of her thoughts.

"Clarion!"

She looked up to see Petra fighting her way to the foot of the dais, her red hair blazing bright beneath the sunlight. The sight of her comforted Clarion more than she expected. Before she could open her mouth to greet her, Petra launched herself forward and seized Clarion's forearm. Something as familiar as embracing her in public would raise eyebrows, but she felt all the warmth and relief Petra intended in the steady pressure of her grip.

"You're all right," Petra breathed. "When I heard what happened, I . . ."

"It's all right. *I'm* all right." Clarion offered her an uncertain smile. "Mostly."

Petra withdrew her hand, instead letting it curl protectively in front of her chest. "What's wrong?"

Clarion's gaze darted to Elvina, who had begun speaking with Aurelia and Iris in hushed tones. Artemis, standing dutifully at the foot of the dais, *of course* noticed her feeble attempt to be sneaky. She narrowed her eyes at Clarion, as if to say, *I know you're up to something.* After her disappearance two nights ago—and the attack in Autumn—she supposed she'd never slip away from her guard so easily again.

"Not here," Clarion said. "Follow me."

Petra groaned.

Clarion led her toward the door of the throne room. Artemis immediately began to follow them, close enough to keep an eye on them, far enough to stay mostly out of earshot. As inconvenient as it was at times, Clarion couldn't deny how safe she felt with her shadow falling over them. Petra cast surreptitious glances her way every now and again, the color on her cheeks deepening with every passing moment. Sometimes, it was impossible to tell if she wanted to run *from* Artemis or *toward* her.

When they made it to the lawn of the palace grounds, a sprawling stretch of green spangled with buttercups and wood sorrel, Clarion settled onto the grass. This early in the morning, it was still cool and damp with dew. The entire field sparkled beneath the sunlight. Clarion couldn't help thinking it looked like frost.

"What is it you've brought me out here for?" Petra asked.

"What do you make of Elvina's plan?"

Some of the concern faded from Petra's face. Comfortable in the realm of logistics and her own expertise, she said, "She's spoken to some of the tinkers about it already. The roots of the Pixie Dust Tree can't be destroyed easily, so it won't be as simple as setting the woodcutting-talents on it. But if there's some way to imbue an axe with magic, then theoretically . . ."

Petra began sketching out the theory for her, but Clarion processed little of it. She could not stand the thought of governing-talent magic and tinker ingenuity being used in such a way. Of

Milori, who'd sought out her help, being so summarily shut out. More than anything, Clarion could not bear the idea of wasting this opportunity. If she had even a small chance to mend the rift between their worlds, how could she turn away from it?

"I have to stop her," Clarion said.

Petra's face went deathly pale, and her voice came out as little more than a squeak. "Stop her? Why?"

Clarion sat up straighter. "Because it isn't right to abandon the winter fairies to the Nightmares! Do you even know what will happen if the bridges are destroyed?"

"No one will be able to cross into Winter again," Petra replied. Judging by her frown—and her hesitant tone—Clarion's protests did compel her. "But the dustologists confirmed that there are other root systems connecting Winter to the Pixie Dust Tree. They'll be fine. Just alone."

Is alone truly fine? Clarion wondered. She shook her head. "There has to be some other way."

After how dismissive Elvina had been of her ideas, Clarion harbored no delusions of being able to dissuade her. Which meant she had to talk to Milori.

"I haven't seen that look in a while," Petra said, with equal parts fond admiration and wariness.

Clarion blinked, startled out of her own thoughts. "What look?"

Petra put on something like a scowl and gestured to her own face. "This look. It means you're going to do something reckless."

Clarion smiled innocently, if only to hide that she did indeed plan to do something reckless. "I would never! I've outgrown such things."

Petra buried her face in her hands. "Why don't I believe you?"

"I'm just going to talk to Elvina," she lied. "Don't worry."

"Why would you say that? That's going to make me worry more!"

But Clarion had already turned her mind to plotting. Elvina's new decree had given her the perfect opportunity to sneak out. Until further notice, no one would be out and about at night. No one would know to miss her. No one except Elvina.

And Artemis.

Clarion dared to look over at her, half-hidden with her earth-colored tunic against the trunk of the Pixie Dust Tree. As if called—as if she could sense the ill-advised scheme brewing in her mind—Artemis met her eyes with a wary frown.

For the good of Pixie Hollow, Clarion would have to find a way around her.

8

All week, Clarion could focus on little else but the sun inching gradually westward. In the daylight, life continued as normal. But as the afternoon frittered away to evening, dread gathered over Pixie Hollow like a storm cloud. Even Clarion found herself flinching at every distant cry of an animal. Today, she was even more painfully aware of the lengthening shadows. Because once the sun dipped below the horizon, the week Milori had offered her would be gone.

Impatience lodged itself like a splinter in her mind. Her duties had consumed her every spare minute lately, and today was no exception. During the council meeting, she stared at Rowan's empty chair as representatives from the scouts and healers presented their updates on the Nightmares. The only words she truly absorbed were *no trace* and *no cure*. It only further confirmed what she suspected: there was nothing the warm seasons alone could do.

She needed to speak to Milori.

Her schedule was mercifully clear after this, but Artemis would no doubt prove to be an obstacle. In the wake of Elvina's decree, she'd been particularly *attentive*. Any click of a lock or creak of a door, and Clarion felt the weight of the scout's eyes like the tip of a blade pressed to her spine. If she couldn't sneak past her, she would have to try a different tactic: asking permission. Clarion might not have known Artemis as well as she knew Petra, but she knew her values. More importantly, she knew her heart. If anyone could understand the burden of wanting to keep Pixie Hollow safe, it was her.

As soon as the meeting adjourned, Clarion determinedly ignored Elvina's assessing stare and hurried back to her room. She unlatched her balcony doors and stepped out into the late-afternoon warmth. Artemis, predictably, was perched in the forked branches of a moss-covered tree limb, her polished wooden sword resting in the crook of her neck and shoulder. Her arms draped lazily over the knee she'd drawn into her chest. The angle of the sunlight cast half her face in shadow and set the shades of blue in her dark hair alight.

Absently, Clarion noted that the Pixie Dust Tree had sprouted a single Neverberry just above the scout's head, as though offering her hospitality while she kept her lonely watch. Every now and again, it took notice of its inhabitants and their moods. Once, after a particularly difficult day, the branches just outside her window had blossomed riotously with golden butterfly magnolias.

"Your Highness," Artemis said by way of greeting, her voice as coolly deferential as ever.

Clarion rested her elbows on the balcony railing, doing her very best to appear casual. It occurred to her that she so rarely did such a thing—what a concept, appearing *casual*—and had little idea what to do with her hands or face.

"I have a free afternoon," she said. "I was hoping to go out."

Artemis eyed her warily. "Where do you want to go?"

"The border of Spring and Winter?" As soon as the words left her mouth, she winced. She'd meant to sound confident, but it came out as more of a question.

Artemis grimaced. "I don't think Her Majesty would like that very much."

"No, I don't think she would."

Artemis seemed relieved. "Then we're agreed."

"*If*," Clarion added brightly, "she knew that I went."

Artemis straightened up, now catching on to Clarion's game. She laid her sword across her lap and turned to her with a look on her face that could only be described as incredulous. "You want me to lie to Her Majesty for you."

Well, that was much easier to broach than she'd expected. "If you want to put it like that . . . yes."

"Surely—" As if on cue, the branch of the tree bearing the fruit drooped onto Artemis's shoulder. Bewildered, she plucked it and stared down at it. "What is this?"

Clarion bit down on a smile. "A bribe, I think. Did it work?"

Artemis did not look impressed, nor did she dignify their antics with a reply. "Surely there's somewhere else you might like to go." After a moment, with a touch of hopefulness in her voice, she added: "Perhaps Tinker's Nook?"

Clarion met her gaze with all the conviction burning bright within her. "Nowhere else would suit me better than the border."

Artemis, clearly sensing that Clarion would not be moved with good sense, sighed deeply. "Permission to speak freely?"

"Of course."

Artemis stood and, with a flutter of her wings, came to land gracefully on the banister. The leaves cast dappled shadows over her face. "Your Highness, my orders are to keep you *safe*. Given the circumstances—and frankly, knowing you—the border is the very last place I should allow you to go."

Clarion had expected that answer. Artemis, after all, was the most duty-bound fairy she knew—and far more devoted to her than Clarion deserved. As much as it frustrated her, it touched her. Artemis would not be so strict if she didn't care. "I wouldn't insist if it weren't important. Trust me."

Artemis hesitated. Whatever she saw in Clarion's expression

must have softened her, because she sat so that they were nearly eye level again. She took a bite of the fruit and chewed thoughtfully. "What's at the border that you want to see so badly?"

"The Warden of the Winter Woods."

Shock flickered in Artemis's eyes, as subtle a change as shadows passing over the moon. Warily, she asked, "Why would you want to meet with them?"

"I think he knows how to defeat the Nightmares." Clarion frowned. "Cutting Winter off from the rest of Pixie Hollow isn't an option. If I can save more fairies, then I have to try."

Artemis looked more conflicted than Clarion had ever seen her. With unmistakable fondness, she said, "You always have been so stubborn."

Hope sparked within her. "Then you'll let me go?"

"I shouldn't—for your own good. I am no stranger to what happens when someone leads with their heart over their head." Artemis smiled ruefully, as if lost in some reverie. "Queen Elvina and Commander Nightshade gave me a second chance by appointing me the royal guard. If any harm befell you, I don't know what it would cost me."

It surprised Clarion, both Artemis's vulnerability and her confession. Artemis had been such a steady presence, it shocked her to realize that she'd had a life before Clarion even arrived. There were things about her she did not know—and might never know. "I can't imagine you ever leading with your heart."

"That was a long time ago," said Artemis.

When she looked up at Clarion again, her stoic façade was back in place. But just for a moment, Clarion had truly seen her. It all but confirmed what Clarion had long suspected. Artemis had not chosen this: the cosseted life of a queen-in-training's personal guard. How many times had Clarion caught her staring longingly after patrols? How many times had she caught her whittling her already-sharp blade for a battle that would never come? Indeed, the most *alive* Clarion had ever seen her was when she shoved her out of the way of that beast.

Maybe she could imagine a reckless version of Artemis, after all. She was not the sort of fairy who could let others risk their lives—especially not if she could take on the risk herself.

"No harm will befall me," Clarion said softly. "I swear, I would never do anything intentionally to jeopardize your position."

Artemis raked a hand through her hair and blew out a long sigh. "If you truly believe this is the better path forward, then I trust you."

I trust you. How long she'd yearned to hear those words. She could hardly believe them, now that she had.

"I do," Clarion said hastily, if only to keep the emotion out of her voice.

Artemis already looked as though she regretted it. "Go, then. If Her Majesty comes looking for you, I will give your excuses."

Clarion grabbed her free hand and squeezed. "Thank you."

Artemis stared down at their hands with an oddly flustered expression. Then, she extricated herself and rearranged her features back into a mask of professionalism. "Just be back before full dark."

With only a few minutes until sunset, Clarion waited on the bridge that spanned Winter and Spring. She sat on the damp moss that carpeted the root, letting her feet dangle over the water. Her reflection stared up at her, haloed by the soft aura of her wings in the gloaming. Here, despite the danger the night promised, she felt almost at peace. With the quiet burbling of the river below her and the steady snowfall on the other side of the border, it was—

"You came."

Clarion gasped, nearly toppling into the water.

When she recovered, she looked up to find Milori standing a few feet away from her. When had he gotten there? It was as though he'd appeared out of the snow itself. She opened her mouth to speak, but something about the soft surprise on his face stole away her words. She did not know if it offended her or endeared him to her. Then again, she supposed she'd given him no reason to expect her.

It occurred to her a moment too late that she was half-sprawled on the ground, staring slack-jawed up at him. It did not help matters that he looked almost *pretty* in the evening light. Snowflakes had gathered on his eyelashes and sparkled against his white hair so that he seemed to be gilded with frost. Clarion sincerely hoped the heat rising in her neck did not reach her face. To be caught so undignified . . . it would not do.

With a flutter of her wings, Clarion straightened to her full height and hovered off the ground. Primly, she dusted the grass off her skirts. "I did," she said. Then, more gently: "It took longer than I thought it would. I had to find out how to make it here again."

"Of course," he said. "You did mention your obligations the last time we spoke."

That wry edge returned to his voice. Clarion very much resented the implication. Whatever notions he had of Pixie Hollow's royalty, she really *was* quite busy. "It hasn't been easy. I've been kept under lock and key, and our new curfew complicates things."

His expression softened with concern. "A curfew?"

"Yes. We were attacked." It felt too insufficient of an explanation for what had happened. The memory of it made her stomach curdle with dread—and guilt. If only she'd been able to stop it. "Eleven fairies have fallen into some sort of slumber. Our healers are working on reviving them, but . . ."

"I'm sorry." He sounded as though he meant it. Worse, he sounded as though he believed it was his fault. "A number of winter fairies have met the same fate. We haven't been able to develop an antidote, either."

A terrible somberness fell over him, and Clarion had to fight back the impulse to . . . what, exactly? She had no comfort to offer him. But if nothing else, she could understand him. There was little worse, she thought, than being helpless when others depended on you.

Clarion smiled ruefully. "Do you still think I can help you?"

"I do." He hesitated. "I just didn't think you would come back. Why did you?"

"Because I want to hear your plan." She crossed her arms to ward off the chill that emanated from the border—and from the news she had to share. "Since no one knows how to destroy the monsters, Elvina intends to trap them in Winter. She's going to sever the bridges that bind Winter to the other seasons. You'll still have your supply of pixie dust, but . . ."

Milori went as pale as the snowbanks. It felt less isolating, she thought, to see someone react with the same horror she felt. A hundred emotions and thoughts passed over his face, but in the end, all he said was "You disagree with her?"

"Of course I do. I saw the monster myself." When she closed her eyes, she could still see the Nightmare, like an afterimage seared into her mind. She might not have been plunged into sleep, but it still tormented her dreams. "I won't leave you to deal with them alone. I wasn't strong enough to protect anyone, but when my magic struck it . . . I don't know what happened, exactly. It seemed almost afraid. Elvina forbade me from getting involved, but I refuse to let her go through with this if I'm capable of destroying them."

"No one in Winter has been able to drive them back," he said, almost wonderingly. "You really could be the key."

The key. He would not say that if he knew just how little she'd mastered of governing-talent magic.

"I don't know about that." She glanced away. "The only other thing I can offer is that they're called Nightmares. Elvina at least told me that much. But you already knew that, didn't you?"

"Yes," he said reluctantly. "I know what they are."

Your predecessor has not been forthcoming with you, he'd told her.

No, she certainly had not been.

Clearly mistaking her silence for betrayal, he added, "My knowledge is incomplete, but I believe the Queens of Pixie Hollow have information that I don't. But when I realized you knew even less than I do . . ." He frowned, as if searching for the right words to make her understand. "There has not been much goodwill between our realms. I feared you wouldn't trust me unless you heard it from Queen Elvina herself."

"I understand," she said quietly. He wasn't wrong, she supposed. His shoulders slackened with relief. "How did you find out about them?"

"There is a frozen lake deep in the Winter Woods that has long been used to contain Nightmares." As Clarion studied his face, she noticed just how exhausted he looked. The shadows feathered beneath his eyes suggested that he had not slept well in days. How long had he lain awake, worrying about his own subjects? "They've finally escaped."

"Like a prison," she murmured. Suddenly, the realization struck her. "Then you—"

"Yes," he said wearily. "That's why I'm called the Warden of the Winter Woods."

What a heavy burden, she thought. No wonder now that he'd seemed so guilty. Did he truly believe this was *his* fault? Some part of her longed to reach out to smooth away the tension in his brow—to lay a reassuring hand on his arm. This was no longer his problem to shoulder alone. But she resisted the urge and instead, with a gentleness that surprised her, said, "I want to help you. Tell me how."

A small measure of relief softened the worst of his despair. "There is a place called the Hall of Winter, where a copy of every text in Pixie Hollow is stored. It's presided over by a fairy known as the Keeper of Fairy Knowledge. There's a book in his collection that neither he nor I am able to read. He believes that only governing-talent magic can unlock it."

Every text in Pixie Hollow? How spectacular. Clarion would never want for answers again. But the suggestion of her magic being the key cut through her excitement. With the little scrap of power she could summon, she was a governing-talent in name only. When it truly mattered, she would let him down. But there was no sense telling him that now.

"Easy enough." She forced a smile. "Will you bring it to me?"

"It's too heavy to carry. Besides, the Keeper is . . ." Milori grimaced, which told her far more than words ever would. He must have been a fearsome sparrow man, indeed, to inspire such deference in the Warden of the Winter Woods. "I do not know what he would do if it were exposed to the elements. It's a very old book."

Well, that would certainly pose challenges. "What do you suggest, then?"

Without hesitation, he replied, "You'll need to come to Winter with me."

Her first thought was *absolutely not*—and her first instinct was to laugh—but at least her training in queenly disinterest had proven effective enough to conceal her reaction. He wanted her to *go to Winter with him*? It was entirely out of the question, assuming it was even possible. She could not keep the incredulity out of her voice when she said, "And how do you propose I do that?"

"The Keeper has told me that warm fairies used to cross to Winter," Milori said uncertainly, as though he had a hard time believing it himself.

If they had, it certainly wasn't in Elvina's lifetime. Milori was not exaggerating when he said the Hall of Winter contained *all* of fairy knowledge, then. The idea that others had crossed sent a thrill through her. All the times she had wondered about the bridges' existence and admired the carvings of Winter's insignia throughout the palace . . . It made sense. Perhaps their realms truly *did* belong together.

"If you can find a way to protect your wings from the cold," he said, "you should be able to cross for a brief period of time."

Theoretically, that was true. As long as her wings remained

insulated, they wouldn't freeze. Clarion blew out a long, steadying breath. She could not believe she was even *considering* such a dangerous plan after the promise she had made to Artemis. But if it would protect her subjects—both in Winter and the warm seasons—she had no other choice.

"All right. I don't know how I'll manage it yet, but . . ." Before she even finished her sentence, the solution came to her. *Petra.* If there was one fairy she could count on to devise a clever invention, it was her.

Anticipation kindled Milori's gray eyes. "You have an idea."

"Yes," she said reluctantly. It would only involve conscripting the most risk-averse fairy in the entirety of Pixie Hollow into perhaps the most ill-advised scheme Clarion had ever concocted. "I can't guarantee anything, but I'll try."

"That's all I ask. Thank you."

He spoke so sincerely, so *hopefully*, that it made her feel almost flustered. His gratitude—and the knowledge that someone was counting on her so deeply—felt like a precious thing, indeed. She wanted to hold it close. "Of course."

He, too, must have felt the weightiness of the silence. He glanced away before breaking it. "I suppose we don't have any way to contact each other in the meantime. If you'd like, I can continue waiting for you here at sunset."

"Every night?" Clarion raised an eyebrow "Does no one miss you?"

He tilted his head. "What do you mean?"

"No one keeps track of you?" she prompted. Heat spread across her cheeks as she realized what exactly she'd said. "I mean . . . no one minds that you come to haunt the border of Spring like a ghost?"

"Ah." If he was offended, it did not show. If anything, he seemed to enjoy this rapport they'd fallen into. "If the winter fairies knew that I was—what did you say, haunting the border?—then they might not be pleased. But it's spring now, so things are quiet. Besides, who is there, really, to mind what I do? No one is above me in station but you."

No one but you.

Her heart tripped over itself as she turned over those words. It felt as though he'd woven some spell, one that made the world narrow to this: the snow settling gently over the earth and the steadiness of his gaze on her.

She tucked a strand of hair behind her ear—and refrained from reminding him again that she was not yet queen. She found herself hungry for more details of how exactly things worked in Winter, if only to shake off this . . . *flutteriness.* "Was there a Warden of the Winter Woods who trained you?"

He shook his head. "He left behind his notes. That's all I had."

"Oh." Clarion could not imagine how difficult it would be to have to cobble things together from what someone else had left behind—and to do it entirely alone. The Seasonal Ministers in the warm seasons were the same: one faded before another arrived, the two never overlapping. But the queen served as a guiding light and a steady rock, there to help a new arrival to their feet. Here was yet another way they'd left Winter to fend for itself. Guilt sat heavy in her stomach.

Milori, clearly sensing the dark turn of her thoughts, offered her a small smile. "They were very thorough notes, rest assured."

That startled a laugh out of her. The mental image of a newly arrived Milori, harried and riffling through a centuries-old tome to find the answers, had cut through her gloom like the abruptness of a summer rain.

"Well," she said, "I hope they were well organized."

"By topic," he replied solemnly.

"Good." Clarion hesitated, suddenly reluctant to leave. "Well, I shouldn't linger. My guard will be beside herself if I don't return by full dark."

He glanced up. "You should hurry, then."

Indeed, she should. The moon had shimmered into view overhead, a thin waxing crescent, like an eye cracking open. "I'll see you as soon as I can."

"Take care, Clarion."

The sound of her name sent warmth flooding through her. But it was short-lived. When she blinked, he had gone again. He'd left behind only a swirl of snow glittering in the scant moonlight.

9

Come morning, Clarion found Artemis settled in the branches just outside her balcony. The Pixie Dust Tree, evidently possessed by some spark of impish whimsy, had grown a veritable orchard in miniature above her. Neverberries in every shade hung enticingly from its boughs, perfuming the air with a subtle sweetness. Artemis, either completely unaware or pretending not to notice, had apparently decided to occupy herself with whittling. Her thin blade winked in the morning sunlight as she worked. Watching her filled Clarion with renewed fondness.

Few were so dependable.

Last night, Clarion had shut her balcony doors behind her

just as full darkness settled like heavy snowfall over Pixie Hollow. The moment the lock clicked behind her, she caught the streak of a fairy's glow in the corner of her eye. Artemis, slipping out of the tree, as if finally able to rest.

"Well?" Artemis asked now without looking up. "Did you find your Warden of the Winter Woods?"

Clarion did not appreciate the way her traitorous stomach flipped at her choice of words. Milori was certainly not *hers*. It wasn't as though Clarion had snuck out for some sort of tryst. "I did."

At last, Artemis glanced up at her. There was an unmistakable glimmer of hope in her eyes. "And did he have the information you wanted?"

"Not exactly. He has an idea of where to find it, though." Clarion rested her elbows on the banister and frowned as she propped her chin up on her fists. Now, there was just the small matter of breaking the news of what exactly *finding it* would entail. She'd just barely convinced Artemis to let her *visit* the border. Conscripting her into a plan to cross it . . . Well, she would ease into that. "On that note, there is someplace I'd like to go today."

"Is that so?" Artemis looked so dismayed, Clarion couldn't help laughing. It was rare to get such an open display of emotion from her.

"Nowhere dangerous, I promise. This time, I *would* like to go to Tinker's Nook. I need to ask Petra a favor."

Artemis perked up at that but quickly arranged her face into neutrality. "A favor?"

Best to get it over with, she supposed. "I'm hoping she can make something that will allow me to cross into Winter."

Artemis nearly dropped her knife. She fumbled with it for a moment before fixing Clarion with a look of pure and utter disbelief. "What?"

"For a very short time!" Clarion added hastily. "I need to read a book for him."

"Read a . . . ?" Artemis trailed off and pinched the bridge of her nose. When her arm fell limply back to her side, it revealed an expression that suggested she'd decided it best not to ask too many questions. When she spoke again, she made a noble effort to sound diplomatic. "Your Highness, are you *sure* that is a good idea? I trust your judgment of character, of course, but that is a very dangerous trip to undertake."

"I know—and I know I'm asking for a lot. But I don't see any other way forward."

With a resigned sigh, Artemis pocketed both her whittling knife and her misshapen little sculpture. "Shall we pay the tinker a visit?"

Clarion, nearly boneless with relief, slumped against the banister. "Yes. Thank you."

Together, they left for Tinker's Nook, soaring far above the trees. From this vantage point, Pixie Hollow was a quilted sprawl of verdant green and glittering blue. The air was aglow with ribbons of pixie dust as fairies whizzed by. The distant sounds of their laughter reached her from this height, and her chest constricted with sudden emotion. Something so precious needed to be protected.

Here and there, Clarion caught glimpses of scouts clinging to the tallest boughs of the pines. They nodded in silent acknowledgment as they passed. "Have they found anything yet?"

"No," Artemis said grimly. "Not that I've heard."

"It seems impossible that something that size could just vanish without a trace."

"Even if they did find something . . ." Artemis looked troubled. "That thing didn't even flinch when it was struck by my arrows. But I saw what your magic did."

Clarion warmed at the open reverence in her voice. In truth, she hardly knew what she'd done. One moment, she'd felt almost resigned to her fate: that if she were to die, she would go down protecting someone else. The next: golden light, as brilliant as a felled star. She hadn't known Artemis had even seen that, considering she'd promptly tackled her to the ground. The scrapes on her elbows still stung.

"So you understand," Clarion said quietly. "Why I'm doing what I'm doing."

"I don't think you have any idea what you're doing, but I have placed my trust in you." Artemis offered her a faint smile, then seemed to remember that she'd been almost *cheeky*. In a grave tone, she added, "With all due respect, of course, Your Highness."

It wasn't exactly the vote of confidence Clarion had hoped for, but for now, it would have to be enough.

They flew in silence until they reached Petra's cottage in her lonely corner of Tinker's Nook. In the morning light, the dew beaded on the moss-thatched roof glittered invitingly. When they landed on her porch, Artemis ran her fingers over the house's rough stone face. With genuine wonder in her voice, she said, "I didn't realize the tinker was so enterprising."

Clarion allowed herself a small, private smile. "Have you never seen her focused on something? It's actually quite frightening."

Considering Petra's pale, freckled face hadn't appeared in the window yet, she likely was in one of her fugue-like states as they spoke. Indeed, all the blinds were drawn, shutting out the light. Really, she could be so *intense*. Most of the other tinkers stayed well out of her way when she was engrossed in a project. She became a different fairy entirely.

Clarion knocked. No answer came from within, but she could hear the bright clang and clash of metal on metal. Oh, Petra was almost certainly lost to the world by now.

"Shall we come back another time?" Artemis asked.

"Oh, no need." Clarion tried the handle and found the door unlocked.

Artemis glared at the ajar door with a look of baffled consternation. Clearly, she had a few choice words about security that she was electing to keep to herself.

Clarion eased the door open and was greeted by a blast of

heat and the distinct smell of welding. Sweat immediately began to prickle at the back of Clarion's neck. Pixie dust twinkled in the stuffy darkness of the room. All sorts of tools Clarion did not have names for floated in the air, as if borne aloft on the current of a river. And there, bent over her worktable and bathed in the warm glow of her forge, was Petra. Her red curls were wild and her freckles were hidden behind streaks of gold and soot. She hammered a fine sheet of molten metal, shaping it with a focus so complete, Clarion thought for a moment that she had not registered their presence at all.

"Clarion." Petra's voice was preternaturally calm. She pointed at some contraption hovering just out of her reach. "Hand me that."

Artemis stationed herself by the door. Clarion smiled at her encouragingly before she complied with Petra's request. As she handed her the tool, she said, "I need to ask you a favor."

Petra made an absentminded sound to indicate she was listening but did not look at her. At least, Clarion did not *think* she did. She was wearing the safety goggles she'd devised with the help of a water-talent last year. They'd affixed dewdrops—dyed black with hawthorn berries and walnut husks—to metal frames. Like this, Clarion couldn't see her eyes at all.

"I need you to help me cross into the Winter Woods."

"Gah!" Petra stumbled back from her worktable and nearly crashed into the wall. Her safety goggles fell askance on her face, and the dewdrop lenses burst from their rough treatment. The water dribbled down her cheeks and left blackened stains behind, but so great was her shock, she hardly seemed to notice. "What?!"

"I said—"

"Oh, I heard you," said Petra darkly. At last, she smeared away the remains of her goggles with the back of her hand. "What I don't understand is why you'd want to go to Winter."

"Because it's for a really, *really* good reason?" Clarion tried.

"But it's against the rules!"

"Crossing the border isn't forbidden." It wasn't, technically. It was, however, deadly without proper precautions, which made it something of an unpopular destination.

"Maybe not for me," said Petra. "But it almost certainly is for you."

"I'm inclined to agree," Artemis said dolorously from the back of the room.

Petra shrieked in surprise. Then, when she realized who exactly had spoken, the color drained from, and then rose high, in her cheeks. "You! What are *you* doing here?"

Artemis glanced over her shoulder, as though there might be someone else who had provoked such a reaction. When she turned back around, she wore a rather flustered expression. She cleared her throat, then said, "Accompanying Her Highness, who was quite insistent on this course of action. Can you help, or can't you?"

Petra gawped at her. "You're in on this?"

Artemis sighed. "Unfortunately. And now, so are you."

"No one will have to know it was *you* who helped me," Clarion cut in before she well and truly lost control of the situation.

Petra jabbed her hammer in Clarion's direction. "I haven't agreed yet! You always have some harebrained scheme, and this time, I—"

Clarion caught her wrist, lowering it. She'd begun waving the hammer around quite menacingly. "The Nightmares came from Winter. If I can cross the border and investigate, perhaps I can stop anything like what happened from happening again. More importantly, I can convince Elvina that she doesn't need to go through with her plan."

"That does not make me feel better." Petra groaned. "If anything, it makes me feel *worse*. You could have died the other day, Clarion, and now you want to throw yourself in its path again? I won't be the one who lets you do it."

Tenderness and frustration knotted up within Clarion. "And you want to live your whole life like this? Worrying that you might be attacked at any moment? Being escorted around everywhere you go?"

"No," Petra said quietly.

"I can stop it," Clarion said, squeezing her forearm. "But I need your help. Please?"

Petra rubbed her eyes with the heels of her palms. "Why me? I'm not a sewing-talent. If you want to keep your wings insulated, the easiest way is to dress for the cold." As if she had realized something for the first time, her expression brightened. "Why don't you ask Patch? Then we can pretend we never had this conversation."

Patch was a sewing-talent who had made a number of Clarion's gowns over the years. But a winter coat? Patch would never agree to such a ridiculous request without an explanation—and she would tell Elvina immediately if Clarion provided one. Patch also had a tendency to stare unblinkingly when spoken to; it unsettled Clarion, to feel as though her very soul were being measured with every word.

"I could," Clarion drawled. "But Patch isn't the best tinker in Pixie Hollow."

Petra preened. "Well, I . . ."

Clarion snatched one of her tools from where it hovered in midair, then twirled it absently between her fingers. "Unless, of course, you don't think you're up for the task."

"Put that down," Petra groused. "And of course I am. It won't be a challenge on a practical level. It may not *look* stylish, but . . ."

"I don't care about that," Clarion said, perhaps too eagerly. "You can do it?"

"I have a lot of other things going on, you know. But I guess I can do it." Petra paled, then buried her face in her hands. "I cannot believe I'm doing this. Please don't make me regret it."

"I won't." Clarion leaned her head against her shoulder. "Thank you."

"You owe me," Petra muttered. "You owe me so much."

Clarion smiled despite herself. "I know."

That evening, Clarion went to the border. She didn't know what possessed her, exactly. It wasn't as though she had anything terribly pressing to share with Milori, but she couldn't deny the giddiness that had welled up within her at today's small victories. For the first time since the Nightmares emerged, they had a path forward. Besides, there was something about the thought of him, haunting the border in solitude until she returned once more. He'd done it every night for a week, of course, but it seemed so terribly *sad*.

If she so chose, neither of them had to be alone.

She arrived just as the sky began to flush with muted shades of pink. Across the border, the pines and birches carved jagged silhouettes against the sunset. This time, Milori was already there. He sat on the bridge, with a book propped open in his palm. The waning light veiled him in gold and danced atop the fresh-fallen snow, until all the world seemed to glitter.

Never before had it struck her just how beautiful Winter was.

Milori turned toward her at that exact moment, as though she'd called his name. Clearly, there had been no time to armor himself, because his expression morphed into something she didn't know how to read. He looked almost dazzled, as though he'd been staring directly into the sun itself. For a moment, she forgot how to draw breath. But when she blinked, his face had settled back into pleasant neutrality. Perhaps she'd imagined that starry-eyed look altogether. Convincing herself of that made it far easier to recover her senses.

Clarion alighted on the bridge. Doing her best to keep her voice even, she said, "Good evening."

"Good evening." He closed his book. A quick glance at the cover revealed it to be . . . something she did not recognize, but the slender, gold-painted spine reminded her of the volumes tucked away in the poetry section of the library. She thought to ask him about it, but he said, "I didn't expect you again so soon."

He didn't sound displeased, but the acknowledgment embarrassed her more than she cared to admit. Perhaps she should have waited a coy night or two before she came rushing back here. But if they were going to work together effectively, expediency was surely nothing to be ashamed of.

She put on a mock-offended tone. "Then you've underestimated me."

"A mistake I won't make again." A wry smile played at the corner of his lips—one Clarion tried very hard not to notice. "What have you achieved in a day?"

She smoothed an invisible crease in her skirts. "I've found a way to cross, but it may be a few days before I'm able to attempt it."

"That's great news." He frowned pensively. "You haven't run into any trouble? You mentioned obligations."

"Right." She sighed glumly. "Those."

Silence descended over them as she considered what to tell him. Quiet had never discomfited her, but Clarion found herself yearning to fill it. She and Milori could never be anything resembling *friends*. But here in the twilight, the space between them as good as a solid wall, nothing felt wholly real. What did it hurt to pretend?

Slowly, Clarion settled on the bridge beside him until they sat almost shoulder to shoulder. The magic flowing through the Pixie

Dust Tree's roots warmed her palms, grounding her. This close, she could see the snowflakes gathering in his white hair and the feathered shadows his eyelashes cast on his cheekbones. That troublesome thought resurfaced, unbidden: *Beautiful.*

And dangerous, she reminded herself.

"I never appreciated how much went into planning for a coronation." She rested her chin in her hands, gazing down at her wavering reflection on the surface of the river. "Everyone wants my opinion on every detail, but I can hardly process it's going to happen at all. The expectations . . ."

"It sounds like a great deal of pressure."

Clarion glanced up at him, startled by the genuine understanding in his voice. Self-consciously, she tucked a loose strand of hair behind her ear. "It is. . . . But you didn't come here to listen to my troubles. It isn't all stress. There's the Coronation Ball on the night of the next full moon, just a week before my coronation."

Milori's lips parted, as though he wanted to say something but stopped himself. In the end, he said, "We'll hold one the same night."

Clarion perked up. "Really?"

"Of course." His eyes glimmered with quiet mirth. "Your impending coronation deserves recognition. We never miss an opportunity to celebrate in Winter."

She snorted incredulously—and inelegantly. But she couldn't bring herself to care all that much. She'd learned Milori had a subtle sense of humor, but she could not imagine him at a ball. In the warm seasons, parties raged on for hours, full of spectacle and dancing and *noise*. Winter and its warden, meanwhile, seemed to her like the still waters of a pond. "Even you?"

"Even me," he replied, with a somberness that surprised Clarion. She heard clearly what he'd left unspoken: *once upon a time.*

She found herself missing the warm glimmer of amusement in his eyes—and thinking of what she could do to restore it. She adjusted her skirts so that she could sit cross-legged and angled herself to face him. "And what sorts of things do you do at a Winter ball?"

Milori smiled at her enthusiasm. "I imagine the same sorts of things one does at a warm-season ball."

"I'm not so sure." Curiosity bubbled up within her, too urgent to tamp down. "I'll remind you that I know absolutely nothing about Winter."

Milori went quiet for a few moments, his gaze searching hers. "What do you want to know?"

Everything. Admitting to him that she'd always felt some pull toward his realm—it made her feel terrifyingly exposed. But now, she could finally have answers to all the questions she'd had since she first arrived. But where to even start? "I don't know. What kinds of talents do you have?"

"Far too many to list. We have frost-talents, snowflake-talents, glacier-talents, icicle-talents . . ."

Clarion's head spun as he continued to rattle them off. How many intricacies could there possibly be in frozen water? "And you?"

Surprise softened his features. "I don't know if there's a name for what I am."

"Surely there is."

Every talent had a name—and in the rare instance a fairy's innate talent developed into something more specialized, they almost always intuitively knew what to call it. How strange, then, that it should elude him. Warden-talent seemed to be the simplest name, but it seemed . . . ill-fitting. Something about it grated against her, like a picture hung crooked on the wall or a sweater that did not fit quite right. Besides, it left too many things unaccounted for.

"Watching over the Nightmares cannot be the extent of what you do," she pressed. "Who welcomes new arrivals?"

"I do."

His response electrified her. She sat up taller. "And who coordinates preparations for delivering winter to the Mainland?"

"I suppose I do," he said warily. "But it's a very small part of my role. My duties as the guardian of the Winter Woods take precedence over all else."

"You have similar responsibilities to Elvina." As the realization struck her, Clarion turned to face him fully. His eyes reflected her glow, burning brighter with her excitement. "Perhaps you're a governing-talent as well! Were you born from a star?"

Milori hesitated. "I wasn't, no."

"I see." Of all things, *disappointment* surged up within her. Clarion swallowed it down as best she could. How silly, to hope that there would be someone like her besides Elvina. As the aura around her dimmed, she offered him an uncertain smile. "There goes that theory. I'm sorry I couldn't be of more help."

"There's nothing to apologize for. Not knowing doesn't bother me," he said gently. "Are you all right?"

"I'm fine." Clarion turned her gaze out to the Winter Woods, unable to meet the unbearable earnestness of his stare. Snow pirouetted in the wind, melting the instant it neared the border. "I thought that maybe there would be someone else like me in Winter. It makes sense that there isn't. To be a good queen is to be as cold and distant as a star."

From the corner of her eye, she caught a glimpse of his reaction. His entire body shifted backward, as though the words had physically struck him. "Is that what you believe?"

What she *believed*? What she personally believed was immaterial.

"That's what Elvina has always taught me." She knotted her fingers together in her lap. "But I've never been like that. I've always wanted things I shouldn't. It's my greatest shortcoming."

"Is it? I understand the necessity of that worldview, but . . ." When she dared to look up again, the sight of him stole away her breath. The setting sun painted him in stark shadows. "What is the harm in wishing things could be different?"

The necessity of that worldview? Clarion felt the weight of his words like a knife to the heart. Perhaps he was not a governing-talent like her. Perhaps they had not endured exactly the same things. But in that moment, it didn't matter. The shape of his pain matched her own.

Milori was just as lonely as she was.

She yearned to rest her hand atop his, but she felt anchored in place. For so long, she'd wished for someone to see her—*truly* see her. Now that someone might, she understood just how terrifying it would feel to allow it—and just how much more complicated that would make this entire mission.

I've always wanted things I shouldn't.

Never had that felt truer.

10

After three agonizingly long days of waiting, Petra sent her an update. It happened while Clarion was lying in bed, once again awake before the sun had fully risen.

The sky outside her window was a velvet swatch of purple stippled with fading stars. Even from here, she could see the barest sliver of white-capped mountains, peering in at her. A small torment, when all she could think about was how soon she would stand beneath their shadow—and how soon she and Milori would exist on the same side of the border. Maybe then, she could convince herself that all of this was truly real.

There came a soft rapping on her balcony doors.

Clarion shot bolt upright as panic doused her like a sudden rainstorm. This early, someone on her doorstep portended nothing good. Another attack, or—

When her eyes adjusted to the darkness, all the fear bled out of her. Something between annoyance and sheer relief took its place when she noticed Artemis standing there. Her guard stood on the balcony, her silhouette traced by her own glow. Clarion dug the heels of her palms into her bleary eyes. What could she possibly want this early?

Artemis knocked again, more pointedly this time.

Clarion threw off the covers and crossed the room. She cracked open the door, letting in a sigh of cool air and the faint sound of the dust-keepers' chatter as they prepared to distribute morning rations. She did her best to glare at Artemis, although she imagined its effect was somewhat diminished by her dishabille. She was still wearing her nightgown, and her hair hung unbound down to her mid-back. "Good morning."

"Good morning," Artemis replied dutifully. "Sorry to disturb you at this hour, but I thought you might want this."

She held a thin roll of parchment tied off with green twine. Clarion accepted it from her outstretched hand and unfurled the note. Immediately, she recognized Petra's handwriting, as well as the telltale stains of soot and grease and something she sincerely hoped was not blood. Sewing could not be *that* dangerous, even to someone unpracticed, could it? The message itself, however, was uncharacteristically short—and unsigned.

All it said was *It's done.*

Clarion's heart skipped a beat, and she hugged the parchment to her chest. The giddy anticipation that had been building for days seized upon her. After so many years of staring out at it, after so many years of wondering, she could be going to Winter as soon as *tonight*. It took a great deal of restraint to keep herself from twirling through her room. Artemis would hardly know what to do with her.

She settled for beaming up at her—only to find Artemis looking at her with a peculiarly soft expression. When Artemis realized Clarion had noticed, she rearranged her features into the very picture of composure. "Something good?"

"We can pick up my coat."

"Ah." Artemis grimaced, clearly still not thrilled about the prospect of letting her charge wander into Winter. "Good news, indeed."

After a moment, something occurred to Clarion. She considered the letter in her hands. "Where did you get this?"

The faintest flush crept up from beneath Artemis's collar. "The tinker gave it to me."

"I didn't realize you spent so much time around Tinker's Nook," Clarion said, trying for a conversational tone. Artemis and Petra had known each other for years through Clarion, but as far as she knew—much to her dismay, considering how *obvious* it was Petra fancied her—they'd never spent any time together without her. This was a new development, indeed.

"We only ran into each other," she replied hastily. "That is, I found myself nearby."

"Oh?" Clarion pressed, unable to keep the interest out of her voice now. "What for?"

"Before I go home, I do my own sweep for Nightmares."

Clarion nodded. "Did you find any in her house?"

"No, I . . ." Artemis looked flustered now. She raked a hand through her roughly shorn hair. "I suppose I was curious about what she was making. It's something that would make scouts' jobs much easier."

Satisfied, Clarion smiled innocently and folded up the letter. "I see. Well, we can take another look later today."

"As you wish, Your Highness." She gave her a sour look, which nearly made Clarion laugh. Perhaps she should tease her more often. She was far too easy a target. "We can go after your meeting with the Minister of Spring, which is in an hour, in case you've forgotten."

She groaned. She *had* nearly forgotten. Hopefully, Iris would not keep her for *too* long. Only she stood between Clarion and Winter.

When Clarion had gotten ready, she and Artemis made their way to Spring Valley. Although she always felt the most at home in Summer, Spring never failed to delight her. It was the domain of Pixie Hollow's garden-talents, fairies capable of making flowers bloom. Clarion could see their handiwork everywhere she looked: trees dripping with citrus fruits, golden forsythia, delicate sprays of wisteria, wild strawberries ripening in warm patches of sunlight. As they flitted through the woods, Clarion caught glimpses of their houses cradled in the branches, all of them with roofs of fuchsia and trumpet flowers.

They arrived in Springtime Square, the heart of Spring Valley. At this early hour, gauzy skeins of fog drifted off the Never Sea and filled the clearing. Two massive cherry trees framed a view of the water—and a moss-covered stone from which a single flower bloomed: the Evergreen. Its soft white petals were folded around itself like a slumbering fairy's wings. It bloomed only on the spring equinox, when spring was due to arrive on the Mainland. Each year, every fairy poured into this clearing for the queen's final review of Spring's preparations. Despite the long days of work ahead, some stayed up until dawn to watch its petals unfurl with the sunrise.

One day, Clarion hoped to see it herself.

Iris waited for them beside the Evergreen, limned in the sunlight. Today, she wore a gown of crocuses, with long bell-like sleeves that enveloped all but the tips of her fingers. Her hair flowed down her back like a sheet of dark water. Her face—uncharacteristically pensive—brightened upon seeing them.

After the three of them exchanged pleasantries, Iris sighed. "I'd hoped to have more to show you today. Thank you for coming anyway."

Clarion frowned. "What do you mean?"

Iris's lips parted in surprise. "Did Her Majesty not tell you?"

Clarion's heart sank. "Tell me what?"

Iris hesitated. "It might be easier to show you. Come see."

With a flutter of her wings and a shower of pixie dust, Iris took flight. She led them deeper into Spring Valley until they came to an open field. What Clarion saw made a shiver of horror run through her. A line of decay carved through the meadow—and headed straight toward Winter. Or perhaps more accurately: *from* Winter. Whatever had passed through here seemed to have drained the very color from the foliage. Wilting, desiccated blooms and the shattered remains of what looked to be a trellis were scattered among the trampled grass. The faint scent of rot reached her even from here.

"By the second star," Clarion muttered.

"The scouts came by this morning to assess the damage." Iris wrung her hands together fretfully. "No one was hurt. No one besides the flowers, anyway."

Clarion could tell even the flowers' deaths pained her. Most spring fairies, after all, could commune with them. She glanced at Artemis and hoped her meaning was clear: *Did you know about this?*

Artemis shook her head.

Yet another thing Elvina hadn't seen fit to inform her of. And yet another reminder how urgently she and Milori needed to figure out how to destroy the Nightmares.

"I'm very relieved to hear that no one was hurt," Clarion said softly. "I'm sorry about the field."

"You're very sweet to say that, Your Highness," Iris said, clearly trying to sound more chipper than she felt. "*I'm* sorry that some of the work we did for your coronation was ruined. But Her Majesty will take care of the Nightmares, and we'll have everything fixed in no time. In the meantime, let me show you what my water-talents have been up to. You're going to *love* it."

Clarion scarcely had time to reply before Iris shot off in another direction. Clarion followed as quickly as she could. If only she had so much energy at this hour.

Iris guided her a short distance before diving back through the canopy. They landed on the banks of a river just as a group of dragonflies darted by in a flash of iridescent wings. When Clarion regained her bearings, she drank in the sound of the water-talents' domain: burbling water, the croak of frog-song and the drone of insects, and her subjects' laughter, as sparkling as a brook flowing over stones.

Clarion had always loved to watch the water-talents at work. Some of them drifted on the current on boats made of birch bark and lily pads, encouraging the golden fish drifting just beneath them. Others lounged on half-submerged logs, shrouded by curtains of cattail and fern. Others still skipped across the surface, leaving the barest ripples in their wake. It made Clarion's breath catch with equal measures of wonder and nerves. As a rule, fairies could not swim; waterlogged wings were too heavy. But the water-talents were fearless and joyous—and perfectly at ease.

At least, until they noticed her. When she passed by, they fell abruptly silent. Clarion was torn between the impulse to smile encouragingly and look away so that they didn't feel scrutinized.

"Here we are," Iris said brightly.

It took a moment for Clarion to register what she was looking at. They stood before a vast spiderweb strung on a frame of branches. It was beaded with more dewdrops than Clarion could fathom, each of them stained with dye. It was, she realized, a mosaic—one fashioned to look like her. When the sun struck it, the water refracted the light and scattered multicolored patterns on the forest floor.

"What do you think?" Iris asked.

"It's spectacular," Clarion said quietly, and she meant it. To see herself represented with such care stirred within her a feeling she could not entirely place.

Clarion would have sworn she felt more than heard the collective sigh of relief behind her. As though the entire clearing had been holding its breath, the sound of splashing and chatter resumed.

Iris clapped her hands together. "Oh, good! Your coronation is going to be incredible, Your Highness. Just wait until . . ."

The sound of Iris's voice faded to a drone as Clarion stared up at her own likeness, a version of herself more queenly and poised than she knew herself to be. She could hardly bring herself to focus on any of the beautiful things Iris was describing for her. Her coronation somehow felt entirely insignificant in the face of the threat against Pixie Hollow. As much as she longed to enjoy the talents of her subjects, as much as she wished she could believe in Elvina, all she could think about was how precarious everything felt. All she could think about was the winter coat waiting for her in Tinker's Nook—and how tonight, she would cross into Winter.

"Your Highness?"

Clarion startled. Iris was frowning at her with a look of genuine concern on her face—and also disappointment. Clarion felt guilty to have gone somewhere else so obviously. Clearly, this mattered a great deal to Iris.

"I'm so sorry, Minister," Clarion said. "Did you ask me something?"

Iris folded her arms and fixed her with an appraising look. "Is there something on your mind?"

"A few things," Clarion said sheepishly. "There's so much to prepare for the coronation. Sometimes, I don't feel ready."

Surprise flickered across Iris's face before she smiled. "Your Highness, are you *nervous*?"

Clarion winced. "A little."

"Really?" Iris sounded genuinely shocked, if not somewhat delighted. "I never would have guessed. You always seem so composed."

"It's a careful illusion," Clarion said wanly.

"It's normal to be nervous." Iris tapped her chin. "But you really do look exhausted. Are you sleeping enough?"

She almost certainly was not. "Well, I—"

"I know just the thing." Iris brightened. "I'll send you home with some skullcap tea."

Both her exuberance and generosity caught Clarion off guard. "That would be lovely. Thank you."

"You're so welcome," said Iris. "Tea fixes *almost* everything. But if you'll listen to some advice, think about it like this. You're like a bulb flower."

That . . . did not sound like a compliment. Clarion wrinkled her nose. "Oh?"

With a casual curl of Iris's finger, a flower bulb in miniature appeared in her hand, glimmering with pixie dust. "In Pixie Hollow, of course, flowers bloom whenever we ask them to. But on the Mainland, these types of flowers are planted in autumn, just before the soil freezes. You'd think that would kill them, but they lie dormant all through winter. Then, as soon as spring arrives . . ."

Hyacinths sprung from the earth all around them in shades of white and vibrant pink and soft purple. They gave off a damp, green scent, as ethereal as spring itself.

"Spring is all about renewal," Iris said serenely. "When things seem impossibly dark, bulb flowers are sparks of hope. It takes time for things to bloom. You just have to be patient and nurturing." After a considering pause, she jabbed a finger at Clarion. "So be nice to yourself. You'll grow into it, I promise."

For a moment, Clarion felt too stunned to reply. "Thank you, Minister. Truly."

"Anytime," she said sweetly. "Now, about those floral arrangements . . ."

By midafternoon, Clarion and Artemis had made it to Petra's lonely stone cottage. Predictably, she did not answer when they knocked, but Clarion could see the faint orange glow of the forge through the dew-streaked windows.

She nudged the door open and called, "I'm here."

As always, Petra's projects cluttered every surface—and most of the floor. But strangely, her metalworking tools lay still and inert, catching faint glimmers of the firelight. Today, Petra's workshop looked like it belonged to a sewing-talent—if that sewing-talent had emptied their entire ration of pixie dust over their workspace. As Clarion made her way deeper into the room, she had to dodge air-borne needles and shears. She touched a spool of thread, watching as it sailed lazily across the room, unraveling as it went. Everywhere she turned, it was a riot of colorful fabrics and buttons.

Petra stood in the eye of the storm she had created, fussing with a coat she'd wrapped around the metal shoulders of a dress form. She looked about as well rested as Clarion did, which was to say: not at all. She wouldn't be surprised if Petra hadn't slept since she began this project. To say she was single-minded was a gross understatement.

"Are you all right?" Clarion asked tentatively.

"It took days to make a pattern that was even remotely usable," Petra said, her tone almost trancelike, "and several hours of harvesting spider-silk to convince Patch to teach me basic stitches. But after three prototypes, I've done it. Finally."

Clarion peered over her shoulder and could not help her soft sound of surprise. The coat was far beyond *remotely usable.* She should have known that Petra was incapable of making anything less than spectacular. It was a spill of thick golden fabric, glittering faintly with pixie dust. A fringe of white fur lined the hood and the cuffs of its sleeves.

"It's beautiful," Clarion said.

"It'll do." As dismissive as she sounded, Petra looked proud. "Try it on."

Petra removed the coat from the dress form and held it out. Clarion slipped her arms into the sleeves, drew it around her shoulders, and immediately fought to hold in her laughter. It was *enormous*. She was all but drowning in fabric, but at least her wings fit comfortably.

Petra looked at her fretfully and tugged at the lapels. "The fit is dreadful. I realized too late I never took any measurements."

Clarion snorted. "It's warm. That's all I need."

"Maybe if I—"

"It's perfect." Clarion took her hands to still her. "Thank you. Truly."

"Don't mention it," Petra said gruffly.

"I have to take it off immediately, though. It's always so hot in here."

"It's not that hot," Petra protested. "Oh! I have other things for you."

As Clarion shrugged out of the coat and folded it over her arm, Petra rummaged around on her worktable. A whittling knife fell off and hit the ground with a metallic ping. After a few moments, Petra foisted a pair of mittens and boots on her, as well as a strange set of what looked to be badminton rackets. Clarion let the latter dangle from her fingertips by the leather straps attached to them. "What are these for? To play games?"

"Don't be ridiculous. They go on your feet."

Clarion inspected them more closely. Skeptically, she said, "I think *you're* the one being ridiculous."

"They're snowshoes," Petra said wearily. "They harness the properties of flotation by distributing your weight over a greater surface area so that . . . Actually, it doesn't matter! The point is that they'll make it easier for you to walk on the snow."

"Incredible," Clarion murmured. "I never would have thought of that."

"I know." Petra flashed a smile at her, clearly pleased by her praise. After a moment, it faded. "Just . . . be careful, will you?"

"Don't fret," said Clarion. "When have I not been careful?"

Petra gave her a speaking look. "You know I love you."

Clarion did not like where this was going. "Of course I do."

"You're my oldest friend." Clarion could hear plainly what Petra left unsaid: *my only friend.* "For the longest time, you were the only one who would talk to me."

Clarion grinned at her. "I seem to remember that you were afraid of me."

"Well, you're intimidating," Petra replied. "And you've never backed down from what scares you. You used to drag me into so many things I would've rather avoided."

Clarion remembered those days fondly: two inseparable outcasts, running wild through Pixie Hollow. Yes, she supposed she had dragged Petra into quite a bit of trouble over the years. There was the time they took the two fastest, most willful mice from the tinkers' stable and rode them through the fields at a gallop. Or the time they'd gotten lost in a rabbit warren after Clarion suggested they go spelunking. Or the time she'd convinced Petra to fashion a hummingbird-drawn carriage, which was—unsurprisingly, in retrospect—a disaster.

But Petra didn't seem to be in the mood for reminiscing. In fact, she seemed to be working herself up to something. "Where are you going with this?" Clarion asked.

"Now that I've done this for you, I need you to leave me out of it. Don't tell me what you're doing. Every time I think about it, I . . ." Petra paused for a moment to collect herself. "It's better for both of us if I pretend that you're not going anywhere near Winter."

"Right." It made sense. And yet, it stung. It felt . . . isolating, to know that she could not talk to her about something so important. "I can do that."

"Good." Petra frowned. "You do know what you're doing, don't you?"

When Clarion closed her eyes, she saw the ruined fields of Spring burned on the backs of her eyes. Her subjects falling out of the sky, struck unconscious by a single drop of the Nightmare's venom. Clarion had only a vague and terrible sense of what she was up against, and an even vaguer idea of Milori's plan. But if it meant protecting Winter—if it meant proving herself capable—then she had to keep moving forward.

Clarion smiled as encouragingly as she could. If she had to lie to Petra going forward, she might as well practice. "Of course I do. You have absolutely nothing to worry about."

11

Minutes before sunset, Clarion stood at the border, draped in her new coat. She stared hard at the other side: the dwindling light glittering on the snow, the shadows pooled beneath the firs, the dense swirl of flurries. Her fingers trembled as she did up the delicate buttons of her coat, and she couldn't entirely tell if it was excitement or nerves that had her so rattled.

"A very practical solution you've found."

Clarion startled at the sound of Milori's voice. The snowshoes slung over her shoulder clattered together at the sudden movement. "Please don't sneak up on me like that!"

Milori landed on the bridge with the faintest glimmer of

amusement in his eyes. "My apologies," he said, although he really didn't sound all that sorry.

She was beginning to suspect he really *did* appear with the wind. She laid a hand over her chest and confirmed that her heart was indeed still beating. "It's all right."

In truth, she found it rather difficult to muster a glare when he was looking at her like this. The mirth had faded from his expression, and he studied her now with a curious mixture of hope and trepidation. A gust of wind brushed the loose snowfall from the branches and swept his white hair over his shoulder. "Are you ready?"

Was she ready?

The prospect of crossing frightened her more than she cared to admit. The sensible part of her, smothered as it was beneath her excitement and determination, worried about the dangers. She trusted Petra, but not even she could make a coat impervious to things like tears or water. One careless mistake could cost Clarion her wings. But deeper down, she worried what it would feel like to finally cross the border. Would Winter still hold its allure once she set foot in it?

"Just a moment." Clarion hastily tugged on her boots and mittens, then strapped on her snowshoes. When she finished, Milori took a step back to give her clearance. She stared down at the border, where the very tips of her boots grazed the lacy line of frost. She willed herself to cross, and yet, she felt rooted to the spot.

"I can't do it with you staring," she blurted out.

"Would you like me to turn around?"

She scoffed. "Don't be ridiculous."

She closed her eyes and did her best to ignore him. She stood close enough to the border that the faintest sensation of cold washed over the tip of her nose. All she had to do was take a single step forward. She would be *fine.* Clarion drew a deep breath and sighed it out—then realized a moment too late that she probably looked extraordinarily foolish. When she opened her eyes, Milori was watching her with another one of those curiously teasing looks.

"What?" she demanded.

"Nothing at all." His eyes glittered, and her treasonous heart fluttered at the sight of his smile. "Do you need help?"

"No, sir." She tried her best not to sound offended. "I do not need your help."

"Perhaps a pull is the better word?"

That did not sound any better, but she refrained from comment. Milori extended a hand to her. Clarion could do nothing but stare at it for a few moments. "What is this?"

He held her gaze. "Just trust me."

Very tentatively, she took it—and was surprised to find that his skin was pleasantly cool. She didn't know what she was expecting. That he would be carved from ice, too? That his very touch would freeze her, even through her mittens? No, he was just like her: flesh and bone. Both of them lingered, their hands a bridge between worlds.

Then, with a gentle tug, he guided her through.

As Clarion passed through the veil of snow, she bit down a

gasp; the temperature plummeted as Winter enfolded her. When she opened her eyes again, she had left everything she knew behind. Despite herself, she let out a breathless laugh and looked up at Milori. This close, she was struck by the true color of his eyes: a stormy gray, with the faintest touch of glacial blue. She could see his expression softening as he gazed back at her, and—

She was still holding his hand.

Heat flooded her face. Clarion all but snatched her hand back. "Sorry—and, um . . . thank you?"

"It's not worth mentioning." He flexed his fingers as if working out a cramp, then took a single step back from her. The snow crunched beneath his weight.

Snow. She was really in the Winter Woods.

Some of her embarrassment forgotten, Clarion tipped her head back to the sky and spun in a slow circle. Clouds drifted overhead in a thick gray sheet, limned by the fiery light of sunset. She opened her mouth to catch the falling snowflakes, and they melted on her tongue almost instantly. She was so strangely delighted with it all; she didn't know that she'd ever felt so . . . giddy.

"Is it what you expected?" There was a touch of surprise in his voice.

Her breath plumed in the air, and even that was wondrous. "It's beautiful."

For a moment, he did not reply. If she didn't know better, she'd say he looked almost flustered. "There's a lot more to see. Follow me."

"All right," she said, hoping she didn't sound too eager.

And with that, he led her into the forest.

Only the crunch of their footsteps and the soft rustle of wind-stirred branches filled the silence. Clarion found she didn't mind it. The quiet here wasn't eerie but almost cozy, as though all the world were asleep. She had expected desolate landscapes and swathes of monochrome, lifeless earth. But everything was spectacular, from the intricate pattern of frost on the leaves to the sunlit icicles hanging from the trees. Here, everything sparkled, as magical as pixie dust.

Soon, the terrain grew rockier—and steep. Her breaths came heavier, puffing out of her in little white clouds. Wind rushed down the mountainside, sending the tails of her coat whipping behind her. The fur lining of her hood tickled her cold-stung face. She was certain she was bright red. Milori, meanwhile, remained as pale as the snow-covered earth; he flushed neither from exertion or the chill. Even as they ascended, he did not fly but insisted on walking alongside her.

Stubbornly chivalrous, she noted.

After what felt like hours, they crested the peak of one of the mountains. What she saw stole her breath away. From here, she could see all the Winter Woods sprawled out before them. It was a land of brilliant white and deepest green, with rivers and lakes clearer and bluer than she'd ever thought possible. In the distance, she could see the winter fairies' homes carved from ice and molded from snow, gleaming in the moonlight and glowing softly from within.

How had anyone thought this place so terrible?

"Here it is," he said softly.

She could hear the reverence in his voice so plainly—one she felt, too. What was there to say, really? She'd never seen anything quite like it.

After a moment, he added, "Our destination is the Hall of Winter. You can see its glow from here."

He pointed, and Clarion squinted to see a faint aura of blue gilding a distant mountainside. "That's a long way to walk."

He flashed her a small smile. "There's a faster way to travel."

"If you suggest carrying me—"

"Certainly not." He looked almost insulted, which made her grin. "I take it you don't have sledding in the warm seasons."

"Sledding," she echoed.

"Mm." He approached the base of a fir, where a few wooden planks carved into circles leaned against its trunk. He dusted the snow off two of them and carried them over to her.

Clarion did her best not to look utterly perplexed. "What are those?"

He plopped them down on the ground at her feet. "Sleds."

"I see," she said, but she did not see at all. "And what do we do with these?"

"We ride them down the mountain."

"We . . ." Clarion gawped at him. "What? That's absurd."

He shrugged and climbed onto one of them. "We'll see. It's been a very long time since I've done this."

"You're serious, then," she said disbelievingly. All she could think about was just how high they'd climbed—and just how slick the hard-packed snow beneath her feet was. Forget Nightmares. This would surely be the end of her. She couldn't deny that the obvious foolishness of the prospect made it more enticing. When was the last time she'd gone on a *real* adventure? "This is a common pastime among winter fairies?"

"During happier times, yes." He looked up at her through his eyelashes. "Of course, if you'd prefer, we can walk . . ."

"No! No need." Clarion did indeed feel ridiculous as she perched on the other sled. There were rough-spun ropes looped into holes drilled onto each side—what Milori informed her were meant to pass for handholds. "And now what?"

"We go."

"What does—hey!"

He did not wait. With a *smirk*—one she very much resented, given how it made her stomach twist into an impressive knot—he pushed off the ground. His sled edged closer to the slope of the mountain and then careened down. Well, there was nothing else to do but follow him. Determined not to think about how dangerous this was, Clarion went after him. The terror—and the *rush*—was immediate.

She had never flown this fast in her life.

The forest rushed by in streaks of green and white, and the snow hissed below her. Her stomach bottomed out as the sled skipped over the snowbanks and slick ice, threatening to overturn midair, but she kept a steady course. The wind whipped at her face and tore her hair from its braided coronet. It came loose around her shoulders, fluttering wildly around her. Snow, knocked from the branches overhead, crashed to the ground.

At the bottom of the slope, Milori was climbing out of his sled—too slowly. Clarion was going to crash headlong into him.

"Look out!" she shouted.

He glanced up. Without hesitation, he took flight, neatly avoiding her. She whizzed by him—only to strike an embankment. The sled soared into the air, then hit the ground hard. The force of the impact threw Clarion from her seat. With a cry of surprise, she went tumbling out of the sled and landed directly into a cushion of deep snow.

"Clarion!"

For a moment, she lay there, staring dazedly up at the sky. "I'm alive."

"That's good." Milori's face soon eclipsed her view. "And you're all right?"

"I think so."

When her senses returned to her, she crawled out of the Clarion-shaped hole she'd left in the ground. He offered a hand to her. This time, she took it without hesitation and allowed him to pull her to her feet. Snow caked her wild hair and clung to her eyelashes. His expression was so full of concern, she couldn't help laughing. How *exhilarating* that had been. She couldn't remember the last time she'd had such pure, silly *fun*. For just one minute, she was not the soon-to-be Queen of Pixie Hollow. She was just a fairy playing in the snow.

Milori stared at her with a peculiar expression.

"What is it?" she asked.

"Nothing," he said hastily. He reached for a loose strand of her hair, and she stopped breathing entirely. For a moment, she thought he meant to tuck it behind her ear or brush off the ice that clung to it. But he must have thought better of it, for his arm dropped back to his side. She reminded herself sharply not to be disappointed. "It's just . . . you seem different here. It suits you."

"Oh?" Clarion took a step closer to him and injected a challenge into her voice, if only to conceal that thwarted spark of yearning. "What is *that* supposed to mean?"

"Ah," he said. "There you are."

She glared up at him, but he did not back away from her. If anything, the space between them seemed to shrink as he considered her.

"I only mean to say that you seem happy here." His tone turned almost gentle. "It's nice."

How could she not be? In the gathering dark, with someone who saw through her, this seemed to her a place she almost belonged. An entire world made of starlight, glittering and silver. It occurred to her that no one had ever said that about her before. *Was* she unhappy in the warm seasons?

"Thank you." She tucked the wayward strand of hair behind her ear. "Shall we keep going?"

Side by side, they set off for the Hall of Winter. Moonlight filtered through the bare branches of the trees and cast Milori with a silver glow. He had a preoccupied frown notched in his brow, as though searching for a way to break her pensive silence. At last, he said, "I must ask. How did you enjoy sledding?"

It surprised her enough that she let out a soft laugh. How serious he made it sound. "I loved it."

"Despite your crash landing?"

"Maybe even because of it. It made me feel more alive than I have in a long time. I confess, I . . ." She trailed off. If she finished that sentence, he would almost certainly mock her for it—or at the very least think her ignorant. But she supposed he'd chipped away enough at her armor tonight. "I didn't think Winter would be so much . . . fun?"

He raised an eyebrow. "What, did you think we stood around like ice sculptures?"

"It's a reasonable assumption." She tried and failed to keep the indignation out of her voice. "We've only seen you during seasonal transitions. And at a distance. I'll have you know we thought you all to be rather standoffish."

He let out a soft huff of laughter. "The feeling is mutual, rest assured."

She smiled despite herself. "I asked the queen what she knew of the Winter Woods, and she told me it was a place crawling with monsters."

Just then, another gust of wind lifted the fresh snowfall from the ground. It enshrouded them in white—and pierced her through with cold. Clarion shivered, half from the chill, half from the knowledge that in full dark, Nightmares could emerge from the shadows at any moment.

"Crawling with monsters," Milori echoed with some wonderment in his tone. "So why did you agree to come here with me if that's what you thought? You could have been attacked. Or I could have spirited you away."

"Could you have?" Clarion asked, unable to keep her own amusement out of her voice. "I mean no offense, but you're not very frightening."

"No?" He tilted his head at her, and his eyes were practically aglow with something like mischief. "How do you find me, then?"

Her face burned, and her heart fluttered. How infuriating, she thought, that a single look from him was all it took to fluster her. "Impertinent, for one."

Milori seemed quite delighted, judging by the tiny smirk he was clearly trying to keep off his face. "My apologies, Your Highness."

"You're forgiven," she said primly, with a cant of her chin. After a moment, she dropped the act and sighed. "Truthfully, I've always wanted to come here. I can see this very mountain from my room. Every night, I look out at it, and I've always thought . . . I don't know. It must seem silly to you, but I thought it looked sad. I'm glad to know that it's not."

"It's very much not."

Indeed, this close to the village, the twinkling sound of

laughter and work songs reached her. Clarion drank it in eagerly. Through the trees, she spied flashes of a river frozen solid. Here and there, she could see fairies dancing across its surface with . . . knives attached to their feet? It was all too puzzling—and entirely magical. "What are they doing?"

Milori steered her away from them by the shoulders. "Another time, perhaps. You've fallen enough today."

The trees gradually thinned, then gave way to a clearing at the foot of the mountain. Clarion stopped dead at the tree line. A massive door, made entirely of ice, loomed before them. It was carved with a snowflake insignia and washed blue in the ethereal light emanating from behind it.

"This," Milori said, "is the Hall of Winter."

"Wow," she breathed.

He guided her toward the door. Great pillars of ice rose from the earth and towered over them, marking the walkway from the woods to the entrance. When they stood before it, Clarion reached out to touch the pane of ice. Milori grabbed her wrist and stopped her. Before she could protest, he said, "Before we go in, I should warn you about the Keeper."

Clarion stilled. He'd mentioned the Keeper once before, in a tone that suggested he commanded respect—and maybe a healthy dose of awe.

He paused for a moment. Then, he settled on his warning: "He's eccentric."

That was . . . not what she expected. That could mean *anything*, but she supposed it was not worth pressing the matter. She would see for herself soon enough.

"Right," she said. "Understood."

Satisfied, Milori laid his hands against the massive doors. The intricate carvings responded to his touch; they lit up, so bright it bathed his face in blue. With a groan, they opened. Clarion tried not to gasp as they passed through the threshold. It was a palace made entirely of ice. The ceiling towered above them, supported by columns of ice and dripping with wickedly gleaming icicles. Sculptures of snowflakes hung suspended above them, emitting that same eerie blue glow. Even the floor was solid ice. It took a moment for her to find her balance and not go sprawling with every step. All around her, the walls were lined with shelves of dark wood. Each one was filled to bursting with books and scrolls and tablets.

"This is incredible."

Milori was surprised, clearly, for he smiled a little. "It is."

His voice, quiet as it was, resonated through the hall, deep and rich. The light played across his face. Clarion had to avert her gaze to keep herself from staring at him.

Just then, a long shadow fell across the floor. A terrible sound tore through the silence: a growl. Then, the sound of claws dragging viciously across the ice.

A Nightmare.

12

Clarion reached for her magic—and braced herself for the helplessness that would come when it did not answer her. But when the beast emerged from the stacks, it did not bear the sinister aura of a Nightmare. It was not made of oily shadows—but of flesh and bone and fur. Hardly reassuring, Clarion thought, when it was staring them down with its lips pulled back from its teeth in a snarl. It stood almost three times their height, with a thick gray coat and yellow eyes that bored into the very heart of her.

Clarion instinctively scrabbled backward. "What is that?"

Milori said, "That's only Fenris."

Only? How could he be so calm in this situation? "You've named it!"

"*I* didn't." Milori extended his hands, as though calling the creature to him. "He's the Keeper's wolf."

The wolf—Fenris—slunk toward Milori on his belly with his ears pinned flat to his head. When he reached them, Fenris laid his massive chin at Milori's feet and swished his tail against the ice. Clearly, the two of them were friends.

Clarion laughed breathlessly, if only to dispel the tension building within her. She had roped Petra into some dangerous schemes, but even she had her limits—or perhaps a scrap of self-preservation. "And do *you* have one of these beasts?"

"No." Milori patted Fenris's muzzle. "I've always been partial to owls myself."

"*Owls*?" Clarion could not keep the horror out of her voice. They were dangerous predators—at least in the warm seasons.

"The Keeper has a soft spot for misunderstood creatures," Milori said after a moment. Now that neither of them was paying attention to him, Fenris let out an aggrieved-sounding sigh. The force of his breath swept Clarion's hair back from her face. "Fenris here is quite harmless. He's still a pup. But even as adults, wolves are skittish—and easy to befriend if you have food."

"I don't have anything for you." Clarion tentatively scratched his ear. It flicked, as though a fly had landed on it.

"Fenris," a good-natured voice called from somewhere in the stacks. "What is all this fuss about? Oh!"

A winter fairy flitted into the atrium. He was short in stature, with a kindly face and hair like a tongue of white fire. He was wearing a rather serious-looking suit, but when his eyes landed on them, his expression lit up with an unbridled, unselfconscious enthusiasm. "Milori!"

"Keeper." Milori's entire demeanor changed. His answering smile made him seem instantly lighter. "I've brought you someone."

This was the Keeper?

Clarion had expected the Keeper of Fairy Knowledge to be more . . . retiring. The Keeper, however, was exuberant. He turned his attention to Clarion, adjusting his spectacles as he came closer. "A warm fairy, eh? It's been a long time since one of those has crossed into Winter."

"You've *seen* warm fairies before?" Clarion asked.

"Oh, no. I wish! I've read stories, though." Fenris trotted over to the Keeper, his tail wagging, and whined softly. The Keeper absently patted the top of his head. "Apparently, warm fairies used to come here all the time, way back when. Do a little ice-skating, make snowfairies . . ."

"That sounds delightful." Clarion had no concept of skating or snowfairies, but the fond way he spoke filled her up with wonder. "I'd love to read those."

The Keeper brightened. "Well, I—"

"Perhaps later," Milori interjected, clearly sensing a tangent. "She isn't just *a* warm fairy. Clarion is the Queen of Pixie Hollow."

"Queen-in-training," Clarion amended, with a pointed look in Milori's direction. He looked far too pleased with himself.

The Keeper gawped at her. "Then . . ."

Milori smiled at him, almost indulgently. "Someone can read our book at last."

Our book. Clearly, this was something they'd been working on together for a long time.

The look on the Keeper's face could only be described as exultant. "You can?"

"I hope so," said Clarion. The thought of crushing his hopes was almost unbearable. "But I'm not sure yet."

"Excellent!" The Keeper grabbed her by the arm and all but dragged her deeper into the library.

"Keeper," Milori groaned, with the long-suffering resignation of someone who knew it was pointless to protest.

He followed, with Fenris padding along just behind him. The labyrinthine shelves seemed to rearrange themselves the farther they went. Clarion absently studied them as they passed, the gilded titles illuminated by the ice sconces glowing with soft blue light. At last, they arrived at their destination: a square of empty space, hemmed in on all sides by the stacks. A table filled much of the area, cluttered with piles of books and quill pens.

"Wait just one moment," said the Keeper.

The Keeper released her and retrieved a set of gloves from his pocket. After pulling them on, he soared upward, nearly to the ceiling, until he found what he was looking for. He freed a massive leather-bound tome from the shelf—and almost dropped from the weight of it. Clarion held her breath until he brought it safely back to ground level. With utmost care, he laid it on the table.

No wonder Milori said he couldn't bring it to the border. It was indeed ancient, with thin, yellowing pages. The cover was peeling and worn, and while Clarion could see there had once been an illustration, the paint had faded with time. All that remained now were strange shapes carved into the leather, shimmering faintly with dormant power.

"What is this?" she asked.

"I don't know," the Keeper said, far more cheerfully than she would've expected. "It's been in the collection for a long, *long* time. It's written in a lost language. But it's filled with illustrations of Nightmares."

A shudder passed through her. "What do you need me to do?"

"It's sealed with runes that respond to governing-talent magic," the Keeper replied. "I suspect it's like a cipher. Once you unlock it, you should be able to understand the language it's written in."

Dread constricted her throat. "I've never learned to unlock anything with governing-talent magic."

"Try," he said encouragingly. "It should come naturally."

If only. "All right."

She reached out to take the book from him, but he gasped. "Swap out your gloves first, if you don't mind. It's very fragile."

Milori muttered something that sounded like *archivists.*

Clarion peeled off her damp mittens and slipped on the pair of gloves the Keeper handed her. The book was delicate beneath her touch, the spine groaning as she cracked it open. It promptly coughed up a cloud of dust. She leafed through the delicate pages, skimming over the illuminated drop caps and the strange little doodles of monsters in the margins. The illustrations were indeed striking, framing handwriting in a language she had not seen before. Amorphous black shapes with cruel violet eyes stared back at her. Here and there, golden swirls of magic pierced the darkness.

She closed the book again, staring down at the gilded runes shining on the front cover. But nothing about them grabbed her. They did not rearrange themselves into meaning. She'd let them down. How could she have ever thought otherwise? She should have told Milori from the start that she couldn't access the full range of her governing-talent magic. Her stomach twisted with shame. "I'm sorry. I don't think I can help you."

Both their faces fell.

"I suppose it was a long shot." Milori's brow furrowed in thought. "But then . . ."

"You have an idea?" the Keeper asked.

"The runes on the Hall of Winter's doors activate at my touch," he replied. "Perhaps the book will respond to Clarion's."

The Keeper shrugged. "It's certainly worth a try."

One more try, then. Clarion slipped off her gloves and set them aside. She drew in a deep breath. This was it, she supposed. If this—whatever *this* was—didn't work, then how could she ever hope to master her magic? *No. Just one more try.* With trembling fingers, Clarion laid her palm against the surface of the book.

Golden light shot out from it.

The Keeper shouted, half in surprise, half in delight. Even Milori's face was bathed in its warm light, his eyes sparkling with triumph.

Clarion withdrew her hand, but something of their wonder had seized hold of her, too. She felt almost giddy, watching the air twinkle with lingering magic. "What's happening?"

"Not a clue!" Once again, the not-knowing seemed to thrill the Keeper. "Try reading it now."

When Clarion opened the book again, the writing on each page glowed gold with her magic. Pixie dust lifted from the ink, glimmering in the darkness like starlight. Through the scintillating haze, the words slowly took shape in her mind.

"Long ago, when the Pixie Dust Tree was still but a sapling, children's dreams—both good and bad—traveled over Pixie Hollow," she said—or did she? Clarion could hardly tell if the voice she heard was her own, because the words certainly were not. They slipped out as though by recitation; the story unfolded in her mind so clearly, she could almost see it like a reflection on still water.

It was a legend, she realized. It went like this:

> Each night, as they crossed the skies above the Never Sea, those dreams knotted together and lit up the night like an aurora borealis. In those times, there were dream-talent fairies who gathered up the

dreams like shorn fleece and brought them back to their homes. All through the night, they spun dreams into thread on their spinning wheels. Come morning, they gathered up their thread and wove it through the branches of the young Pixie Dust Tree so that the children's hopes and wishes protected and nourished the tree as it grew.

Spinning dream-thread was long, arduous work; nightmares had to be separated out in the process, for they contained a sinister power. They lay on the workroom floor like scraps of black fabric. In the daylight, they burned away, but one night, a tenacious few escaped the notice of the dream-talents. With that glimmer of freedom, they tore through Pixie Hollow.

They could change shape like smoke but seemed to remember the shape of the fears that birthed them. Monsters, insects, vicious dogs—any beast a child could conjure—attacked that night. They lashed out with rending claws and teeth. But more terrible still was their magic. Any fairy who was struck by it fell into an unbreakable slumber, tormented by their worst fears. And just before daybreak—when the Nightmares would burn away like fog—they found refuge in the darkest places, biding their time until night fell once more.

The Queen of Pixie Hollow was consumed with worry for her subjects—and for the fragile Pixie Dust Tree, only just a sapling still putting out its first leaves. The dream-talents could not destroy the Nightmares, and so, they advised the queen to build a prison, one they would seal with a barrier woven from dream magic. The only question that remained was where to put it.

She and her ministers debated for hours—until the queen's dear friend, the Lord of Winter, offered to house it deep in Winter, as his realm was farthest from the vulnerable tree. He would watch over it himself to ensure that no Nightmare ever again escaped.

With that one act, he gained a new title: the Warden of the Winter Woods.

One night, the dream-talents set a trap for the loose Nightmares, ensnaring them in nets of dream-thread. They transported them to the Winter Woods, where the frost-talents had bored a hole into a frozen lake. They plunged the Nightmares into those dark waters, then laid the tapestry of the dream-talents' barrier. The moment the frost-talents repaired the ice, sealing away the Nightmares' terrible power, the slumbering fairies awoke. From that day forward, all Nightmares were transported to their watery prison in the Winter Woods.

There, the monsters squabbled among one another like starving animals—until, on one visit, the dream-talents realized they had fallen unsettlingly quiet. Over centuries, the oldest of the Nightmares, feeding on all that trapped bitterness and despair, had grown powerful enough to unite them. Like a queen bee at the center of her hive, it commanded the others, mindless but for their longing to escape—to destroy. It terrified the dream-talents, what they had allowed to fester.

When the Pixie Dust Tree grew to its full size, dreams no longer lit the skies. Over time, fewer and fewer dream-talents arrived in Pixie Hollow—until there was one, then none at all.

"Such is the way of nature," Clarion murmured. "Things rise and fall according to its designs."

With that, the book ended. The magic coursing through her went dormant, and the pixie dust cloud shattered, raining softly over the table. Its warm glow on the ice faded, and the eerie blue light filled the room yet again.

None of them spoke at first.

Clarion could hardly process it: an entire talent of fairy, lost to time, that could have roused her subjects and contained the Nightmares. What were they meant to do now?

Milori's thoughts, evidently, had followed the same path. He frowned at the Keeper. "Have you ever heard of dream-talent fairies?"

"No!" He was practically vibrating with excitement. At least *someone* was heartened by what they'd learned, Clarion thought. "This is an entirely new discovery."

"It makes sense now." Gloom settled over Milori. "The barrier they created is deteriorating, and there are none of them left to fix it. There's nothing we can do."

Clarion pulled her hand back from the book and worried her lip with her teeth. Perhaps there were no more dream-talents, but if she had learned anything from Petra over the years, it was that there were no unsolvable problems. They just hadn't landed on the right solution.

"There must be *something*," she said. "When the Nightmare attacked the Autumn Forest, I was able to drive it off. It was almost as if it was repelled by my magic. I'm not entirely sure why, but . . ."

"Queens of Pixie Hollow are born from stars, aren't they?" the Keeper asked. When Clarion nodded, he continued. "Sunlight burns them, so it makes sense to me that the Nightmares are repelled by your magic. The sun *is* a star, after all."

Hope sparked in Milori's eyes. "Then you can destroy them."

Clarion held up her hands. "No. I can't."

"But you just said—"

"I can't control my magic." The confession slipped out before she could stop it. "All my life, I've tried, but I can't. It has never come easily to me, and I fear it never will. I'm very sorry to disappoint you."

She blinked hard against the threat of tears. How humiliating, to be so overcome in front of them. Milori looked as though he was about to protest, but the Keeper rested a hand on his shoulder to still him.

"Maybe there's something else you can do," the Keeper said. After a brief pause, his glow intensified as another idea struck him. "If memory serves, queens aren't born from just any star, but a star that a child has wished upon. Maybe dream-talent magic lives on in you—in all governing-talents. It's possible you could repair the barrier. If there's one thing stronger than fear, it's hope."

"Maybe," she said quietly. How desperately she wanted to believe that. But now that the magic had bled out of her, she was becoming painfully aware of the chill in the air. Her teeth chattered, and her wings felt stiff beneath her coat. Every breath was a thin wisp of white in the dark.

Milori laid a hand against Clarion's elbow. His touch was featherlight—almost tender. "You're shivering."

Clarion forced herself to smile. "It's nothing to worry about."

"It isn't nothing. We need to get you back to the warm seasons."

For the first time, with that iron and ice in his voice, she understood why his forebears had once been known as Lords of Winter. Clarion tried to glare at him but found she had little fight left in her.

"Take Fenris," said the Keeper, his demeanor turning serious. "Go."

Relief softened Milori's voice. "Thank you. Come, Fenris. Clarion."

With that, he flitted toward the exit, and the wolf obeyed. His nails clicked on the ice floor as he trailed after Milori. Clarion passed the gloves the Keeper had given her back to him. Her fingers had gone quite pale, which she did her best not to notice. "Thank you, Keeper."

He tucked them into his pocket. "Anytime, Your Highness."

She lingered for only a moment before following Milori, tugging her mittens back on as she walked. As soon as she stepped out into the winter night, a gust of icy wind tore at her. Her entire body ached from how violently she shivered, and the tips of her ears burned with cold. She pulled her hood over her ears and nestled deeper into the fur lining. How sweet it would be to crawl underneath her covers with a cup of tea.

Milori stood a few paces away, illuminated by the spill of moonlight and the glow of the ice. Fenris lay at his side, his yellow eyes narrowed and fixed on Clarion. It froze her where she stood. The sight of Milori—practically luminous, the starlit space between them glittering—made her heart flutter. Her boots crunched in the snow as she approached him. He offered his hand to her. She accepted it, and with her free hand, she took a fistful of Fenris's fur.

"Up you go." With that, Milori took flight. He pulled her upward and steadied her as she clambered onto Fenris's back. The wolf gave a half-hearted growl to show his displeasure.

Clarion patted his shoulder. "Sorry, boy."

Fenris huffed. As soon as she was settled, he rose to his feet.

The shift of his weight threw her off balance, and she had to cling to his fur to keep herself from falling. "Whoa!"

Milori was beside her in an instant, hovering midair and braced as if to catch her. When it seemed she would not plummet—rather humiliatingly, she thought—into the snow, he relaxed.

"I suppose I should have warned you to hold on," Milori said, only a little apologetically. "Let's go."

He took off, and the wolf chased after him gamely. For the second time that evening, she felt as though she were soaring, even with her wings bound. Out in front of them, Milori was little but a glimmer of light against the darkness of the woods, weaving and dodging through icicles and branches heavy with snow. Clarion nearly laughed as she processed what exactly she was doing. If anyone from the warm seasons saw her like this . . . Imagining their stunned reactions delighted her far more than it should have. At the very least, it chased away some of her gloom.

Milori led them to the border of Winter and Spring. As soon as Fenris lay down, Clarion slid off his back and hurried over the bridge. When she crossed into Spring, she undid her buttons with numb, trembling fingers and let her coat pool at her feet. The chill of Winter still lingered on her skin, but she unfurled her wings: stiff—but still golden and whole.

Milori's anxiety dropped off him, and the relief brightening his face made her feel oddly flustered. He descended from where he hovered and sat on the bridge. "How do you feel?"

"Physically? I'm all right." She rubbed her hands together, pleased to find that the sensation was slowly returning to her fingers. She withdrew a few paces backward, until she stood far enough away that the chill emanating from Winter could not reach her anymore, and sighed. "I'm only disappointed I couldn't be of more use. I don't know where we go from here. But knowing our realms used to be so close . . ."

They couldn't let Elvina go through with her plan.

"I know." After a moment, more hesitantly, he asked, "What do you make of what the Keeper said?"

If there's one thing stronger than fear, it's hope.

Clarion absently plucked snow from her hair. "That he has more faith in me than I do myself."

Milori frowned at her. "I think you're capable of far more than you know."

Her chest constricted with the sudden force of her emotion. "How can you say that? You've only just met me."

As if it were the most obvious thing in the world, he said, "Because you were made for this. I feel it, when I look at you. Perhaps it's your magic. Perhaps it's you. Whatever it is, you have an aura about you. You command respect, yes, but more than that, you inspire hope. It is the first time I have felt it in a very long time."

Clarion's face warmed. She felt overwhelmed—so much so, she forgot how to speak entirely. "Oh."

Milori's expression went endearingly blank, as though it occurred to him belatedly that he'd said all that aloud. "Forgive me," he said hastily. "I don't mean to—"

"No," she cut in. "Please, don't apologize. That's the kindest thing anyone has ever said to me."

Was she made for this? Clarion had never believed it. But with his gray eyes steady and earnest on hers, she could almost convince herself it was true. Maybe, if she allowed herself to entertain it—if she pretended, just for one moment, that she was equal to the crown that would soon be hers . . .

Maybe she could do this.

A Pixie Hollow, fully united and safe, was worth fighting for. As much as it frightened her, she had to try. For the sake of the winter fairies. For the sake of Rowan and the others. If there was any chance that they could break the Nightmares' spell over their subjects, it was worth the risk.

"Tomorrow," Clarion said, with far more conviction than she felt, "take me to this prison. I want to put the Keeper's theory to the test."

13

When Clarion awoke, her pillow was damp with melted snow. If it weren't for that, she might have believed she'd dreamed her excursion into Winter. But then: there was the coat shoved into the very back of her closet. All of it had been real. A library carved from ice. Riding a wolf through the snowy thickets. A book describing talents long gone. And a white-haired boy who ferried her through the cold.

I think you're capable of far more than you know.

Maybe dream-talent magic lives on in you.

It seemed too much to hope for. But tonight, she would find out for certain whether she could seal the barrier and wake her subjects from their slumber. They weighed heavily on her mind this morning. And so, as soon as she readied herself, she asked Artemis to escort her to Feverfew Fields, where the healing-talents performed their work. It was one of the most peaceful corners of Summer, a meadow carpeted with feverfew and dotted with clear springs. Drinking from them had a calming effect, so the healers always kept vials of their water on hand.

Clarion couldn't help feeling a twinge of relief that it was still untouched. Not all of Pixie Hollow was so fortunate. Yesterday, a swarm of Nightmare-aphids had descended on Autumn's pumpkin patches and Cottonpuff Fields, draining the very life from them. She had not seen it herself, but Artemis had relayed the rumors she'd overheard from the other scouts.

By the time the sun peered above the horizon, Clarion and Artemis had arrived at the clinic, a space nestled into the hollowed-out trunk of a maple. They landed on one of the toadstools that served as the clinic's front porch, which was cluttered with an assortment of rocking chairs. Lights burned in the window, even at this early hour. Healing-talents took shifts at all hours to ensure they were always available to help fairies in need.

Clarion hesitated in front of the door, breathing in the bitter-citrus smell of the feverfew. A terrible mixture of nerves and guilt roiled in her stomach. She had not come to visit Rowan or the others since they'd been attacked, and she did not know if she could face them.

"Ready?" Artemis asked gently.

Her voice and steady presence grounded her. *Ready* was perhaps a strong word. But she could do this. Clarion nodded.

She knocked, and a healing-talent opened the door. She wore a fluted white gown of calla lily, and her black hair was tucked into a nurse's cap. Only a few wavy strands escaped and settled against her ochre skin.

"Good morning," she chirped, then visibly startled when she registered exactly who was standing on her doorstep. "Oh! Your Highness. I wasn't expecting you as well. What brings you here?"

"I'd like to visit the Minister of Autumn." Although she already knew the answer, Clarion couldn't help asking, "Has there been any change in his condition?"

The healer's wings drooped, as did her smile. "No, sadly. I'm sorry to not have better news. We've been working hard on an antidote, but I—"

"I know you're all doing your best," Clarion said gently. "Will you take me to him, please?"

With a bow of her head, the healer led her and Artemis to the sick ward, past a curtain of string-of-pearl succulents. Clarion stopped dead in the doorway as nausea threatened to overtake her. She had never seen this room so full. Eleven cots, dressed with moss and milk thistle seeds, were laid out on the floor with eleven too-still bodies on them. The eerie silence of the room settled over her like the chill of Winter.

"I'll leave you two to visit," the healer said.

Clarion moved quietly through the rows, her glow tracing

the haunted features of each fairy they passed, until she stopped at Rowan's bedside. His brow was furrowed as he dreamed his troubled dreams, and his auburn hair fell in a messy spill across his pillow. The sharp lines of his cheekbones looked even more prominent. The sight of him like this made her heart squeeze. It frustrated her as much as it pained her, to feel so helpless.

"I'm sorry," she whispered.

When she closed her eyes, something brushed against the very edges of her awareness. She couldn't place the sensation, exactly. It was as fleeting and inexplicable as a shudder in broad daylight—a sense that something was amiss, even when nothing appeared to be. With each passing moment, it—whatever *it* was—swirled into focus in the theater of her mind. A wisp—cold and dark, giving off little sparks of sinister light—wound itself around Rowan's mind.

Was this the magic that bound him in his slumber?

When she focused her attention on it, she reeled back with shock. Chills erupted over her skin, and her lungs emptied in a rush. Her ribs constricted, so tightly she felt she could not draw another breath. Clarion had never known what his fear had looked like, but she imagined it felt something like this. She stumbled back a step from the minister.

"Your Highness." Artemis was beside her in an instant, steadying her by the elbow. Her gaze was fixed warily on the minister. "Are you all right?"

It took a few moments for Clarion to find her voice. "I think so."

Slowly, Artemis eased her hold on Clarion's arm. "What happened?"

"I don't know, exactly." Clarion rubbed her temple. With some distance between them, terror eased its grip on her—enough for her to think more clearly. She'd been able to *see* the Nightmare's lingering power, like a knot or heavy chains binding him into the realm of his nightmares. Could this confirm the Keeper's theory? However small, she had *some* connection to the dream-talents' faded magic. She just had to hope it was enough to repair the fraying barrier they'd left behind.

For all their sakes, she could not fail tonight.

"You've come to visit."

Clarion startled, and Artemis bowed her head with a murmur of "Your Majesty."

Elvina had emerged from a back room with a healer, her hands folded and her expression solemn. The succulent curtain rustled softly behind her. Here in the early-morning light, Clarion noticed just how exhausted the queen looked.

"Yes," Clarion said. "I wanted to check on them."

Elvina only nodded. They'd had the same idea, after all. It struck Clarion that this, at least, connected them; no matter how their ideas differed, they shared both grief and love for their subjects.

After a moment of silence, Elvina said, "You have a meeting with the Minister of Summer tomorrow."

Clarion sighed at the reminder of her schedule. "I do."

"Later that day, you'll have a consultation for your coronation ball gown—and the final fitting for your coronation gown. You've only two more weeks before—"

"I know," Clarion cut in, with a touch of impatience.

Elvina stared at her, stunned.

When it occurred to her that she had interrupted the Queen of Pixie Hollow, she lowered her gaze deferentially. She hadn't *intended* to be so rude, but the thought of ball gowns and menus and ceremony . . . She could not bear it, not when she was surrounded by all the fairies she had failed to protect. But what else could she do but pretend? "I mean . . . Yes, I'm aware. Thank you."

Elvina composed herself and gestured out over the sickroom. "It is good of you to worry for them, but I want to ensure your focus is on your coronation—and mastering your magic before then. I am handling the Nightmares."

"I have been focused—"

Elvina arched an eyebrow. "The Minister of Spring told me you seemed distracted when she saw you last."

"It's only nerves." Clarion hesitated, crossing the room so that she floated beside Elvina. "And I can't help worrying some. Even if your plan succeeds, it won't awaken these fairies."

Elvina's expression darkened, but she laid a hand on Clarion's shoulder. "We will find a way. In the meantime, we will ensure no one else falls. My plan is progressing. Our royal tinker has been assisting me."

"Petra," Clarion said, half on reflex. Elvina seemed incapable of remembering her name. "Right."

Rationally, she *knew* she should not have felt disappointed. It wasn't as though Petra could disobey the queen so easily—not when her position as the royal tinker could be taken from her. And yet, it still stung.

"That's good," Clarion managed. "She is very talented."

Elvina seemed to relax some at that. "Then try not to trouble yourself too much. I am handling this."

"Of course," she said.

But all she could think was, *No. I am.*

Just before sunset, Clarion threw her coat, mittens, and boots into a bag. She pushed open her balcony doors and stepped into the golden-hour light. Sunshine trickled thick as syrup through the branches of the Pixie Dust Tree, patterning the earth with dappled shadow. The leaves sighed softly in the breeze, as if wishing her farewell.

"Off again, Your Highness?"

Artemis sat in her usual perch, leafing through a book. Already, Artemis had grown so accustomed to their routine, she could not be bothered to glance up from . . . whatever it was she was doing. Clarion squinted at the cover; the title looked suspiciously like *The Love Language of Flowers.*

Clarion snorted. "What are you reading?"

"Nothing." Artemis snapped it shut and glared. Then, recovering her decorum, she cleared her throat and added, "Please do not stay out too late."

"I won't." She smiled innocently. "She likes daffodils, by the way."

Artemis flushed. Clarion waved, then took flight toward Winter.

By the time she arrived, Milori was already waiting for her—and he wasn't alone. A snowy owl, twice as tall as he was, stood beside him. Her blood ran cold with apprehension. Ever since she was a new arrival, it had been drilled into her that birds of prey were among the greatest threats to fairykind. And here was Milori, patting it as though it were as docile as a mouse! Truly, winter fairies feared nothing.

"What," she said, "is that?"

"This is Noctua," Milori replied, as though that were a perfectly comprehensive answer to her question. After a moment, he added, "She's a snowy owl."

He *had* told her he was partial to owls. "You weren't joking."

The owl's yellow eyes gleamed in the gathering dark. She moved with the cagey erraticism Clarion had never much trusted in birds, her head swiveling unnaturally on its neck. She was tethered by one of her terrifyingly clawed feet; Milori held the end of it like a leash.

"I would never joke about owls," he said solemnly.

"Then you're mad."

Milori only smiled. "Would you like to meet her?"

Clarion swallowed her groan of dread. "Oh, yes. I'd love nothing more."

She dropped her bag and retrieved her winter gear. Once she'd fastened the last button on her coat, she stepped over the border and let the cold of Winter flow over her like water. As she approached, she couldn't help thinking Milori looked the warmest in the setting sun, with his wings shot through with shades of burnished gold and faintest red. And now that she forced herself to look closely, she could not deny that Noctua was a beautiful creature. Her feathers gleamed as white as the snow—as white as Milori's hair. A crystal charm dangled from a cord wound around her neck; reins hung down her back.

"We're going to ride her, aren't we?" Clarion asked, as cheerfully as she could manage.

"Well . . ." Milori took hold of the reins and untethered Noctua's leg. "It *will* be faster than walking."

"Are you sure about this?" Clarion asked.

"You're about to face Nightmares willingly," he said, "and you're afraid of an owl."

She resisted the urge to smack his arm. "I'm not afraid of her."

He gave her a wry half smile, as if to say, *Right*. To his credit, he only asked, "Shall we?"

"If we must," she muttered.

With a resigned sigh, Clarion climbed onto the owl's back. Noctua swiveled her head 180 degrees to fix her with an inquisitive yellow stare. Clarion considered immediately throwing herself to the ground again. If this beast took off with Clarion still on her back, she would plummet to her death with her wings bound down as they were. Never had a fairy been afraid of heights until now.

Fortunately, Milori soon joined her. "Hold on."

Clarion locked her arms around Milori's waist. He nudged the owl onward; without hesitation, Noctua took flight. The wind buffeted her face. Her stomach lurched. Clarion held in her scream as they soared toward the darkening sky. She pressed her forehead between his shoulder blades, if only to keep herself from watching how quickly they were leaving solid ground behind.

"I hate this!"

Milori laughed, a warm sound that almost made it all worth it. *Almost.*

When she finally allowed herself to look, the view was spectacular. They'd flown high enough that Clarion felt as though she could reach out and pluck the pale moon from the sky. Noctua's wings cut through the low-hanging clouds, dragging trails of white behind them. Then, they dove. Her hair whipped wildly around her, dancing among the thickening flurries.

Milori guided Noctua to a branch and slid off her back. Then, he offered Clarion a hand and helped her down into the snowbanks. Clarion spun in a slow circle, drinking in their surroundings with a mounting dread. In this section of the Winter Woods, the trees grew strange. Their pale trunks rose in straight, stark lines, and their bark was whorled and knotted with dark shapes that looked like eyes. The branches overhead clawed at the sky—and just ahead, she could see a break in the trees.

A shudder worked its way through her, and something deep in the back of her mind said, *Run.* It was the same voice she'd heard when she'd been confronted with the Nightmare in Autumn, towering over her with its horrible violet eyes.

Something about this place was *wrong.*

"Where are we?"

"A place few go," Milori said grimly. "Follow me."

When they emerged from the shadow of the birches and into a clearing at the foot of the mountains, it took a moment for Clarion to process what exactly she was looking at. A vast lake stretched out before them, frozen solid and glaring up at the moon like a solid black eye. Everything in her balked at it.

Run.

"This," Milori said, "is the Nightmares' prison."

When he stepped onto its surface, Clarion reluctantly followed him. Faint protective magic glimmered and winked within the ice, but she could vaguely make out the churning of dark waters beneath. The empty, void-like depths unsettled her more than she cared to admit. And then, a flash of something—a violet eye, she realized, fixed balefully on her—caught her attention and made her blood run cold. No, that wasn't water.

Whatever was underneath the ice was *alive.*

"The Nightmares are beneath the lake."

"Yes," Milori said. "That's right."

Clarion's heart twisted at the bitterness in his voice. She could not imagine the burden he carried. Not only did he need to worry about his subjects—but also these creatures he was utterly powerless against. What would it be like to know you were responsible for them? To spend your days listening, watching, waiting, for something you could not prevent?

"Milori . . ." She trailed off. What could she truly say to comfort him?

He looked toward her, his lips parting as though he meant to reply.

But just then, it felt as though every Nightmare in the lake turned toward her. The awareness of them prickled along her skin. That instinctual desperation to flee rose up within her again and sent a racking shiver down her spine. She mastered it as best she could and followed Milori toward the center of the lake. With each step, the Nightmares seethed. They seemed to shrink away from her every footfall.

"Here we are."

Instantly, Clarion saw the problem: the ice was fissured. In the daylight, it would hardly be noticeable. But here in the darkness, it was seamed with a sinister glow, as though whatever was contained beneath was beginning to bubble up. She crouched beside the shattered surface to examine it more closely. She could make out the golden threads of the dream-magic barrier. Here, it had grown as thin and tattered as an old quilt. A few Nightmares had slipped through the magical barrier and pooled just beneath the ice like a spill of ink, hungrily gnashing their teeth.

Terrible understanding unfurled through Clarion. "They're going to shatter it."

"Exactly," he said. "I've tried to seal the cracks with ice, but each time I return, it's as though I did nothing."

It didn't surprise her to hear that. Although the larger ones remained trapped beneath the net of dream-thread, these would persevere until they created a gap wide enough to escape through. The others only had to bide their time until the magical barrier deteriorated enough to let them through as well.

Unless, of course, she could fortify it.

Clarion closed her eyes and concentrated on the frayed, ancient fibers of dream-talent magic. She could see them, bright as starlight, shimmering in the darkness behind her eyelids—the same way she'd been able to detect the Nightmare's power in Rowan's mind. When she imagined closing her fingers around that golden thread, happiness bloomed within her. She wanted to draw it around herself like a sweater, to nestle into its comforting warmth. It really did not feel so different from her own magic. But she could also sense how faint this dream's power was now.

If she could weave starlight into the holes time had worn into it . . .

She called on her magic. As golden light emanated from

her skin, a hiss—muffled beneath the thick layer of ice—rose up beneath her. Cold sweat gathered on the back of her neck as she focused her energy into her hands.

Her first thought was not *control* but *protect*.

Her magic threaded itself into the tapestry of dream magic. As the Nightmares howled in rage, her power illuminated all the world in gold. Milori stared at her with open awe, his lips parted softly. She had to tear her eyes away from him to maintain her focus. Once she finished stitching the threadbare segment of the barrier, Milori could freeze over the shattered ice.

Something rumbled deep within the prison. The ice shuddered beneath her feet. Her magic flickered like a guttering candle, and she felt her work unraveling like a row of knit stitching pulled loose. A jolt of panic shot through her.

"Can you hold on?" Milori shouted.

"I think s—"

A resounding boom echoed through the clearing as a Nightmare threw itself against the barrier. Clarion wobbled, then lost her footing on the slick ice. Her stomach bottomed out as her feet slipped from beneath her. The connection with her magic snapped, and she landed hard on her back. Her breath whooshed out of her, and a sharp pain radiated through her wings. It *hurt*. And yet, all she could dwell on was the frustration. She'd been so close. All that remained of her attempt was a fine layer of pixie dust on the moonlit ice, its glow fading like a dying ember. The shadows swam menacingly underneath her, exuding a palpable malice.

"Clarion!" Milori called. "Are you all right?"

Before she could respond, there came the low sound of splintering ice. Just behind Milori, a dark shape rose like smoke from the depths of the lake. It swirled, then expanded like a drop of ink in water. Clarion could make out the shape of wings; they unfurled and blocked out the meager light of the moon.

"Milori," she whispered.

All the color drained from his face. Slowly, he turned to face it.

The smokelike form of the Nightmare writhed and bubbled until it took recognizable form: a raven. One by one, ten violet eyes blinked open on its body; all their pupils rattled, as if struggling to focus. Its talons flexed experimentally. Then, it beat its wings—once, twice—sending a fetid gust of air their way. It rose higher into the sky, with all its eyes fixed on her. The Nightmare-raven shrieked, then dove toward her.

She did not think. She rolled. A bright pain seared through her, but the Nightmare's talons drove into the spot where she'd been lying only moments before. The beast recovered almost instantly, rounding on her again. Her heart pounded so loudly in her ears, she could scarcely hear the sound of her own ragged breaths. Its very presence was skin-crawling, muddying her mind with nothing but the steady refrain of *run, run, run*.

The Nightmare launched itself at her. The terror she'd tried to suppress simmered far too close to the surface. She couldn't stop it. She couldn't do this. She couldn't—

A blast of frost knocked it off course. The raven landed in a heap on the ice, dissolving into smoke before it re-formed, more horrific than before. Its wings sprouted, many-jointed and dripping viscous shadow as it took to the skies. It let out another cry, so piercing that Clarion felt it resonating in her very bones. It dove, its talons outstretched toward Milori.

"Noctua!" he shouted. "Now!"

Noctua screeched, a sound of pure fury. She descended on the Nightmare like a snowstorm, all thrashing wingbeats and rending talons. They tore across the sky, a scrabbling tangle of black and white. Clarion watched with her heart in her throat until Noctua managed to free herself, with a trail of smoke dripping from her beak like blood.

Clarion decided that perhaps she would have to revise her opinion of owls.

The Nightmare seized its opportunity. With a beat of its crumbling wings, it ascended until it was silhouetted by the pale face of the waxing moon. Then, with a final cry, it dove and vanished into the woods.

Clarion crumpled to her knees, then drove her fist into the ice with a shout of frustration. How could she have been so *inept*? She'd had it, and then she'd let it escape. As the adrenaline wore off, she began to shiver all over with nerves. Her heavy breaths misted in the air.

"Clarion." Milori kept his voice level, but Clarion recognized strangled panic when she heard it.

"I'm so sorry. I never should have—"

“Clarion,” he repeated, more firmly this time. “You’re bleeding.”

She glanced down. A stain of red blossomed on her arm. Now that she’d noticed it, the pain—and the cold—flooded in. She clutched her wound to stanch the bleeding but shivered at the sensation of her wet skin already cooling. “Oh.”

Her coat sleeve had torn.

Don’t panic. Clarion blew out a steadying breath. As long as her wings remained insulated, she wasn’t in any danger.

Milori soared over the short distance between them. “Are you all right?”

“It’s only a scratch,” she said hastily. A deep one, yes, but it wasn’t life-threatening. “I’m sorry. I wasn’t able to do it.”

“No. *I’m* the one who should be sorry.” Milori’s expression was agonized. “I put you in danger.”

Milori carried far too much guilt already. She refused to let him add her to his ledger. She jabbed a finger at him. “*You* didn’t do anything. I put myself in danger, and as the soon-to-be Queen of Pixie Hollow, I won’t hear otherwise.”

He looked very much like he wanted to press the matter, but he’d thought better of it now that she had pulled rank on him. “I’m going to repair the damage they did to the ice. After that, we should get you to a healer.”

Clarion clutched her forearm tighter, shuddering at the feeling of blood weeping through the gaps in her fingers. “Yes, I think that’s a good idea.”

Milori hesitated, as though she would keel over if he looked away for even a moment. With a frown, he turned away. Clarion watched the rise of his shoulders as he drew in a deep breath. Swirls of ice crystals poured from his extended hands like mist, sparkling in the moonlight. Frost bloomed across the ground in fractal patterns, then crystallized over the shattered ice, like broken ceramic repaired with gilt.

When he finished, he whistled for Noctua. The owl came to him immediately, hooting softly in acknowledgment. As soon as she landed, he leaned his head against her beak and murmured, "Thank you." Noctua fluffed out her feathers contentedly. Seeing the bond between them—and just how quickly Noctua had leapt to protect him—hit Clarion somewhere tender.

"She's incredible," Clarion said softly.

Milori brightened. Even Noctua seemed to preen.

"She really is." Milori's smile faded after a moment. "Can you get on? I'll have her take us to the healing-talents."

"I think so." Clarion clambered onto Noctua's back as gracefully as she could. When she steadied herself, she frowned down at her arm. "I might have a hard time holding on, though."

"I'll make sure you don't fall," he replied without hesitation. Never had Clarion met anyone in the habit of making such solemn oaths so readily.

She couldn't dwell on it, for when Milori joined her, he wrapped an arm securely around her waist. A flush crawled up her neck at his sudden closeness. No, she supposed she wouldn't fall. The scent of pine and cold water and the promise of snowfall radiated gently from his skin. His presence blunted the skin-crawling sensation of the Nightmares' wrath boring into her. Like this, she could almost believe she was safe. Without thinking, Clarion turned her face into the crook of Milori's neck and tried not to notice the way his breath hitched.

14

Noctua brought them to a sprawling holly bush where the winter healing-talents had established their clinic. All of its leaves were sharp and silvered in the flood of moonlight, and sprays of red berries dripped from the snow-covered branches. Everything was impossibly quiet at this hour. Clarion heard nothing but the flutter of Noctua's wings as she landed.

Milori helped her down from her seat and led her through a hollow cut in the holly branches. Pale light filtered in through the gaps in the leaves, patterning the hard-packed ground and setting the frost aglow. As they walked, the path began to slope downward.

"It's underground?" Clarion asked, with some surprise.

"Just slightly," Milori replied. "It keeps it insulated from the wind."

Clever, Clarion thought. It was noticeably warmer in here than it was outside. Even so, her every breath plumed in the air. The cold seeped through the tear in her coat, but she clenched her teeth to keep them from chattering. They came to a stop in front of a curtain of lichen. She tried not to notice the blood beading on her fingertips—and how it pattered onto the ground.

"Hello?" Milori called softly.

The curtain parted, and a healing-talent's face appeared. She had umber skin and white hair that framed her face in tight curls. Like the healers in the warm seasons, she wore a gown of white; this one, Clarion noted, was made from primroses.

"Milori—" Her smile faltered when she took in Clarion, and it was replaced with momentary shock. Clarion knew she must have looked quite a sight. Blood had dried on her hands and soaked into the beautiful coat Petra had made her, staining the gold a livid red. Half her hair had come loose from its braid and hung bedraggled and partially frozen around her shoulders. "Who is this?"

"This," he said wanly, "is Princess Clarion."

Clarion watched at least ten emotions pass over the healer's face before she settled on dismay. "And how, may I ask, has she ended up in this condition?"

He winced. "We ran into some trouble."

"I can see that." Concern bled into her voice. "And you—"

"I'm fine," he said quickly, holding up his hands.

"Good." The healer rearranged her expression back into stern displeasure, but Clarion could see the fondness she had for him: a kind of familiarity born from knowing each other for a long time. It astounded Clarion how casually Milori's subjects spoke with him. "Do be more careful with her going forward."

Chastened, he replied, "I will."

"I like her," Clarion whispered to Milori, unable to help her teasing smile.

"I thought you might," he said. "This is Yarrow."

"I'm honored to meet you, Your Highness," Yarrow said with a bow. "I only wish it were under better circumstances."

"Me, too," Clarion said, momentarily stunned. How unusual, to be treated with both respect and warmth. How she wished the warm seasons were more like this.

Yarrow ushered them through the lichen curtain and into the ward. Clarion froze in the doorway, her hand clasped to her chest. The room was filled with cots built from platforms of snow and covered with a latticework of twigs. All of them housed fairies trapped in their tormented dreams. There were far more of them here in Winter. Clarion's heart ached for them—and for Milori, who surveyed the room with an expression of pure guilt.

It's not your fault, she wanted to say, but Yarrow urged her along. She stationed Clarion on a cot piled high with blankets. Clarion pulled one around her shoulders and sighed in relief.

Milori leaned closer and murmured, "Will you be all right alone for a few minutes?"

"Of course," she said encouragingly. "Go."

He nodded, gratitude plain on his face. Within a few moments, he'd flitted across the sickroom floor and begun speaking with another healer in low tones. Every now and again, he cast a worried look out at the slumbering fairies.

Yarrow, who had been fussily arranging the blankets and pillows around her, said, "He's been in here every day, you know. Are you warm enough?"

Clarion tore her gaze away from Milori, embarrassed that she'd been caught staring. "I am, thank you. Has he really?"

Yarrow nodded. "There's nothing he can do, but . . ."

But he feels responsible, Clarion filled in. She knew that particular feeling well. "I know he cares a lot."

"Yes. He's beloved in Winter." Yarrow paused for a moment, as if choosing her next words carefully. "I'm glad he found you. It's been a long time since we've seen him so . . . hopeful."

Clarion tucked a strand of hair behind her ear. She regretted it when she felt her skin warm with a blush. "It's nothing *I've* done."

"As you say." She smiled knowingly. "Well, let's take a look at you."

Clarion let the blanket slide off her shoulder and offered her arm. The sight of the blood made her stomach turn, but she had not inspected the wound closely. The torn fabric of her coat clung to her skin, concealing the worst of the wound from view.

Yarrow clicked her tongue disapprovingly. "You can't remove your coat, so I'm going to need to cut the sleeve to get a better look."

Clarion cringed. Petra was going to kill her for brutalizing her masterpiece this way, but that was a problem for another time. "That's fine."

Yarrow nodded and withdrew into another room in the clinic. Here in the main room, it was dark and cozy in the candlelight. Everything sparkled in the light refracted through the icicles dripping from the ceiling. The shelves lining the walls were cluttered with books and kettles, acorn shells filled with tinctures and sea-glass bowls of dried herbs. The air smelled earthy and green. Until now, Clarion had never realized just how many things grew in Winter. How had anyone ever believed it was devoid of life here?

She let her attention drift back to Milori, who had begun assisting the other healing-talent. They moved from bedside to bedside, helping each fairy drink sips of water. Her heart fluttered with a terrible fondness. How had she ever thought him cold, even for a moment?

A few minutes later, Yarrow returned with a woven basket, a stone mug that steamed in the cold, and a delicate set of fabric shears. She cut away the blood-mottled sleeve, and Clarion hissed in pain as the wound was exposed to the freezing air. Yarrow set down the scissors on a side table with a clack and bent down to inspect her more closely. She turned Clarion's forearm carefully this way and that. "It's clean, but it's fairly deep. I'm going to need to stitch it for you. It should heal quickly, but you'll need to keep a wound dressing on for tonight."

Clarion felt a small measure of relief that she would not have to explain away her injury or commit to the questionable choice of wearing long sleeves in Summer. "All right."

Yarrow rummaged through a basket and procured a thin hooked needle, as well as a poultice of juniper, usnea, and linseed wrapped in a leaf parcel. She worked in silence, cleaning and suturing the wound. Clarion stared resolutely at the wall, willing herself not to flinch with every tug of the thread through her skin. When Yarrow finished slathering on the poultice and applying a bandage, she handed her a mug.

"What is this?"

"Balsam fir and wintergreen," Yarrow said. "It will help with healing and inflammation."

Clarion brought the cup to her lips. It smelled resinous—and tasted it, too. But it warmed her hands, and right now, that was all she could ask for. "Thank you."

Yarrow gave her a stern look. "Try not to irritate the wound before it closes. Don't do anything strenuous."

"I won't."

"I'll send you home with this poultice, too. Apply it once per day." She narrowed her eyes. "Don't forget."

Clarion could see how Milori allowed himself to be fussed over. Yarrow was quite forceful. With a laugh, Clarion said, "I won't."

"Good." Yarrow studied her pensively. "I hope you'll come back soon, Your Highness—although maybe not *here*. There's a lot to see in Winter that has nothing to do with that dreadful lake." She paused, and her expression brightened as something occurred to her. "Milori is a very talented ice-skater, you know. I'm sure he'd teach you."

Clarion beamed. "I would love that."

She just had to figure out how to stop the Nightmares before Elvina's plan took shape. She could not abandon the winter fairies to the Nightmares. She refused. That conviction filled her up with a determined fire.

As soon as Yarrow moved on to the next patient, Milori reappeared at her side. "How are you feeling?"

Clarion offered him a small smile. Yarrow had cleaned the blood from her skin. Now, all that remained was a neat line of stitches. She caught him studying it, a lock of white hair falling out of place as he tilted his head. She resisted the urge to right it.

"Much better," she said. "A little cold."

"We should get you home."

Home. More and more, she dreaded leaving Winter. "Right. Good idea."

Outside, Noctua waited for them, her white feathers fluffed and gleaming coldly in the moonlight. The two of them climbed on, and this time, when Milori hooked an arm around her, Clarion found herself grateful for the close contact. Her bare forearm stung in the cold, and the wind slipping beneath the tattered half sleeve chilled her to the very bone. Noctua took flight toward Spring, and the thickening flurries swirled around them. Even in darkness, Winter was breathtakingly beautiful. Endless forests of pine dusted in snow reached toward them.

Clarion tipped her face toward Milori's until she could see his profile limned by starlight. Like this, unguarded and lost in thought, he looked so serious.

It's been a long time since we've seen him so hopeful.

She couldn't believe she'd had that effect on him. And yet, if it was true, she wanted to pull him out of his gloom as much as she could. "Well, that didn't go entirely as planned."

She startled a laugh out of him. It was a nice sound, made sweeter for how rare it was. "No, it certainly didn't."

"But we'll find a way," she said. "Next time will be better."

"Next time," he echoed, as solemn as a promise.

"I'll need to get my coat repaired first." She plucked at a loose thread on her sleeve. "I'm not sure how long it will take. It took a few days for her to make it the first time."

"I don't mind," he said. "I'll wait for you."

Clarion frowned as he fixed his gaze straight ahead. There was something terribly vulnerable on his face. *Loneliness.* How could he not be? He spent his time poring over unreadable books or standing at the border or patrolling a prison he could not guard. He was so duty bound—and forever bound to fail.

"I could come visit you," she said—and immediately wished she could rephrase. It sounded far too eager to her own ears. She cleared her throat and added, "If you're going to be there waiting anyway. We can strategize on what our next steps are."

Matching her feigned nonchalance, he replied, "As you wish."

She gave him a look that said, *As I wish?*

Apparently unable to maintain the façade, he relented. "I would like that."

She did not mistake the faint pink burning on the tips of his ears. "Well, then," she said. "I'll see you tomorrow."

His lips curled into a soft smile. "Tomorrow."

A strange lightness—a sort of *giddiness*—filled her up inside. Even though they soared high above the Winter Woods, Clarion had the distinct sensation of free-falling. Between the Nightmares and Milori, she'd landed herself in far more trouble than she'd bargained for.

The next morning, Clarion and Artemis stood outside Petra's door at first light. Despite the danger she'd found herself in, Clarion had awoken in a strangely good mood. That was, of course, until she processed that she was about to ruin Petra's day, if not her entire month. In her pack was the ripped, bloodstained coat Petra had so generously sewn for her. If there was any good news to be taken from the entire ordeal, it was that the boots had escaped the scuffle with little more than a scratch.

"Are you going to knock?" Artemis asked.

Clarion realized she had been staring at the door—and that she'd been clenching her jaw. She willed her face to relax. "I'm mentally preparing myself."

Artemis shot her a look that landed somewhere between sympathetic and pitying. "Surely she'll understand."

"We'll see," Clarion replied skeptically. Even Artemis didn't sound fully convinced by her own words. "You may have to intervene."

"I stand at the ready."

"Good." With a sigh, she knocked. "Petra, it's me."

Barely a second passed before Petra flung open the door. She looked weary—but like she had been up for quite some time. Her face was already streaked with grease, and the heat of her forge emanated steadily from within. "Do you have any idea what time it is?"

Clarion smiled innocently. "Dawn?"

"Exact—" She cut herself off with a strangled squeak when she spied Artemis. "Oh. Good morning."

"Good morning," Artemis replied stiltedly.

Clarion let her gaze volley between them for a moment, trying not to let her exasperation show. "Are you going to invite us in?"

Petra groaned but stepped aside to admit them. "You have that look in your eyes again. What is it this time?"

Best just to get it over with, Clarion decided. She cleared a new pile of detritus from Petra's kitchen table, then upended the contents of her bag onto its surface.

Petra let out a soft wail of dismay. "What have you *done*?"

Clarion winced. "I might have gotten into a little accident."

Artemis pinned her with a flat stare that said, *You could have handled that better.*

"All my hard work, ruined! Completely ruined!" Petra picked

up the jaggedly cut sleeve of the coat. After a moment's inspection, she hurled it across the room with a yelp of surprise. "Is that *blood*?"

"Keep your voice down," Clarion hissed. "Yes, it's blood. It's nothing to worry about."

Petra seized Clarion's shoulders and shook them. Out of the corner of her eye, she saw Artemis shift, as though debating whether or not to intervene. In the end, she let out a long-suffering sigh and folded her arms behind her back.

"What do you *mean* it's nothing to worry about?" Petra demanded. "There are monsters on the loose, and you've suddenly decided to gallivant around the Winter Woods, and now you show up on my doorstep with blood on your clothes?"

As much as she resented the suggestion that she was *gallivanting*, when Petra put it like that, Clarion supposed it sounded a little bad. "It looks a lot worse than it is. I'm not hurt. Not badly, anyway."

She pulled up her sleeve to show Petra the thin strip of gauze bound to her forearm. Mercifully, it concealed the stitches underneath. Petra let her go and slumped heavily into an armchair. Something in the far corner of the room tipped over and clanged to the ground. Petra hardly flinched. "I know I said I didn't want to know, but I've decided the not-knowing is much worse than the alternative. What is going on with you?"

There was something in her voice deeper than her usual anxiety. There was a real plea there, and Petra was staring at her with an accusation in her eyes: *I feel like I don't know you anymore.*

She hated disappointing Petra—and not knowing how to stop.

But if she couldn't be honest with her, what friendship did they really have anymore? Clarion couldn't lose her after everything they'd been through together.

"If I tell you," Clarion said, "you have to promise not to tell anyone."

"I didn't tell anyone you were going into the Winter Woods before," she said defeatedly. "I hate keeping secrets, though, Clarion. You know I'm terrible at it, but . . . I'll try. For you."

With as much levity as she could muster, Clarion said, "You have to promise not to scream, either."

Petra glared at her, which Clarion chose to take as agreement.

"About two weeks ago, when the Nightmare was first spotted in Pixie Hollow, I went to the border of Winter. I thought I'd find a trail there. I didn't, but there was something else there . . . well, *someone*." She took a deep breath. "The Warden of the Winter Woods."

Petra looked on the verge of either fainting or combusting. "The Warden of the Winter Woods? You met *the* Warden of the Winter Woods?"

"Just listen." Clarion took hold of her elbow. "I was a little skeptical at first. He isn't all that bad once you get to know him."

"How reassuring." Petra laughed breathlessly, the sound fraying at the edges. Then, something dawned on her. "You've met multiple times, then?"

"A few."

Petra gasped. "Did you cross the border to see him?"

Clarion flushed. "Yes. But—"

"You're sneaking out to see a *boy*?" Petra sounded positively disgusted, but there was no real bite to it. She'd never had much of an eye for sparrow men; the very notion of finding one comely enough to risk life and limb for was surely confounding.

Artemis made a sound that sounded suspiciously like a stifled laugh.

"It's not like that!" Clarion protested, and she realized too late it was not exactly a denial. Petra's eyes gleamed with vicious triumph. "We've found a way to stop the Nightmares. Which is why I need your—"

"And this is what stopping them looks like?" Petra jabbed a finger at the coat crumpled in the corner. "You should have no part in it. It's too dangerous."

Clarion could not keep the frustration out of her voice. "I'm so tired of being told things are too dangerous."

"But they *are*. I know it's never been a concern for you, but some of us are happy tucked away in our nooks."

"Petra . . ."

"No. Don't use your queen voice on me," she said, almost pleadingly. "I won't do it. I can't watch you come home like this again. I'm a tinker, not a healer. I can patch up your coat, but not *you*."

For a moment, they remained in brittle silence, staring at each other across the darkness of Petra's workshop. Clarion felt monstrous, indeed. Was this really what Petra thought of her? That she was some kind of reckless instigator who had ignored her discomfort all these years?

Artemis, clearly sensing they needed space, wordlessly slipped out through the door. When it clicked shut behind her, Clarion found her voice again. She had to fight to keep the hurt out of it. "I wouldn't ask if I had another option. There's no one else I can rely on."

Petra sighed fretfully. "Both you and Elvina are depending on me for your schemes to work. Being in this position isn't easy for me."

"I know." Guilt plucked at Clarion. "But her plan is misguided. It's the duty of the queen to ensure the well-being of her subjects—not to leave an entire realm to fend for itself."

Petra frowned and absently picked up a pair of sewing shears, the conflict clear on her face.

"I'm sorry that I've put you in this position," Clarion continued, "and I'll be as careful as I can. But I can't walk away from this. I won't, whether I have your support or not, because for the first time, I feel like I'm doing what I'm supposed to be doing."

Petra groaned: a telltale sign that her surrender was nigh. "Fine. *Fine.* Consider it my coronation gift. But if it comes back to me in tatters again—"

"It won't," Clarion cut in breathlessly. "Thank you, Petra."

"Keep your gratitude." She turned back to her worktable and began rearranging her tools. "Just live."

Clarion's breath caught in her throat. "I will."

15

"Your Highness?"

Clarion startled awake—and found herself rather undignifiedly slumped over her writing desk. At least she managed to avoid falling out of her chair in surprise. She turned toward the door, where a harried-looking sewing-talent hovered over the threshold. Artemis loomed just behind her, wearing an apologetic expression that seemed to say, *I tried to stop her.*

"Hello," Clarion said blearily.

Her fingertips tingled with numbness from her pillowing her head on her forearm. Late-afternoon sunlight poured through the window, a fact Clarion felt a small measure of dismay about.

She'd been asleep for hours, and she could hardly recall when, exactly, she had drifted off. She certainly hadn't intended to take a nap.

Hazily, she retraced her steps. After her spat with Petra this morning, she'd arrived late to the weekly council meeting, where she proceeded to spill the contents of her teacup all over her notes as well as the Minister of Spring's new gown. When she returned to her room, still hot with embarrassment, she'd attempted to decipher the swirl of tea and ink in her notebook. . . .

That must have done it. Clearly, staying up late and waking up early were not agreeing with her.

"I don't mean to interrupt," the sewing-talent said delicately. "But you have a dress fitting."

She had entirely forgotten that she had a dress fitting today. Patch, the royal seamstress, would no doubt be displeased at her lateness. She'd already made a gown for her coronation, but Clarion would need a new one for the ball.

"Thank you." Clarion dug the heels of her palms into her eyes. "Shall we go?"

The sewing-talent led her to Patch's studio. Helper-talents—including dusting-talents and polishing-talents—bustled through the corridors and trailed after organizer-talents. Clarion had taken to calling the latter Elvina's Trusted Circle of Decorators. They flitted through the palace, barking orders at their assistants and appraising every detail of others' work. She noted that her sewing-talent guide conspicuously—and expertly—avoided them.

When they at last arrived, they were greeted with an abrupt "There you are!"

Patch floated in the center of her studio. She was of narrow frame, angular features, and a birch-white complexion, as though she had not seen the sun in some time. Her dark brown hair was woven into a neat braid that lay neatly against her elegant cloak of black calla lily. A length of tailor's tape was draped around her neck like a serpent.

While Patch styled herself in dark garments, there were bolts of fabric in every imaginable shade piled on the shelves that lined the room. Half-finished garments covered the dress forms scattered throughout the space, and the whole studio seemed to glow in the sunlight, which reflected off the mirror sitting in its ornate frame—and glimmered on the skeins upon skeins of spiderweb Patch had gathered in baskets. Just outside the window, a vast web stretched between the branches of the Pixie Dust Tree, each strand like a thread of gold in the afternoon light. This was where Patch sourced the silk for her spectacular embroidery and lace. No doubt, Fil—her orb weaver companion—was basking in the center of her web.

But what struck Clarion when she entered the room was the Minister of Summer. Aurelia sat in an armchair, drowsing in the wash of sunlight with one elegant hand propping up her chin. She wore a gown of sunflower petals; their vibrant gold contrasted with her deep black skin. As always, she looked as radiant and luminous as summer itself.

"Minister," Clarion said, surprised. "What are you doing here?"

Aurelia's golden eyes rested on her curiously. "I missed you earlier."

Realization dawned on Clarion. She'd missed her meeting with Aurelia, all because she'd fallen asleep. "Oh, no. I am *so* sorry."

"It happens." Aurelia waved a dismissive hand. "It's nothing I can't discuss with you here. I wanted to get your opinion on the menu for the Coronation Ball. I've brought some of my cooking-talents, but Patch has banished them from this room."

Patch skewered the minister with a glare. "Because if they smudge that gown, I—"

"Peace." Aurelia stifled a yawn. "It can wait until you're finished."

"Good."

Patch wasted no time in ushering Clarion behind a privacy screen. There, her gown for the Coronation Ball waited for her. The fabric glittered brilliantly and moved through her hands like water. Clarion slipped out of her gown, doing her best to conceal her injured arm from view. Patch, if she noticed it at all, did not remark on it. She laced her into the ball gown with a practiced ease, then guided her by her shoulders to the mirror in the main room.

"What do you think?"

In truth, it was the most beautiful thing Clarion had ever owned. The skirts of the gown were a spill of golden fabric, unfurling into a long, elegant train. The sleeves, made of sheer fabric, trailed to the floor. When she moved, they billowed behind her like a cape. In this, she almost felt like a queen. "It's perfect, Patch. I love it."

Clarion saw both Aurelia's and Patch's approving gazes reflected back at her.

"Excellent," Patch said, clearly pleased. "I'll just make a few final adjustments."

The twenty minutes passed in a blur. While Patch slid pins into the hem and sleeves, the Minister of Summer excused herself for a moment—only to return with her retinue of cooking-talents. Patch radiated a palpable discontent as they set up what seemed to Clarion an entire tea service in the corner of her studio.

"If I find a stain on anything, even so much as a *drop*—"

"You won't," Aurelia said, completely unperturbed.

The two of them began to bicker, but Clarion could hardly focus on what they were saying. With no one speaking to her directly, all the things she tried to keep at bay closed in on her: her looming coronation, the Nightmares, Milori.

She had to get back to Winter as quickly as she could.

Eventually, once Patch finished sticking her gown full of pins, she led her back to the privacy screen so that she could change back into the gown she'd arrived in. Patch folded the ball gown almost reverently over her arm, then called: "She's all yours, Aurelia."

When Clarion reemerged, Aurelia had installed herself at the table the cooking-talents had set up in the corner. Atop one of Patch's ornate spider-silk lace tablecloths was one of the most decadent spreads Clarion had ever seen. A tiered stand showcased an impressive display of tarts, some filled with thin rounds of squash and tomato, others with slivers of apricots and blackberries. Beside it was a bowl of watermelon gazpacho, garnished with a sprig of mint and a drizzle of olive oil. There was even a plum cake, with pockets of jam that smelled of cardamom and cinnamon.

Everything burst with the colors and scents of summer. It evoked pure joy—or it should have. Looking at it all made Clarion feel oddly cold. How could she sit here planning a party after what she had seen in Winter? So many fairies depended on her to save them. But right now, Aurelia sat before her with something like anticipation in her expression.

Clarion forced herself to smile as she took her place across from Aurelia. "Everything looks incredible."

Aurelia relaxed some. "We can make any adjustments you'd like."

Clarion stared down at the spread. She hardly knew where to begin—and hardly knew how she would manage to get through this, when stress had stolen most of her appetite. Still, she filled her plate with a small sample of each dish and began to eat without tasting much of anything.

Halfway through her first mouthful, Aurelia let out a sigh. "Your Highness, is something the matter? I can see that you're somewhere else."

Clarion swallowed without fully chewing. "No, nothing."

Aurelia fixed her with an assessing golden stare. "The same thing that kept you from our meeting, perhaps?"

She winced. "It's just . . . everything is happening too quickly."

Each day, coronation loomed larger over her, and she felt more and more as though she could not keep her commitments to everyone. Time slipped through her fingers. And now, she feared not even her closest relationships were solid anymore.

"Ah." Aurelia grew pensive. "Especially on the Mainland, summer is a season of opposites—a time where you want to do nothing and do everything. Humans are equally likely to spend an entire day lying in the grass as to stay up all night dancing beneath the stars. The heat has that effect on them."

How she wished she had such luxury. "I see."

"What I mean to say, I suppose, is that summer encourages us to savor our time, in whichever way we choose to."

Clarion lowered her eyes to her plate and absently pushed a tart with her fork. Perhaps it was sound advice, but she could think of no way to apply it. There was far too much pressure and far too much at stake for her. "I'm finding it difficult to savor this time."

Aurelia frowned at her. "Like summer, this brief moment before you ascend the throne is fleeting. Think of it, then, as a time to be awake to what you want—and who you want to become."

I've always wanted things I shouldn't, she'd told Milori once.

But now, she wasn't so certain. When she allowed herself to dream, she thought of Pixie Hollow, united and safe. She thought of the warmth of Winter, where respect did not mean distance. She thought of Milori.

Those moments of freedom and happiness had felt something like power. What *would* it be like if she got out of her own way? If she trusted her instincts? If she did what felt right, not what she had been taught? Conviction felt like sunlight, illuminating her from within. Maybe her heart had never really steered her wrong.

That evening, Clarion returned to the border. Here, sitting cross-legged on the bridge between Spring and Winter, she could feel the barest whisper of the cold over her skin—and the snow-laced breeze winding itself around her wrist. It felt as though it beckoned her closer, inviting her to drift over the pale grass, frozen stiff with lacy hoarfrost. She'd never escape the pull of it now that she'd experienced firsthand what a magical place it was—one where there were libraries carved from ice and mountains you could traverse by sled and fairies who made friends of wolves.

How sad that no other warm fairy had experienced what she had.

Clarion shivered when she sensed another presence. When she looked up, she caught the exact moment Milori began descending from his flight. Clearly, some part of her was attuned to him—or perhaps sought him out. He landed delicately on the earth beside her, the glow shed from his wings silvering the snow like moonlight. This time, she did not admonish herself for the answering lurch of her heart.

What harm was there in allowing herself this?

"You're back." It warmed her to see his pleasantly surprised expression and know he had looked forward to this meeting as much as she had.

"I did promise I'd be here tonight," Clarion countered. "Besides, Yarrow told me you could teach me to skate. I have to come back for that."

"Did she?" Surprise flickered across his features, before he schooled them into composure. "I imagine that's because she didn't see you fall off your sled. Who knows what will happen when we put you on the ice?"

Clarion glared at him, but she found she could not muster much heat at the twinkling in his eyes. Slowly, he lowered himself to the ground beside her. They sat almost knee to knee in the darkness, close enough to touch. The very thought prickled along her skin like electricity. *Ridiculous,* she scolded herself. They'd been far closer than this last night. But then, that had been out of necessity. Somehow, this felt far more vulnerable. Especially when he was looking at her like this. Clarion could not name what exactly she saw there, but it made a terrible longing rise up within her.

"I'll teach you one day." His voice was low, almost wistful, as though he'd lost himself in a reverie. It took a moment for Clarion to recall what they'd been discussing.

"I'll hold you to it," she said, only a little breathlessly.

Milori traced the very edge of her sleeve. "How is your arm?"

"Fine." Clarion pulled the fabric to her elbow and turned her arm over. She'd removed the dressing earlier and had been shocked; the wound beneath looked days older than it was. No swelling, no complications. She offered him a teasing smile. "You should put more faith in your healers."

He huffed out a breath. "I do. But I'm aware of how lucky we are it was only a minor wound. If anything worse had happened . . ."

"Milori." Clarion reached across the border and rested her hand on his forearm. He went terribly still, then raised his eyes to hers. Her glow bathed his face in gold and set his pale eyes ablaze. For a moment, she was acutely aware of the sensation of his skin, cool and smooth against her own—and of the bitter cold of winter, like another comforting hand laid atop hers. The thought made her chest ache.

"Please don't blame yourself," she continued. "It was my choice to cross. I knew the dangers. And even if I had been seriously injured, it would have been my fault—not yours."

Just like it was her fault what happened to Rowan. She breathed through the sudden rush of shame.

"That isn't true," he protested.

"It is. If I had a better handle on my magic, we wouldn't be in such a precarious position. No one would be trapped in a nightmare. Neither of our realms would have to worry. But I don't, and so I can't save anyone." She had not known these feelings were so close to the surface. She could not bear to look up at him with them pouring out of her. Now that she had opened the floodgate, she found she could not stop herself from giving voice to them. "What kind of queen will I be? I am the only fairy in the entirety of Pixie Hollow who can't do the one thing she was born to do."

Milori laid his hand over hers, chasing away the familiar chill of the air. She hadn't realized she'd begun digging her fingers into his arm. She certainly hadn't realized how close she had come to weeping. Slowly, she loosened her grip on him, and she was left with nothing but the blunted edge of her despair. After a moment, he let her go, and Clarion withdrew her arm to the warmth of Spring. The lack of contact felt more like a loss than it ought.

"You mustn't blame yourself for things beyond your control," Milori said.

She laughed thickly, blinking through the rheum of tears that threatened to spill. She swiped her fingertips beneath her eyes. "You can't just turn my advice back on me. Not until you take it yourself."

"In that case, I retract it." He smiled, just barely. "You're not the talentless queen you believe yourself to be. You *can* use your magic, even if it isn't to your standards. I saw it myself."

"So rarely," Clarion protested. "Besides, I'm barely conscious of it when I do manage to wield it. That hardly counts."

"Start there, then."

Clarion let out a startled laugh. "Are you really going to give me a magic lesson?"

"Humor me." He angled himself toward her, drawing one knee into his chest. "What do you feel in those moments?"

"In the moments it comes easiest?" Clarion sighed, leaning back onto the palms of her hands. She tipped her head back toward the sky and watched the light slowly drain. "Fear. During the Nightmare attack in Autumn, it came to me in an instant."

Milori leaned forward, intrigued. "And when it slips away from you?"

Where exactly was he going with this?

"I remember myself. I remember to master my fear. To control my will and shape it. Drawing on my power, I think, is easy. It's molding it into anything useful . . ." She trailed off at his expression, caught somewhere between incredulous and concerned. "Why are you looking at me that way?"

"It's nothing." He hesitated. "It's only that it seems to me that trying to suppress your fear is hindering you. In fact, you seem to access your power easiest when you're trying to protect others—when you're afraid for others but brave enough to act."

He was giving her another meaningful look—one that seemed to say, That *is the kind of queen you will be.* Clarion averted her eyes. He had an inconvenient knack for challenging her worst opinions of herself. He made her sound almost noble.

"Maybe." She frowned. "But that's what Elvina told me I should do. She said that our power is easiest to access when your mind is clear."

"Perhaps she conceptualizes it differently than you do." Milori held out a hand. In an instant, the very air before him began to sparkle. Delicate ice crystals glimmered in the sunset, swirling and coalescing into an orb of ice in his palm. "No one taught me to do this. That is the case for most winter fairies. I don't say that to confirm what you fear, but . . . Forgive me for speaking out of turn, but it's possible that advice might have done you more harm than good. You already know how to harness your magic. All fairies do. What would happen if you let go of what she told you?"

Stubborn resistance flared to life within her. Elvina wouldn't have misled her. At least, not intentionally. All Clarion's life, Elvina had been the image of a perfect queen—everything she knew she should model herself after. Naturally, that extended to the way she wielded her magic. But Milori's assessment made a terrible kind of sense. Every time Clarion tried to control whatever spark of magic she'd clawed from the wellspring of starlight within her, the walls in her mind slammed down. It baffled her that someone who had known her for such a brief period of time had pierced to the heart of her.

Think of it as a time to be awake to what you want—and who you want to become.

"I'm not sure how."

"It will come to you," he said. "You *were* made for this."

His reassurance made that voice within her—that nasty self-doubt that had plagued her for weeks—settle and fall quiet. "Encouraging," she replied. "But hardly practical."

Milori considered it for a moment. "You said your magic comes to you most easily when you're afraid. Maybe it's not fear—but when you're fully immersed in a moment, whether it's positive or negative."

"You're suggesting I stop thinking so much?"

He smiled that wry little smile again. With a curl of his fingers, the orb of ice in his hand shattered into a fine dusting of frost. It sparkled against his skin until the wind carried it away. "Something like that."

It wasn't a terrible theory. "You want me to try now?"

"If you'd like," he said.

Why not? She had nowhere else she wanted to be.

Clarion closed her eyes and tried to—No, she could not *try*. That rather defeated the purpose, when the entire point of the exercise was to simply be. And yet, it was so difficult to be fully present when she could feel Milori there. Self-consciousness would make this entirely impossible. She opened her eyes again, prepared to tell him she couldn't manage it, when the sight of him silenced her every protest.

He was gazing at her like she was something to marvel at. His expression went soft and unguarded when he noticed her staring back at him, as though he hadn't expected to be caught but did not mind it overmuch. There was no mistaking the wide-open yearning in his eyes. He had looked at her like this once before, she realized: the very first time she'd crossed into Winter. She wondered exactly how long he had wanted to kiss her—and felt very foolish, indeed, for being so oblivious.

And yet, Milori sat as if frozen.

Snow fell only an inch away from her in a glittering, tantalizing whirl. This close to the border—to him—her breath was a soft plume of white in the air. Clarion shifted closer, until the cold washed over one shoulder, then the shell of her ear. It was a strange sensation: half of her safe in the warm seasons, half of her nipped with cold. Carefully, almost reverently, she let her fingertips trace the line of his jaw and tipped his face toward hers. The space she held between them was a question—one he answered readily. His hand came to cradle the side of her neck, and although his touch chilled her skin, warmth flooded through her.

Clarion leaned fully into Winter and kissed him.

As his lips moved against hers, something bubbled up within her like spring water until it spilled over completely. *Happiness*, she thought, far purer than any she had ever felt—and magic. She felt it trilling in her bones and weaving through her fingertips, eager to apply itself. This time, it did not feel like something she had to master. It felt like a river—like a deep and inexhaustible well. It flowed forth until her entire body radiated a soft golden light.

Milori drew back, just barely. His forehead rested against hers as they shared the same tremulous breath. Her eyes fluttered open, and she would have sworn that the stars above them shone brighter. Their brilliance was reflected in the pale gray of his eyes—and sparkled all around them, as though the constellations had been drawn down to earth. Pixie dust glimmered on her eyelashes and the sleeves of her gown. It danced joyfully through the air and gathered in Milori's hair like snowfall, painting all the world in gold.

Had *she* done this?

When he spoke, his voice was low and full of wonder. "You're incredible."

For perhaps the first time, she believed it.

16

A few days before the Coronation Ball, Elvina summoned Clarion to her study. Clarion's first thought was *She knows.*

Clarion did not know *how*, exactly, but she supposed she should have expected it all to come crashing down eventually. Milori was not an easy secret to keep, after all—especially not since that night on the border.

Perhaps Elvina had noticed how distracted she'd been and sent someone to follow her. Or perhaps there was something undeniably different about her. On a foolish impulse, Clarion had inspected her face in the vanity mirror, searching for some evidence of what she'd done written in her features. She'd traced the curve of her lower lip, still chapped and aching with the memory of his kiss. She could still recall every detail as though he stood before her now: the cold of his skin, the heat of his gaze, the brightening glow of the stars all around them. Nothing had changed—not truly—and yet, she felt consumed by the immensity of it.

It might drive her mad, just how often she dwelled on it. Her stomach dipped and churned almost constantly, for the very thought of him threw her into sudden free fall. Her heart was sent aflutter at the slightest provocation. She'd scarcely eaten a thing since they parted, too full of nerves or excitement or . . . whatever feeling this was. She did not wish to examine it too closely, for as much as it thrilled her, it terrified her.

She'd resolved not to see him until her winter gear was repaired; some distance, she reasoned, would restore her to her senses. But Petra had delivered the repaired coat to her just an hour ago, and Clarion's good sense had not returned—had not so much as glanced back since it left her. Even in his absence, Milori was haunting her, just as he was undoubtedly still haunting the border of Spring.

Unless, she thought, *he regrets it.*

Because surely, he did. It had been impulsive and ill-advised, considering the dangers that Pixie Hollow faced. They'd both gotten swept away in the moment, and tonight, she would have to confront the bitter reality that anything between them was impossible. Oh, what was she going to—

"Your Highness?" Artemis asked. "Is everything all right?"

Clarion startled, banging her knee on the underside of her desk.

Hissing out a pained breath, she swiveled around to face her guard. Artemis stood beside her bedroom door, wearing a rather peculiar expression. It belatedly occurred to Clarion that Artemis had informed her of Elvina's summons some minutes ago.

"Yes, of course!" Clarion smiled sunnily, if only to hide her embarrassment. "Why do you ask?"

Artemis seemed to be struggling with a polite way to respond. After a moment, she said, "Your glow . . ."

"My . . ." Clarion glanced down. Now that Artemis had pointed it out, she supposed it was much brighter than usual and tinged with a rosy flush. And had the sunlight intensified since she last checked? Now, she supposed she understood why Elvina always cautioned against getting carried away by passion.

"Also," Artemis said, with the air of someone about to deliver grave news, "the Pixie Dust Tree is blooming."

Clarion stood and approached the glass doors of her balcony. Indeed, the branches just outside frothed with forget-me-nots and delicate white roses. She glared at them. The tree could be so cheeky sometimes.

"It's nothing to worry about." Clarion drew the curtains, eager to block out all the reminders of her *mooning*. "I was lost in thought."

Artemis nodded, obviously unconvinced. "Shall I escort you to the queen?"

Clarion supposed there was no sense avoiding it, but she was not exactly keen to hear whatever choice words Elvina had in store for her. "What do you think she wants?"

"I imagine she wants to discuss the scouts' reports," Artemis replied, with only a touch of confusion. "One of her helper-talents had them delivered earlier. You reviewed them . . ." She trailed off, as if she were not entirely convinced on that last point.

"Of course I did."

According to scouts' reports, the Nightmares had not stopped their onslaught. Just last night, one shaped like a cat had chased away an entire stable of mice on the outskirts of Tinker's Nook. The stalls and carriages both were now little more than wreckage. And two days before, a fish-shaped Nightmare, enormous enough to swallow the reflection of a full moon, had swept a number of water-talents' houses from the bank of the river. Everyone mustered as much cheer as they could, but Clarion could sense the unease that had begun to creep into even the daylight hours.

But she did not dare hope that Elvina wanted her opinion.

"Well," Clarion said with a resigned sigh, "let's go."

Clarion found the door to Elvina's study ajar. Bracing herself, she announced her presence with a soft knock, then stepped inside. Artemis trailed after her as she slipped past the rows of royal portraits and into the flood of afternoon sun.

Elvina was seated on a chaise longue, reading through a document. Today, she'd forgone her crown, and her hair fell around her shoulders in loose, soft waves. Clarion could see the thin strands of silver, seeming to glow like cold starlight. She looked far more relaxed than Clarion had seen her in some time. Some of the tension bled out of Clarion, replaced with a faint twinge of affection.

So much—too much, really—weighed on her. Clarion had not fully appreciated just how heavy the crown sat until now.

"You wished to see me?"

Elvina set aside the document she'd been reading, and when she looked up, she smiled. "Clarion."

When was the last time she'd been greeted so warmly? Clarion tried not to let the surprise show on her face as she took a seat in an armchair. It seemed her secret was still safe—and that Aurelia had not told the queen about their missed appointment.

Thank the stars.

A teapot stood steaming on the table between them, along with a small jar of honey. Elvina leaned forward to pour them each a cup. "I apologize for how busy I've been," she said, passing one to Clarion. "I would have called on you sooner."

Clarion drizzled honey into her tea from a wooden dipper and inhaled the earthy scent of carrot blossom. "There's nothing to apologize for. We've both been busy."

She took a hasty sip of tea to conceal her expression—and the flush surely blossoming across her face. It was only partly a lie. She had kept up with preparations for the coronation, of course, and spent a good deal of her time worrying about how little she could do until Petra repaired her coat.

Only a beat of silence lingered before Elvina set down her teacup. "I have good news to share."

Clarion perked up. Now, that was a welcome announcement; good news seemed in short supply these days. "What is it?"

"My plan is nearly ready to put into action."

Clarion had made the grave error of taking another sip of tea just after speaking. She nearly choked on it now. "It is?"

"It took some trial and error," Elvina continued. "The magic woven between our realms is strong, of course. But magical bonds can be severed like any other—with the right tool and technique."

Clarion's blood ran cold. "And what is that?"

"No simple tool could sever it—and my magic alone is too weak."

Elvina rose from her seat and drifted to her desk. Clarion had not noticed it before, but an elegant metal object rested on a cushion there. It was only when Elvina picked it up that she realized what it was: the bladeless hilt of a sword. The cross guard was intricately wrought, fashioned into the shape of interwoven branches putting out leaves, because of course Petra would make even a weapon a work of art. Affixed to its heart was a sunstone, its glass-like surface swimming with orange light. If she looked closely, she could see a flame blazing bright within it. Clarion had encountered only one other gem like this: the moonstone used to transmute moonlight into blue pixie dust.

"But on the summer solstice, a day of great significance for governing-talents, our power will be at its height. Petra has built this to channel our magic." The gem shone with the golden light of Elvina's magic—and a blade of pure starlight flickered to life. "If you wield this blade on the solstice, you will be powerful enough to cut through the bridges. After that, nothing and no one will be able to cross between Winter and the warm seasons."

Petra had done it. Of course she had.

Normally, Clarion might have been proud of her friend's brilliance and her uncanny ability to solve seemingly unsolvable problems. Besides, this was what she had always wanted: for her inventions to be of value. And yet, Clarion could feel only horror at what Petra had wrought.

But then, it struck her what exactly Elvina had said.

"When *I* wield it?"

Beneath the harsh brilliance of the blade, Elvina's face was blanched a severe white. "It has to be you. It will be an auspicious start to your reign and instill confidence in your subjects. They will see that you have guaranteed Pixie Hollow's safety from the Nightmares forever."

Not all *of Pixie Hollow,* Clarion thought.

She could not manage a reply. She could hardly fathom such a terrible thing: a blade powerful enough to rend open the very fabric of Pixie Hollow. No matter the dangers the warm seasons faced, this could not be right. Once, she might have yielded. She might have even agreed. But after everything she and Milori had been through—after how close they'd come—she could not hold her tongue in the face of such a misguided plan. "This can't be the only way."

The starlight blade faded until Elvina was left holding the empty hilt once more. Without the light glittering in her eyes, Elvina's expression grew unreadable, almost cold. "You're displeased."

Clarion stood up so quickly, her chair scraped against the floorboards. If Elvina was shocked by the sudden outburst, she did not let it show on her face. "Of course I am! I can't understand how you're satisfied with this course of action. You have taught me how to rule. You know very well that we work to ensure each season arrives to the Mainland when it should. This goes against the natural order of things."

If she had learned anything these past few weeks, it was that each season was essential. Milori had not shared with her Winter's wisdom the way the other ministers had, but he hadn't needed to. She'd seen it for herself firsthand. Winter taught endurance—how to hold on to hope, even in the longest, darkest nights.

Elvina regarded her impassively. "Perhaps you were right, when you confronted me before. I have not taught you everything you need to know."

Her unruffled calm made the heat of Clarion's anger fizzle. Guardedly, she asked, "No?"

"I have told you before that Winter is self-sufficient. It is for the best that they remain that way." Elvina placed the sword's hilt on her desk and folded her hands. "There is a story passed down among queens. It is time I shared it with you."

Slowly, Clarion settled back into her chair. As furious as she was, she could not deny her own curiosity. Elvina's stiff shoulders relaxed now that she'd wrested back control of the conversation.

"Once, as hard as it may be to believe, the warm seasons and the Winter Woods lived in harmony." The cadence of Elvina's voice changed, as it always did when she shared a story of Pixie Hollow's history. "Of course, it was a very long time ago—a time no one alive remembers. Understanding the danger the Nightmares posed, the first Queen of Pixie Hollow arranged for them to be imprisoned deep within the Winter Woods. She also entrusted the Warden of the Winter Woods with the responsibility of guarding that prison. For a time, everything was peaceful. But eventually, he grew resentful of his duty. He gathered his scouts and organized a rebellion against the queen."

"What?" Clarion cut in. "But why would he do such a thing?"

Sensing that she now had Clarion's full attention, Elvina smiled wryly. "The full details of their conflict have been lost to time, unfortunately. Perhaps he grew bored, or perhaps he believed he should rule over all of Pixie Hollow. The Queens of Pixie Hollow have a great many responsibilities and much power. Perhaps he was dissatisfied with his lot, having no jurisdiction over anything but his barren realm."

None of those explanations satisfied Clarion. Their realms could not have been driven apart over something as petty as ambition or boredom. She couldn't believe that—not after she had visited Winter herself. Not after she had fallen in love with it. *Barren* was the very last worst she'd use to describe it. It was beautiful and vibrant—a season that anyone would have been proud to rule.

"However," Elvina continued, "I have a theory of my own. I believe that Nightmares have an influence over winter fairies."

She paused, letting that ominous statement hang over them like a blade waiting to fall. It slid beneath Clarion's skin like winter's chill, filling her with a terrible, prickling unease. "An influence?"

"You have seen how insidious Nightmares are—how they can sink their claws into a fairy's mind. Who's to say they cannot do it while you're still awake?" Elvina smoothed her hands over her skirts. "Besides, I cannot imagine what effect it must have, living beside so many for so long. If the prison has weakened enough to release them into the world, surely their power has leaked out as well."

Clarion felt sick at the implication—at the thought of all the fairies she'd met at the mercy of monsters. "You believe the Nightmares caused the warden's betrayal."

"It's possible, yes." Elvina approached Clarion with slow, measured steps, then perched on the edge of her chaise longue. Now that they were at eye level again, the weight of her words felt suffocating, inescapable. "It is a shame. It means that the Warden of the Winter Woods can never be fully trusted."

Clarion couldn't believe it. She *refused* to believe it. She dug her fingers into her knees, if only to keep herself from fleeing. "Why didn't you tell me this before?"

"I did not want to overwhelm you with too much information at once, especially when you already seemed so concerned about the winter fairies." Clarion felt those words like a slap. They were all but a confirmation of her worst fears: Elvina did not think her capable of handling the truth or her duty. Elvina leaned over and rested her hand on Clarion's arm. Elvina's skin felt feverishly hot, as though each of her fingers were a searing brand. "But now, you know everything that I do. And on the day of your coronation, you will fulfill the very last of our inherited duties: the Queen of Pixie Hollow must guard the warm seasons against the Nightmares' influence."

Clarion's boldness, briefly suppressed beneath the weight of her old insecurities, flared viciously back to life. She could not listen to another word of this. "If that's true, then we should help the Winter Woods, not cut them off!"

"We are in no position to help them." Elvina's tone brooked no argument. "It's far too dangerous. We do not know how to combat them."

"And so you'd force me to abandon the winter fairies to their fate?" Clarion's voice trembled. "Shall I let the Nightmares destroy their homes? Pick them off one by one? This is not pragmatism, Elvina. This is monstrous. I will not do it."

Elvina stared at her with open shock. When she recovered, Clarion was struck at how quickly she gathered her royal bearing around her like armor—how she could wear a simple robe like her full regalia. Her tone was frosty when she spoke again. "This is for the greater good. I know you have an interest in the fairies of the

Winter Woods, but you must put them out of your mind. They have survived this long on their own, in the most brutal of conditions. They will endure this as well."

But they shouldn't have to. Clarion bit down on her tongue.

Taking her silence as acquiescence, Elvina sighed, as though trying to collect the fragments of her shattered patience. "You will understand in time, Clarion. Your kindness is an asset, but it is also a heavy burden to carry. You cannot hurt so much for others."

"I will take that into account," Clarion replied. "Now, if you'll excuse me. I feel suddenly ill."

She did not wait for Elvina's reply before fleeing her study. Once she made it to her room, she pulled the box Petra had sent her from where she'd hidden it beneath her bed. She untied the fastidiously knotted ribbon, then yanked off the lid. Inside was her coat: pristine and whole. Clarion could not help hugging it against her chest. She did not care how ridiculous she looked, kneeling on the floor with her face buried in the fur-lined hood. It wasn't as if there were anyone here to witness it.

Once she'd breathed through the worst of her panic, she tried desperately to sort through the jumble of her thoughts. Whether or not what Elvina told her was true didn't matter. All she knew was that Elvina had handed her a problem almost too overwhelming to shoulder.

She and Milori had only until the summer solstice to seal the Nightmares' prison—or Elvina would doom the Winter Woods to an eternal isolation.

17

Every minute that Clarion waited at the border passed at a glacial crawl. She paced restlessly along the riverbank, the hem of her mended coat billowing behind her. As she watched the tree line, all she could envision were Nightmares unspooling from the shadows, a ravening, bilious black. Winter sealed away as if behind a wall of glass. The roots binding them together severed by her own hand. She could not stomach this vision of herself, the cold and remote queen who weighed lives like grain on a scale. A blade of starlight held above her head, smoking with her power. The magic of the Pixie Dust Tree, emptying into the river like blood from a mortal wound.

Monstrous, she'd told Elvina.

The dark churn of her thoughts only served to compound the dread of seeing Milori again. She'd spent so many hours reliving that kiss—and imagining what she might say to him when they met again. Such concerns felt terribly far away now. And yet, her anticipation built with every second that slipped away.

Thankfully, she did not have to suffer long. Milori was never late.

In fact, he was early.

The sun had not yet begun to set when he arrived. Snow swirled around him as he landed on the bridge between their realms with silent grace. Despite it all, her heart fluttered at the sight of him. She'd hardly realized how desperately she'd missed him until he was standing here before her. Clarion found herself torn between the impulse to armor herself with distance and to run headlong into his arms. The guarded look on his face and the rigidity of his shoulders, at least, made her choice easy. It wounded her, to see such plain confirmation of what she'd feared.

Nothing could exist between the two of them.

Clarion drew her coat tighter around herself as she stepped onto the bridge, sighing at the feeling of magic humming beneath her feet. Words evaporated as she stared up at him. As always, his stark beauty was like a blade of ice to the heart. Frost glimmered on his pale eyelashes, which were drawn low over his gray eyes. He was avoiding her gaze.

"Clarion." He spoke her name with such careful formality, it was as though he'd called her *Your Highness.* It prickled her all over with its chill.

"Milori."

The uneasy silence stretched thin between them. When she could bear it no longer, she blurted out, "There's something you should know," at the same time he said, "I wanted to—"

Their eyes locked, and heat bloomed across her face. His lips were still softly parted, whatever confession he'd been prepared to make hanging in suspension. A look of singular vulnerability passed over his expression, Clarion could not help wondering if she'd been mistaken. Hope welled up within her—but no, she could not allow herself to read anything into it. It was only that their halting exchange had flustered them both.

After a moment, he shook his head and said, "Please. You first."

Clarion drew in a breath to compose herself. Now that he'd ceded the initiative to her, she felt more clearheaded. Where to begin? Somehow, the dangers Elvina's plan posed to the Winter Woods felt like safer skies to navigate than her feelings. "I spoke with Elvina earlier."

Clearly, that was not what he had expected her to say. Milori blinked, disoriented, as if rousing himself from a troubling dream. Some of his nervous energy fizzled out, but she could see him wrestling with the desire to ask for more details. Ever patient, he replied, "I see."

Even in Spring, she felt impossibly cold at the memory of what she and Elvina had discussed. She crossed her arms over her chest to ward off a shiver. "She told me that the first Warden of the Winter Woods attempted to overthrow the Queen of Pixie Hollow. In her mind, that is the reason our two realms have nothing to do with each other anymore. Worse, she believes the Nightmares held some sort of power over him. That it might be possible for it to happen again, and . . ."

She could not force the words out. She did not want to even say it, nor did she want to ask him the questions fear had sparked within her.

Do you think it's true?

Do you harbor the same resentment the first warden did?

Clarion watched his expression fill with certainty, slowly, then all at once; he looked as though he'd at last pieced together something that had been puzzling him. "You worry that it might be true," he said. There was no accusation in his voice, only a resigned sort of understanding.

Guilt pierced through her. How could she believe that, when he and his people had been nothing but kind to her? She clasped her hands together to keep herself from reaching for him. "Only to the extent that I worry for you. You've never given me a reason to doubt you."

He frowned as confusion overtook him once more. "I have never seen a Nightmare hold any power over someone who was still awake. I don't think it's possible."

"That's a relief," she murmured. "Surely, there would be some sort of sign. You haven't noticed anything . . . ?"

Milori shifted on his feet, his gaze skirting away from hers again. "I haven't slept well in days. Other than that, no."

Dread pooled within her. "You don't think—"

"It isn't Nightmares that keep me awake, Clarion."

His voice was impossibly gentle—and so soft, for a moment, she thought she had misheard him. When he turned his eyes back to her, the intensity and earnestness she found there made her ears warm. The sense memory of their kiss awakened, skipping across her skin in heated trails and stoking her glow to a rose-colored blaze. There had been something like devotion in the way he'd cradled her face, an oath sworn in every brush of his lips against hers. Oh, she had been such a fool to believe a sparrow man like Milori would do a single thing without the intention of committing himself fully.

"Oh." It was a bare exhalation of sound.

"You didn't come back." Equal parts pain and relief suffused his every word. "At first, I worried that something had happened. Then, I convinced myself that you regretted it."

"No," Clarion said, through a humorless laugh. "I didn't regret it at all. I only regret that I panicked—and that my fear has given you cause to worry."

That was what frightened her the most: the feeling that her heart now beat outside her chest. He stood before her, close enough to touch. And yet, it wasn't close enough. Clarion feared she might never be satisfied until they could truly share in one another's worlds. And now that she knew Elvina's plan . . . It terrified her, to think that the two of them could be separated forever.

She could not avoid telling him what she'd learned any longer.

"There is much more to say, I know." She took a step closer to him, until she could feel Winter's cool caress her face. She closed her fingers around his forearm and squeezed gently. "But that isn't everything Elvina told me."

As he drank her in, the hope faded from his eyes. "What is it?"

"Elvina is close to putting her plan into motion. We have until the summer solstice before the bridges between Winter and the warm seasons are destroyed."

All the color drained from his face. When he recovered enough to speak, he said, "I didn't think it was possible."

The despair in his voice chilled her. "I didn't, either. But we still have daylight left. I'm ready to try again."

If she failed . . .

No, it hardly bore thinking about. She would not fail a second time.

Gathering her nerve, she said, "I think you and I were meant to do this together—to solve the problem of the Nightmares for good."

"You and I," he echoed, as solemn as a vow.

Perhaps it was a bold declaration. But what they'd found felt a little like destiny—especially when the space between them crackled with possibility.

"If we seal the prison before the sun fully sets, none of them will have a chance to leave for the night." She canted her chin, hoping to project more confidence than she felt. Milori watched her through hooded eyes, some of his initial resistance giving way to something like . . . admiration? Clarion continued before she could lose her nerve. "After that, everyone under the Nightmares' spell should awaken, just like when the dream-talents first sealed the Nightmares away."

"Very well," he said, with only a touch of reluctance. "But if we're going to make it to the prison before sundown, we'll need to fly."

At that, Clarion's façade faltered. "You mean with Noctua."

"Of course, we don't have to," Milori said, with the tiniest of smirks playing on the corner of his mouth. "However, we would need to reconvene tomorrow and begin hiking much earlier in the day."

She bit down on a groan. "Fine. Call her."

Milori looked far too pleased. He brought two fingers to his lips and whistled. The sound cut through the serene stillness of the woods. Somehow, the silence deepened, as though the entire forest were holding its breath. Only a few seconds passed before Noctua appeared, bursting from the cover of pines and carving a dark shape against the reddening sky.

With a defeated sigh, Clarion did up the buttons on her coat and stepped into Winter. Noctua ruffled her feathers and let out a soft hoot as Clarion approached. This time, at least, she did not shrink back.

"I think she likes you," Milori said. "If you want, you could ride alone this time."

The suggestion filled her with unwelcome visions of plummeting to her untimely end. She reached up to take hold of the reins. "No, I very much do not."

Milori rested a hand on her waist, prepared to lift her. The cold of his touch seeped into her coat, and Clarion had to battle the urge to lean into him. His tone all fond amusement, he said, "The Queen of Pixie Hollow has truly met her match."

Two could play at that game. Clarion flashed him a coy smile. "Or maybe I want to be close to you."

That, apparently, silenced any smart reply. Feeling a flush of triumph, Clarion began to climb onto Noctua's back. With a boost, she found her seat easily—and did not flinch when Noctua swiveled her head to appraise her from the corner of her golden eyes. Perhaps she imagined it, but Clarion could have sworn she saw a glimmer of approval there. Milori settled behind her. He locked one arm around her and gathered the reins in his free hand.

"Ready?" His breath ghosted against her ear. A pleasant shiver worked its way down her spine.

"Ready," she replied.

With that, they took flight. They dodged through snow-laden pine boughs and around the icicles refracting the shell-pink sunlight. When they broke through the canopy, the view stole Clarion's breath away. Endless expanses of snow and cold waters glittered, illuminated in the golden hour. Everything was so small from this height—and with her wings bound beneath her coat, exhilaration prickled at the edges of her wonder. Cold wind sent her hair snapping behind her and nipped at the tip of her nose. Flurries danced wildly before her, each snowflake stained in warm shades of pink and gold as the sun settled like a lit ember in the crook of the mountains.

Then, they dove toward the shadow of the woods. Below them, the round eye of the frozen lake locked on to her, as though every Nightmare seething beneath it sensed her presence and loathed her. Instinctual terror quickened her pulse, and the wound on her arm throbbed with the memory of what had happened last time they had come here. But she could not afford to lose her nerve now.

The pines enfolded them, and Noctua landed on a low-lying branch. Even from here, the miasma that settled like dense fog over the ice crawled over them. The hairs on the back of her neck stood on end. Even Noctua fluffed out her plumage with unease. Without thinking, Clarion scratched the top of her head to soothe her, then slid off the owl's back. Her boots crunched in the deep snowfall.

Milori landed beside her, his gray eyes fixed on the prison lurking just beyond the row of gnarled birches. Another wind gusted through the trees and shredded into her coat with icy claws. A veil of snow lifted off the ground, blotting out the fading sun. All of it felt like a warning: *Leave this place.*

"Shall we?" she asked Milori.

"One moment." He threaded his fingers in hers, and Clarion did her best not to melt. His touch grounded and thrilled her more than she cared to admit.

Hand in hand, they trudged through the snowbanks until at

last they emerged onto the edge of the frozen lake. As long as she lived, she would never grow accustomed to the sheer *presence* of it. The silence here was unnatural, as though the lake swallowed all the sound. Dread settled over her shoulders like a mantle of steel. Clarion did her best to breathe through the weight of it.

She stepped out onto the ice. Its treacherous surface gleamed, but she could still make out the hazy shapes of Nightmares rippling beneath her boots like dark water. As she and Milori made their way to the center, the Nightmares shrank back and lashed out by turns. She avoided the thin cracks in the surface, which groaned beneath her weight. She shuddered to think of what would happen if she fell into the lake's depths.

By the time they made it to the center of the lake, the daylight was a bare sliver of red on the horizon. She could practically feel the Nightmares' hunger and anticipation bubbling up from the cracks. They swirled together, reaching longingly for their freedom.

It was now or never.

Reluctantly, Clarion let her hand drop from Milori's. She crouched beside the new fissures in the ice, letting her awareness drift to the dream-magic barrier just underneath—to its thinning strands and loosening weaves, just barely holding back the beasts it contained. It had grown even more threadbare since they were here last. Her magic itched to mend it.

Her first instinct was to reach for what felt familiar and comfortable: to master herself, to focus, to strain. Instead, she closed her eyes and felt her feet planted on the ice, the way her chest rose and fell as she breathed. Perhaps if she tried to see herself the way Milori did . . .

You were made for this.

Calm certainty filled her up. Energy crackled just beneath her skin, and her glow intensified. Clarion rested her palm flat against the ice and let her magic surge through her. Golden light swirled down her arm and coalesced in the palm of her hand. Milori's awe-struck eyes reflected the glow of her power.

Clarion let it soar.

Starlight flowed into the ice and wove itself around the fraying dream-threads. It fortified them and, stitch by stitch, spanned the tears. Her magic lit the ice from within, bathing her in marbled golden light.

As the Nightmares roiled within their prison, their shrieks rattled her very bones. They lashed out with torrents of negative emotion: the sting of rejection, the stomach-churning sensation of humiliation, the sharp terror of something come back to haunt her. All she could see were gnashing teeth and baleful eyes. All she could think of was that terrible future version of herself, isolating Winter with a single cut. All her worst fears felt too close to the surface, urgent and undeniably real. Pressure built behind her eyes. Her hands began to tremble.

But with one last loop pulled taut, her work was done. The repaired barrier shimmered like a layer of spider-silk gauze. Through the stitches, she could just barely see the Nightmares, snarling and snapping as they shrank back from their new confines.

"Milori," she called. "Now."

He extended his hands, and frost bloomed across the shattered ice. The wails of the Nightmares grew more muffled until she could not hear them at all.

The light of the barrier dimmed beneath the frozen surface of the lake, and night settled softly into the space it left behind. As her vision adjusted to the starlit dark, she gazed out at their handiwork. The ice itself seemed to glow. With the prison sealed, the oppressive atmosphere lessened, and Clarion imagined this was what this place had been like centuries ago.

Beautiful.

Milori let out a soft sound of disbelief. When Clarion turned to him, she was struck with another pang of longing. Moonlight gilded the ice and draped itself over him. Like this, he was lustrous—an effect not helped by the way he was *beaming* at her.

"We did it."

She couldn't help grinning back at him. "We did."

She could hardly believe it. After weeks of fear and uncertainty, they'd freed their subjects from the Nightmares. She barely had time to process it. Because with a flutter of his wings, Milori lifted off the ground. He took both her mittened hands in his own—and then flew backward, until she was gliding along the ice after him.

"Milori!" she protested through a laugh. She had half a mind to dig her heels in, but his joy was infectious. She surrendered and let herself skate across the surface.

He spun her to slow their momentum, one hand coming to rest against her waist to steady her. "Come with me. I want to show you something."

When he was so unguardedly happy, how could she possibly deny him anything? "Of course. Anywhere."

Milori took her to a vista atop another mountain's peak. It afforded a view of the Winter Woods—most strikingly, the vast frozen lake. The mirror-smooth ice now sparkled with veins of gold. Soft golden light illuminated the surrounding darkness. Beyond it, she could see the Hall of Winter, gleaming cold in the moonlight, and the enclaves of winter fairies' homes glowing like fireflies in the dark. And there, luminous and golden, was the Pixie Dust Tree. It seemed impossible that she should be standing here, staring back at the place she'd spent all her life—a place she believed she would never leave.

But it was not the view Milori had brought her to see. On a precipice overlooking the Nightmares' prison was a massive sculpture carved entirely from ice.

Clarion approached it, tipping her head back so that she could appreciate it fully. The statue was of a sparrow man, with his hand resting on a sword at his hip. A diadem—carved with the snowflake insignia of Winter—sat on his brow. A cloak trimmed in the fur of an animal billowed behind him. His wings, shot through with moonlight, glittered like winter itself. He looked strangely familiar . . . almost like *Milori*, with his stoic countenance and weary eyes.

"Here it is," said Milori. "This is the first Warden of the Winter Woods. It's said that this statue was commissioned by the Queen of Pixie Hollow herself."

"The Lord of Winter," Clarion murmured.

"Yes," he said, after a pause. "I suppose he was also known by that title."

This did not look like the memorial of a sparrow man who had risked everything for the sake of his pride. It looked like someone who, even in death, had not forgotten his duty.

As she circled the statue, her gaze snagged on the plinth. It was covered in lichen and densely packed snow, but she could see something written just beneath it. She knelt beside it and scraped off the rime with her mitten. Piece by piece, it fell away. She scrubbed until she could make out the carved inscription.

IN THE ICE AND IN THE HEARTS OF ALL OF PIXIE HOLLOW,

THE MEMORY OF THE LORD OF WINTER,

A TRUE FRIEND AND STEADFAST PROTECTOR,

IS PRESERVED FOREVER.

Just beneath the final line was a faint carving. Clarion recognized it as the royal insignia: the Pixie Dust Tree framed by the wings of a monarch butterfly. Clarion's heart ached at the sight of it. This was not the sort of statue built for the living—which meant Elvina's story was completely wrong. There had been no rebellion that had driven their realms apart, no treachery. It comforted her as much as it puzzled her.

"What happened, then?" she asked. "How did we end up this way?"

"I don't know." Milori crouched beside her and gazed up at the statue. "In his writings, he emphasized that the Nightmares were not something the queen should worry about. I suppose his successor wasn't as close with the queen's—and so, perhaps we just drifted apart over time. I suppose it's a trait we all share, to want to shoulder this burden alone."

I understand the necessity of that worldview, Milori had told her when she shared Elvina's philosophy.

Clarion rested a hand on his arm. "You haven't."

"I haven't." He smiled ruefully. "You are not the only fairy in Pixie Hollow who believes they can't do what they were born to do. For generations, every Warden of the Winter Woods has upheld their duty unfailingly, except for me. What happened to both our subjects is entirely my fault, and I asked you to fix my mistake."

Entirely my fault. Hadn't she thought the exact same thing, kneeling among the wreckage of the Autumn Forest? But listening to him say it, she realized how terribly unfair it was. No one should take on so much.

"I owe you an enormous debt," he said. "And as you share the news with your subjects, if you want to blame me—"

"How can I blame you?" she cut in. "What could you have done?"

He fell silent.

"You owe me nothing. If anything, I owe *you*." She took his hands in hers. "So forgive yourself. This would have happened one way or another. You and I were just the unlucky ones who had to fix what our predecessors couldn't. For so long, you and I have wasted our energy trying to live up to them. But you are good enough on your own merits."

Milori lifted his gaze to hers once more, and all the world grew as still as deepest winter. The snowfall seemed to slow to a halt; the wind ebbed to a bare whisper. The emotion glittering in his eyes knocked her breathless, and it occurred to her then just how close they were. Her breath misted in the narrow space between them.

"I hope you know the same is true for you." Milori carefully tucked a strand of hair behind her ear. His knuckles lightly traced her cheekbone as his hand fell away. "You will be an excellent queen."

And although her heart soared to hear him say it, the reminder of her coronation made reality crash over her like a wave. It felt cruel, to meet him just before she would have to let him go. Gone would be her days of sneaking into Winter. Gone would be whatever this was between them. Because the moment that crown was placed upon her head, she would spend the rest of her life in the palace, her days taken up by meetings and hearings and ceremonies.

She would become the cold star, high in her tower, looking down on all that she'd sworn to oversee from a distance.

As Clarion, she could care for him. But the Queen of Pixie Hollow could never truly be with him—or anyone else.

Milori clearly sensed the turn of her mood. "Is everything all right?"

"Yes." She forced a smile. "I'm only cold."

He did not look convinced, but he said, "Then let me get you back to Spring."

Clarion kept her silence on the journey back to the border. He did not push her, even though she could feel his concern washing over her. It was only when she stood on the edge of the bridge that she whirled around to face him. She could not force both of them to languish without closure—not again. Besides, she had promised him that they would finish the conversation they'd begun.

"I have to confess," she said, "that I lied. Everything is not all right."

"Oh," he said, in a tone that suggested he did not know whether he ought to feign surprise. "Can I ask what troubles you?"

She couldn't decide if she should laugh or weep. How could she possibly answer that question? Now that they'd done what they set out to do, they had no reason to see each other anymore. "I'm going to miss you."

"Is that all?" he asked. "You can come back tomorrow."

"I can't." Frustration and longing both bubbled up within her.

If only it were that simple. "My coronation is in just over a week, Milori. Our duties as rulers will keep us apart from one another."

Her words landed like a sucker punch, sending him reeling. Milori shook his head, just barely. She could see he wanted to argue, but he only said, "I see."

"I like you," she continued breathlessly. "Far, far too much."

"Then I don't understand why—"

"It scares me." *How much I want you. How painful it would be to lose you*. "I meant what I said. I don't regret a thing. I am glad it happened, but it cannot happen again. Going forward, we should maintain a formal distance between us. Before it becomes too painful."

As the seconds ticked by, the stricken look on his face softened gradually. He took a wary step closer to her, as if he were afraid of chasing her away. With his voice pitched low, he said, "I do not think I've been subtle about it, but I feel I should tell you that I like you, too."

Clarion couldn't help laughing, even through the threat of tears constricting her throat. She leaned her forehead against his shoulder, if only to hide how much his words had affected her. She supposed she had known for quite some time how he felt, but to hear him admit it aloud . . . It made *this*—whatever it was—real: something she could lose. "Is that all you've taken away from what I've said?"

"I don't believe our duties require that we stay away from one another. But I shall argue my point another time." When she dared to glance up at him again, he averted his gaze. If she did not know better, she'd say he looked nervous. "I wanted to invite you to Winter's coronation ball. It is to be held in your honor."

The quiet vulnerability in his voice, hidden behind that veneer of courtly grace, took a hammer to her defenses. Must he always make things so *difficult*? "Milori . . ."

"You can attend in an official capacity, of course, as our guest of honor," he hastened to add. "Your subjects in Winter are very eager to meet you."

She considered it. Good sense dictated that she should decline his invitation. It would be far simpler to make this a clean break—to not torture herself any further by being around him. But if she wanted to bridge the distance between Winter and the warm seasons, she would have to learn to endure it. With time, perhaps these feelings would fade to little more than a memory. In the meantime, she would have to practice.

Attending, of course, would pose a logistical challenge. But how difficult could it really be, to sneak away from her own coronation ball? Once she fulfilled her ceremonial duties and exchanged pleasantries with the right fairies, no one would notice if she slipped away for an hour or two. She would be back before anyone knew to miss her.

Clarion plucked at the sleeve of her coat. "I don't have anything to wear to a Winter ball."

Clearly, he knew he had already won, because a smile curled on his lips. "You are the queen. You can wear whatever you'd like."

A terrible fondness bubbled up within her chest. "Then I suppose I'll have to go."

"You will?" As soon as his excitement sparked, he smoothed it over. "Everyone will be very happy to see you."

"Well," she said, "the feeling is mutual."

Too late, she registered that she had not withdrawn from him—that she had not wanted to, despite the distance she knew very well she should hold between them. It would be a simple thing, to rise onto her toes and kiss him as she had the other night, to thread her fingers into his snow-white hair.

His gaze trailed down her face and lingered, just for a moment, on her lips. He was right that he had never exactly been subtle; Clarion knew, down to the stardust in her bones, that he would let her. And yet, he stood as still as a sparrow man carved from ice.

"You're going to get cold if you stay much longer," he murmured.

Before she could think better of it, she said, "I've been told it suits me."

It took only a moment for him to realize that she had turned his own words back on him. A glimmer of bittersweet yearning lit his eyes, and Clarion knew then and there that she had crossed a line she might never recover from. Perhaps it would have been better not knowing what she was missing.

Perhaps it would have been better to pine than to mourn.

18

Since they had sealed the prison, no Nightmares had descended on Pixie Hollow as they slept. No one had awoken to find their work destroyed. No one else had fallen prey to their terrible spell.

No one had stirred from their Nightmarish slumber, either.

When Clarion had visited the clinic, the eerie silence of the room settled over her. Staring out at the sleeping fairies, she'd gone numb with uncomprehending shock. But the devastation that followed was like an icy wind, slicing through her and hollowing her out. She did not understand. They'd sealed the prison, so why hadn't it worked as it had in the past?

Perhaps she should have known better than to put so much faith in stories. She and Milori might have prevented any more monsters from escaping, but until they found a cure for their spell, this nightmare was far from over. And now they had only one week to end it.

At the very least, Pixie Hollow had finally, tentatively, let down its guard. Although the new development clearly confounded Elvina, she had announced the curfew would be lifted for tonight's Coronation Ball.

Clarion, however, did not feel much like celebrating. She could not content herself with what she'd achieved until she made sure that this was well and truly over—until she saw Rowan and the others awaken and autumn arrive on the Mainland with no delay. There had to be some way to free them.

But how?

Clarion turned over the question as she dressed for the ball, alone and melancholy in her quarters. It still did not feel entirely real that in one week's time, the crown would be hers. Perhaps it never would until she'd proven herself worthy of the title.

Her balcony doors were ajar, letting in a cool wash of evening air. The delicate, grassy scents of lady's mantle and freesia reached her faintly. Purple and yellow flowers waved on the branches, as if trying to catch her eye. The Pixie Dust Tree had put out new growth over the last few days; in the language of flowers, it said, *I am here for you*. Clarion marveled at how attentive it was being lately. She could not help wondering if it knew she was trying to protect it.

She stood in front of her mirror, feeling utterly ridiculous—and decidedly unqueenly. She had stepped into her gown after severely overestimating her ability to do up all the tiny buttons that ran along her spine. The fabric gaped open on the back and threatened to slide off her shoulders.

As if on cue, two sharp knocks sounded on the door. Relief flooded through her. Someone had come to rescue her at last. "Who is it?"

"Artemis, Your Highness."

"Oh, good," she replied. "Come in."

The door swung open. Artemis stood on the threshold, dressed in her full scout's regalia. Clarion admired her jacket, all tailored lines and black fabric and gleaming golden buttons—and noted that her sword was not purely ceremonial. She wore the same blade she always carried at her hip, but she'd tucked it into a more ornate scabbard. It was filigreed in intricate whorls of gold in the shape of flowers. To Clarion's great shock, she'd even done something about her hair. It shone like the polished shell of an acorn, slicked back and tucked neatly behind her ears.

Despite her immaculate uniform, she looked weary—and a little sad. Clarion supposed she understood. Tonight, there would be a knighting ceremony for scouts who had risked their lives on patrol over the past few weeks. It was the highest honor they could achieve, bestowed by the queen herself. Clarion did not need to ask to know it was something Artemis wanted—and something she deserved, after she had saved Clarion's life.

Artemis took in the scene before her. Evidently moved by Clarion's plight, she asked, "Do you need help?"

Clarion shot her a grateful look in the mirror. "Please."

Artemis flitted over, then immediately set to work fastening the buttons with practiced, efficient ease. When she finished, she adjusted the train, letting it fan out like a spill of water. Now, Clarion could appreciate the full effect of the gown. The fabric glittered as bright as starlight, its brilliance casting a twinkling, ever-changing glow on the walls. Just minutes before, she'd plaited her hair. One of the garden-talents had left a garland of forsythia and daisy petals for her to weave into her braid. All that remained now was to apply her maquillage.

"You look lovely," said Artemis.

"So do you." Clarion warmed at the compliment, but she could not shake just how bittersweetly *pensive* her guard looked. "How are you?"

Artemis seemed somewhat surprised but replied, "Fine."

Clarion raised an eyebrow. "Really?"

There was a moment of silence as Artemis registered the question behind her question. Her mouth twisted into a moue of discomfort. "Ah."

Honestly, Clarion thought. Scouts and their determined stoicism. Perhaps it was unprofessional to push the matter, but her well-being mattered to Clarion. "You deserve recognition, too, you know."

"It doesn't matter," Artemis said hastily. "I have done my best to help in the small ways I can. All I want is the good of Pixie Hollow."

Clarion turned away from her own reflection and fixed Artemis with a meaningful look. No one could truly be so selfless. "But you want more than that."

Artemis hesitated. "I suppose I do."

For the second time in all the years they'd known each other, Clarion had dragged Artemis to the very edge of her vulnerability. She did not know if she could convince her to take the leap. She perched on the edge of her bed and placed her chin in her hands. "Once, you told me that you'd led with your heart over your head. That's why you were assigned to be my guard. What happened, exactly?"

For a moment, Clarion thought she might change the subject entirely. But Artemis heaved a long sigh and settled on the bed beside her. The mattress dipped beneath her weight. Artemis sat with her spine rigidly straight and her hands clasped over her knees.

"Back when I first arrived in Pixie Hollow," she said, "there was something of an ongoing situation. A hawk had happened upon us and tried to establish its territory in the Autumn Forest. None of the animal-talents could manage it or convince it to go elsewhere, so it was up to the scouts to handle the danger it posed.

"I was something of a firebrand back then." At this, Clarion suppressed a snort of laughter. Artemis gave her a wry smile, but it faded quickly. "I'd gotten into a skirmish with it—and I was poised to drive it off. I had it in my sights, after me and a friend in my unit cornered it. But she'd underestimated her pixie dust ration. She fell."

Fairies' wings could not support their weight without pixie dust. And if they were battling a hawk, no doubt they'd found themselves high above the forest floor.

"Oh," Clarion murmured.

Artemis bowed her head, and her black hair curtained her face. "I saved her—but I let our target go. Others were lost as a result of my mistake. My superiors determined that I was not levelheaded enough to make the right decisions in battle. My instincts meant that I was better suited for guard duty."

A good queen must focus on the task at hand, Elvina had said once, *and help at scale.*

Her heart lurched at the pain in Artemis's voice, a pain Clarion knew intimately. She could not have turned her back on someone she could have saved, either. Was that really what it meant to be responsible and levelheaded? To protect the hypothetical many over the one in front of you?

"I'm not sure I would call that a *mistake,*" Clarion said softly.

Artemis looked up at her, a startled hope shining in her eyes. Had no one ever absolved her of this? Soon enough, Clarion would be able to officially reinstate her. She'd been punished—and she'd punished herself—for long enough.

"I don't know that I would have done any differently. It was brave, what you did." Clarion knocked her shoulder against Artemis's. "You have a good heart, Artemis. We need more fairies like you in the scouts."

A faint smile curled on Artemis's lips. Haltingly, as though she did not trust herself to speak, she said, "That's kind of you to say."

Clarion returned the smile. "It's true."

Before Artemis could reply, another knock sounded on the door.

"It's me."

Clarion brightened at the sound of Petra's voice. It was something of a tradition for them to get ready for balls together, but between their schedules and the tension over Winter, she hadn't known whether to expect her.

"The door's open," Clarion called.

Petra entered the room, and Clarion felt as much as she heard Artemis's sharp intake of breath. She could not blame her. Petra was always beautiful—but tonight, she was utterly resplendent. The bodice of her gown was fitted, but the skirt flared into graceful tiers of ivy. Her red curls had been tamed and gathered into an elegant knot at the nape of her neck, with a few ringlets artfully framing her face.

When Petra's gaze landed on Artemis, she let out a strangled sound of surprise. Artemis rose to her feet automatically, and the two of them stared across the room at each other in silent awe. It took all of Clarion's strength to refrain from commenting. Instead, she moved from her bed to her vanity.

Artemis broke the silence first. "You look . . . nice."

A flush crawled up Petra's neck, and self-conscious panic overtook her. She nearly stumbled into the wall behind her. "What? Why do you say that? Is there something on my face?"

"No, I . . ." Artemis blinked, clearly unsure how to handle the situation. "I said it because I meant it."

"Right." Petra still looked deeply skeptical—but almost pleased.

"So," Clarion interjected.

Both of them startled, as though they'd forgotten she was there entirely.

"Petra and I need to finish getting ready." Clarion picked up a cosmetic brush, then a shallow pot of eye paint. Inside was a gold pigment made from a mixture of clay and pixie dust. "Do you want any, Artemis?"

Artemis examined her as though assessing a threat. "No, thank you. I'll leave you to it."

Clarion lifted one shoulder. "Suit yourself."

Petra shrank back against the wall as Artemis brushed past her. When the door clicked shut behind her, Petra crossed the room in a flutter of ivy skirts and fire-bright curls. "You didn't tell me she was going to be here."

"She's always here." Clarion twisted the lid off her eye paint. Unable to resist, she added, "She's off duty tonight, you know."

Petra's face lit up. "Really?"

Clarion gasped. She had not *intended* to catch Petra out, but now she'd all but confirmed what she'd suspected for years. She jabbed the brush at Petra. "I knew it!"

"There's nothing to know!"

Petra looked ready to snatch the brush away from her, or else flee out of the nearest window. It did nothing to tamp down the spark of mischief. "Oh, I think there is."

"It doesn't matter, anyway." Petra buried her face in her hands. "She's terrifying."

Clarion resisted the urge to roll her eyes. "Just ask her to dance. She's not going to bite you."

"She might stab me, though," Petra said darkly.

Clarion grinned. How easy it was to fall into this pattern with her. It felt so normal that she'd nearly forgotten about their last fraught conversation. She'd nearly forgotten that tonight, she would have to slip past her.

Both you and Elvina are depending on me for your schemes to work. Being in this position isn't easy for me.

The memory—the reminder of the distance wedged between them—twinged painfully. If Petra knew she planned to sneak out to Winter tonight, she would try to stop her. And now that it was clear their plan hadn't fully succeeded, she needed to speak with Milori more than ever. There had to be something they could do—anything to prevent Elvina from using what Petra had armed her with.

Petra's expression softened with concern. "What is it?"

"There's just a lot on my mind lately. Coronation things." Clarion forced a smile. In an effort to busy herself, she shuffled a few glass bottles of fragrances around. They clacked together, too loud in the fragile silence. "Come here. Sit."

Petra perched gingerly on the edge of her bed.

Clarion swiveled to face her, nearly knocking their knees together. She dabbed her brush in the eye paint, then took Petra's chin in her fingers. "The usual?"

"Yes." After a moment, she added, "But it has to look especially good. For no particular reason."

"Of course not," said Clarion, with only a touch of impishness.

Bracing her wrist against Petra's cheekbone, Clarion daubed gold onto Petra's eyelids. Her bracelets clinked together softly, and Petra's steady breath fanned out against her skin as she worked. Clarion fell into a practiced rhythm, feathering and layering the pigment across her brow bone. When she finished with Petra's eyes, Clarion switched to her fluffiest brush and dusted pixie dust across Petra's cheekbones. It was all she needed. Anything else would conceal her freckles.

"Open your eyes," Clarion said.

She did—and Clarion's heart skipped a beat. The gold of the paint and the fierce red of her hair drew out every shade of green in her eyes. They were the color of a sunlit summer forest.

"Perfect." Clarion set down her brush emphatically. "She's going to fall in love with you."

Petra wailed inarticulately in protest, and despite the fear and the stress, Clarion laughed. For a few more hours, maybe she could pretend everything was as it always had been.

By the time they arrived at the ball deep in the heart of Summer, the festivities were already in full swing. Clarion, Petra, and Artemis passed beneath the Fairy Circle—a ring of red-capped mushrooms—and into the ballroom, announced by the bright, resonant tone of a herald-talent's voice.

The sight of it stole her breath away.

Glowworms, suspended from low-hanging branches, cast a soft blue aura over the grass. Every so often, fireflies pierced the darkness with pinpricks of light as they drifted through the air. Even without their aid, the entire clearing was impossibly bright, bathed as it was in moonlight. At its center, a spring burbled, made into a spectacle by the water-talents gathered around it. With a wave of their hands, droplets rose from the surface and refracted the light of the moon. Delicate strands of water wove through the air and dissipated into a shimmering curtain of mist.

In the very back of the ballroom, Clarion spotted her destination: a makeshift dais on the moss-covered stump of a sapling. From here, Clarion could make out the hooked points of Elvina's crown and the radiance of her wings. When she craned her neck to get a better look, she glimpsed Commander Nightshade hovering just beside her. Soon, she would stand beside them as Elvina presided over the knighting ceremony.

They passed by banquet tables, each of them piled high with the cooking-talents' hard work. Every dish was as good as a love letter to summer and its bounty: honey cake topped with honeycomb, blackberries, and slivers of fig; delicate blueberry tarts sprinkled with coarse sugar; peach jam and golden bread; tomatoes sliced thick and served with a dusting of salt and basil; glasses of redcurrant wine; pickled radishes and rainbow chard; sweating jars of water flavored with orange blossom and mint; rhubarb and strawberry streusel. Clarion's mouth watered as she looked at it all.

But most striking were her subjects, all of them dressed in their finery. Fairies lounged on the petals of night-blooming flowers, preening beneath the light of the full moon. Others sprawled atop the mushrooms or fluttered aimlessly through the air, speaking in low tones with their friends. Normally, their excited chatter would all but drown out the sound of the orchestra's music. But tonight, the atmosphere was tinged with melancholy.

The slumbering fairies, clearly, were on everyone's mind.

As they navigated their way through the clearing, the crowds parted for her and conversations fell to a hush. All around her, Clarion could hear deferential murmurs of "Your Highness." Many curtsied or bowed to her as she drifted by. Artemis was a comforting presence beside her, guiding her toward the dais like a pirate ship's prow cutting through the waves of the Never Sea. Clarion gave her a quick nod of acknowledgment before floating up to join the queen and the commander of the scouts. Elvina raked her gaze over her, with her ceremonial scepter clutched loosely in her hands.

Whatever she saw there satisfied her, for she said, "You look like a queen tonight."

The pride glimmering in her eyes made Clarion feel off-kilter. How long she'd yearned to be told as much—and how strangely hollow it felt to hear it now, when Elvina did not know what she had done. "Thank you."

Elvina turned toward the gathered fairies. The orchestra played one last, shivering note that dissipated into the humid summer air, and with that, the silence was complete.

"Welcome, all. Thank you for coming to the Coronation Ball held in honor of Princess Clarion, who will be crowned your queen one week from today." Elvina paused when her voice faltered. Clarion frowned. She'd never seen Elvina waver, especially in front of her subjects. But now that Clarion was studying her closely, she could see that Elvina's face was quite wan. "It has felt like a long time since we could all gather like this. While those injured in the attack are at the forefront of our thoughts, the dark shadow that has fallen over Pixie Hollow is finally lifting."

A smattering of tentative applause broke out across the clearing. When it died down, Elvina continued. "And so, I would like to begin the evening by honoring some of our brave scout-talents. They have worked tirelessly to ensure our safety. Each night, they risked their lives by patrolling the skies. They evacuated areas as needed, provided thorough reports, and helped with the repair of any damages the Nightmares caused. Tonight, they will be recognized with the highest honor a scout can achieve: knighthood."

Clarion glanced at the scouts, standing in neat, orderly rows just in front of the dais. Although most of them were beaming, she could focus only on Artemis. She stood in the back of the group, with such open longing on her face that Clarion had to look away.

"All Knights of Pixie Hollow, please join me."

A small collection of scouts rose into the air and came to hover behind Elvina in a semicircle. Each of them wore a pin on the lapel of their coat: an iridescent shard of abalone in the shape of a star, glistering against black fabric.

"Please step forward when you're called," Elvina intoned.

Clarion watched as one by one, the chosen scouts stepped forward and knelt before Elvina. Even with their heads bowed, she could practically feel the happiness emanating from them. They deserved it—truly. But Clarion could not help the bittersweet feeling curdling within her, knowing Artemis had missed out on what she so desperately wanted.

"I hereby induct you into the honorable order of the Knights of Pixie Hollow." Elvina tapped both of their shoulders with her scepter. "Rise, knight, and be recognized."

When the last of them had been knighted, the crowds broke into whoops and cheers. In the chaos, a serving-talent flitted up to the dais and handed Clarion a delicate flute. It chilled her skin, and when she glanced down, she saw that it was a glass of lemonade garnished with a sprig of rosemary.

"Now," Elvina called out over the noise, "your future queen will speak a few words."

Clarion's throat went dry as all the attention in the clearing focused on her. She floated forward and swept her gaze out over her subjects. This was the very first time she would address them on her own, and she found the reality of it far more intimidating than the idea of it. The languid heat of summer settled over her—or perhaps it was her own nerves making her feel so *hot*.

"Good evening," she said, her voice uncertain. "I want to echo what Her Majesty said in thanking you for coming tonight. I will save my speeches for Coronation Day, but in the meantime, I will say that I appreciate your coming to celebrate this occasion more than I can say. Enjoy yourselves tonight, and dance in my honor. So . . ." She lifted her glass. "To all of you—and to brighter days ahead."

The glittering sound of glasses clinking together traveled through the clearing. Clarion swallowed a sip of her lemonade, if only to dispel the bitter taste in her mouth. She did not deserve to be celebrated when she still had not roused the slumbering from their spell.

As the orchestra struck up another tune, Elvina rested a hand on Clarion's shoulder. Although she did not speak, Clarion understood her meaning: *You did well.*

"Go on," said Elvina. "Enjoy the rest of your night."

"I will." A bolt of anticipation shot through her. Now, with her obligations fulfilled, she could pay a visit to her subjects in Winter. All that remained was slipping away undetected.

As she flitted through the ballroom, she watched fairies

pirouette through the air to the soaring tune of the music-talents. The dance would wear on late into the night, until all the world was alight with showers of pixie dust and starlight. All her life, she'd known very well what it felt like to be lonely in a crowd. But she had never felt it more acutely than she did tonight. Seeing the others holding hands, twirling and laughing as they switched partners, reminded her of all the things she would never—*could* never—have.

A hand locked around her arm, yanking her from her thoughts. When she whirled to face whoever had accosted her, she found herself staring down at Petra. Clarion's stomach twisted into a knot.

Just my luck, she thought. How was she going to escape now?

"I saw a pretty isolated corner over that way," Petra said, sounding as though she had been talking for a few seconds already. "What do you think?"

"Actually," Clarion said, extricating herself from Petra's grip as gently as she could, "I'm not feeling well."

"Oh, no. You can't use that excuse if I'm not allowed to. You're not allowed to abandon me here, where people could *talk to me*"—Petra shuddered—"or *worse*."

"What could possibly be worse than that?"

"A lot of things! For example—" Petra cut herself off. "No, don't distract me. If you're leaving, I'm going with you."

"No," Clarion said hastily. "I mean . . . no, you don't have to do that."

Petra regarded her suspiciously. "Why?"

"Because . . ." She groped for an excuse. "I just want to get some air for a few minutes. You should stay and enjoy the party."

"Enjoy the—*Enjoy*?" Petra spluttered. "You know I don't enjoy parties. What is really going on here?"

Clarion laughed, a brittle sound even to her own ears. "Nothing is going on."

"Oh, really?" Petra planted a hand on her hip. "Then why are you trying to run away from me?"

She could be so stubborn sometimes. "I'm not," Clarion said, trying to keep her mounting frustration out of her voice.

Evidently, she failed, because Petra regarded her with a somewhat stung expression. "Have I done something?"

"No, of course not." Clarion glanced over her shoulder fretfully. She really needed to go. "I just want to be alone."

Color rose in Petra's cheeks. "I can't apologize to you if I don't know what you're upset about."

A few nearby fairies cast curious looks their way. Clarion grabbed Petra's wrist and steered her toward the very edge of the Fairy Circle, where the shadow of the woods reached between the archway of the mushroom caps. The light from the party glittered on the pixie dust on the bridge of Petra's nose and set her red hair ablaze. Yet here in the near darkness, Clarion felt oddly chilled. She wrapped her arms around herself and fixed her gaze on the ground. Clearly, she was not going to escape without being honest.

"I'm not upset with you. It's only that you didn't want me to talk to you about Winter."

Petra took a reflexive step backward. "This is about Winter? What business do you have there? The attacks have stopped."

"But no one has woken up," Clarion countered. "And Elvina showed me what you made for her."

"Oh."

Oh. Was that really all she had to say? When Clarion looked up, Petra was staring back at her, her face as pale as Winter.

"I told you how I felt about her plan, and I thought you agreed with me." Clarion's voice wavered with an emotion she hadn't realized was so close to spilling forth. There were so many things she wanted to say, but she did not want to lash out when she was hurting. It was not Petra's fault. Her obligation was to the Crown, not to Clarion. Even so, Petra's involvement had made things quite difficult for her. "It doesn't matter. I'm doing the best I can to solve the problem my own way."

Slowly, Petra's wounded expression morphed into one of determination, but the flush did not fade. High emotion always stained her face bright red. "And that's really what you're planning to do *now*?"

Clarion did not appreciate the judgment in her voice. Guardedly, she said, "I've done everything expected of me tonight. I'm trying to keep Pixie Hollow safe."

Petra let out a soft, frustrated sound. "In a ball gown, Clarion? I'm not naive. You're not going to investigate a cure. You're going to see the warden."

Clarion reeled back. Did Petra resent Milori for taking up

Clarion's time, or did she truly think Clarion lovesick enough to put a boy over her duties? Either way, she bristled all over with indignation. "And what does it matter if I am?"

Petra stared at her disbelievingly. "Your coronation is in a week."

"Which means I must stay inside until then," she replied bitterly, "and speak to no one you disapprove of."

"No. It means you need to be more responsible. It's too dangerous to play these games!" Petra's glow intensified, burning orange at the edges. "You've already gotten hurt because of him. You've become distant, and you're exhausted all the time. And sneaking off tonight, when everyone is looking to you to reassure them that things will be all right? It's a bad idea. But you have *never* listened to me. Then again, who does? No one takes me seriously, because I'm just the one who's afraid of everything."

The pain in her voice doused the hottest flames of Clarion's anger. But Petra's words had cut deep.

You think I'm being selfish. You think I'm not taking my role seriously.

Clarion held those words behind her teeth. She could not remember the last time they'd fought like this. As much as she was burning to defend herself—as much as she wanted to fix whatever had broken between them—she did not have time for this. No matter what Petra wanted to accuse her of, this was about Pixie Hollow as much as it was about her feelings. She did not owe her an explanation.

Clarion squeezed her eyes shut, as if that could prevent her tears from falling. Furiously—and as carefully as she could—she swiped them away. She could not reapply the gold to her eyes, and she could not meet the winter fairies looking as though she'd just been crying. "I have to go."

"Clarion, *please*—"

Swallowing down her hurt, Clarion slipped into darkness and headed toward Winter.

19

If only Petra had just let it lie. If only she had not goaded Clarion into a confrontation she wasn't prepared for.

If only, if only, if only. Clarion stewed in her thoughts while she fetched her coat from where she'd stashed it in the knothole of a nearby tree. She hugged it to her chest, inhaling the familiar scent of Winter clinging to the fur trim. It brought her no comfort; it only served as a bitter reminder of how much she owed to Petra.

Drawing in a deep breath, she did her best to fold up all her hurt feelings and file them carefully away. She could not afford to become maudlin right now. Tonight's journey into Winter, after all, was purely to fulfill her royal duty. She could manage her emotions, as any competent queen could. And yet, all she wanted was to retire for the evening—to brood over how she'd officially torn apart her relationship with her best friend.

Although the sun had fully set, Clarion could have found the border of Winter and Spring blindfolded by now. Her wings knew the way: every stone jutting from the earth, every turn of the river, every branch elbowing out into the path, guiding her to the only place that felt like home. Spring seemed to sense her sadness tonight. Willow branches trailed soothingly along her arms, and she could have sworn the cherry blossoms bloomed wilder than they had before. Their petals tangled in her skirts and settled gently on the surface of the moonlit pond she passed.

When she made it to the border, Milori was waiting for her. Slowly, she descended from her flight. The train of her gown pooled around her, and as the hem dissolved into pixie dust and motes of golden light, it stained the water and ice with brilliant gold.

In the full dark, Milori was a sketch in charcoal beneath the glow of a star-flecked sky. She found she couldn't look away from him. She'd never seen him in the trappings of his rank before. He wore a cloak of spider-silk brocade, dyed a pale blue and embroidered with frost-like patterns in delicate silver thread. It was fastened around his shoulders with a brooch of solid ice, gleaming coldly against the fabric. A circlet of icicles, both fragile and imposing, was nestled in his white hair. He'd left it unbound, so it fell like a spill of moonlit water down his back.

For a moment, they stared at each other, the air thickening with all the things left unsaid between them. How had she ever believed she could keep her feelings out of it when they reunited?

Perhaps Petra hadn't been *entirely* wrong.

At last, Milori broke the silence. The fur-lined hem of his cloak shifted as he bowed to her. "We're here to escort you to the ball."

"We . . . ?" She trailed off when she spotted Noctua. She was perched in the branch of a spruce a few yards away, watching them with a look that veered too close to exasperation for Clarion's liking. If even an owl could sense the tension, things were bleak indeed. "Of course."

He nodded at the coat draped over her arm. "May I help you with your coat?"

She hesitated. She'd wanted—well, *wanted* was a strong word, but the point stood—to maintain some distance between them, but what harm could there possibly be in so small a gesture? She handed it to him. "I don't see why not."

Milori held it out for her so that she could slide her arms into the sleeves. Once she had let it settle over her shoulders, she fastened the buttons. She knew she must have looked rather ridiculous, wearing this patched-together coat over the most elegant ball gown she owned. But when she glanced up at Milori again, he was watching her as if the entire ensemble were the most striking thing he'd ever seen.

"What is it?" she asked.

"Nothing at all." He offered her his arm. "Shall we?"

She tucked her hand into his elbow. "How proper."

"It is the first time Pixie Hollow's royalty has graced this realm in an official capacity," he said, only a little winkingly. "I intend to make a good first impression."

He turned, and as she moved to follow him, she slipped into Winter. The cold that washed over her felt cleansing. Summer and her coronation ball seemed terribly far away now.

As he led her toward Noctua, Milori let his shoulder knock gently into hers. "Is there something on your mind?"

For a moment, she considered lying. "Is it so obvious?"

Milori's response was a half shrug that said, *Painfully so.* After a moment, he asked, "Is it the Nightmares?"

"In part." She worried the inside of her lip. "I'm sorry. I'd meant to check in with you sooner. The attacks have stopped, but . . ."

". . . no one has woken up."

Clarion ached at the somberness of his voice—at the weary shadows still carved beneath his pale eyes. How she yearned to take away some of that burden. "I don't understand what we did wrong."

"You didn't do anything wrong." Milori kept his gaze fixed straight ahead, seemingly lost in thought. "The instructions weren't exactly clear. Besides, there was always a risk that the legend would lead to a dead end, but it wasn't for nothing. Sealing the prison has given your subjects peace of mind for the first time in weeks. Tonight is evidence of that."

"I suppose so," she murmured. "Still, I can't help feeling guilty—like we've forgotten the slumbering. It feels wrong to celebrate without them."

"I'm not sure it's wrong to hold what moments of joy we can find."

Her heart gave an answering flutter. That low, gentle tone of his felt almost . . . pointed. It was a lovely sentiment, one she wished she could believe applied to her—to *them*. Clarion held her silence, lest something regrettably whimsical or melancholy slip out. With her current mood, she couldn't be sure which it would be.

"At any rate . . ." He barreled onward. The tips of his ears burned red. "The Keeper and I have begun searching for other texts that might provide some answers. It could take some time, however. The Hall of Winter is vast . . . and admittedly rather disorganized. Each Keeper has had their own system of classification, and none of them has managed to make it consistent across the entire collection during their tenure. There is still an entire section with shelves arranged by color."

Clarion almost smiled at the thought. How magical, that an entire library could be transformed into a rainbow. "I wish I could help."

"Me, too." He hesitated. "If you'd like, I can write to you with our findings."

After her coronation, she supposed there would be no one monitoring her correspondence. "All right."

He nodded. "There's something else troubling you?"

Clarion let out a heavy sigh. Her breath unfurled in a white cloud. "I'm afraid it will sound ridiculous in comparison. Petra and I got into an argument at the ball, and it's weighing on me."

When they reached Noctua, he took her reins—these ones, she noted, were made of a much finer material; apparently, even birds had finery—and hesitated. "Do you want to talk about it?"

Did she? Some part of her did, of course. But she feared that once she picked open the wound, there would be no stemming the tide. She would have to think about how Petra had almost enabled the worst possible outcome for Winter. But worse still, she would have to consider the role she herself had played in driving a wedge between them. It wasn't as though Petra's concerns were unreasonable. Venturing into the Winter Woods as a warm fairy *was* objectively dangerous. Perhaps she should have spoken to her instead of throwing up walls.

Perhaps she had not listened to her properly for a long time.

Grimacing, Clarion shook her head. "It will pass soon enough."

He did not look terribly convinced, but he did not press the matter. "As you wish."

She and Milori climbed onto Noctua's back—something that was becoming almost second nature to her now, she realized. She no longer had to hold on for dear life when the owl beat her wings, carrying them into the skies. Here, nestled safely in Milori's arms,

Clarion felt something like peace. She dared to look down. Beneath the veil of night, all the snow was stained a muted blue.

It took her only a few minutes to realize that Milori was steering them to an area she had never seen before. Below them was a river, frozen solid and gleaming like a vein of glass. From this height, she could make out the milling crowds atop the ice—and scattered here and there along the riverbanks, a few booths, lit from within with a cheerful orange light.

Milori slowed Noctua; she beat her wings to hover nearly in place. When he spoke, Clarion could feel his voice, rumbling in his chest and curling softly over the shell of her ear. "I should warn you that this might be somewhat overwhelming."

She shot him a wry look. "You doubt me?"

"Never," he said softly. "It's only that they know what you've done for them."

"Oh." She supposed that *would* make things different. In the warm seasons, no one knew that she and Milori had sealed away the Nightmares. "Thank you for the warning. But I think I'm ready."

A spark of mischief glittered in his eyes. "Then prepare to make quite an entrance."

They made quite an entrance, indeed.

Noctua dove, descending on the Winter ball in a swirl of white feathers and pixie dust. The owl slowed their fall with a few flaps of her wings, kicking up the topmost layer of snow; it eddied wildly around them as they landed just outside the festival grounds.

Even over the rush of the wind, Clarion heard the winter

fairies' cheers. In an instant, the crowds pressed in around them, and she caught snatches of her name, spoken not in a reverential hush but with . . . excitement? It was such a foreign concept, she could hardly make sense of it.

"Our guest of honor has arrived," Milori called out over the commotion.

Somehow, the noise intensified. Clarion could only laugh breathlessly as she stared out over their faces. She did not think anyone had ever been so happy to see her. She could only hope she did not disappoint them.

Milori leaned close enough to murmur in her ear, "I *did* warn you."

"You certainly did."

As Clarion dismounted, the wind tugged loose glittering trails from the hem of her gown. Together, she and Milori waded into the veritable sea of fairies. They could make little progress toward the river, however, when she was stopped every few paces.

"Welcome to the Winter Woods, Your Highness." A fairy with an elegant white braid draped over her shoulder beamed at her. "I wanted to give you this, if you'll accept it."

She held out a jasmine blossom encased in frost, glittering and perfectly preserved. It was beautiful—and an incredibly kind gesture. It must have been difficult to fetch it; jasmine grew only on the very edge of Winter and Spring.

Clarion took it gently, afraid to snap the delicate petals off. "Of course I will. Thank you so much."

The words had no sooner passed her lips than a sparrow man took the fairy's place. He offered her a figurine carved from ice. "A small token of our gratitude, Your Highness, that you risked your life to protect ours."

"Oh," she said, a little overcome. She accepted the figurine gingerly, cradling it in the palm of her mittened hand. It would melt if she held on to it—if not now, then when she returned to the warm seasons. She marveled at the fragile beauty of these ephemeral things. "It's my pleasure."

By the third fairy who approached her, Clarion realized that something of a line had formed. It astonished her to see so many fairies waiting to speak to *her*. Her interactions blurred together eventually, a whirlwind of clasped hands, exchanged names, and gifts—so many, she did not know how she would get them home, or where to put them even if she could. Winter fairies, so long separated from the warm seasons, were apparently keen to share what they had to offer. Their generosity and warmth astounded her. Between this reception and her fight with Petra, the world felt far too raw, all her emotions just a pinprick from spilling forth.

This had been overwhelming, indeed.

When the initial excitement died down and the crowds thinned, a kind fairy loaded her things onto a sleigh and offered to take it to the border after the festivities. The very last of her subjects waiting to see her was Milori. Clarion felt no small measure of relief to see him.

"How are you holding up?"

"Perfectly," she said—and she meant it. "A little tired, though."

He looked a little apologetic. "Shall I take you home?"

"No," she said, perhaps too hastily. In truth, she never wanted to leave. "Not yet. I haven't visited any of the booths."

"That is a must before you go." Milori offered her his hand. Giddiness, irrepressible and bright, unfurled through her at the sight. "Come with me, then."

She took his hand. "All right."

He led her toward the frozen river. As they approached the festival, the night brightened. Candles burned on every available surface—stones, tables of ice, logs—and cast everything in rosy hues. The river absorbed all the candlelight and seemed to glow in the darkness. All along its embankment, the winter fairies had set up painted wooden booths, their roofs iced like cakes with a thick layer of snow and dripping with icicles. Each one offered something different: spiced cider, butternut squash soup garnished with fragments of pomegranate seeds, salads of dark greens and delicate slivers of beets, candied nuts chopped into fine pieces, pastries glazed with citrus, toffee puddings in caramel sauce. Clarion insisted on trying some of everything.

All around them, fairies skated across the ice and drifted through the air as they danced. They wore clothes of pure white and deepest red. Clarion paused to admire the frost lacework and ice gems glittering at their ears and wrists. How different even their fashion was here!

"Would you like to join them?" Milori asked.

Clarion whirled to face him, flustered to have been caught staring with such . . . yearning. It took her a moment to process that his question sounded suspiciously like an invitation. "Do you dance?"

"I *can*," he said, "theoretically. But I find I rarely have reason to."

"I'm shocked," she replied with a grin. She could hardly imagine him dancing. "Me neither. Well, I suppose that isn't entirely true. I've always *wanted* to dance."

He made a pensive sound. "Why haven't you?"

"Queens don't dance."

"In Winter, they might." He met her eyes meaningfully, and her throat went dry. "Besides, you aren't queen yet."

Clarion flushed to have her words turned back on her. She shook her head at him in fond exasperation. With every moment that passed, it became more and more difficult to remember why exactly she'd insisted on maintaining some semblance of distance between them. What he said was true: she wasn't queen yet. And he was looking at her with such hope, it seemed almost cruel to deny him.

Why not allow herself one last night of freedom?

Putting on airs of defeat, she sighed. She drew a step closer and tipped her chin up to meet his gaze. "I suppose I can't argue against that."

Milori's lips parted mutely. Clarion felt a small thrill that she seemed to have rendered him speechless. Clearly, he hadn't expected her to acquiesce so easily. But after a moment, he recovered enough to ask, "Then may I be so bold as to ask for your first dance?"

It took all her strength to maintain her teasingly aloof tone. "You may."

Distantly, she registered that the music-talents had struck up another song. Slowly, she rested one hand on his shoulder; the other slid into his. He settled into the frame of the dance, drawing her closer with a hand on the curve of her waist. The familiar, comforting chill of his skin enveloped her, along with the scent of evergreen and fresh-fallen snow. And although he claimed he rarely danced, he guided her through the steps with practiced ease. They were among the only couples on the ground; it was freeing, to take up so much space, to never fear colliding with someone else. The fabric of her gown billowed around them as they twirled, gathering up snow and starlight.

"How have you enjoyed your first Winter ball?" he asked.

"It's incredible. It's so . . ." She struggled to find the exact word, but the most paradoxical one fit best. "Warm."

Milori seemed pleased, but his expression soon grew thoughtful. "This is what it could be like, if you wanted it to be."

For the first time, Clarion allowed herself to envision it. When she was queen, it would be within her power to change things in the warm seasons. Although Elvina had imparted her wisdom to Clarion, her time in Winter had shown her it was not the only way forward. How sweet it would be to rule not from an impartial distance but with *warmth*. Perhaps, then, she would not have to be alone. The very thought filled her up with a yearning greater than any she'd ever known.

When the song ended, Milori did not let her go immediately. Clarion resisted the urge to lean her head against his shoulder. But while her heart longed to stay, the cold had made itself known. Her fingers were going numb, and the tips of her ears stung. "I should get back to Summer before they notice I'm gone."

If he was disappointed, it did not show on his face. But she could read his reluctance to let her go, broken only by the shiver that gripped her. Even after he dropped her hand, his palm still rested steadily on the small of her back. "Of course. Let's get you out of the cold."

A solemn mood had come over them both; the flight back to the border passed in silence. Clarion could focus on little but the feeling of finality. Milori clearly felt it, too. He held on to the reins with a white-knuckled pressure, as though he could cling to these last few moments. She leaned her head back against his shoulder, letting her eyes fall half-lidded. From this vantage point, she caught glimpses of his loose white hair, unspooling like ribbons into the dark.

Noctua alighted, then immediately fluffed out her feathers. Her head seemed to recede into them. With the sun long since sunk below the horizon, the temperature had plummeted. Ice floes drifted on the river's current, as glossy as sheets of black glass in the moonlight.

When Clarion dismounted, her boots sank deep into the snowdrifts. She hesitated, tipping her head back to peer up at Milori where he remained perched on Noctua's back. In his diadem, frozen into jagged points, he looked so much like the statue of the Lord of Winter: as forlorn as he was formidable. Wind swept through Winter like a mournful sigh. It set his cloak billowing, and the thickening flurries drifted between them like a curtain.

She could not bring herself to say her goodbyes.

This is what it could be like, he'd said, *if you wanted it to be.*

After everything, did they not deserve happiness?

"Milori," she began, at the same time he said, "I . . ."

He cleared his throat. "Go on."

Clarion let out a shaky breath. "Will you come down first?"

Without hesitation, he dropped into the snow beside her. She still had to look up at him, but here on level ground, it felt less like he would slip away from her. She tugged her mittens off, one after the other. Gathering her nerve, she said, "I've been thinking."

Milori's voice was barely audible. "About what?"

"About what you said. I . . ." Her words left her in a rush. Any hope of being articulate had fled her entirely. Her mittens fell to the ground. She twined her fingers in the fabric of his cloak where it met at the dip of his collarbone. Holding his gaze, she said, "I don't want to leave."

Milori looked as though he had been waiting his entire life for those words. A dam had given way within him, and the emotion burning in his eyes broke over her like a wave. His hands came to rest over hers, his fingers encircling her wrists. She could feel the wild thrum of his heart beneath her touch, the chill of his skin seeping into hers.

"Then don't," he murmured into the bare space between them.

Don't. As though it were the simplest thing in the world.

What else was there to do? She stood on her toes and kissed him.

For a moment, they remained suspended in a sort of tender disbelief. Then, his lips parted beneath hers, and Clarion felt herself catch flame. She tasted cocoa and cinnamon on her tongue, swallowed the hitch of his breath as she melted into him. His fingers threaded into the hair at the nape of her neck, angling her chin up toward him as he deepened the kiss. The pins holding her flower crown in place came loose, showering the earth at her feet with white petals and sweet pollen. His every touch set her nerves alight with both languid heat and searing cold.

Breathless, she pulled back. But even that small distance pained her. How she resented her own limitations right now—her body's inability to tolerate his realm for long. "I'm freezing."

"We can't have that." His lips brushed against hers with every syllable.

Neither of them seemed willing to part.

He gathered her into his arms and slowly walked her backward. Clarion laughed unsteadily, winding her arms around his neck for balance. He stopped only when they were bridged between worlds: her feet planted on the frost-laced moss, his in the shallow dusting of snow. But even here in Spring, the cold clung to her. Snow sparkled against her eyelashes, and the breath she shared with him plumed softly in the air.

This, she thought, was enough. They could make this work.

In that moment, there was nothing and no one but the two of them.

And then, a familiar voice cut through her joy: "Clarion!"

Elvina.

20

Elvina descended on them like a falling star, her glow blazing bright with the force of her anger. Milori did not let go of Clarion immediately; his fingers curled almost protectively around her upper arms. As much as she appreciated it, she would have much preferred to vanish entirely. To dissolve and be carried away like dandelion seeds on the wind.

This could not be happening.

When Elvina landed on the edge of the riverbank, Clarion nearly shrank back from her. Over the years, Clarion had seen many sides of Elvina; although she was an understated fairy, Clarion had come to understand and anticipate the subtle shifts of her emotions.

Far too many times, she had seen her disappointment—but never anything like this. Her face was contorted with barely leashed fury, all the planes of her face carved in stark shadow and orange light.

But what stung even more was the sight of Petra and Artemis behind her. Petra hovered a short distance away, halfway concealed behind a blueberry thicket. Even so, Clarion could see how distressed she looked: her hands knotted together, her hair pulled loose from its elegant updo, her lip bitten raw.

Clarion cut her gaze to Artemis, who gave a subtle shake of her head. Clarion read her meaning: *I had nothing to do with this.*

There was no doubt in Clarion's mind what had happened, then. After their fight at the ball, Petra had told Elvina where Clarion had gone. Mortification had churned sickeningly within Clarion. But now, betrayal seared through all her humiliation, all her indignation. As much as it wounded her, it did not surprise her.

"What are you doing here?" was all Clarion could think to ask.

This, apparently, was not the expected or desired reply. Elvina's aura flared brighter with outrage. "Am I to understand that *this* is what has consumed you over these last few weeks? *This* is what has made you so curious about Winter? I expected better of you, Clarion."

"This is my responsibility," Milori cut in. There was no trace of coldness in his voice—only an unbearable earnestness. Despite the diadem around his brow, he seemed willing to kneel.

Clarion shot him a disbelieving glare. Of *course* he would attempt to take on the brunt of Elvina's wrath himself. "It is *not*—"

"I sought her help in remedying my mistake," Milori continued, undeterred. "Everything she has done has been at my behest. Forgive me, Your Majesty."

Elvina stared at him as though he were little more than an insect, far beneath her notice. The disgust on her face made anger spark bright within Clarion. Now that she knew what Elvina believed of winter fairies, she knew it was pointless to argue. No matter what he said, it would never satisfy or convince her.

Still, Clarion could not allow Milori to accept the blame for this. He could not martyr himself any longer; he had already done so in a hundred different ways. He was meant for so much more than that. For too long, winter fairies had been ignored and maligned for something they had nobly volunteered for. Clarion could not stand here and be complicit in it any longer. The burden the Wardens of the Winter Woods had taken from the Queens of Pixie Hollow was immense; they deserved to be honored for it.

"You're wrong about him." Clarion stepped in front of Milori, as though she could shield him from Elvina's open disdain. "About all of them. The Winter Woods are nothing at all like we believed."

"We will discuss this at home," Elvina said through clenched teeth. "Come with me. Now."

"No."

Her voice rang in the silence, and the stars above seemed to punctuate it, flaring brighter with the force of her emotion. Elvina reeled back. She looked almost baffled, as though she hardly knew what to do or what petulant creature had replaced Clarion, her collected and controlled heir. Clarion herself hardly knew where she'd summoned the nerve from.

"I'm afraid you don't have a choice," Elvina said.

"He's been working with me to stop the Nightmares! If you would just listen to me—"

"Clarion," Elvina said warningly.

"Everything I have done has been to protect Pixie Hollow. Can you say the same?"

Elvina recoiled as if slapped. "Excuse me?"

Clarion's hands shook with the sudden rush of adrenaline. She barely recognized herself. This righteous anger felt as though it would incinerate her. But it burned like a wildfire, and she could not very well stop it now. "You have had no regard for your subjects in Winter. You planned to turn your back on them and leave them with an impossible task! Governing-talent magic is the only thing that can stop the Nightmares, but you have been completely uninterested in—"

Elvina let out a single note of humorless laughter. "You have no idea what you're talking about."

"I do," Clarion insisted. Now that she had begun, she would not be silenced. "Winter fairies have too long been the victims of our incomplete understanding of history, and I will not see it stand. Mil—the Warden of the Winter Woods is not what you thought him to be."

"No," Elvina said darkly. "He is young. He hasn't yet had a

chance to grow into what he might become: ambitious, like his predecessor, or corrupted by the beasts that poison everything they touch. You are not safe with him."

Beside her, Milori winced.

So that was it? She would disregard everything Clarion had said? "I have never been anywhere safer."

Elvina advanced toward her. By the look in her eyes, it seemed she was ready and willing to drag Clarion off this bridge herself. "He's already turned you against me."

"No, *you* have turned me against you!" The words slipped out before she could stop herself, halting Elvina in her tracks. Her voice trembled. And yet, it was the truth she had not wanted to admit. "I have tried to live up to the standard you have set, all in the hopes that I would be worthy of the crown. I have tried so hard to be just like you. But I'm not. This is what Winter has taught me."

Her magic flared within her, rising with the tide of her emotions. She was made luminous with the force of her conviction. Even through her coat, the radiance of her wings washed Elvina's stunned face a pallid white.

"No. You are certainly not," Elvina said—but it was not horror in her voice. It was something like wonder.

"I don't mean to interrupt," Petra said quietly, peering out from the thicket she'd hidden behind. Her face had gone ashen. "But I think there's something wrong."

She pointed, and Clarion's gaze followed the path she'd

indicated to the sky. Now that she mentioned it, something *did* feel wrong. Sometime in the last few minutes, the darkness of night had deepened.

The clouds hung low and threatening, clotting over the full moon and all its attendant stars. Energy crackled through the air and prickled along her arms. The weather-talents had said nothing about a rainstorm, but . . . No, this wasn't the promise of lightning. It felt worse, almost sinister. She shuddered.

And then, something shot across the sky: a gold streak of pixie dust, impossibly bright against the thickening gloom. As it drew closer, Clarion realized it was a scout-talent from Winter, hurtling straight for them.

Although the sparrow man was still dressed in his finery, he clutched his bow in his white-knuckled hand. His chest heaved, and his eyes were wild—and glassy, as though still staring out at something not truly there.

"Milori," he choked out at last. "There's been an attack."

Milori's studiously calm expression splintered. "What?"

"The Nightmares," the scout wheezed. "They've flooded the festival—more than we've ever seen. My unit is leading as many fairies as they can to the Hall of Winter, but . . ."

Clarion felt his pause like a physical blow. She felt as though she were free-falling, plunged into a mire of confusion and guilt. This shouldn't have happened. But wasn't that what she'd believed about the fairies still locked in their eternal slumber? What she and

Milori had accomplished was nothing more than a handful of sand shored up against the rising tide. They hadn't accomplished anything at all.

This is all your fault, her self-doubt hissed.

Just how many had they lost to the Nightmares' spell this time?

Resurfacing from her shock, Clarion demanded, "How could they have broken free again?"

Understanding broke open Elvina's stupor. "You attempted to seal them away."

"I . . . I don't know." Milori shook his head. Clarion had never seen him so rattled, but he gathered his resolve enough to speak steadily: "I have to go."

Clarion seized hold of his elbow and held his gaze. "I'm coming with you."

The gratitude that lit Milori's eyes knocked her nearly breathless.

"Clarion." A pleading note knifed into Elvina's voice. "Don't do this."

Clarion spared only a glance backward. Her gaze landed on Petra, whose eyes were wide open and shining with an emotion she could not place. Perhaps she and Elvina were right: her feelings for Milori had made her reckless. But with this protective, righteous fury burning within her, she'd never felt more attuned to her purpose.

"I'm sorry," she said softly. "I have to."

Turning her back on her friends and her mentor, she followed Milori into the bitter chill of Winter.

Please don't let us be too late.

Clarion clung to that plea like a lifeline as they soared toward the festival grounds, as tightly as she did to Milori. He held fast to Noctua's reins, guiding them through the brewing storm. This high up, the clouds—a near black in the dark—drifted over her vision like a smear of wildfire smoke. Heavy snowfall buffeted her, clumping heavily in her eyelashes and stinging her face like volleys of ice. Every gust of wind knocked them off course, and Clarion could have sworn she heard a voice carried on it.

Fall, it whispered.

For the first time in all her crossings of its border, Winter felt hostile.

A flicker of shadow in the corner of her vision snagged her attention. Clarion whirled toward it—only to see something hurtling toward them: a winged shape, traced in the violet glow of the Nightmares' power.

"Milori!" she called. "Look out!"

His head snapped toward the Nightmare. A flash of lightning split open the sky, illuminating the beast for one terrible moment.

He jerked the reins, and Noctua veered out of the Nightmare's path. Milori flattened himself against the owl's back to maintain his balance, dragging Clarion along with him—just in time to avoid the creature's talons reaching toward them. She pressed her forehead against his shoulder blades and let out a tremulous breath, horrified at how close she'd come to losing both her seat *and* her head. Staying astride Noctua for a casual flight was one thing, but combat was quickly proving to be another entirely.

Clarion looked up to see the Nightmare circling around again. It had contorted itself into the shape of an owl: a grotesque mockery of Noctua. Its beak curved over a set of unsettlingly human teeth, which were bared in an empty smile. Worse, just beyond the shadow of its wingspan, she spied a dark cloud moving toward them with alarming speed. A chittering sound, distant at first, swelled to a high-pitched shriek that resonated through her very bones. No, not a cloud—but a group of Nightmares, carried on insects' wings. Even from here, Clarion could *feel* their hunger.

Fear skittered over her. They'd never survive if the swarm reached them. There had to be hundreds of them. Had *all* the Nightmares broken free?

"We need to land," Clarion shouted over the wail of the wind. "Now."

Milori stared out at the encroaching Nightmares, a muscle feathering in his jaw. "All right. Hold on."

Clarion obeyed. With that, Milori gave Noctua the reins. The owl tucked her wings into her body and dove headfirst toward the forest below.

Clarion's eyes watered as the bitter claws of the wind and cold tore at her. Milori's hair streamed behind him, lashing against her face, as they plummeted. In a matter of seconds, Noctua broke through the canopy of the forest, knocking loose snow and knife-sharp icicles as she went. Branches snared Clarion's coat and hair viciously, but she hardly felt a thing through the sheer rush of adrenaline. Just a few feet from the ground, Noctua beat her wings to slow their fall.

By the time they landed, Clarion's heart was beating wildly in her throat. None of the Nightmares had followed them this far, but she could sense them, shifting just beyond the latticework of branches overhead. She remained frozen in place until the horrible drone of the insects faded. The slivers of sky she could see were still stained a baleful shade of gray—but nothing glared back at her. Breath by shallow, shaking breath, terror eased its grip on her, and the skin-crawling sensation of the Nightmares' presence lifted.

For now, they'd escaped.

She and Milori slid off Noctua's back. When they were safely on solid ground, she turned to face him. He'd lost his diadem at some point during their flight, and chunks of hail and snapped twigs were caught in his hair. But mercifully, he seemed whole and relatively unharmed. A thin scratch had opened on the side of his face.

She cupped his jaw, smearing away the blood that had welled up with her thumb. "Are you all right?"

"I am," Milori replied. His eyes roved over her, searching her for injuries. He apparently found none, for she saw some of the tension drain from him. "Are you?"

"I think so." On trembling legs, she spun in a slow circle to get her bearings. Nothing felt familiar to her anymore. "We should keep moving."

Milori nodded. He led their grim trudge, deeper into the forest, deeper into the storm; his glow, shining faintly silver in the gloom, guided her path. She carefully fit her boots into the shape of the footprints he left behind. Through the darkness and the thickening flurries, she could hardly see her own hand an inch away from her face. Every branch that pierced the curtain of snow reached toward them like claws, and her growing unease made bared, dripping fangs of the icicles hanging from the trees. How she hated to see her beloved Winter Woods transformed into such a haunted place.

It was always quiet here, all the sound muffled by heavy snowfall. But this was an unnatural sort of quiet, as if all the forest were holding its breath, too terrified to move. Their footfalls crunched too loud in the crust of ice that glittered coldly over the snow.

Then, she heard it: screams.

Clarion's blood turned to ice. Neither of them said a word; they did not have to. Spurred on by that sound of terror, they broke into a run. When they burst through the cover of beeches and firs, Clarion drew up short.

The wreckage of the festival lay before them. The booths they'd wandered among not long before were completely destroyed—nothing but skeletons of splintered wood. Embers smoldered on their remains, having caught fire from candles that had never been extinguished. Jagged shards of ice sculptures were scattered on the river's surface, glinting among the trampled mess of flower petals and wreaths.

But Clarion could not look away from the dark shapes of slumbering fairies sprawled on the ice. They looked like statues: perfectly still amidst so much destruction. Snowfall had already begun to accumulate over them.

Here was evidence of her failure laid bare.

Nightmares pooled around the fairies like spills of oil, bubbling as they struggled to take shape. They swirled through the air, as dark as smoke. Others prowled in their animal forms, riddled with arrows. Dimly, Clarion watched as another arrow sank into the eye socket of a misshapen bear. It roared in outrage, spittle—no, she realized, venom—flung from the lethal points of its fangs.

That brought Clarion back to herself.

Scouts zipped overhead, their bows drawn and voices raised in battle cries. Although they couldn't fight the Nightmares off, they were risking their lives to save as many fairies as they could. A few goaded Nightmares into pursuing them, dodging and weaving through streaks of darkness, while their comrades ushered civilians toward the Hall of Winter. Clarion's heart lurched to see such selfless bravery.

A low growl rumbled behind her.

Clarion gasped, whirling around. She stood face to face with a twisted version of Fenris: a wolf, its mouth bristling with too many teeth and a second set of eyes mounted above the first. Before she could move—before she could even open her mouth to scream—the beast went sprawling across the ground in a spray of snow and writhing shadow. It lay motionless on its side, pierced through with an arrow. Viscous black liquid oozed out around the shaft, and smoke curled slowly up from it as though it had been singed. A faint golden light glittered around the edges of its wound.

Slowly, Clarion turned—and what she saw nearly brought tears to her eyes.

Petra stood a few yards away, brandishing some kind of weapon Clarion had never seen before. The look on her face was caught somewhere between triumph and horror. Her hair was bloodred under the cover of night, with snow gathered like a smattering of stars in her curls. Artemis stood beside her, a slash of darkness against the expanse of white, one hand resting on her hip.

"Nice shot," she said. She looked begrudgingly impressed. "And good reflexes."

Clarion could hardly believe they were really here. Had her mind not been otherwise occupied, she might have been concerned about innocent bystanders catching a stray arrow. She did not think Petra had ever aimed a weapon in her life. But right now, she could feel nothing but overwhelming gratitude.

"Go," Milori said softly. "I'm going to help the others find their way to the Hall of Winter."

"I'll be right behind you." She held his gaze, seized with a sudden bolt of fear. If anything happened to him . . . No, she could not even think about it. "Be careful."

Milori nodded tightly. "You, too. I'll see you soon."

He turned, the fabric of his cloak snapping behind him, then took flight. Clarion could not completely swallow down the knot of anxiety in her throat as his glow was muted by the heavy snowfall. Milori could handle himself, she assured herself. She'd be at his side again soon enough. Tearing her gaze away from where he'd vanished, she ran through the snow to Artemis and Petra.

"What are you doing here?" After a moment, something more pressing occurred to her. "*How* are you here?"

Petra let her weapon drop to her side. As if it were the most obvious thing, she said, "We weren't going to let you do this alone. As for the how . . . my prototype coats might be ugly, but they get the job done well enough."

Clarion drank them in. The two of them *did* look ridiculous; they were drowning in fabric. The coats were oversized patchwork monstrosities, clearly made of whatever Petra had found lying around Tinker's Nook. Clarion couldn't help laughing through the burn of tears at the back of her throat.

"She also wanted a chance to test her other prototype." Artemis stared covetously at Petra's weapon. She lifted her own, which—while otherwise more or less identical—looked held together with a dream rather than anything concrete. To Clarion's untrained eye, it seemed to be a scout's bow nailed into a thin wooden block. A long groove ran down its center, where an arrow would be nocked. The bowstring, once pulled taut, was held in place by a mechanism released by a trigger. "Or at least, *mine* is a prototype."

"That's why you need to stay close to me," said Petra, with an almost roguish smile. "All my efforts have finally paid off."

"Your efforts to ruin a perfectly good bow and arrow," Artemis muttered, with no real heat behind it. "It takes all the artistry out of it."

Petra jabbed an accusatory finger at her. "There *is* artistry! You just don't appreciate—"

"Wait." Clarion's stomach twisted into a knot. "*This* is what you've been working on? Not the sword?"

Artemis and Petra fell silent. The tension fizzled in the air between them.

"Of course." Petra gave her a wobbly smile. "I would have told you earlier, but I never exactly got the chance."

Clarion flinched at the reminder of their fight, but before she could speak, Petra barreled onward. "I mean, I was working on Elvina's sword, too. But after a certain point, most of my time was spent making it look convincing."

Clarion furrowed her brow. "Convincing?"

"It doesn't work." It burst out of Petra, a confession of guilt she could no longer contain. "If she finds out—"

"She's not going to find out," Artemis interjected, a little wearily. This had the air of a conversation they'd had at least twice before.

"—then I'll be exiled for real this time!"

"It doesn't *work*?"

Petra paused to consider it, collecting herself. "Well, I suppose it works insofar as sunstones channel sunlight. So it's not a stretch to think it would work on the starlight governing-talents wield. . . ."

The mention of governing-talents, evidently, reminded Petra of her more immediate concerns. "The point is, it won't do what Elvina wants. I was going to tell her, but you seemed to think you knew what you were doing, and—"

The rest of her sentence fizzled into nonsense. All Clarion could latch on to was this: "You lied to Elvina?"

Petra's face went very pale, then vaguely green. "I guess I did."

But Petra *never* lied. Clarion could hardly process it. "Why did you do that?"

"I don't know." Petra dragged her hand down her face. "By the time I'd done it, it was too late. And now, when she finds out—"

Artemis sighed. Diplomatically, she said, "We both believed in you." She slid her gaze pointedly to Petra. "Even when we worried about you."

Guilt chased away Petra's panic. "I'm sorry about earlier. I shouldn't have been so . . ."

"Judgmental?" Clarion supplied.

"Right. That." Petra winced. "I'm sorry for involving Elvina when I knew that was the very last thing you wanted. I panicked, just like I always do. I worried you would do something foolish. I didn't want you to get hurt."

"I know. And I suppose you weren't wrong," she choked out through a laugh. Clarion could have wept then and there—from relief or regret, she wasn't entirely certain. There were still so many things knotted up between them, but for now, this was enough. It had to be, when she did not know if they would make it through the night. "I'm sorry, too. I shouldn't have—"

"We'll talk later," Petra said softly.

"Later, then." Clarion did her best to swallow down the sudden wave of emotion. She gestured vaguely at the weapon Petra was holding. "What exactly is this thing, anyway?"

Petra brightened. "Oh, this?"

Apparently, it was some sort of Nightmare-vanquishing contraption. At least, that was what Clarion gleaned from the enthusiastic—and very technical—description Petra had launched into.

"I've decided to call it a T-bow. Or maybe an X-bow? I'm still working on the finer details, but you can load it with pixie dust–infused arrows. Obviously, it isn't quite as potent as governing-talent magic, but I hypothesized . . ." Petra trailed off, her face going pale. "You know, I don't think the science behind it matters right now."

The end of her sentence broke off in a squeak. Clarion turned to see the Nightmare Petra had shot earlier beginning to knit itself back together. Its mist-like form collapsed and bubbled as it attempted to rise to its feet. They didn't have much time before it could strike again.

"What's the plan?" Artemis asked, ever pragmatic.

"Most of the winter fairies have taken shelter in the Hall of Winter," Clarion replied. "We need to ensure their safety first and foremost. We'll meet Milori there, secure the entrance, and regroup. Understood?"

Artemis saluted. "Understood, Your Highness."

Petra loaded another arrow and locked the string taut. The tip of it sparkled, filling her eyes with golden light. Her face had taken on that familiar, eerie calm; she'd entered the same mindset as when a deadline loomed so close, it left no space for panicking. "Let's do this."

Standing between them and the Hall of Winter was a veritable sea of Nightmares. They would not reach it without a fight. But as Clarion looked back at Artemis and Petra, their eyes blazing bright with determination, she decided it felt like one they could win.

21

They set out for the Hall of Winter, carving their path through knee-deep snow and dark thickets of trees. On foot, it was maddeningly slow going. The blizzard raged on, all lashing snow and rending winds. Ice scraped against the exposed skin on her face, and cold, as sharp as a blade, slipped into her very bones. Clarion did not know if the weather was the influence of the Nightmares, or Winter itself howling its battle cry.

"It's not too much farther now," she called back to Artemis and Petra.

How she hoped that was true. It was difficult to tell where, exactly, they were going. But the sound of skirmishes reached her:

shouts and roars made distant as the storm snatched them away. Although she could see and hear little, the Nightmares' power lingered like a low-hanging fog. It slithered over her skin, setting her every nerve alight with dread.

Here and there, she caught glimpses of Nightmares flying overhead: skeins of writhing shadow blotting out even the darkness of the clouds. They took no notice of the trio as they doggedly pursued the fleeing winter fairies. Panic constricted Clarion's chest.

She sent up a silent wish to the stars: *Let them fly fast.*

It had been a mistake, Clarion thought, to let Milori forge ahead alone.

By the time she spied the Hall of Winter—its ice-hewn doors gleaming with the soft blue light of its runes—she was burning with anticipation. They stood at the top of a hill, staring down into the bowl of the valley where the Hall was carved into the mountainside. From here, Clarion could see the chaos unfolding before her.

The Hall of Winter was completely besieged by Nightmares.

Scouts ushered terrified fairies inside the cracked-open doors, doing their best to manage the frantic press of the crowd. Another group soared through the air, goading on the Nightmares as they lured them away from the Hall. And there, at the center of it all, surrounded by a phalanx of scouts, was Milori.

Her heart leapt as admiration and relief tangled together within her. She had never seen him move like this, with an efficient, ruthless grace. He unleashed blasts of sheer cold, the air bristling with ice crystals as it froze Nightmares mid-strike. The beasts jittered and raged beneath the frost, threatening to break free, and more still descended from the skies.

For now, they were holding. How long could they fend them off?

Artemis reloaded her bow. Her dark eyes glittered as she scanned the scene below them. "There's so many of them."

Clarion understood clearly what she'd left unsaid: *Too many.*

"We only need to hold them off until daybreak. They'll need to hide from the sunlight."

But daybreak was still hours away.

The runes etched in the Hall of Winter's doors shimmered as a Nightmare struck the ice. The protective wards were powerful, but against an onslaught of monsters . . .

"Until daybreak, then," Artemis said, her expression cool and undaunted. "Your orders?"

"Cover me. I'm going to the doors. After that, help the scouts keep the Nightmares occupied. Don't do anything risky." When Artemis gave her a wry half smile, Clarion added, "Just stay alive."

They charged forward, into the fray. Her friends flanked her: Petra, her red hair trailing behind her like a comet; Artemis, her lips pulled back in a feral snarl.

Here in the valley, the oppressive atmosphere was as unbearable as it had been at the prison. All the negativity the Nightmares exuded pressed down on them like a smothering hand. Cold sweat prickled on the back of her neck, and the stale tang of fear burned at the back of her throat. All around them, Nightmares rippled like swaths of dark, tattered fabric. Scouts sailed past, their haunted expressions made skeletal in the orange light of their own glows.

The hordes were seemingly endless. Nightmares peeled off from the shadows and materialized out of the snowfall like wraiths. Together, Clarion and her friends picked off the Nightmares that drifted into their path. They fell to arrows and starlight. Under the heat of Clarion's magic, some of them began to disintegrate, but they skittered toward the shadow of the woods.

Cowards, she thought.

Out of the veil of snow, a dark shape appeared. A deer loomed behind Artemis, its antlers dripping with shadowy venom.

"Artemis!" Clarion shouted.

Artemis jerked in surprise. On reflex, she unsheathed her sword and stabbed into the beast's leg. Its form rippled like water as the blade passed harmlessly through it. Slowly, the shadows of its flesh solidified around her weapon and wrenched it away from her. As its hoof came down to dash her against the ground, Artemis dodged with only the softest intake of breath. A second blade materialized in her hand. She was twirling it through her fingers, preparing to swipe at the deer again, when Petra skewered it with an arrow blazing bright with pixie dust. The deer bellowed, staggering away from them as oily blood poured from its wound.

"Thanks," Artemis said gruffly.

That had been too close for comfort.

Clarion studied the two of them. A thin line of scarlet had opened across Artemis's cheek, and while Petra looked calm, her arm was trembling from supporting the weight of her bow. Even Clarion felt exhausted, with her magic fizzling within her.

"Go," Petra said. "Don't worry about us."

Reluctantly, Clarion nodded. She ran toward the Hall of Winter. Through the clamor and seething of battle, she found her true north: Milori.

A group of Nightmares burst forth from the blizzard, descending on her. She stumbled backward, nearly tripping over her own feet. Without thinking, she threw her hand out, unleashing a bolt of starlight. The beasts reeled back from her power, contorting themselves to avoid being burned. By the time they scattered, she was panting heavily with exertion. She did not know how long she could keep this up.

"The queen is here!" a scout shouted from overhead. "Fight on!"

Rallying cries broke out through the valley. Clarion looked down at her trembling hands before curling them into fists. Her power was a symbol of hope. Right now, maybe that was all they needed.

Clarion sprinted the rest of the way to the Hall of Winter, unleashing another beam of starlight at a Nightmare readying itself to lunge at Milori. It was knocked aside, screeching in anguish. He whirled toward her, shock and gratitude plain on his face.

She rushed to his side, and in the brief lull, she took stock of him. "You're all right."

His fingers skirted along her jawline, just for a moment, before his hand fell back to his side. "As are you."

She had no time to reply, for the Nightmares she'd disoriented had recovered. They prowled closer, their low growls and the clacking of their talons against the ice echoing off the mountainside. Clearly, they hesitated to draw too near to her. None of them had regained their forms completely. Some slunk haltingly toward them; others rose like wildfire smoke and encircled them, swathing them in a veil of darkness.

Clarion and Milori exchanged looks before pressing their backs together. Frost swirled around him as gold pooled in her palms. As the Nightmares lashed out at them, they fell into the rhythm of battle. She wielded her magic like knives, slicing through the Nightmares as they lashed out. They offered little resistance against her; her light sheared effortlessly through the darkness. But she'd never drawn so much on her power; with every beast she felled, the more she faltered.

One in the shape of a rat struck her with its tail, and she was knocked hard against the mountainside. Her breath escaped her in a rush, and white exploded across her vision. She recovered just as a blast of ice knocked it away from her.

Milori pulled her to her feet and did not let go. His eyes were wild with concern, and his fingers curled urgently around her forearm. "You've done enough, Clarion. You should go inside."

"No," she forced out through gritted teeth. "I can keep fighting. We have to hold them off until daybreak."

There was something almost resigned glimmering within his eyes. Clarion saw the truth there: he did not expect to last until dawn, but he did not intend to stand down. A knot of emotion pulled taut within her. She could not deny it looked hopeless. Carried by the storm raging behind them, more and more Nightmares were pouring in.

Clarion rested her hand atop his and held his gaze. "I'm not leaving you. You can't ask that of me."

She saw the moment his restraint gave way. His expression crumpled, and for one torturous moment, he leaned his forehead against hers. Quietly, he said, "We've evacuated as many as we can. We should recall everyone still outside and prepare to make our final stand."

Final stand. Those words sent a shudder through her. Nevertheless, she nodded. "You get the scouts. I'll find Artemis and Petra to make sure they make it back on foot."

He took to the skies, shouting the retreat order. Clarion searched for her friends in the chaos. Eventually, she spotted Artemis and Petra locked in battle with a Nightmare-bobcat.

She darted across the field toward them. The shrieks of Nightmares filled her ears. She dropped into a roll as something sprung at her. A bolt of gold soared down her arm and knocked it back. Her heart in her throat, she scrambled to her feet—just in time to see the beast sink its teeth deep into Artemis's shin. Artemis screamed in agony. It shook its head viciously, thrashing her; Artemis's body snapped back and forth like a rag doll.

"Artemis!" Petra shouted.

She sent an arrow flying toward it; it narrowly missed its

shoulder. The bobcat swiveled toward Petra. Petra's eyes were wide and glassy with fear.

A Nightmare-bat swooped toward Clarion. She gathered starlight in her hand and shot it down—only for another to pull her down to the ground. The monster pinned her beneath its weight. She struggled wildly for a moment before magic erupted from her. The beast wheeled backward, freeing her from its crushing grip. Clarion crawled forward before hauling herself back to her feet. Her bones ached. She'd cut into her own lip with her teeth. Her hands trembled too much to channel magic in anything but spurts. But she could not stop.

A short distance away, she saw the faintest glimmer of pixie dust falling out of the sky: another one lost. It sent a wave of agony through her, but there was nothing Clarion could do for them now. She could focus only on Artemis, her face gone ghostly pale and glistening faintly with sweat, her leg crunched into an odd angle—and gleaming bright, visceral red.

The Nightmare-bobcat had advanced toward Petra. Venom coated its claws, gleaming violet in the darkness. As Petra struggled to nock another arrow into the bow, the Nightmare swiped at her. She went soaring, then slammed into the trunk of a tree. A sickening crack split the silence. Her weapon clattered to the ground and skidded across the ice, far out of her reach. Petra lay very still, her red hair splayed out in the snow like a bloodstain. Her eyes were closed and her face was fixed in a mask of horror.

Entrapped in the Nightmares' spell.

No, Clarion thought. *No, no, no.*

How many fairies had fallen today? How many more would? She'd lost so many. And now, she'd lost Petra.

The force of her emotion tore through her, then exploded outward in a blinding arc of light. Her magic reflected off all the ice and snow until the valley was as bright as day in the dead of night. All the beasts swarming the Hall of Winter howled in agony. It was almost pitiful, how they scrabbled to escape. They writhed and contorted themselves into a thousand different shapes, desperate to be free of the ruthless illumination of her power.

Within its splendor, all the Nightmares were revealed: small and cowering and pathetic, exposed for the small things they were. Magic poured out of her relentlessly, incinerating them. When the light finally faded, wind sighed through the valley. What remained of the Nightmares scattered, carried through the air like grains of black sand.

And Clarion collapsed onto her knees.

22

Clarion felt hollow, as though someone had scraped the very marrow from her bones. The glimmer of starlight she usually sensed within her chest had gone as cold as ashes in a hearth.

Although exhaustion dragged her down, although her vision flickered black, she crawled toward Petra. When she at last made it, she let out a choked sob. Petra's freckles seemed to disappear into the waxy pallor of her complexion. Her eyes roved behind closed lids, haunted by something Clarion could not see—something she could not save her from. Clarion could not bear it. She could not bear the weight of her failure any longer. She wanted to curl up in the snow beside her and surrender. She wanted to sleep for an age.

It would be so easy to sleep.

She did not know how long she knelt there before she heard the crunch of footsteps in the snow beside her. Clarion tipped her head toward the sound. Milori and Yarrow stood above her, wearing twinned looks of concern. She felt cold in a way not even the longest, most bitter night of Winter could manage. She felt it down to her very soul. It made her blood sluggish—and her thoughts even more so. Everything felt so unreal, she could not be certain if they were there at all.

"See Artemis first," Clarion murmured. The words felt thick in her mouth; she could hardly force her lips to make the shape of them.

"The healers are seeing to her," Milori replied softly.

"Good." Her eyes fluttered shut. "It's so cold."

Distantly, she registered that Milori was speaking to Yarrow in low tones. She caught only fragments: ". . . too pale . . . do something . . ."

He was talking about her, she thought. Clarion forced herself to focus on Yarrow's reply.

"I can't do anything if there's no wound to treat. The strain she's put on herself . . ." The healer trailed off. "It's bad, Milori. She's entirely depleted. She needs to go back to the warm seasons immediately. Their healers will know what to do with her."

Am I dying? she wondered. She felt so disconnected from her own body, the prospect hardly frightened her.

"Neither of her friends is in any condition to take her back," Milori said. "I can get her to the edge of Spring."

"And if you can't find any warm fairies?" Yarrow demanded, her hands curling into fists at her sides. "Our scouts warned them of the attack. I can't imagine anyone will be waiting at the border."

His expression darkened. Clarion did not like the determined set of his jaw, the resigned squaring of his shoulders. An inchoate feeling of dread swirled through her, far worse than anything the Nightmares had inflicted on her. "Then I'll do what I must."

"Milori," Yarrow said warningly.

"I understand the cost."

"Do you really?"

Clarion caught a glimmer of the pain that lit Yarrow's eyes—and how she offered no further protest when Milori knelt beside Clarion. He slid one arm underneath her and hoisted her up into his arms.

He beckoned over a scout-talent and whistled for Noctua. In an instant, the owl fluttered down from her perch. With the scout's help, Milori hoisted Clarion onto Noctua's back, then climbed on with her. The downy warmth of Noctua's feathers comforted her.

As they took to the Winter skies, Clarion's vision began to fade in and out. She could only faintly make out the planes of his face, gilded in moonlight, and his hair, a streak of snow white against the starlit sky. The storm had cleared, she thought hazily. He looked so beautiful—and so sad. Sensing her gaze on him, he glanced down at her. The worry creasing his brow broke her heart. More than anything, she wanted to take it away from him.

But in this moment, she was powerless.

She felt nothing but emptiness within her. A disconcerting numbness had taken over her entire body. If she let go, she thought she might drift away. It sounded so very tempting. Her eyelids were impossibly heavy. Through the snow matted in her eyelashes, she watched the stars dim. They were calling her name.

Clarion.

Or was that Milori?

"Clarion," he said firmly. "Stay with me."

She was so tired. But if Milori had asked her to stay . . . well, there was little in this world that she would deny him. Anything in her power to give was his. Her words were slurred when she said, "Talk to me."

There was a moment of silence before he let out a breathless sound, as though he could not believe what he was about to say. "Did you know that I saw your star fall?"

At that, the tiniest spark of warmth kindled in her. Blearily, she smiled. "Really?"

"Really."

She forced her eyes open at the tenderness in his voice. Haloed in celestial light, he seemed almost otherworldly. He gazed down at her with fierce desperation, equal parts adoring and pained. It made an ache bloom within her, an emotion she could not name bubbling to the surface of the murky pond of her thoughts.

"I didn't know at the time that it was bringing us a new queen. I'd never seen a shooting star before; they fall so quickly. But I caught the exact moment it soared across the sky. I remember feeling so . . ." He trailed off, his voice softening. A bittersweet smile stole across his face. "I had not felt hope in a long time, but I felt it on that night. I even made a wish."

A wish? One was not supposed to share their wishes, she knew. It tended to render them powerless. But surely, if it had been made upon her own star, she could keep it safe for him.

As if he sensed the turn of her thoughts, he answered. "I wished that there could be a different future for me in Pixie Hollow," he said quietly. "One where I was not bound to the Nightmares. Where maybe our worlds were not so divided."

A beautiful wish. When she allowed herself to envision it, her heart filled with longing. He threaded his fingers into hers and brushed his lips against her knuckles.

"There will be," she whispered. "I promise."

If it was the last thing she did, she would make his wish come true.

The stars overhead glittered brighter. Wonder filled Milori's expression as their light danced on the snow fluttering around them. When his gaze found hers again, she could not remember how to draw breath. How beautiful, to see the exact moment he fell in love with her. Perhaps he had always loved her, on some level, ever since that night he allowed himself to hope again. But with darkness encroaching—with her mind floating somewhere beyond her—she could not convince herself she hadn't imagined it.

Surely, she thought, something so lovely had to be a dream.

By the time her vision came into focus again, they had landed.

Clarion was curled on her side, still nestled safely in Noctua's feathers. It took her only a moment to realize they'd stopped at the border of Winter and Spring—and that Milori was no longer beside her. With a jolt, she struggled to lift herself onto her elbow. But with her strength sapped, she collapsed once more. She could only groan weakly as the world tilted on its axis.

From this vantage point, she could see little but snowflakes gathering in her hair and twirling lazily before her. White moonlight glittering on the surface of the river. And there, along its banks, deep trails of footprints, layered over top of one another. Milori had been pacing, she thought—was *still* pacing. He trudged into view again, wearing an expression that verged on despondent.

What happened?

Clarion's head ached with the effort of remembering. Here, with the cold making its home within her, the answer eluded her. Everything seemed so far away, as though she were observing herself from a great height.

"What are you doing?" Clarion managed to ask. Her own voice sounded garbled.

Milori startled, clearly shocked to find her awake. After a

moment, his features settled into grim composure. "Nothing. Where are your healers?"

She furrowed her brow, struggling to concentrate. "Feverfew Fields."

"Where is that?" Desperation clawed into his voice.

The answer clearly mattered to him. She could hang on to consciousness, just for a little longer. "The edge of Summer and Autumn."

Milori drew in a steadying breath. "All right, then."

At the resolve in his voice, it occurred to her—far too late—why he had asked. Memories flooded back. The swarm of Nightmares. A detonation of light. Milori, determined to return her to the warm seasons. A bolt of urgency cut through her delirium: *He can't.*

If he crossed the border, he would break his wings.

There had to be some other way. If she could find the strength to walk, or even stay astride Noctua . . . But no, she could hardly twitch a finger. Even her trembling had stopped, as though her body had given up hope of ever getting warm again. Her only chance was her magic. Although she had never managed to teleport, Elvina had taught her the theory behind it. If she could manage it just once in her lifetime, it had to be now. She reached deep within herself and felt as though she scraped her nails against the bottom of a dry well. A soft gasp of pain escaped her. There was nothing left.

And so, there was no other option.

"Leave me," she rasped.

As he drank her in, his panic slowly melted into agony. Both of them knew that in this state, she was far more likely to fall than to make it to the healers intact. "Your glow is almost entirely extinguished."

She supposed it was, now that he mentioned it. Distantly, she noted her sallow skin; the night, without a glow to push it back, settling over her like a pall. Clarion felt no pain, but the look in his eyes gutted her: utterly helpless. It was as though he were dying along with her.

There was some argument she'd intended to make, but it was slipping away from her. It was too hard to force the words out. Too hard to cling to consciousness. As her eyes fell shut, he let out a strangled sound. With a flutter of his wings, he floated onto Noctua's back and gathered her into his arms.

"Milori . . . stop."

He did not answer her. He only took the reins in one hand and snapped them, urging Noctua into flight once more. He did not even flinch as they soared over the border. Passing into Spring felt like plunging into hot water. As it flooded over her, Clarion wanted to sob in both relief and horror. A winter fairy had no protection here.

"Please." Her lips formed the word, but it came out as a bare wisp of sound.

Had he heard her at all?

With her head lolled against his shoulder, all she could see was his jaw set in determination and his steely gaze fixed straight ahead. His pale skin had already begun to flush. Sweat beaded at his temple. Leaned against him as she was, she could feel his heart racing.

The heat was too much for him.

"Your wings." Her voice was thick with emotion. When had she begun crying? It had come on so suddenly.

"Clarion." He said her name like a plea. "Weighed against your life, they are nothing to me. I would make that trade every time."

Those words nearly broke her. Tears slipped freely down her cheeks, but she had no strength left to brush them away. She could hardly focus on him; the world swam, marbled by the rheum in her eyes. "Why?"

"Pixie Hollow needs you," he said quietly. "As warden, I have a duty to defend Pixie Hollow. That means protecting you."

If only she had the wherewithal to argue with him . . . She would rail against him with everything she had. How could his own safety mean so little to him? But she'd been reduced to a captive in her own body, forced to watch as he sacrificed himself for her. It was the worst kind of torture she could imagine.

"Be angry if you must," he said, "but I can't lose you."

Miserably, she understood she would do the same.

What fools their hearts made of them.

Clarion knew the moment they crossed into Summer. Below them, it was a blur of lush greens and golden blooms. But its heat sighed over her skin as though welcoming her home. Water trickled down her neck as the snow tangled in her hair melted. Slowly, sensation returned to her extremities. She did not want it, not when it felt like a thousand needles piercing her once-numb skin. The warmth of the air, however, did nothing for the cold within her. Her chest was as dark and empty as the space between stars.

Milori's breathing grew ragged, stirring the hairs curling around her face. This was, by far, the most dangerous place in Pixie Hollow for him. At night, at least, it was only muggy—nothing like the sweltering afternoons beneath the punishing sun.

The familiar scent of feverfew wafted up to her. When Clarion turned her bleary gaze outward, she saw every white petal drenched in moonlight. Never before had it looked so beautiful, or so horrible.

"There," she said miserably.

When they alighted in the field, Milori slid off Noctua's back and landed heavily, as though he could barely support his own weight. He approached the door to the healer-talents' clinic with slow, staggering steps. Clarion could not look away from his wings. They were folded against his back, but they seemed to be . . . wilting.

No, she thought. *Melting.*

They dripped from the ends like icicles in the thaw of early spring. The very sight of it made her stomach roil with nauseous waves of guilt. She could not imagine the resolve it took to push through that kind of pain. He knocked, his fist falling weakly against the door.

Within moments, a healing-talent appeared on the threshold, backlit by the illumination filtering out from within. Clarion could not hear what they were saying from here, but she could imagine the general shape of their conversation. She watched the emotions tear through the healer as Milori spoke: confusion giving way to shock—and then to the grim calm born from urgency.

She nodded to him, then disappeared back into the clinic. The door, she left ajar. A messenger firefly crawled through the gap and set off toward the Pixie Dust Tree, its belly blinking with the emergency signal.

Milori returned to her. "I'm going to have to move you."

With a soft grunt of effort, he lowered her from Noctua's back. He scooped her into his arms and carried her into the clinic. His skin, usually so cold against hers, felt feverishly hot. Candles burned dimly, melted down to puddles of wax in their shallow dishes. The soothing smell of healing herbs—minty chickweed and acrid burdock root—perfumed the air. The only thing she could concentrate on was the rhythmic *drip, drip, drip* of his wings against the floorboards.

"Back here," someone called to Milori.

Milori made his way haltingly through the clinic. In the near dark, Clarion couldn't make out much, but she knew when they passed beneath the curtain of succulents. Their waxy leaves clattered together and brushed almost tenderly across her face. He took her to the room reserved for fairies in critical condition. It still did not feel quite real, even as he laid her in the cot. Her teeth chattered. Milori unfastened the brooch at his throat and laid his cloak over her. Thinking of her, even now.

"Go," Clarion whispered. "Please."

He looked stricken. "I can't." He knelt at her bedside. "Not yet."

"*Please.* Milori." She fumbled for something, anything, to sway him, but she had nothing. She could barely make sense of the sounds that had come out of her mouth. Through her delirium, she could see the sheen of sweat on his face. She could hear the healers shouting at one another. Clarion registered only fleeting sensations. Cool water at her lips. Glimmers of pixie dust. The prick of a needle. And warmth, slowly, slowly returning. She did not know if it was minutes or hours or days that had passed when she heard a voice.

"Warden?"

Elvina, she thought. Her tone was guarded but held nowhere near the hostility she'd lobbed at him earlier this evening.

Clarion cracked open her eyes, just barely, to stare up at the candlelight thrown onto the ceiling. It wavered hypnotically as the flame danced atop the wick. How strange, to be shrouded in such complete darkness. Her wings were as transparent as darkened glass. Only the faintest motes of starlight glittered within them.

"I needed to know if she'll be all right," Milori replied, his voice hoarse.

Elvina made a sound, somewhere between admiration and disbelief. "You must leave now. Return to Winter before it's too late."

Neither of them spoke. For a moment, Clarion believed they had been nothing but figments her addled mind had conjured, now vanished.

But then, Elvina said, "Thank you."

She did not need to clarify.

"She'd do the same for me," Milori said.

Clarion scrabbled to cling to those words. But darkness crept in at the corners of her vision. The last thing she heard before she slipped under again was:

"She's worth protecting."

23

When Clarion awoke, the soft glow of lanterns filled the private recovery room with warm light, shining on the vials and jars lining the shelves. The skies outside her window were striated with bands of deep blue and orange as the sun peered out from the horizon line.

I'm alive, she thought hazily.

She'd lived to see daybreak after all.

Even beneath the covers, the cold lingered below her skin and coiled around her heart. Experimentally, she curled her fingers. Still attached, mercifully. Nothing had been lost to frostbite. She peeled back the blanket and breathed a sigh of relief to see her wings twinkling faintly in the predawn dark. The whorls of gold threaded through them had returned, even though the radiance they emitted had dimmed.

When she rolled onto her side, her gaze snagged on the cloak draped over the bedside chair.

Milori.

The very thought of him was an icicle lanced through her heart. When she closed her eyes, burned there was the memory of his wings wilting as they dripped onto the floorboards of the clinic. The devotion and agony knotted together in his voice when he told her, *I can't lose you.*

Maybe Elvina was right.

If she cared for no one, if she'd kept herself removed as she ought, none of this would have happened. If Milori had left her on the border, the stars would have righted their mistake. Perhaps another star would have fallen that very night to replace her. Another fairy with golden wings, with a heart that matched her talent: one poised and practical, one who did not yearn for things she couldn't have.

Instead, he'd ensured Pixie Hollow would have her, in all her imperfections, for the entirety of her long life. She wanted to scream. She wanted to swipe the vials from the shelves and listen to them shatter. She wanted to turn back time—to do everything in her power to save him from his own selflessness.

How could he have done this?

No, how could *she* have done this? If anyone was to blame for this, it was her alone. She'd been selfish enough to pull him into her orbit. A queen was not meant to live among her subjects. She could not mingle and embroil them in things beyond the scope of their talents. She had always been destined to be alone.

It was time she stopped fighting it.

"Clarion."

She startled, blinking hard at the sound of her name. In her disorientation, it took her a moment to process that the room had brightened. Late-morning sunlight poured through the window, softened as it filtered through the leaves, and bathed her face gently in its warmth.

She must have fallen asleep again.

Blearily, she touched her cheek. Tears had dried on her skin, stinging her face with salt. She swiped at them with the back of her wrist. As her vision adjusted to the daylight, Elvina came into focus. She sat in the bedside chair with a deep exhaustion written into every line of her face. A pang of guilt dropped into Clarion's stomach. Had she kept vigil over her all night?

"You're awake," Elvina said, her voice thick with relief. "Thank the stars."

Clarion propped herself up on her pillows. "Where are Petra and Artemis?"

A small smile tugged at the corner of Elvina's lips, as though she had expected such a question. It faded just as quickly as it arose, replaced with a queenly mask—the one she reserved for relaying bad news with calm detachment. "They're both here. I saw the warden briefly before he left for Winter. He asked us to send healers to the border to collect them."

Of course, she thought. Even when he was suffering, he'd thought to coordinate with Elvina on how to get them home. "How are they?"

"Artemis will have a long road to recovery, but she's in stable condition. Petra is asleep, like the others."

Clarion's throat constricted. "And Milori?"

Elvina hesitated. "He did not look well."

"I see."

Clarion squeezed her eyes shut. As much as she wanted to believe he had returned unharmed, she could not be so naively optimistic. No winter fairy could remain in the warm seasons without consequence. If she thought about it any longer, she did not know that she could hold it together.

Elvina watched her rein in her emotions. When she had composed herself, Elvina said, "You were right, Clarion."

Clarion gathered up the corner of her blanket and dabbed at her eyes. A humorless laugh escaped her. "About what?"

"About the warden." Her mouth twisted into a little moue of displeasure, as though it wounded her to admit that she was wrong. After a moment, she sighed. "About everything. My plan was shortsighted at best—and incredibly dangerous at worst. Our realms should be working together."

Clarion had wanted to hear those words for so long. And yet, she could hardly believe them. "Where is this coming from?"

"He saved your life," Elvina replied matter-of-factly. She folded her hands in her lap. "For that, I owe him a debt."

Then there was still a chance to make this right.

Perhaps her magic had not been powerful enough to bind the Nightmares as the dream-talents' once had. But the Keeper's book had also spoken of a Nightmare dwelling in the depths of its prison like a queen bee in her hive. One powerful enough to command its drones—to hold all of their power.

Clarion's starlight had obliterated every Nightmare outside the Hall of Winter. If she defeated the Queen Nightmare, surely its slumbering spell would break. But she was still recovering. And besides, every attempt she had made to help had only worsened things in the end.

"You can help me. Together, with our governing magic, we can destroy the Nightmares," Clarion said.

"I can't." Elvina smiled ruefully. "My power is waning."

"Waning?" Her voice sounded terribly small to her own ears, almost childlike.

Elvina opened her hand. Starlight bloomed like a rose in her palm, unfurling slowly. It burned steadily—but certainly not as bright as Clarion was accustomed to. Elvina closed her fingers, extinguishing it. "I can't manage much more than this anymore."

She had never heard of a fairy's talent *lessening* over time. "Why?"

"It is the way of things," said Elvina. "Soon after your coronation, I will return to the stars, just as all the queens before us have."

"I don't . . ." Clarion shook her head. She could not process it; she refused to. Elvina's words blurred into meaninglessness.

If that were true, then surely she would have seen the signs.

Elvina looked no different, did she? But then, Clarion could hardly remember what she'd looked like when she first arrived in Pixie Hollow. Was there new gray in her hair? Had she always looked frail, her bones birdlike and delicate beneath her pale skin? Fairies lived long lives, queens even more so than most. But they were not supposed to simply die of something as mundane as *age*.

"I don't understand," Clarion said at last.

"I'm sorry, Clarion." Elvina's voice wavered, just barely. Her brow furrowed with the pain she tried and failed to master. "There are so many things I should have told you. I should have told you sooner, but I didn't know how."

Clarion did not want to hear this. For so long, she had wanted Elvina to trust her with the truth. Now, it felt like too much to bear. Tears burned in Clarion's throat as Elvina reached out and brushed a strand of hair behind Clarion's ear.

"I have never been to the Mainland myself, but I have heard extensive reports about it. Humans love their children from the moment they are born. They raise them in the hopes that they will be better than their parents ever were." Elvina's fingers lingered on Clarion's chin. "When I saw you rise from that star, I think I understood something of what mothers must feel. I know how difficult and confusing it is to be told from the moment you draw your first breath that the world depends on you. And how you know it in your heart to be true.

"I saw so many ways that you were like me, but I saw many more ways that you were not. Experience had taught me many lessons, most of them hard-won and painful. I wanted to protect you from it. I did not want you to get hurt. You are precious to me." Elvina let her hand fall away. "The weight of a queendom is heavy, and our lives are long. And all the fairies you love will eventually fade away while you remain unchanged. I kept myself apart so that I might not grieve more than I could bear. I encouraged you to do the same, although I could see how much it pained you. And you tried so hard for me."

Clarion's heart ached for her, more than she ever thought possible. She saw Elvina as the girl she'd been and the woman she was now—one with an existence long and lonely and shaped by loss. Elvina had tried to shield her from harm. In the end, her best efforts had only left a new kind of scar—a distorted mirror of Elvina's own wounds. But at last, Elvina had set them both free. Clarion could choose for herself what kind of queen she wanted to become.

I wished that there could be a different future for me in Pixie Hollow, Milori had told her.

The thought of him—of a wish she carried safe within her—stirred something in her. Starlight kindled in the cold hollow of her chest, swirling through her like the comforting warmth of a fire in Autumn. Perhaps she could make that dream a reality for them both. Perhaps a good queen *was* like the star from which she was born. Not one cold and distant—but one that carried her subjects' hopes forward.

If it was the very last thing she did, she had to make his sacrifices matter. She had to protect Pixie Hollow—and everyone she cared for—with all she had. That, she decided, was the kind of queen she was.

"I think I understand now," Clarion murmured. "Thank you, Elvina. For everything."

"Of course." She looked somewhat surprised. "Now rest and recover your strength. We will find a way forward together."

Together. It sounded like such a sweet concept. But this, she had to do alone. No one else would be hurt because of her failures.

When the door fell shut behind her, Clarion held to that determined spark of hope within her. It glowed, warm as an ember, then fanned itself brighter. To end this, she would have to face the Queen Nightmare alone—before it broke free.

She would have to go beneath the ice.

On the third day of her convalescence, Clarion plotted her escape.

She did not know if she would ever truly be ready to face the Nightmares again, but if her impending coronation had taught her anything, it was that one would never feel entirely ready for difficult things.

She waited until sunrise stained the horizon line bloodred

and the morning sounds of Summer filtered through the cracked-open windows of the clinic. By now, Clarion had become attuned to the rhythms of life here. In these twilit hours, the healers kept up a steady stream of chatter in the next room over, gossiping about some workplace drama or another. Nothing terribly interesting, from what Clarion could gather. The cheerful cry of finches and soft calls of mourning doves filled the lulls in their conversation.

It was now or never.

Her winter coat lay folded at her bedside, and when she shook it loose, it was intact, notwithstanding a few bloodstains. It would survive at least one more trip into Winter. All that remained was leaving the clinic without being spotted. Which meant she would have to clear the last hurdle of governing-talent magic: teleportation.

She had never managed it before. But right now, with starlight burning steadily within her, she felt nothing but calm certainty. Clarion shrugged on her coat and jiggled the window the rest of the way open. Best if her first real attempt was not through a solid object, she decided. She drew in a deep breath and closed her eyes.

Now, if she just imagined herself growing lighter and lighter . . .

A radiance emanated from within her. When she lifted her hands to eye level, she could see her edges growing fainter and feathering out into golden sparks. The knee-jerk bolt of panic was quickly replaced with delight. Bit by bit, she dissolved into a shimmering cloud of pixie dust. As if summoned by her whims, the breeze kicked up. It danced through the leaves and carried her on its gentle current. She drifted through the open window, as soundless and shapeless as mist creeping down the mountainside. She drifted over the feverfews and made her way to the tree line. As soon as she was safely ensconced in the shadow of the woods, she allowed herself to take shape again.

She had done it.

Clarion laughed, a disbelieving sound. She felt disoriented and unsteady on her feet, but a quick glance down confirmed that all of her had indeed made it through. No limbs left behind—a success in her book. But she had no time to marvel at what she'd done.

Clarion took to the skies and set off for the border. Now that the spark of starlight within her had rekindled, the cold that had burrowed into her bones had begun to lift. Her glow was nowhere near its usual radiance, but the sunlight soaking into her wings felt almost healing. With every wingbeat, golden sparks danced through the air around her.

Below her, Needlepoint Meadow was a vast sea of green. Sprinting Thistles winnowed through the tall grass, occasionally knocking into one another in their haste. It was unusual to see so many of them crowded together, but Clarion soon saw the reason: a long, blackened strip of field, like a scar carved into the earth. The thistles must have been flushed out of their homes by the Nightmares. Determination flared within her, fanned by her anger.

Once and for all, she would end this.

When she arrived at the border, she felt a pang of both relief and sadness that the bridge stood empty. *Good,* she thought. It would make her task easier if she did not have to convince Milori to stay behind.

Clarion fastened the buttons of her coat and crossed into Winter. She stepped off the bridge and tipped her head toward the sky. For a few moments, she lingered here: breathing in the crisp air and the scent of the evergreens, savoring the nip of cold at her cheeks, watching the snowflakes tumble wildly down. She'd never seen the Winter Woods in the daylight. The snow glittered as though it were inlaid with diamond, and the ice scattered golden light across the ground.

Beautiful, she thought.

It amazed her how a place could carry both such joyful and painful memories. But she wanted to remember Winter like this: a friend, holding its companionate silence with her. The wind wove through her hair, tugging almost playfully at the ends.

"It's time to set you free," she murmured.

From here, it was a long journey to the Nightmares' prison. If only she could summon Noctua . . . Clarion frowned as the idea came to her. It certainly couldn't hurt to try. She brought her fingers to her lips and whistled.

Nothing happened.

Slowly, she dropped her hand to her side, feeling quite foolish for having attempted it. But then, an inquisitive hoot sounded just above her.

Clarion gasped. "Noctua!"

The owl swiveled her head to inspect Clarion. Somehow, she managed to look quite incredulous. Clearly, she had not expected *Clarion* to call her. Nevertheless, she hopped down from her perch and ruffled her feathers in greeting.

Too giddy to remember her fear, Clarion all but skipped forward and trailed her fingers against Noctua's beak. Her hand looked so fragile against the deadly point of it. How quickly, she thought wryly, she had lost her every instinct of self-preservation. Perhaps Milori had been a bad influence after all. Hopefully he would not mind terribly if she borrowed his pet.

"Sorry," she said softly. "It's just you and me today."

Noctua blinked slowly. Clarion could not be certain, but it seemed like acceptance.

Clarion stared up at her as a terrible realization sank in: she would be riding alone. But she'd practiced enough, surely. And the risk of falling was far outweighed by that of hiking. She *did* have to make it there before nightfall, after all.

"All right," she reassured herself, "you can do this."

Taking hold of the reins, Clarion climbed onto Noctua's back. Once she'd found her balance, a grin stole across her face. That wasn't so difficult. Now, what was it Milori did to make her go? Ah, that was right. Tentatively, she snapped the reins.

Noctua took off like an arrow. And because she was alone, Clarion did not bother to stifle her scream.

They burst from the canopy in a shower of snow and pine

boughs. The sun reflected off Noctua's wings, painting the edges of her feathers with an iridescent sheen. The owl barreled forward at full speed as the reins slipped uselessly through Clarion's fingers.

She bent low over Noctua's neck, her unbound hair whipping wildly behind her. After a frantic moment of scrabbling, she seized hold of the reins and choked up on them. Noctua tossed her head in protest.

"Whoa!" Her voice was thready, half terror and half delight.

With control wrested back, Clarion steadied herself. It took all the strength of her thighs and forearms to keep her seat, but she was doing it. With a flush of triumph, she urged Noctua onward to the Nightmares' prison.

Now she understood why Milori loved to fly owlback so much.

They soared high over the pines and birches, diving only once Clarion spied the eye of the frozen lake. They landed on the shore, and Clarion dismounted. Her legs wobbled, and she steadied herself against Noctua. She lingered at the owl's side, staring out over the glittering expanse of the lake. Even in the cold light of morning, that oily feeling of dread bore down on her more relentlessly than it ever had before. She fought to suppress her shudder.

"Wish me luck."

Noctua pecked at her shoulder, which she decided to interpret as well-wishes.

Clarion walked toward the shore with slow, unsteady steps. The ice seemed thinner than it had the last time she was here; it shifted and popped beneath her weight. But it was only when she reached the center that Clarion saw the wreckage of the barrier she and Milori had created. Shards of ice glittered like a mess of broken glass, and the delicate strands of starlight had been snapped as though they were nothing more than spiderwebs. The prison had cracked open wide enough to release all but the largest Nightmares. Perhaps governing-talent magic truly was incompatible with dream magic, or perhaps the Nightmares had grown too powerful to be contained any longer. Whatever the reason, Clarion would ensure they never harmed another fairy again.

In the daylight, whatever remained beneath the ice was eerily still. But Clarion could feel their eyes boring into her as she stared down into the world beneath the lake. Would it be freezing inside? Would there be water after all, ready to drag her down to its darkest depths? The uncertainty clawed at her. She had made it this far, and there was really only one way to find out.

She jumped in.

24

Clarion anticipated a splash, a rush of cold. But as she slipped beneath the ice, there was nothing but open space and blackness enveloping her. Her fall slowed, then stopped entirely. Even with her wings bound beneath her coat, she floated somewhere above the bottomless abyss, suspended in total darkness. A crawling sensation spread over her skin, akin to the feeling of a predator's eyes fixed on her from the underbrush.

Something was watching her.

Clarion suppressed a shudder and tipped her head back. From here, she could see the crack in the prison she had entered through—and just beyond, spears of gauzy light filtering down.

The sun illuminated the ice from above, casting strangely beautiful patterns around her. The world above was blurred and tantalizingly out of reach. She could almost understand why the Nightmares wanted to escape so desperately. There was nothing at all down here: no light, no sound, no scents. It unsettled her terribly.

Then, there came a steady *drip, drip, drip.*

Clarion's breath caught in her throat. It sounded too much like . . . Shaking her head to dispel the thought, she demanded, "Who's there?"

No reply but *drip, drip, drip.*

The sound ricocheted through her mind, maddeningly loud. With every drop, guilt and horror climbed up her throat like bile. She whirled toward the sound and channeled her power. Starlight pooled in her palms, but the curtain of shadows did not lift. The sensation of unbearable pressure—of malice—intensified. But she saw a thin wisp of white against the dark.

Milori.

She caught only a glimpse of his hair streaming behind him as he retreated with slow, faltering steps. It reminded her too much of how he had looked the other night, dragging himself up the stairs to the healers' clinic.

"Milori?" she called. Her voice echoed endlessly in the darkness.

He did not acknowledge her.

Abruptly, her feet struck solid ground. She stumbled as she caught her balance. Nothing had appeared beneath her that she could see, but with every step forward, the blackness rippled under her feet as though she'd alighted on the surface of a still, dark pond. Gradually, she broke into a run. She had to catch up to him.

What was he *doing* here? And where was he going?

"Milori!"

She chased after him. But no matter how quickly she moved, no matter how far they traveled, he never seemed to get any closer. The darkness churned around her, the shadows slithering and swimming and closing in.

A shift in the air pressure. Then, something lunged at her.

Clarion ducked, barely dodging the snap of teeth as they closed over her head. She fired a bolt of starlight at it. Whatever it was shrank back, hissing its fury at being thwarted.

Her heart pounded in her throat; her hands, set aglow by her magic, trembled. How was she supposed to fight when she could hardly see her enemies? But she could not dawdle here; she could not lose Milori in a place like this.

When she looked up, she saw him standing in the near distance, staring at her with those piercing gray eyes. Clarion charged toward him. The closer she got to him, the more the world began to take shape around her in shades of charcoal.

Silhouettes of trees loomed out of the dark. Grass sprouted, waving in a wind she could not feel. Her feet knew exactly where to carry her, which obstacles to step over, as though this were a dream she had wandered through many times before.

This wasn't Winter anymore.

Milori turned and walked away from her with purpose, heedless of what the heat would do to him. No, she thought. What it had *already* done to him.

She could not watch this happen again.

Clouds gathered overhead, limned by a sinister violet glow. It felt like the moment before a lightning strike—like the moment before a Nightmare attack. Every hair on the back of her neck rose, and her skin crawled with a formless anxiety. Her mind had emptied of every thought but *I have to stop it.*

The air thickened and settled heavily in her lungs. It smelled like decay: a foul, sickly-sweet vegetal smell that made her stomach turn. She recognized this place now: the last stretch of woods before she would reach the river that divided the Pixie Dust Tree from Summer.

As she pressed onward, she would have sworn she heard screaming.

Briars surged from the earth, barring her path. Clarion shoved her way forward and tripped, her boot catching on an upturned vine. She sprawled across the ground, skimming the skin clean off her hands. Blood welled on her palms and dribbled down her wrists. But the pain hardly touched her. When she looked up, what she saw rooted her to the spot. It made her entirely numb with horror.

The Pixie Dust Tree was rotting.

Viscous black liquid dripped from the ends of its branches, and all the leaves had gone slick with decomposition. A sickly rot licked up the sides of the trunk, bubbling and oozing. But worst of all, it had put out feeble new growth: wispy clusters of rhododendrons and black roses, barely managing to unfurl.

Danger, it said. *Despair.*

Help me.

Pools of Nightmares rose from the spongy ground at its roots, clawing their way toward the Pixie Dust Well. Everything about the fairies' world depended on the survival of the tree. Without it, there would be no pixie dust. No home. Nowhere for newborn fairies to land. Pixie Hollow would be gone—and without Never Fairies, what would happen to the Mainland?

"No," Clarion choked out. "No, no, no."

Clarion forded the shallows of the river, nearly frantic in her desperation. She was sweating in her winter coat. Why was she wearing a winter coat at all? The few Nightmares she saw, she blasted insensately, hardly even looking to see whether her blows landed or if they stayed down.

When she reached the other side, she grabbed the first fairy she saw by the shoulder. "What happened?"

He recoiled from her, disgust plain on his face. There was something in his eyes that she had never been confronted with: hatred. It contorted his features into a horrible rictus and set his eyes aglow. The sight of it rattled her to her very core.

"You did," he spat.

Me?

He wrenched away from her. Clarion whirled around to find that a small group had gathered behind her, huddled close as they watched the heart of their queendom putrefy. All of them glared at her with pure loathing. Mutters spread through the group, low and baleful. She could pick out a few words here and there:

Cold. Uncaring. Undeserving.

Mistake, mistake, mistake.

It rang in her head: the confirmation of all her worst fears.

No, she could still do something. She could still save them. Hadn't she come here to save them? Panic obliterated all sense as she fled to the base of the Pixie Dust Tree. Fairies lay scattered across the roots, still as corpses beneath the Nightmares' spell. Some of them had begun to sink into the rotting earth. And there, against the stain of black rot, was the spill of Petra's red hair.

"Petra!"

The earth bubbled like bog water, dragging her down into the depths. Clarion plunged her hands in, gagging on the stench, and dragged her out.

"Petra," she said pleadingly. "Please, wake up. I'm sorry."

Petra's eyes cracked open. Clarion let out a strangled sob. If nothing else, then there was some good in this world. Some small mercy.

"You," Petra said, full of venom. She sat up slowly, staring unblinkingly at Clarion. "You did this to me. You refused to listen to me when it mattered the most. You are so *selfish*."

Clarion scrambled backward—directly into someone else's

shins. She craned her neck and found herself staring directly into Elvina's dispassionate face.

"You are an utter disappointment," said Elvina with a curl of her lip. "Why did the stars send *you*?"

"I don't know," she whispered, curling in on herself. "I don't know."

She wished they hadn't. The weight of the crown had always been too much to bear. How had she ever thought she could shoulder it all? Being born a governing-talent was a mistake. No matter what she did, it would never get any better. It was always destined to end up this way.

Pixie Hollow, ruined. Her, alone and reviled.

Darkness flowed off the river, encircling her like fog. What was the point in fighting back?

"Clarion!"

She knew that voice, but from where? She dared to lift her head, but it felt so heavy—and her eyelids even more so. All she saw were the cruel faces of those who loved her best and hated her most bitterly. At least they were vanishing slowly, as this darkness closed in around her. If she let herself, she could drift off to sleep forever.

"Clarion." The voice sounded far more strained than it had before, edged now with a hint of desperation. "It isn't real. You have to wake up."

Milori. What was he doing here?

He couldn't be here in the warm seasons. And yet, hadn't she seen him only moments ago . . . ?

No, she realized. She wasn't in the warm seasons at all. She was beneath the ice, deep in the Winter Woods. The fog had enshrouded her entirely, so choking, she could barely draw breath. If she focused, she could see the violet light of the Nightmares' magic threaded through her surroundings. *An illusion.* Like all those fairies trapped in their slumber, she'd been cast into the Nightmares' realm.

She bit down on the inside of her lip, hard enough that the pain startled her awake. The horrible nightmare version of Pixie Hollow fell away, revealing nothing but the swallowing darkness beneath the lake once more.

Clarion fought through the malaise and harnessed her power. Starlight poured from her in beams, and the darkness binding her fell away, like fabric sliced to ribbons. She fell to her knees, landing hard on the invisible, glass-like water beneath her. Her teeth rattled together. But with the light of the magic reflecting off the ice overhead, she realized now what had taken hold of her: a sickly purple smoke, curling upward from a massive creature's nostrils. She let out a shaky breath and scrabbled backward to get some distance.

A guttural hiss cut through the silence. Two reptilian eyes blinked open—and locked on to her with a vengeance. She saw now what had been lurking in the deepest recesses of the prison.

The Queen Nightmare.

A dragon.

Clarion could not fathom how such a thing existed. She did not know how she was supposed to face something like this. Her terror rooted her to the spot. Her hands trembled violently, and that spark of starlight within her felt terribly small in the face of something so immense. Fear was not only raw, instinctual terror, or death nipping at your heels. It was this, too: despair.

The dragon opened its mouth to reveal row after row of serrated teeth, and a sulfuric light spilled into the darkness between them. It took her only a moment to realize that it was a ball of fire, ready to be unleashed.

"Clarion!"

Clarion startled at the distant sound of Milori's voice. She looked up to find Milori, banging on the ice from above. His face was indistinct, but she could see the desperate *belief* shining out of him.

"Don't forget what you promised me!"

It jolted Clarion out of her stupor—enough to startle the faintest laugh from her. It had been such a beautiful wish—one worth fighting for.

No, she could not surrender now.

Within her, she carried the dreams of the thousands who had seen her star falling. For one moment, they'd felt hopeful or desperate enough to shed their cynicism and entrust their wishes to her. As long as she had them, she could not succumb to despair.

As the flames rushed up the dragon's throat, Clarion squared her shoulders. She was the Queen of Pixie Hollow. And this beast? It was a child's fear, given shape and left to fester for far too long.

In the harsh light of day, it was nothing at all.

Clarion burned like a star: inexhaustible and obliterating. Golden light exploded outward, filling the prison. The dragon bellowed as, strand by strand, the horror and doubt that had made it unraveled. Threads of darkness unspooled, crumbling into ashes as they floated through the air.

In the end, nothing but this remained: twinkling motes of starlight, transforming what had lain empty into the endless brilliance of the night sky.

25

When the starlight winked out, Milori pulled her from the depths of the lake. As soon as he guided her onto solid ground, the ice knit itself shut behind her, like a wound finally healing—and underneath, Clarion could see dark waters churning. Just like that, it was as though the prison had never existed at all.

She had done it.

Slowly, she eased herself back onto the smooth mirror of the lake's surface and stared up at the sky. Cold seeped in through her coat, but she found she didn't mind. Time had slipped away from her beneath the ice. Night had fallen like a curtain over Winter, but it was positively luminous with celestial light. An aurora borealis unfurled through the sky in broad, billowing ribbons. Once upon a time, perhaps, dream fairies would have soared beneath them, gathering them into their baskets. But now, they shimmered tantalizingly out of reach, their magic as wondrous and mysterious as the night itself. They haloed Milori, painting him in soft greens and blues.

"How did you know to come here?" she asked, unable to keep the wonder out of her voice.

"You stole my owl," he said, with a touch of amusement. "Who else but the queen would dare do such a thing? It wasn't particularly difficult to figure out where you might have taken her."

Clarion flushed. "To be clear, she let me steal her."

Milori laughed. He looked so boyishly, uncomplicatedly happy, she couldn't help laughing, too. She took hold of his arm and pulled him down on the ice beside her. He came willingly. For a moment, the two of them lay side by side like a couple of stargazers. Slowly, Clarion splayed her fingers out across his chest and propped herself up to peer down at him. His hair pooled around him, a spill of white against the muted blue of the ice.

For just a little longer, she wanted to stay here, where nothing existed but the two of them. Clarion traced his jawline with the tips of her fingers. She leaned over him, her hair spilling over her shoulders to curtain them.

"You have your wish," she murmured. "What will you do now?"

Milori gathered up the weight of her hair in one hand, brushing it back from her face and draping it over her shoulder. Despite the chill of his skin, her entire body warmed at his touch. "Truthfully, I don't know. It's felt like such an impossible dream for so long. I've never let myself consider what would happen if it came true."

Fortunately, she had given this some thought in the hours she'd spent trapped in bed. "Well, if I'm going to grant your second wish . . . I want you on my court. Not as the Warden of the Winter Woods—but as the Lord of Winter."

Milori blinked in surprise. His voice was wary, but his expression was full of tentative hope. "We have not had a Lord of Winter in a long time."

"And that is a shame." She would hear no argument. Clarion sat up and offered her hands to him. When he accepted them, she tightened her grip on him, as though she could press her confidence into him. "You deserve your ancestral title returned to you. We have three Seasonal Ministers and no involvement in Winter. It makes no sense to exclude you."

"Your other ministers may not feel the same," he said, but she could tell she'd won.

"They will see reason." Clarion canted her chin, earning herself a smile from Milori. On aching limbs, she stood and helped him to his feet. "Or I will make them see reason as soon as I am queen. Each of us has resources and expertise to share."

"Very well. I will accept your offer." He put on a good show of sounding deferential, but the smallest of smiles curled on the corners of his mouth.

"It will be my first decree," she said. "Never again will our two worlds be at odds with one another."

"Never again," he agreed softly.

In the ensuing silence, reality pierced through the dreamy bubble of their victory. There was still much to do to make this vision a reality. And now that they were safe, now that he was standing here in front of her, she had to address what had happened. Reluctantly, she let his hands go.

"How is . . . ?"

Her words failed her, but she did not need to finish her question. His eyes filled with terrible, somber comprehension.

"It's broken," he said.

He turned around, and the quiet joy of this stolen moment evaporated. Her gaze followed the delicate, whorled patterns on his right wing down to its end. For a moment, the horror of it was something her mind refused to process. The bottom half of it looked as though it had melted completely, then frozen again into jagged edges.

The force of her emotion knocked the breath from her. Guilt and shame were shackles around her wrists, dragging her down toward despair once more. "Milori . . . I'm so sorry."

"Clarion," he said, with some iron in his voice. "I don't regret what I've done, nor do I blame you for what happened. I'd do it again if given the opportunity."

Her vision blurred with unshed tears, but she blinked them back fiercely. "You should have left me on the border."

"No." Milori turned to face her, resting his hands firmly on her shoulders. The flash of vulnerability in his eyes devastated her. Beneath his gaze, she could almost believe she was something precious and irreplaceable. "I couldn't have done that. This will be an adjustment, yes. But in Winter, scars like this are a sign of honor, and it isn't as though I'll never fly again. I have Noctua."

She knew, of course, that it was all true. For what he'd done, he'd be recognized as a hero. And yet, this should have been so *avoidable*. "You didn't even hesitate. Why?"

"I think you know why, Clarion."

His voice was low and gentle—and so achingly bittersweet, she could hardly stand it. Of course she knew why. It was the same reason her heart was shattering now.

As she stared up at him, into his earnest gray eyes, the immensity of the feeling that overcame her seemed like both a revelation and an inevitability.

She loved him.

Perhaps she was always bound to, from the very moment she saw him standing on the border. How could she not? She loved his steadfastness, his kindness, even his reckless, selfless bravery. She loved his wry humor and his unshakable devotion to his people. She loved him because he had set her free, too.

And yet, he had broken her heart.

If anything happened to him, she would not survive it. And Milori, loyal to his very core, would throw himself in danger for her time and time again. Now, she saw the full truth of Elvina's wisdom. Love opened you up to too much pain. Love divided your allegiances, your priorities. For most anyone in Pixie Hollow, it would be acceptable, but for the Lord of Winter . . .

It was too dangerous to love her.

"I do," Clarion whispered.

The warmth shining in Milori's eyes faded as he drank in her expression. "I understand if you don't feel the same, but I—"

"It isn't that." Her voice trembled. No, she could not cry now. She could not bear for him to doubt her conviction. But it felt too difficult to breathe through the pain in her chest. She hadn't known it would feel like *this*—as though her heart were truly crumbling. "You can't. It will impede your ability to lead."

"No." Milori looked like a man in free fall, as though he could find nothing solid to hold on to—like everything he believed he had was rapidly slipping through his fingers. "You don't know that—not for certain."

"It will impede *my* ability to lead." It already had. She would sooner see Pixie Hollow rot, her worst nightmare brought to horrible reality, than see any harm befall him ever again. "I would make every decision thinking of you. I would risk anything, *everything*, to protect you. Do you understand? I love you, Milori. It scares me too much."

"I love you, too," he said miserably.

Hearing those words nearly undid her. *Good*, she thought. *Let this pain serve as a reminder of how desperately needed our separation is.*

A love like theirs was ruinous. A broken wing was nothing compared to a broken heart. She could only hope that the pain of both would fade with time.

She armored herself with resolve—with resignation. When she spoke again, her voice was even. "I will ensure the world we both dreamed of exists. But no one else should have to endure what we have. Crossing the border is too dangerous. It should be forbidden. Effective immediately."

There was no blame in his expression, but what she found there—something between a plea and a challenge—hurt to look at. His eyes, usually the placid silver of moonlit water, now seemed to her the slate gray of the Never Sea, deep and wild. They would pull her under.

"If that is truly what you want," he said, with more composure than she expected, "I will uphold your rule."

"It is." Her very soul cried out in protest as she spoke those words. "It is what I want."

But as soon as the last word fell like a stone between them, she realized what a fool she'd been to believe he would make this easy for her. She did not know which of them moved first.

They crashed together, and his mouth was on hers with a desperation that left her breathless. She met him with equal fervor. Her world narrowed to this: His hair, slipping through her fingers like water. His hands, skimming down the ridge of her spine and spanning the curve of her waist. He drew her closer, as if he wanted to erase all the space between them. As if they could ever be close enough. As if she could express the depths of her longing for the time they'd never have.

They broke apart, their breaths ragged. He leaned his forehead against hers and cradled her face in his hands. He traced her cheekbones, the line of her jaw, the bow of her lips, with such reverence, it was as though he was committing every detail to memory. Dimly, Clarion registered the dampness of tears on her face. Whose they were, she did not know. With the pad of his thumb, he swiped them away.

"All right," he said quietly, once he'd set her to rights. His touch fell away, leaving her bereft. "Let's get you back across the border."

Please, she wanted to say. *Just a little longer.* Instead, her voice little more than a whisper, she replied, "All right."

He whistled for Noctua. Within moments, the span of her wings blotted out the moonlight. As Clarion climbed onto her back, she refused to think about how this might be the very last time she ever rode on owlback. She could not dwell on all the winter fairies she would never get to meet and all the wondrous places she would never venture. Never again would she hear the crunch of her footsteps in the fresh-fallen snow. Never again would she feel the dance of the cold northern wind in her hair. Never again would she walk alongside the sparrow man she'd once thought so stoic. He'd never taught her to skate.

Stars, she was not strong enough to do this.

"Will I see you again?" he asked, so softly she almost did not hear him.

"I've decided I want my coronation to take place where *all* my subjects can be in attendance, on the border. So if you'll come . . ."

"Of course," he replied. "I wouldn't miss it."

For a moment, they held each other's gaze. Clarion tore hers away first, if only to keep herself from weeping anew.

When they arrived on the border, a group of fairies was waiting for her on the Spring side. Scouts flitted up and down the riverbank, and there, a bright beacon of gold in the darkness, was Elvina. Even from this height, Clarion could make out shouts of surprise and alarm. It almost made her smile. How sad that none of them would ever know the friendship of an owl.

Noctua landed silently. When Clarion slid off her back, a quiet awe fell over the warm fairies. Clarion wanted to sink to her knees in the snow. She wanted to be alone, if only to allow herself to feel the full weight of what she had done.

But her subjects needed her.

With her shoulders drawn back, she stepped onto the bridge. And when she crossed into Spring, she did not turn around. If she did—if she felt that invisible tether between them snap taut, calling her back to his side—she might just change her mind. But this, she knew, was for the best.

One day, she hoped she truly believed that.

All the way back to the palace, fairies fixed her with curious looks—and, perhaps for the first time in her life, spoke to her unprompted.

The scouts escorting her and Elvina back to the Pixie Dust Tree began peppering her with questions she did not—or could not—answer.

"What is the Warden of the Winter Woods like?"

"How did you manage to defeat them?"

"Will the spell be broken?"

The barrage lasted until they arrived at the palace—until they crowded around the door to Clarion's quarters with their bright, eager eyes.

"Let your queen rest," Elvina said, with a glower that could curdle cream. "You will have quite enough time to interview her later."

With a hurried chorus of "Yes, Your Majesty," they scattered.

Clarion shot her a look of gratitude. With a knowing smile, Elvina ushered her inside. The door fell shut, and Clarion wasted no time in dragging herself to bed. She shucked off her winter coat, letting it pool on the floor at her feet, then flopped face down onto the mattress. It dipped beneath Elvina's weight as she sat beside her.

Even without looking at her, Clarion knew she was waiting . . . for whatever would come out, she supposed. In truth, she herself did not know what she would say until she spoke: "It's finished."

And it was: both the Nightmares and whatever she'd had with Milori. Right now, she felt mercifully numb.

When Elvina did not reply, Clarion turned her head enough to look up at her. It was not pity in Elvina's eyes but an ancient, terrible understanding. It was strangely comforting—and strangely beautiful, to be known without having to speak a word.

There was so much Elvina had not told Clarion about the workings of their world. There was so much more she had not told Clarion about *herself*. Had she been hurt like this, too? It seemed impossible to imagine that Elvina had fallen in love—even more so that she had ever made any sort of fatal mistake or miscalculation. But she'd admitted her wisdom had not come easily.

The gulf between them had felt nigh impossible to bridge for weeks, but now, this shared pain bound them together. Perhaps, with whatever life Elvina had left, she would guide her forward.

Of all things, that was what finally broke the floodgates.

Her tears flowed down her face, hot and relentless. Her sobs racked her body. To her utter shock, Elvina enfolded Clarion in her arms and let her weep in her lap like a child.

"I made many mistakes with you," Elvina said quietly. "Perhaps even with myself. How terribly sad that I can see it only at the end of my life. You were here for only a blink, and yet, you have taught me so much."

"Don't go," Clarion whispered. "Please, please, don't go."

She heard Elvina's soft intake of breath. "Even I cannot defy the stars. But you will be fine without me, Clarion. I feel very confident leaving Pixie Hollow in your capable hands."

Clarion's chest constricted painfully. All her life, she had longed to hear those words. How sweet, to finally have the assurance she'd craved. Only, she was not so certain she deserved it. She had saved Pixie Hollow. She'd mastered her own magic. But she would live the rest of her life with the stain of her mistakes.

How could she ever teach new arrivals to fly? How could she dare to unfurl their wings with the tenderness they deserved when she would always remember the ones she had broken?

Elvina's voice cut through the fog of her despair. "It's good to have a connection with Winter. Unifying the seasons is a very strong way to begin your reign. You will have to apologize to your Warden of the Winter Woods on my behalf."

Hers. No, she did not have the right to claim him any longer. "I don't know if I can see him again."

Elvina frowned. Whatever she saw in Clarion's eyes, she seemed to understand. "Just rest—and I do mean it this time. There is still much to do before your coronation."

In this state, rest would not come easy. But Elvina gently stroked her hair and did not protest when Clarion wound her arms around her waist. Despite how broken and how wretched she felt, it was such a comfort to be held.

"Once upon a time," Elvina began—and whispered to her all the pretty stories she once had back when Clarion first arrived, of valor and love and queens long gone.

Clarion drifted off to the soothing rhythm of Elvina's voice. She dreamed of snow and starlight. Of clear gray eyes, full of forgiveness she would never truly earn.

26

Clarion stirred awake to find her room drenched in late-afternoon sunlight. It disoriented her to have slept so long, but her eyelids still felt heavy enough that she would drift off again if she let them fall. This exhaustion was nothing like her burnout, the devouring cold that had spread through the hollow of her chest, but it was still so tempting to curl up again and . . .

Petra. The thought startled her into full consciousness. She had to check on her and the others.

Clarion threw off the sheets. It had been so sweltering beneath them, even the close air of her room felt cool against her skin. On her nightstand, three things waited for her: a bowl of porridge, gone cold from how long it had been sitting out; her daily ration of pixie dust, bundled neatly in a leaf sachet; and a letter, stamped with the royal seal.

What could Elvina have to tell her?

She retrieved the note and carefully slid her finger beneath the wax seal to open it. Even without the royal insignia, she would have recognized Elvina's perfect handwriting.

Come to the clinic as soon as you're able. The spell has broken at last.

Clarion's breath escaped her in a tremulous rush. Weeks of stress, of worry, lifted from her in an instant. Pixie Hollow was finally free.

And she would get to see her best friend again.

Clarion pulled on the first gown she could find, then poured the pixie dust over her wings. She sighed in contentment as its sweet smell suffused the air. From across the room, she caught a glimpse of her reflection. Flecks of gold clung to her eyelashes and glinted in her loose, sleep-tangled hair. Her eyelids were swollen from crying, and the creases of her bedsheets were pressed into her face in thin red lines. It hardly mattered what she looked like. She could not wait another minute to leave.

She flung open the doors of her balcony. The Pixie Dust Tree greeted her with the soft shift and sway of its foliage, rustled by the breeze. For a moment, Clarion allowed herself to linger. She rested her hands against the railing and leaned out over the edge. Pixie Hollow sprawled before her, vast and beautiful in the golden-hour light.

Soon, all of this would be hers to protect.

And for perhaps the first time, she felt equal to the task.

Feeling lighter than she had in weeks, she took flight. It felt terribly unusual not to be sneaking around for a change. There were no watchful scouts patrolling the skies. No nausea, half from the thrill of it, half from the dread of being caught. No comments from Artemis as she took off toward Winter.

Artemis.

Hopefully she was on the mend as well. Clarion would see her soon enough.

As she soared over the Summer Glade, she grinned to see that Pixie Hollow had returned to normal. The sound of laughter and singing reached her, even from this height. Garden-talents drifted over Feverfew Fields, coaxing new growth to life. As they worked, the scents of rich loam and bitter herbs intensified, carried on the breath of the wind.

Clarion landed in front of the healers' clinic, where the golden-hearted flowers gave way to lush grass. Toadstools sprung from the earth, their wide caps serving as the clinic's front porch. She flitted upward to clear the distance, then alighted on the porch. Immediately, her heart leapt with joy.

"Artemis!"

The scout was sitting in a rocking chair, her right leg extended out in front of her. It was set in a brace made of two thin strips of bark bound together by a grass-woven rope. A staff was propped up beside her, nestled in the crook of her neck and shoulder. Her dark hair was shaggier than Clarion had ever seen it, and her eyes were still shadowed with exhaustion. At the sound of Clarion's voice, her expression softened with relief.

With a flutter of her wings, Artemis rose from her seat, steadying herself with her staff. She did not say a word. She only closed the space between them, the tip of the staff thunking rhythmically against the mushrooms' caps. Then, she pulled Clarion into a hug with one muscled arm slung around her neck. Her grip was crushing, but Clarion did not dare complain. It was unlikely she would ever extract such open affection from her again.

"You did it," Artemis said against her hair.

"I couldn't have done it without you." Clarion drew back and studied her. "How are you feeling?"

"Nearly back to normal, Your Highness."

Clarion gave her a flat look, one that said, *Be honest with me.* Artemis was leaning heavily against her staff. Even though fairies rarely walked, small differences in their weight distribution could make it quite difficult to balance mid-flight. She'd need a mobility aid until the splint was removed, at the very least.

"I have been better." Artemis wilted, clearly displeased at having to admit it. "Do you mind if I sit?"

"Of course not," Clarion replied. "At ease."

Shooting her a grateful look, Artemis carefully lowered herself back into the rocking chair. She stretched out her leg, mindful not to jostle it. "The pain is manageable, and soon, they won't have to stop me from escaping anymore."

"No escaping," Clarion chided. "That is an order, by the way. You need to heal."

"Yes, Your Highness." Artemis smiled faintly. "If you'll approve an exception, the healers have cleared me to go to your coronation. A queen should not be without her guard."

"I do approve, of course." Clarion frowned. "But I think you've more than earned a different post. After I'm crowned, I'm happy to reassign you to—"

"With all due respect," Artemis interjected, "I am happy with my post. If it's all the same to you, I'd like to keep it."

"You want to stay on my guard?" Clarion asked incredulously. "I thought you wanted to return to patrolling."

"I did." Misinterpreting her disbelief as resistance, Artemis hastened to add: "Of course, if you feel I would be better suited elsewhere . . ."

"It's not that," Clarion replied. She had been fully prepared to let Artemis go, but she couldn't deny that, deep down, she'd hoped for this. After so many years together, she hardly knew what she would do without Artemis. "I'm only curious what brought on this sudden change of heart."

"I used to believe that serving as your guard was my atonement. Perhaps even a punishment." Artemis's mouth twisted into a rueful smile. "That regaining my position was the only way I could make a difference in Pixie Hollow. Over the past few days, I've come to doubt that my intentions were so pure. Since my reassignment, I've felt there was something I needed to prove."

"There is nothing you need to prove, Artemis," Clarion said gently. "I've always believed you are among the noblest of fairies in Pixie Hollow."

"I am glad you think so." Artemis tapped her staff against the ground pensively. "If I went back, I would have to quash that part of myself you say you admire. For many years, I've tried to do so. But seeing what you did . . ."

She trailed off, clearly searching for the right words. Clarion warmed under the reverent intensity of her gaze.

"I believe in you," Artemis said. "Your strength. Your kindness. Your vision. Protecting someone like you is a worthy use of my talent."

Oh, Clarion would get maudlin if she kept this up. Teasingly, she asked, "Are you saying you would miss me?"

"I'm saying I don't trust anyone else to be your guard," Artemis countered. Clarion took pleasure in the fact she didn't *deny* her accusation. "With your temperament, it's a more difficult job than one might expect. Even I have not been performing to my own standards recently."

Artemis eyed her. Although she would never say it aloud, Clarion read her meaning plainly: *You look terrible.*

Clarion couldn't help laughing. There was no arguing with

that. Both of them were certainly worse for wear after the events of the last few days.

"Well," she said, "I'd gladly have you. I'd miss you, too, you know."

"Good," Artemis said gruffly. "This injury will not keep me from serving you."

"I have no doubts." Clarion beamed at her. "If you'll excuse me, I'm going to check on everyone inside."

"Of course, Your Highness." Artemis bowed her head. She hesitated, as though uncertain of her next words. At last, she said, "The last I checked, the tinker hadn't awakened. When she does . . ."

Clarion squeezed her shoulder reassuringly as she walked past. "You'll be the first to know."

Artemis's soft "thank you" followed her into the clinic.

The air was redolent with the familiar smell of healing herbs: chamomile, marshmallow root, nettle. As the door clicked shut behind her, it occurred to her that she could hear voices—and laughter—spilling into the atrium. Clarion did not think she had ever heard it so loud in here. For the first time in weeks, the mood was almost . . . joyful. Buoyed by the energy, she hurried past the curtain of hanging succulents that cordoned off the sickroom.

It was *packed*.

Clarion could not help her delighted astonishment. Fairies had piled in with flower arrangements and pots of soup and, of course, the latest gossip. The fairies who had awoken had veritable crowds around their beds. Some chattered and laughed, ready to resume their normal lives. Others wept. Others held their friends close as they emerged from their tormented dreams.

All of them were completely surrounded by love.

So absorbed were they in their reunions, no one noticed her in the doorway—no one but Elvina, who hovered at the back of the room alongside a healer. The queen gave her a gentle smile before jerking her chin toward a cot in the corner.

She's over there, she seemed to say.

Clarion wasted no time in rushing to where Petra lay in her cot. Her red hair was splayed out neatly against the pillow, the curls glossy and perfect as they never were in her day-to-day life. Someone had clearly combed it out and twisted it into ringlets. Tidiness really didn't suit Petra. Clarion smiled, overcome by the affection that welled up within her.

Very gently, she took one of Petra's hands in both of hers. "When you wake up," she whispered, "I have so much to tell you."

And as if she had heard her, Petra stirred.

"Someone send for Artemis!" Clarion called. She only distantly registered a healing-talent reply, "At once, Your Highness!" Clarion could focus on little else but her own relief, the feeling as sparkling and light as sunshine.

Petra's eyes blinked open, glassy and unfocused in her disorientation. Then, when she saw Clarion's face hovering only inches away from her own, they went wide with shock. She let out a shriek and scrambled backward. "Clarion!"

"Petra." Clarion's voice wobbled humiliatingly.

"What are you— Oh."

Clarion threw her arms around Petra and held her close. "You're back. Thank the stars."

Petra relaxed against her. "What happened? I feel so rested. And also like I've been running for days without stopping. The last thing I remember . . ."

Clarion drew back when she felt her shudder. Petra's expression had grown haunted as the memories flooded back in.

"The Nightmares are gone now," she said. "You're safe."

Clarion filled her in on what had happened since she had fallen under the Nightmares' spell. By the time she finished, Petra was staring at her with infinite sympathy in her eyes. Clarion could hardly stand to look at her.

"I'm so sorry," they each blurted out at the same time.

A beat of silence—and then both of them burst out laughing.

"*You're* sorry?" Clarion asked disbelievingly. "Why? I'm the one who needs to apologize to you."

Petra's brow furrowed. "For the distance between us."

"Please don't apologize for that," Clarion said. "You've been nothing but a good friend to me. And I—"

"Hey." Petra rested a hand on her arm. "You don't need to beat yourself up, Clarion. I forgive you."

"You do?"

"Of course I do." Petra smiled at her. "Both of us were caught up in our own things. I know it's going to take some time to figure out how to fit into each other's lives once you're queen. But I'm not going anywhere."

"Thank you."

Before Petra could reply, the curtains over the door of the clinic rustled violently. Both of them turned toward the entrance of the sickroom. Artemis hovered a short distance away, her eyes wild with commingled fear and hope. "Petra."

Clarion had never heard her voice so fragile.

Artemis approached them, navigating the clutter and the maze of cots as best she could with her staff. Even so, she nearly knocked over everything in her haste. A healer standing at her workstation looked dismayed but said nothing. Instead, she busied herself with her mortar and pestle, grinding berries and herbs into a poultice.

When Artemis arrived at Petra's bedside, she glared down at her.

"You—" Petra began, but she was silenced when the scout placed a kiss on her forehead, then, more tentatively, to her lips. By the time Artemis pulled back, Petra's entire face was stained crimson.

"Don't *ever*," Artemis said, "scare me like that again."

"Finally," Clarion muttered to herself. Then, to them, she said, "I'll give you two a moment."

But they hardly seemed to hear her.

Her chest ached with a pang of loneliness—and something like joy, too. If she could not have happiness, then at the very least her friends deserved it. She would not resent anyone for having what she had denied herself. Her heart—and all her devotion—belonged to her subjects now. Clarion turned her attention to the rest of the clinic.

There was still one other fairy she needed to visit.

When she reached the Minister of Autumn's bedside, she sat in the empty chair and studied his face, slack and peaceful in sleep. So, this would end where it had begun.

She did not have to wait long. When he awoke—gently, easily, as though he found he'd drifted off for a nap sorely needed—his eyes found hers immediately, then crinkled into a smile. "Your Majesty?"

"Not yet," said Clarion softly.

He closed his eyes again, a relieved grin stealing across his features. "I always knew you could do it."

27

Coronation Day arrived, and it was a glorious midsummer afternoon.

Clarion waited in the wings of the ceremony grounds, hidden in a thicket of blueberry bushes. The branches overhead drooped, heavy with berries, flushing as they ripened, and delicate bell-shaped flowers. The crowd's excited chatter rose above the sound of the river's burbling—and the sound of her own racing heart. Her anticipation built with every passing moment, especially since she could see nothing through the dense leaves.

"It's time, Your Highness," Artemis said. "They're ready for you."

Clarion turned toward the sound of her voice. Artemis had

appeared beside her, announced only by the soft thunk of her staff against the earth. "That might be the last time I'll ever hear you call me that. It's going to be an adjustment."

"I think it'll be quite natural on my end." Artemis offered her a small smile. "Shall we?"

Together, they made their way toward the exit, a scrolled archway cut into the thicket. Beneath it, Elvina and the three Seasonal Ministers waited for her. The queen's features were composed as ever, but Clarion did not mistake the pride beaming out of her.

Iris gasped. "Your Highness! You're a vision."

Clarion beamed at her. "Thank you."

Her gown was pure, shining gold, with an overlay of translucent spider-silk lace infused with pixie dust. Her hair had been fashioned into the traditional braided coronet and adorned with a crown of snow-in-summer blooms.

No matter how nervous she felt, there really was no denying it: she looked like a queen—and she felt like one, too.

Rowan leaned toward her conspiratorially, the gold stitching in his cloak catching the light as it slid over his shoulder. "Are you ready?"

"We should hope so," Aurelia said drolly, "or she'll miss her own ceremony."

Iris hid a laugh behind her hand.

"I'm very ready," Clarion said. "Let's see what miracles you've worked."

"I think you'll be happy," Iris said in a singsong.

Clarion had the utmost faith in them, of course . . . but still, she had no idea what to expect. When she and Elvina broke the news that—with two days' notice—they would be moving the venue, Aurelia had reacted with a studiously blank stare. If she was disappointed or panicked, Clarion did not know, nor did she have much opportunity to wonder. Iris had twirled into the air, all but cackling in triumph.

Finally, Spring has its moment! she'd cried. *You won't regret this!*

Aurelia had glowered at the Minister of Spring, but the two of them resolved to make it happen. Rowan had seemed rather amused about the whole thing, in a way only someone with no real stake in the issue could be.

Perhaps the only benefit of being asleep for so long, he'd said with a wink.

Elvina cleared her throat, adjusting the scroll she carried in her arms. "Let's not keep them waiting any longer. I imagine they are all eager to see their new queen."

They emerged from the thicket, onto the edge of Spring. When Clarion laid eyes on the ceremony grounds, her breath caught with wonder. Beside her, Aurelia and Iris exchanged pleased glances.

They had outdone themselves.

Honeyed sunlight filtered in through the branches overhead, patterning the earth in dappled gold. Rainbows, carefully painted by Aurelia's light-talents, were draped across the clearing, unraveling across the sky like royal banners. Rows of chairs, arranged in a half circle, faced the bridge spanning Winter and Spring—and all the winter fairies on the other side of the border. Frost-talents had carved rows upon rows of benches from ice, all of them garlanded with mistletoe, holly, and delicate blossoms of snow white. It touched her that Aurelia and Iris had thought to coordinate with Milori.

"All rise," cried a herald-talent, "for Her Royal Highness, Princess Clarion."

In unison, every fairy in Pixie Hollow stood—and turned to stare at her. Never in her life had so many eyes been on her. Never before had they been so full of adoration.

Clarion couldn't help the grin that stole across her face. Murmurs and gasps of delight rang out as she and Elvina made their way toward the bridge, soon swallowed by the sound of the music-talents' instruments as they began to play. The train of her gown hovered just above the ground and billowed behind her as though borne on a river's invisible current.

She and Elvina passed through the aisles and alighted on the bridge, settling beneath an intricate arch that spanned the gap between the seasons. Of all the details her ministers had organized, this was perhaps her favorite. Winter's half of the arch was composed of birchwood, crowned with snow and delicate frost. Spring's half—woven from the moss-covered branches of a sapling—met it in the middle, where their branches twined together like interlocked fingers. Flowers from every season were woven through the structure, bursting with texture and color.

The liminal space of the border comforted her. The chill of

Winter brushed against her tenderly, like the touch of an old friend. A few stray snowflakes caught in her hair before melting. There was nowhere else she would rather be crowned: here, where she'd learned to believe in herself. Here, where she'd met the one who had both mended and broken her heart.

Unconsciously, she scanned the crowds for him. But she did not find him before Elvina began to unfurl the scroll she carried. "Princess Clarion," she said, her voice ringing in the silence, "are you willing to swear your royal oath?"

Her voice did not shake when she said, "I am."

"Do you promise to protect Pixie Hollow with your life?"

"I do."

"Will you rule these fairies gathered before you with fairness and mercy?"

"I will."

"Do you swear to ensure the changing of the seasons faithfully and efficiently?"

"I do."

Elvina nodded, and two helper-talents materialized. One carried the royal scepter; the other, a crown nestled into a cushion. Elvina took the crown first, an elegant diadem of beaten copper that Clarion immediately recognized as Petra's handiwork. Somehow, through all of this, she'd found the time to make something beautiful for her.

Carefully, Elvina nestled it into Clarion's hair. Next, she pressed the scepter into her hands. Elvina adjusted the crown once more, and for one moment, Clarion could have sworn she spotted tears in her eyes—there and gone before she could blink. When Elvina was satisfied, she turned back to the crowd.

"Then all hail the new Queen of Pixie Hollow, Queen Clarion!"

Cheers and whoops echoed through the clearing. Clarion felt her heart lift to meet them. The fairies reached into sachets and tossed pixie dust into the air. A group of fast-flyers swooped from the branches, kicking up a joyful breeze. Gold glittered and swirled through the air. Clarion could only stare out at them with emotion lodged in her throat. She loved them all so fiercely.

That love would be enough to sustain her.

When the commotion died down, she drew in a breath and projected her voice. "If I may, I would like to address you for the first time as your queen."

Immediately, the crowds fell silent. Would she ever grow used to that effect? Would it ever feel natural, filling the space they yielded to her?

"Many of you may not know me well. I have stayed apart from you since I arrived, something I regret deeply. But I would like to change that, starting today. So . . . allow me to officially introduce myself. I'm Clarion.

"I hope to get to know each and every one of you over the course of my reign. Your safety and happiness are my top priorities, so I hope to lead with wisdom . . . and a sense of humor." She smiled tentatively. "Please feel free to come to me with any issues or ideas you have. And don't hesitate to say hello. I cherish any opportunity to speak with you."

She dared to glance over at Elvina, who dipped her chin.

Go on, she seemed to say.

"Over the past month, I have learned a lot about myself and our world. Chief among the things I have learned about are our neighbors, the winter fairies." Clarion glanced over to them, nodding in acknowledgment. "I understand that for many years, they have been thought . . . unapproachable, even untrustworthy. But I have had the pleasure of meeting them. They are a vibrant bunch, with a great deal to teach us. They have welcomed me with more generosity and warmth than I could have hoped for. From them, I have learned how to hold steadfastly to hope, even on the darkest and coldest of nights. I look forward to seeing what else we might achieve together."

Cheers floated up from Winter's side of the border. She waited for them to fade before she continued.

"Without the Warden of the Winter Woods, we would not be here today." Clarion swallowed through the knot of emotion in her throat. "I say this with confidence. I would not have been able to defeat the Nightmares. Many more of us would be under the Nightmares' spell. In time, they might have taken all of us. We owe an enormous debt of gratitude to him."

At least, *she* did. She would never be able to repay him for what he'd done for her.

"And so, my first decree is to unite our realms." Purpose warmed her from within, burning as steadily as a flame. "We will provide them aid, lending them our tinkers to make improvements to their processes. Additionally, the Warden of the Winter Woods will henceforth be known as the Lord of Winter. He has governed over the Winter Woods as my proxy and should be recognized for it. He will formally serve on my council."

She paused, uncertain how the decree would be received. But slowly, applause filled the silence she had left behind. The joy—and sheer relief—she felt buoyed her. It would carry her through her next announcement.

"However," she continued, "as all of you know, their world, though beautiful, is not safe for warm-season fairies, just as ours is not safe for them. And so, today, I am officially forbidding any fairy from crossing the border. Even if we must remain physically apart, know that we are united in spirit and purpose.

"With our partnership, I want to welcome in a new era of a unified Pixie Hollow. One of hope. I will do my best. I know I will make mistakes. But I swear I will give everything I have to you."

The final words of her speech dissipated into the warm spring air. And then, she heard Milori's voice: "All hail Queen Clarion!"

Something pulled taut within her at the sound of her name. As though there were a tether binding them together, her gaze found his in the crowd. How rare it was to see him in the brilliance of the afternoon light. The sunstruck silver of his eyes transfixed her entirely.

Everyone in the clearing had seconded him, bursting into raucous applause. But they sounded muffled in her ears, and everything but *him* faded away. It was as though she and Milori alone had been plunged into some private, shared world—one outside of time, shimmering like a dream. She could not take her eyes off him. She could not guard herself against the pride beaming out of him—and all the longing, too.

She forced herself to return to reality, to focus on the happiness of this day. It was an incomplete happiness, when half of her remained where she could never reach. But right now, showered in the acceptance of her subjects, it was enough.

The party raged on for hours, riotous with joy. While the warm and winter fairies initially kept to themselves, eventually, their celebrations spilled across the border. A few braver—or at least friendlier—souls had drifted to the edge of the riverbank to break the proverbial ice. They engaged in shouted conversations and danced through the air, as close as they dared. They left food for one another on the bridge, inviting them to enjoy what each season had to offer. One enterprising frost-talent had even begun a game of catch, which lasted until the snowball tragically melted.

But as the sun dipped lower and fairies began to make their way back home, Clarion found her mood turning pensive—almost melancholy. There was still one last thing she had to do—the thing she dreaded most.

Saying goodbye.

Though their realms would work together closely, she and Milori would never again meet as they once had.

Clarion stood at the edge of the party, shrouded by a curtain of fragrant wisteria. She nursed a glass of punch: something she objectively knew was bright and tart but that she did not taste at all. Her mind was entirely elsewhere. The flowers woven into her hair had already begun to wilt in the heat, and her earlier happiness seemed quite far away now, as she knew what she had to do. But being queen was not about making easy decisions. It was about making the right ones.

Eventually, Petra found her.

She sidled up to Clarion. "What are you doing over here? Brooding?"

Clarion couldn't help the soft huff of laughter. "I suppose so. Have you come to stop me?"

Petra was dressed in a long-skirted gown of philodendron. Bracelets of polished metal—her own design, of course—clinked on her wrists as she twirled a fluted glass in her hands. With a shrug, she said, "You're allowed, if you really insist. It *is* your party."

"True." Clarion's expression softened. "The crown is beautiful, by the way. Thank you."

"Don't mention it." Petra fell silent for a few moments, contemplative. When she spoke again, there was no accusation in her voice—only a quiet sympathy. "Are you going to talk to him? He's been looking *moony* all night."

"I should. I want to." Did she, though? Seeing him again would hurt, and she'd caused herself quite enough pain today because of her own decree. Here, in the comforting dark with her dearest friend, the question she'd been wrestling with seemed far too urgent to leave unspoken. "Petra, have I done the right thing?"

"Of course you have—you're our queen." Petra frowned, hesitating, as though she were selecting her next words carefully. She studied Clarion's face, and whatever she found there seemed to solidify her decision. "But I don't think you'll ever know for certain."

Clarion sighed miserably. She supposed that was true enough.

"All I know is that we have to protect ourselves in the ways we can—and you have the lives of many others to look out for. You're doing your best." Petra nudged her shoulder with her own. "Go. I'll be fine alone."

"Thank you." Clarion squeezed her arm. "Really. For everything."

Petra offered her a gentle smile. "Good luck."

As she made her way to the border, the sounds of her party—the music, the laughter, the shouts—faded away. Here and there, fireflies shone out of the night. They lit her way, dancing and weaving around her, as if hoping to cheer her. They only parted with her when she stepped onto the bridge. It felt much like the first night she had ventured here: her determination holding back the groundswell of her fear, the cherry blossoms painted with moonlight as they fell.

The moss was cool and damp with dew. The long train of her

gown dragged on the earth. A low mist had rolled in off the river, stirred by the gentle breeze. It had shaped up to be a moody evening, with the promise of rain in the swelling gray clouds.

It took no more than a minute for Milori to arrive, as though he had been watching the bridge, waiting for her glow to appear like a beacon. Dependable, as always—and devastating. His eyes were the brightest, clearest things she had ever seen. They pierced straight to the heart of her with his quiet, kind strength. Her heart gave a terrible lurch. She did not know if she would survive losing him. But whether they stayed together or not, she would lose him. One way or another, the stars would keep them apart.

Best, then, to keep him safe from her.

The breath of space between Winter and Spring felt like an invisible barrier between them. It felt, all at once, as thick as a sheet of ice and like nothing at all.

Milori broke the silence first. "Congratulations, Your Majesty."

The cool formality of his tone knocked her breathless. All their time together, erased: him addressing her with that same impartiality he had on the night they met. It took all her strength to root herself in place, to not close the gap between them or throw her arms around him or beg him to look at her as he had only days before.

Her gaze snagged on the two beads of turquoise pinned to his tunic. They held the quills of two white feathers in place. A new cloak, she realized: one made entirely of Noctua's feathers. It looked like a new pair of wings folded against his back.

She forced herself to meet his gaze again. "Thank you, Lord Milori."

The use of his title made the last of his resistance give way.

"What point is there in pretending?" He sounded absolutely wretched. "I have thought of little else but you since we parted."

This time, she did not bother to deny her worst impulses. She embraced him, and the cold of winter sighed against her bare arms. His heart beat fiercely against her cheek. Her fingers dug into the tops of his shoulders, probably harder than they ought, but she needed something to ground her.

"Me neither," she said. "You made me believe I deserved this, and yet, you have made me feel like I would give anything to be someone, anyone, else. I would give it all back if I could."

"Please don't say that," Milori murmured. "You *do* deserve it. You are going to do incredible things, Clarion. You already have."

"And yet, I will be alone." It slipped out, too quickly for her to stop herself.

Milori tipped her chin up so that he could meet her gaze. "You will have all your subjects to love you. And even if I am not beside you, you will still have me. There will never be a star brighter. I will always love you."

Clarion choked on a sob. It was unbecoming of a queen, she thought distantly, but she could not bring herself to care. "As will I."

She took his face in her hands and kissed him—briefly, selfishly, if only to commit him entirely to memory. The feeling of his lips, soft against her own. The way his breath hitched, no matter how many times they had done this. The pleasant chill of his skin beneath her touch. The scent of evergreen and crisp air. It brought her no relief when it felt so final—and so insufficient.

This was goodbye.

Reluctantly, she drew back just enough to whisper, "Remember to be free, Milori. No more haunting this border like a ghost."

He gave her the most heartbreaking smile she had ever seen. "You, too."

Impossible, she thought. As long as she lived, she would never be free of him. There would never be another. No matter. As the Queen of Pixie Hollow, she could shoulder this pain alone. That much was her duty. Slowly, she stepped back from him. She let her hands slide down his arms, then his wrists, until at last her fingers slipped away.

"Take care, Your Majesty," he said.

She did not trust herself to speak.

When he turned away from her, a soft wind picked up. It danced through his hair and sent his new cloak billowing out behind him. She caught a bare glimpse of his wing. In the moonlight, it shone as bright and clear as a pane of shattered glass.

Clarion stayed on the bridge until he vanished into the tree cover, until the clouds overhead gave way and gentle rain began to fall. She stood alone in Spring as the scent of petrichor rose around her, staring out at the cold emptiness of Winter.

It would call her home for the rest of her long life.

ACKNOWLEDGMENTS

In some ways, I can hardly believe you're reading this. Publishing my fifth book is a milestone I could not have fathomed reaching when I began writing "seriously" in 2016. And if you had told me back then that one day I would write something for Disney Fairies, I don't think I would have believed you. Dreams really do come true.

First, I want to express my immense gratitude for being trusted with such a beloved world. I hope this book felt like a homecoming for some of you. And if this is your entry point to Disney Fairies . . . To quote Queen Clarion herself: Happiness has brought you here. Welcome to Pixie Hollow!

This book exists due to the efforts of many talented people—and, of course, a whole lot of pixie dust. As always, a huge thank-you to my agents, Claire Friedman and Jess Mileo, for always fighting for me. With every book, my appreciation for y'all deepens even more.

To my editor, Katlin Sarantou. You have blown me away with your enthusiasm, communication, and superhuman work ethic. This book would not be what it is without your keen eye for detail, your suggestions, and your support. It's been such an honor working with you on this magical project!

To the rest of the team at Disney Press: Rachel Rivera, Warren Meislin, Nancee Adams, and Jennifer Black—my copyeditors, who heroically kept me in line given all these characters are six inches tall; Cathryn McHugh, managing editor; Hannah Meyer, illustration manager; Jeremy Burton, production manager; Kaia Hilson in marketing; and Crystal McCoy in publicity. Thank you to Charlie Bowater for illustrating this breathtaking cover and to Gegham Vardanyan for designing it.

To my friends! Courtney Gould, my publishing twin and dear friend, you were with me every step of the way. I couldn't have done it without your encouragement and occasional bullying. Jo Schulte, Megan Lally, Kalie Cassidy, Alex Clayton, and Courtney (again), who watched me revise a chunk of this book in Charleston: you were all extremely unhelpful, but you did make me laugh a lot, so I guess it balances out. Charles Keegan, Diane McClamroch, Andrew Oyé, Ana O'Connor: your support, humor, and understanding during a stressful year meant the absolute world to me. Helen Wiley, Audrey Coulthurst, and Elisha Walker: I would be lost without y'all. I love you so much!

PIXIE DUSTED
BONUS CONTENT

QUIZ

WHAT IS YOUR FAIRY SEASON?

Do you dwell in Spring Valley, cheering on the Everblossom's annual bloom and listening to the frogs' chorus at Lilypad Pond? Or perhaps you're a summer fairy, relaxing in Sunflower Meadow or soaring over Summer Glade's grassy fields. Do you specialize in gourd cottages and autumnal coziness? Or do you call the mysterious Winter Woods your home? Select the answers that best fit you.

How do you prefer to fly?

a) With your wings, obviously. It's worth using up your daily teacup of pixie dust.

b) By owl

c) By bat

d) In a sparrow-drawn chariot of your own making

How do you spend your free time?

a) Curled up with a good book

b) Racing leaf boats with your friends

c) Volunteering to take care of the baby caterpillars

d) Taking a joyride on a lynx, sipping some iced chamomile tea

How would you like to spend a first date?

a) Skating across a glimmering lake, mittened hand in mittened hand

b) Having a midday picnic of acorn-butter sandwiches and dill pea tarts

c) Strolling around Beach Cove at sunset

d) Dancing the night away at the Autumn Revelry

You feel most comfortable wearing:

a) a ball gown embroidered with blue tulips.

b) a tailored jacket with gleaming buttons.

c) a practical calla lily shift.

d) a fabulous dandelion-fluff-lined coat.

How did you and your bestie meet?

a) Exploring the forest

b) Learning how to make dewdrop face masks

c) Sneaking some extra acorn cake from the kitchens after hours

d) Competing against each other in the Pixie Hollow Games

Your home is:

a) a cozy burrow with plenty of spider-silk blankets and hot tea.

b) covered in vines and wall-to-wall windows to let in the fresh breeze.

c) a majestic cave surrounded by fir trees.

d) a peaceful spot with views of Havendish Stream.

What type of honor would the queen be most likely to bestow upon you?

a) Head dust-keeper

b) Member of the royal guard

c) Knight of Pixie Hollow

d) Seasonal Minister

What is your worst nightmare?

a) Falling from a great height

b) Getting attacked by a hawk

c) Giving a speech to all of Pixie Hollow

d) Having trouble with your talent

The word that best describes you is:

a) passionate.

b) clever.

c) loyal.

d) helpful.

Which group would you most likely be a part of?

a) Fast-flying, weaving, and leaf fairies

b) Healing, light, and animal fairies

c) Storytelling, cooking, and decor fairies

d) Tinker, garden, and water fairies

CALCULATE YOUR RESULTS

Tally up the points for your answers below, then find your season.

1	a = 2	b = 4	c = 3	d = 1
2	a = 3	b = 2	c = 1	d = 4
3	a = 4	b = 1	c = 2	d = 3
4	a = 1	b = 3	c = 2	d = 4
5	a = 3	b = 1	c = 4	d = 2
6	a = 3	b = 1	c = 4	d = 2
7	a = 3	b = 2	c = 1	d = 4
8	a = 2	b = 3	c = 4	d = 1
9	a = 2	b = 3	c = 4	d = 1
10	a = 3	b = 2	c = 4	d = 1

SPRING

1–12 points: You are a SPRING fairy.

You flourish in Spring Valley—a wild, joyful place teeming with life. On any given day, one can find spring fairies unfurling leaves, bottling spring showers, and flitting from place to place with messages. When you're not gathering in Springtime Square, you're teaching fledglings to fly. Or perhaps you're a garden-talent fairy, making the fields pop with color. Or a fast-flyer, spreading pollen for the bees. Whatever their talent, spring fairies are typically creative and energetic, as well as expert problem-solvers.

SUMMER

13–23 points: You are a SUMMER fairy.

Folks can find you in the warm and lush Summer Glade. Carefree and free-spirited, summer fairies thrive on long, sunshine-filled days. Your work might consist of ripening plums or collecting rainbows for the Mainland. Or perhaps you're honing your healing skills. One thing's for sure: Summer fairies throw the best events. Three-winged race in Needlepoint Meadow, anyone?

AUTUMN

24–32 points: You are an AUTUMN fairy.

In the Autumn Forest, you glow as brightly as the harvest moon. Perhaps more reserved than fairies in the other realms, you take great pride in the beauty of the golden, scarlet, and orange leaves and the perfectly plump pumpkins synonymous with your season. When you're not spending time in the cozy Harvest Promenade, you might be regaling others with your storytelling talent by a roaring fire or sketching pretty patterns on gourds. While wise and logical, fall fairies tend to deeply appreciate sensory experiences—whether digging into a cardamom apple muffin or feeling a crisp breeze on their wings.

WINTER

33–40 points: You are a WINTER fairy.

Whether you're carving snowflakes, exploring the frosty Hall of Winter, or sledding with your friends, the chilled nook of Pixie Hollow is where you thrive. The Winter Woods have long been misunderstood, but you know they're a veritable wonderland filled with snowy owls, arctic foxes, and towering evergreens. Perhaps you're an animal-talent fairy singing lullabies to bears so they can hibernate. Or maybe you're busy frosting the foliage. Whatever the case, winter fairies are known to be confident, resilient, and fun—always making time to skate down a frozen stream or host a snowball fight.

DISCUSSION QUESTIONS

1. Besides being star-crossed lovers, Clarion and Milori are also prominent figures in their respective realms. How do their leadership styles differ? How are they similar?

2. Setting plays a big role in this novel. How do places like the bridge between Winter and Spring or the ball's mushroom-lined Fairy Circle emulate the themes in the book?

3. Clarion and Petra's longtime friendship hits a snag in the course of this novel. How do power dynamics play a role in their evolving relationship?

4 Reflect upon how the plot digs into the idea of history's subjective nature—particularly the different versions of the Lord of Winter's story and how the Winter Woods became cut off from the rest of Pixie Hollow. How do you think stories of the past get rewritten? What effects does this have on the present?

5 They say opposites attract, as illustrated by Clarion and Milori's relationship. Which traits do you think draw these distinct fairies to each other?

6 Consider the quote "What fools their hearts made of them." How do the various characters experience this throughout the story? What is another way to look at love's transformative ability?

7 How does the order of Pixie Hollow resemble that of the natural world? How does it resemble the order of the human world?

8 Which character do you think showed the most growth by the end of the novel?

9 Fairies are born of Mainland children's laughter, arriving at the Pixie Dust Tree with their talents predetermined. What are the pros and cons of this sort of origin?

10 What do you think is the significance of the leader of the Nightmares taking the form of a queen?